"I've been afraid recently. I haven't slept well."

"Afraid?"

She drew a breath and said it. "I keep picturing myself dead."

"How do you know you're dead? Try to recall the image you see."

Darkness yawned beneath her deeper than a grave. She was floating. Pale. Lifeless. Drained. So pale . . . She shuddered. The thought raised the flesh on her arms and made her tremble, even now.

"You remember it, I can see. Tell me what it is."

"I've been bled. Oh, dear God, I've been bled to death!" She hid her face in her hands.

Bled you dry, have I, dearie?

It was the night whisper, again.

Also by Charles Veley
Published by Ballantine Books:

CHILDREN OF THE DARK

NIGHT WHISPERS

CHARLES VELEY

BALLANTINE BOOKS • NEW YORK

All of the characters in this novel are fictitious and any resemblance to actual persons, living or dead, is purely coincidental.

ACKNOWLEDGMENTS

Many people helped with the research and preparation of this book. In particular I owe thanks to Charles J. Lightdale, M.D., for his help with the medical details, to Betty Prashker and Debbie Wichter for their editorial guidance and support throughout the project, to Karl Veley for his suggestions regarding the completed manuscript, and to Pat Guadagno for her ever superlative typing.

Library of Congress Catalog Card Number: 79-8946

ISBN 0-345-29150-6

This edition publshed by arrangement with
Doubleday & Company, Inc.

Manufactured in the United States of America

First Ballantine Books Edition: January 1981

to Unk.

PROLOGUE

The ambulance van came to a stop at the main entrance of Madison Hospital. The headlights glittered against the rainy night. The windshield wipers continued to move. Expecting a new arrival, several people in the hospital lobby turned to watch through the plate-glass windows at the front, but the doors of the van did not open. It waited at the curb, its upright, boxlike frame slowing the late rush-hour traffic that moved up Madison Avenue in the cold February rain. From time to time, as cars pulled around the van, headlight beams caught the drop-lets that clung to its flat, high sides, giving the white enamel a momentary sparkle.

The clock in the hospital lobby read 6:15.

At 6:25 one of the lobby elevators opened and a nurse steered a wheelchair with a woman in it out toward the hospital entrance. The nurse, young and blond, was wearing a starched white cap and a navy-blue nurse's cape. The age of her patient was not easily determined, for the lower part of the woman's face was swathed in white bandages. From the forehead and the brown eyes, which were uncovered, one would have judged the woman to be in her late thirties. Her cream-colored soft leather coat, her lustrous dark-brown hair, and her commanding posture in the wheelchair indicated that she was a woman of position and affluence. She appeared to be in excellent health.

The nurse noticed that people in the lobby were staring at the woman. With purposeful strides she moved the wheelchair and its passenger the remaining distance to the glass doors. "We've completed discharge on Four," she told the middle-aged security guard.

The woman saw the ambulance van parked outside. "Is that ours?" she asked. "I want to get out of here." She spoke sharply, her facial muscles held stiff under their bandages. The pain around her jawline reminded her of the surgeon's instructions that she was not to talk and her impatience increased.

"Let me check," said the nurse. "We're five minutes early. It may be waiting for someone else."

She left the wheelchair by the glass wall to the right of the security guard, where people going in and out would not bother her patient and where there would not be drafts. Then she hurried out into the rain. Opening the ambulance door and exchanging words with the driver, the nurse looked charmingly earnest, and the woman in the wheelchair regretted the sharpness of her tone. A shame, she thought, how being in the hospital could make one so irritable and self-centered. She told herself she would be better when they reached Kingston Spa, the quiet Palisades resort where she would be recuperating from her face-lift. Also, she remembered the nurse had given her a mild injection for traveling. Soon it would begin to take effect, and her mood would begin to lighten. Depression was only a natural reaction to the surgery, quite temporary and to be expected. She reminded herself that the surgeon had commented on how fit she looked.

"He's here for us," the nurse said when she returned.

"Good." The hospital lobby seemed too small, the wheelchair too confining to be borne for another minute. Ignoring the pen and writing pad they had told her to use, she pointed her finger at the door. "Wheel me out of here so I can stand up like a normal human being." She thought what a nuisance it was to abide by the hospital insurance regulations that required departing patients to exit in a wheelchair.

Outside, she stood away from the wheelchair, deftly snapped open her folding umbrella, and marched through the rain to the open door of the ambulance, where the driver was waiting. She was glad to get out. If her husband had been alive, she wouldn't have needed this silly operation. "Are you going to help me?" she demanded of the driver.

He was young and powerfully built. His blue eyes regarded her more pleasantly than she had expected, and with more intelligence. He did not appear to notice her bandages. "Of course, ma'am. We enter at the rear of the van."

He offered his arm and she took it. She felt a bit awkward holding her umbrella over the young man, but she made the attempt to shelter him from the rain, noticing with annoyance that her shoes were already getting wet. The nurse followed. She carried the woman's small overnight bag with the clothes she had worn at the hospital and the medical records that would be needed at Kingston Spa. Other clothes had already been sent on.

The driver stood away from the umbrella to unlock the doors at the back. The rain wet his neat white uniform, and made his thick blond curls shine with beads of water. Quickly he opened the doors and helped the woman climb inside.

She was relieved to see that the van had a fairly large interior, for she was generally averse to confinement and enclosed spaces. At the center, as she had expected, was a narrow emergency stretcher with white sheets and pillows. Two comfortable-looking bucket seats covered in tan leather were positioned on either side. Behind the pillows at the head of the stretcher she saw an upright green console of some sort, with a row of raised, white plastic push-button squares that appeared to be its controls. The woman supposed it to be some kind of emergency life-support apparatus.

"Sit wherever you like." The attendant stepped back to assist the nurse. "We only ask that you do use the seat belts." To the nurse he said, "I have six twenty-seven. We're in good time."

Then he closed the doors. Inside, the woman settled back, finding the leather seat quite comfortable, and buckled her seat belt. She glanced briefly at the nurse, who had seated herself in the other chair, and then at the wall above the green console. "He can't see through that, can he?"

"No, that's sheet metal," said the nurse. "The cabs on these are sealed off." She was looking out the back windows, through the one-way glass, at the oncoming headlights. The woman heard the engine of the van revving up. She watched the lights as the van moved away from the curb and into the stream of traffic, finding it difficult to focus clearly on the cars behind them. She supposed it was because of the rain, or the one-way glass.

Several minutes later, when the van stopped beside a row of cars parked uptown along First Avenue, she was feeling noticeably worse. Her mouth was dry. Her vision had not improved, and she had begun to notice the early signs of motion sickness: shortness of breath and a sense of instability in her abdomen. She tried to focus on the cars outside.

A man in a khaki-colored raincoat was getting out of the car parked behind them. He came toward the back of the van, carrying a small black bag.

"What is he doing?" asked the woman.

"Don't worry," said the nurse. "We're expecting him. He gets on here."

The woman was about to object when one of the rear doors swung open and the man in the raincoat got in. Wasting no time, he slammed the door shut behind him. As though the sound of the closing door were a signal, the ambulance started up First Avenue again, picking up speed.

Too surprised to speak, the woman stared as the newcomer came toward her, keeping his balance easily despite the motion of the van, and sat down, wet and dripping, on the clean white sheets at the foot of the emergency stretcher. The man looked at least ten years older than the driver, his hair dark, his eyes less youthful, his frame even more muscular. Saying nothing, he shrugged off his raincoat. Underneath he wore a physician's white laboratory coat, with a white shirt and tie. He looked exceptionally healthy. The woman noticed that he had recently shaved; from the darkness under the surface of his smooth cheeks, he looked the sort of man who would have to shave several times each day. She immediately disliked him.

He leaned closer. "Well how are we doing?"

Before the nurse could reply, the woman recovered her composure. "I have hired this ambulance," she said. "I have not hired you. You have sixty seconds to explain your presence here to my satisfaction, or I shall have you removed!"

The man looked at the nurse and then smiled, tolerantly. "I'm Garrett, ma'am. A physician. A routine examination and history is part of procedure at Kingston. I was in the city, so I made arrangements to ride along. To save time. Incidentally, you shouldn't be talking so soon after surgery."

As though that settled the matter, he turned back to the nurse. "When did she get her medication?"

"Wait a minute," said the woman. "Why wasn't I told about this?"

"At six-fifteen," said the nurse. "On schedule."

"All right then. It should have been time enough." He reached for his black bag.

"Why wasn't I told?" repeated the woman. She was having difficulty focusing her eyes again, and the small seat seemed to be slipping away from under her. With an effort she pulled herself erect.

Garrett looked at her more closely.

"Damn it, answer me! Why wasn't I told?"

He exchanged glances with the nurse, visibly concerned. "I'm sorry," said the nurse. "I think I forgot to mention it."

"If you'd prefer, we can wait for the examination until we get to Kingston," said Garrett. "As I said, it's routine." He cleared his throat. "All I'm concerned about right now is how you feel. You look like you might be having some reaction to your medication."

She met his gaze. His brown eyes seemed devoid of life, as though made of glass. For a moment she felt a wave of nausea, a sense of falling through darkness.

"Ma'am?" It was the nurse, kneeling beside her.

"She is having a reaction," said Garrett. "We should have had this in her history. Reaction cases show *retention.*" His tone indicated strong disapproval.

"The records are in her bag. There was nothing to indicate—"

"Not good enough." Garrett moved up beside the woman, pressing her fingertips lightly at her throat to get a pulse. His hands were uncomfortably cold and wet from the rain and his touch made her sit up. Her head began to clear a little.

"Try to remember," he said. "Have you ever had this kind of a reaction to any medication before?"

She remembered. "Once," she said. "They gave me an injection when I was in labor. They told me it would make it easier; that I wouldn't remember the pain." She shook her head. "But it just made me more nauseated."

"You *did* retain memories of your delivery?"

"Oh, yes. Yes I did."

She heard the rain against the roof of the van, the whoosh of cars in the opposite lane as their tires cut through the water on the highway. The van seemed to be moving only slowly. Looking out the back windows, she could see they were now on the Harlem River Drive in congested traffic.

"Well that's it, then," said Garrett quietly to the nurse. "We don't have any choice. You know the codes. We'll have to take all of it." His hand moved to rest lightly on the woman's shoulder. The touch was barely perceptible to her through the leather of her coat, but the gesture made her suddenly afraid.

"What are you talking about?" she demanded of the nurse.

"Your medication, ma'am. What to do because of your reaction."

She saw evasion in the eyes even before the nurse had spoken. The van seemed to grow smaller. Garrett's face seemed closer; the lips colder, more repellent. She was aware that her heart had begun to speed up; she could feel the insistent pounding in the blood vessels of her throat, the pain of the incisions beneath her jawline growing more intense. She held her breath to will away the panic. All right, she told herself, you don't trust these people and you're frightened. The medicine—was it like this before, with this *fear?* She tried to remember the blur of images in the labor room nineteen years earlier.

"We're agreed, then?" she heard Garrett say to the nurse.

"I don't want to."

Garrett stiffened. "It's not a question of wanting."

The seat belt. Breathing in short, shallow gasps that dried her teeth and tongue, she forced her hand to move, slowly, so they would not notice, to her lap, where she could unclasp the buckle and then get out of the chair. She kept her eyes on the three lanes of headlights creeping along behind them, her mind fantasizing that one of the pairs of lights would be her son's little red Triumph, that he would have decided on impulse to come home for a visit from college. He would rescue her. Then she thought perhaps she was being foolish and only imagining things. Yet her hand kept moving.

Her fingers were on the buckle when Garrett hit her.

When her eyes opened again she felt wet and chilled. And she hurt. Above her the white ceiling light of the ambulance van shone coldly. Shivering, the woman realized they had stripped her of her coat and outer garments, leaving only her brassiere, slip, and panty hose. The motion of the van told her they were traveling again, and at good speed. She tried to move, but now there was a strap across her shoulders that cut into her collarbone and throat when she tried to raise herself. She moved to pull it away, but they had pinned down her arms on either side. Her wrists were bound to the metal frame of the emergency litter.

Behind her she heard a noise over the sounds of traffic and the ambulance engine. A humming. From the green cabinet she had thought was a life-support machine.

"Good," said Garrett. "She's awake."

He moved the strap away from her neck and she lifted her head slightly. From each of her exposed arms she saw tubes coming out of veins. Instinctively she tried to jerk away, for she had always had a fear of needles. She could not move. The thick plastic straps around her wrists and upper arms held her immobile. The tubes vibrated with the motion of the van.

The tube coming from her left arm was pale, filled with a straw-colored fluid.

The tube coming from her right arm was red and dark.

PART ONE

BLOOD

1

As Dr. Jill Weston reached Eighty-third Street, the whisper took her by surprise.

Breakdown, dearie!

A chill passed through her. She hadn't been paying enough attention, she thought. Someone had gotten close without her knowing. The first rule was to ignore him, and then get away—

Breakdown.

She walked faster, wishing she did not feel so weak and vulnerable. She was too easily fatigued, had been for nearly two months now, and she could scarcely hide her pain from her patients at the hospital. There were moments when she could not seem to breathe; others when she doubled over with abdominal cramps. This afternoon she was on her way to see her doctor.

When she thought she had outdistanced any footsteps, she turned cautiously to look for the intruder. But the sidewalk was empty. Along the edge of Central Park a few pigeons clustered at the feet of a man with a bag of peanuts. An artist on the park wall glanced up only briefly before returning to his sketch pad. The bushes just on the other side of the wall were bare of leaves; no one could hide behind them. Brittle and glazed from rain that had frozen overnight, they caught weak flashes of the pale February sun. The wind was making them creak and hiss, so perhaps—

No, dearie. Inside you. Breakdown time!

The voice seemed to echo one Jill had heard before. One that had awakened her before dawn this morning. Cackling. Ugly.

Breakdown time, dearie. Breakdown breakdown, BREAK—

The whisper stopped.

Fear knotted Jill's stomach. She felt an overpowering

urge to run. Dr. Polder's office was only two blocks away.

In her quiet, book-lined consulting office, Dr. Virginia Polder took three pages of computer-typed paper from a thick manila folder and handed them across her desk to Jill.

"You're concerned, of course, so I want you to see these immediately. This one gives the blood tests, and these two list all the others. They show no evidence of pathology. Here. Read them for yourself."

The data were clear. All normal.

Jill scanned the numbered columns rapidly, trying to understand. She knew the parameters of healthy tissue in each of the tests, after spending several predawn hours reviewing her medical textbooks. She had wanted so badly to help with the initial diagnosis, and to find a cure.

But here were the numbers. They said there was no problem.

And she had not yet told Dr. Polder about the whisper she had heard.

"You're crying, Jill. Are you relieved?"

She handed back the computer sheets, took the offered Kleenex to wipe her eyes, drew a deep breath. "I don't know what to think. I'd been waiting three days for these, and I guess I expected to find something definite. Something to work on. Now we still don't know anything."

"Well I think we can say we've eliminated one problem area. I think we can safely assume that you don't have the malignancy, or the other degenerative diseases that you were worried about."

But there *had* to be something! The way Jill was feeling—"Maybe something went wrong with one or two of the tests," Jill said. "Maybe we ought to run some others. Maybe we ought to think about retesting."

Virginia Polder turned up an empty palm. "Fine. We'll retest, if that's what you want. But I think we have to proceed on another line of thought as well. I take it you haven't had any sudden remission in your symptoms?"

You're going to say mental, aren't you. Even though nothing is wrong with my mind, you're going to tell me that I need to stop practicing for a while and take a nice rest.

"No," said Jill. "No remission."

"All right. Would you listen for a moment or two, while

I read from your file? Here. June, 1970. Height, sixty-four inches. Weight, a hundred and twenty pounds. August, 1971. Height, sixty-four inches, one hundred and twenty-one pounds. In 1972, the last year you came to me before now, you were still sixty-four inches and a hundred and twenty-one pounds."

That was the year she had entered medical school. After that, there had been no time for a routine physical. Medical students were always testing one another, using one another as guinea pigs. Besides, they were young, and it didn't matter. If you could function, you kept functioning. If you couldn't, you found out what was wrong and fixed it. Jill had been one of those who kept functioning. She had not missed a day because of illness since junior high school.

". . . and I did not see you again until your father's funeral, two months ago. Then last month you consulted me. On both those occasions you looked the same, but I am wondering about this weight loss of yours."

"Weight loss?"

"You haven't been following your weight? It's dropped ten pounds since your college days. When?"

"I—haven't been keeping track, really. Maybe there are records somewhere."

"What about your clothes? Those slacks, for example. When did you buy them?"

She remembered. November. A gift from her father. Her friends had wanted her to go skiing that weekend, but she had gone upstate to be with him, just as she had spent all her weekends with him since she had learned of his acute leukemia. She had moved through the whole summer and fall driven by a furious urge to care for him, and still to work harder at the hospital so he could be proud of her. She thought of him as a brave soldier, and at the back of her mind told herself that he would be one of the lucky ones who recovered. Her mother had died when Jill was sixteen. To have her father die had seemed unbearable.

"November."

"And I assume you bought them to fit properly. Stand up, please."

As she stood, too quickly, the weakness struck her as the blood drained from her head. She faltered, grasping the edge of the desk.

She had done all she could, but he had died. And not in tranquillity, not accepting, not at peace with a life well finished. He had been obsessed with the knowledge that he could have done more. That so many others could have been helped by his practiced eye and wide experience. *Do not go gentle,* and Brian Weston had certainly not gone gently. She had watched his fury at the warped, aggressive white cells that had flooded his peripheral blood and bone marrow in their mindless, suicidal growth. He had worked to the end, the anger deepening the lines already etched in his face. Yet none of his patients had ever seen that anger. He had been a professional to the last, to them. Only Jill had seen the human side.

"Turn around, Jill. You're having difficulty, I know, but just please turn around."

The voice brought her back. "It's as I told you. Periods of dizziness. I think that was one just now."

Or something deeper? Something to draw you in?

"The slacks seem loose in the back. Did you buy them that way?"

She could not remember, but she thought the slacks had fit more closely.

"What about your brassiere? When did you buy that?"

During the summer. And it seemed a half size too large.

"Now I want you to think about food intake. And exercise. I want to determine if there has been any change during the past six months. Have you ever done a caloric-intake study on yourself? . . . No? Then we can begin with you describing a typical day's diet during the summer."

Five minutes of calculations later, they had established that Jill's eating habits had remained relatively unchanged, though her appetite had fallen off somewhat since her father's death. Possibly she was not eating everything on her plate these days; she had difficulty remembering, for she generally ate automatically, her mind on the conversation around her or on other things.

"All right. So you may have lost ten per cent of your body weight during the last few months. That's fairly significant. Have you thought much about what else you have lost?"

"I don't know what you mean."

"I think you do," she said, kindly. "I knew your father.

His love for you was very strong. To have it gone now, completely—it must be very difficult."

Jill held firmly to her self-control. "I—still have memories. And he taught me to be independent."

"I'm sure he did. But what love are you getting in replacement? How are you filling the void? Who loves you, Jill?"

She hesitated. "Are you telling me my symptoms are psychosomatic?"

"I'm just trying to learn. I have no diagnosis yet. We all need love. Who loves you? Where do you get love?"

"My patients—they appreciate what I'm doing. They tell me—"

"I know. That kind of love is not to be underestimated. But you had patients before. Who else gives love to Jill Weston?"

The gray eyes maintained their hold on Jill. It's a fair question, she thought. The only reason I'm hesitating is that I'm not really sure of Phillip. "I've been seeing someone when I've had time," she said finally.

"Does this someone have a name?"

Jill nodded. "Phillip. He's a surgeon too."

"And he loves you?" At Dr. Polder's smile, Jill felt suddenly able to talk.

"That's what I was trying to puzzle out just now. He gives me advice, but I don't feel it like love. And he doesn't really seem to need me. Does that make sense? I've never really had time to let myself get too involved outside the hospital. Maybe I haven't given it a chance to work. . . ."

Dr. Polder broke the silence after Jill's voice trailed off. "Let me ask you another question. What about sex?"

Jill looked up in surprise. The image of Phillip beside her flashed through her mind, the feel of his hard, muscular arms drawing her closer. The beginning warmth of her response, and then, lately, the hollowness, the fear.

Virginia Polder's look was understanding. "Why don't you just speak in terms of comparisons. Then and now. Six months ago and the present. Has there been any change in the way you have felt?"

She was giving her time to think, Jill knew. And also being discreet: nothing said about any man other than Phillip during the past six months. Only different feelings about sex. Did she think Jill could have slept with different men? That she could move from one to the next—

No. It was simply a general question. Nondirective. From her doctor.

"I've been afraid recently. I haven't felt well."

"Afraid?"

She drew a breath and said it. "I keep picturing myself dead."

"All right, let's examine that for a moment. How do you know you are dead? What is the cause of your death? Try to recall the image that you see."

Darkness yawned beneath her deeper than a grave. She was floating. Pale. Lifeless. Drained. So pale. . . . She shuddered. The thought raised the flesh on her arms and made her tremble, even now.

"You remember it, I can see. Tell me what it is. You can tell me."

"I've been bled. Oh, dear God, I've been bled to death!" She hid her face in her hands.

Bled you dry, have I, dearie?

And cried. It was some time before she heard Virginia Polder's voice again.

2

Jill thought she had never seen so many boats. For a moment she had a child's impulse to try to count them, but the cold wind off the river stung her eyes and made her blink.

She was still looking at the marina, fascinated, when her heel caught on the rough planking and she stumbled. Phillip's grip tightened on her arm, holding her up.

"Careful now." He raised his voice to make himself heard over the wind and the traffic noise from the highway above them. "It was hard enough getting you to come away from the hospital. We don't want to be sending you back as a patient."

"I'll be okay." She leaned against him while she straightened her shoe. Phillip was tall; his coat of dark-blue cashmere was soft against her hand; the scent of his cologne as her face brushed close to his chest was pleasant.

Why was it she did not love him anymore? Where had the feeling gone? After so many years of giving herself to medicine, Jill had been surprised by her sudden attraction for this handsome southerner. But lately her emotions seemed to be changing.

He took her arm again as they walked toward the water, watching the flight of a gull down to the radio antenna of a twenty-foot cruiser that had braved the choppy Hudson this cloudy February afternoon. "Bet they're cold out there," he said. "See? He's piloting from the flying bridge instead of down inside the cabin. In the cabin it's probably warmer, if he's got a heater. All the good ones do."

"It's funny. I've been in New York nine years now and this is the first time I've ever come down here."

"I've been telling you all along," he said, "to take some more time for yourself. Do you like it?"

"I think it might be better when it's warmer."

"The Hudson gets a little too ripe when it's warmer. And the docks get crowded."

"You've been down here in the summer?"

He shook his head no. "Complete novice. But all the salesmen told me about the river. Do you know some people live on their boats year-round? There's a little colony of houseboats. I think that's it, right over there."

He pointed downriver from where they had stopped, at a cluster of wide-bottomed boats. Jill could see curtains in the windows of some, and wisps of smoke coming up from small chimney pipes.

"Are you about to tell me you bought a houseboat?"

He laughed, full-voiced and confident, his brown eyes suddenly happier, and Jill thought, It must be quite a boat he's bought himself to be so proud. The late afternoon sun broke through a narrow gap between the clouds. Sunlight glittered on the river behind Phillip, touching his light-brown hair with an aura of burnished gold. He's just as handsome as he ever was, she thought. And he's having a good time. I'm not going to spoil it.

"Can you guess which one it is?" He made a sweeping gesture that encompassed the entire marina, from the tarpaulin-covered boats in dry dock down to those moored at the jetties at the edge of the water beyond the fence.

"That one." She pointed to the nearest, not wanting to

play. Maybe it's because he's healthy, she thought. If I felt better or if he felt worse, would I be happy with him?

"Hey," he said. "You're shivering. Let's get you inside away from this wind." He took out a key and opened the steel-mesh door that led down to the nearest jetty. A sign said ONLY OWNERS AND ATTENDANTS PERMITTED BEYOND THIS POINT. "Am I allowed down here?" Jill asked.

He patted a bulge of papers under his coat. "My name's all over these contracts and deeds and things. Official owner." As he helped her down the steps he added, "If anybody stops us, I'll tell him that you're the ship's cook."

"Sexist. Where's it parked?"

"You don't park a boat. You dock it. First you put in, and then you tie up. That's called docking."

"Okay." She shivered again. The planks swayed beneath their feet, rising and falling with the river.

He stopped midway out on the jetty, between two cabin cruisers that were each so tall that Jill could not see over their top decks. "Now which one do you think it is?"

Jill could smell exhaust fumes from a big white-masted diesel yacht coming slowly out of one of the upriver docks. She pointed to the small cruiser ahead of them.

"Wrong again. Let's keep walking."

"I hope you're enjoying yourself."

"Don't you like surprises? C'mon, it won't be long now. That's a promise."

They were almost at the end of the dock. The wind was cold, and the Hudson looked wider from here. She watched the currents and the waves out there, her eyes drawn by the vast gray flow. Such a big river, so wide and dark and cold. If someone were to fall in out there, he wouldn't last a minute.

She wouldn't last a minute.

She saw herself struggling in the chilling water, felt the numbness in her fingertips, her legs and arms like lead, her clothes dragging her down. . . .

No. It was foolish to think that way. If Phillip had a boat, it would be a good one. She would be perfectly safe. She was not going to let herself imagine things. Fear and depression go hand in hand, Dr. Polder had said. The wounded organism fears more perils than the healthy.

On either side of her on the jetty were smaller less-expensive boats, the kind not too far removed from the lake runabouts Jill had known during summers as a girl. "This is more my speed," she said.

The thrumming of the diesel engines took away her words. Phillip called out above the clamor, "What did you say?"

"Looks like something I could steer." She pointed at a small runabout, the last one moored to the dock.

Then she saw what he was looking at.

The white-masted yacht. Its high blue and white sides rose up out of the water above Jill's eye level. As it closed with the dock, it blocked her view of the entire river. On the sides she saw round glass portholes, like those of an ocean liner.

"God," she said. "It's a monster."

He grinned like a little boy. "Do you like it?"

"Phillip. Are you telling me—"

He patted the papers inside his coat again. "I wanted to have it warmed up for you."

"This enormous boat is *yours?*"

"All forty-eight feet of her. She's a Hatteras long-range cruiser. C'mon, let's get in out of the cold!"

He called out to the man piloting the boat, "We're coming aboard! Bring it around!" He explained to Jill that from the end of a dock the only way to board a cruiser of this size was to climb up the ladder astern, so as not to risk damage to the keel. Maneuvering the cruiser in that way was possible here in the cove of the marina, where they were sheltered from the current. If the docks had been extended from another spot open to the flow downstream, no cruiser could maneuver well enough to take on passengers. It would have to stand out in the current and ferry people to and from the shore in a smaller launch.

The boarding ladder was chromed steel, about five rungs high. Phillip reached out and grasped it. "Go ahead on up," he said, grinning.

"No. You first." Mercifully, the pilot of the cruiser had cut the engines so the diesel fumes were gone. Jill drew a deep breath in the cold wind. Even though it stung, the fresh air was making her feel better.

He went up the ladder first. When she reached the top behind him, he helped her onto the deck. "This door goes to the galley and sleeping quarters for the crew. We'll go around on deck and say good-bye to the pilot. Wait till you see the master stateroom."

"He's getting off? You mean you can steer this thing yourself?"

"It's not a thing. It's the *Nirvana*. And I handled her all right last month when I was getting ready to buy her. I don't see why this afternoon should be any different." For the first time he sounded annoyed.

"Then I'm sure you'll do just fine." She gave his hand a squeeze, not wanting to spoil his big moment. But neither did she want to spend time alone in the stateroom with him. She looked at her watch. Four-fifteen. She had promised herself to be back in her office by seven, even though her cases were covered.

Inside he said a few words to the pilot, who had brought the cruiser, and gave him a folded twenty-dollar bill. The cabin was as warm as Phillip had promised.

"How's he going to get off?" Jill asked when they were alone in the cabin.

"Same way we got on. It's no trouble holding her here, where there's no current." He kept his hand on the wheel, gripping it firmly. Jill could feel a slight dipping and rising, more pronounced than on the jetty.

"I've never been on one of these before," she said. "But I'm determined not to be seasick."

"We're the seagoing conquerers," he said happily, and hugged her to him with his free arm. "Look at all we've got here. Radar, modular VHF, sun log, autopilot, digital directional finder—" He watched in an overhead mirror until the man waved to them from the jetty. Then he pulled out a knob on the instrument panel and turned a key. The engines returned to life.

"Is that all there is to it? That looks just like the choke on my father's old Packard sedan."

He showed her the throttle, forward and reverse, and eased the *Nirvana* out toward the middle of the river. "We'll head upstream," he said, smiling. "I always did like to go against the current."

"For a surgeon, you sound pretty philosophical."

He had his chin up, eyes shining, as he turned the pointed prow into the waves. "Actually, I feel like a little kid. What I wish I had was a steam-whistle chain right here. Toot! Toot! I've waited a long time for this."

"I believe you have," Jill said.

"Oh, I know what you're thinking. Conspicuous consumption, low-brow ostentation, all that business about what finer things I could be doing with two hundred thousand dollars. Right?"

"It's a lot of money."

He shook his head. "Not really. You could have two hundred thousand in a few months if you put your mind to it. Your area of surgery is a lot more lucrative than mine."

"Not *that* much more."

"Oh, come on. You could bill a thousand a day, easily, if you weren't so hung up on research. Then if you took the time to look at the markets and make the right investments—"

"Phil, I don't *want* a boat like this. And I don't have the time. I'm really perfectly—"

"Hey, look up there on the Palisades. Look at that ice formation. And over there all lit up. By the shore. Did you know that used to be a ferryboat just like the ones that run to Staten Island? Somebody turned it into a restaurant and made himself a fortune!"

"Why are you telling me this? I'm not looking to get rich."

"I don't want to tell you anything. Here. Take the wheel a minute. See what it's like."

She did. The vibration from the waves on the rudder came through to her hands. Her father's hands, the fingers long and sensitive. He had told her to take her residency in surgery because of those hands. Fine motor skills, he had said. Women have better fine motor skills than men. It's the one area in medicine where you'll have a physical advantage.

She had pointed out that only 2 per cent of American surgeons were female. Because male surgeons are bigots, he had said. They don't want to let women in on the power and the glory. But you'll have to face that whatever specialty you choose. You might just as well choose one where you know you can do a better job than the next person.

"Hey," Phillip said gently. "You see what I mean? Going upriver, the waves coming at you . . ." He let his voice trail off.

She nodded, not about to admit she had scarcely been watching. The river was beautiful and cold. Up ahead the George Washington Bridge framed the horizon.

"Cut the wheel a little," he said. "Just to see."

The rudder responded slowly. "It's like steering a double bed."

"Magic words," he said with a smile, and she wished she had not spoken. "What I'd like to do," he went on, "is take a couple of weeks, maybe three, and head down the inland waterway. See how far we could get. Just turn off the radio and the phone and take off. We could maybe do two hundred miles a day——"

"This is a fantasy, I hope."

"Fantasy?"

"You're saying 'we.' I can't go. That's why I hope it's just a fantasy."

"Look. You're one of the best obstetrical surgeons in the country. You deserve to be able to take some time off. You deserve to have some real money, not just the little bit that hospital gives you to stay on staff. You ought to be in private practice, making some good solid investments, building for the future——"

"I don't have the time." Inside her she heard, *You mean you don't feel up to it. You're exhausted.*

Phillip shrugged. "I publish as much as you do, isn't that right?"

"Probably. I really haven't kept score."

"I spend time with my patients——"

"You have a schedule," Jill interrupted. "Obstetrics is different from oral surgery. Babies make their own schedules."

"Most of your cases aren't deliveries. You let the hospital and the patients make your schedule for you, and then you knock yourself out trying to keep up with their demands."

"It's the way I am," she said, feeling more and more defensive.

"Well I work an eighteen-hour day a lot of the time too. But I'm not knocking myself out. Do I look like I'm overtired?"

"You don't *sound* overtired," she said lightly.

"Someday I'll tell you why," he said. Then he smiled and took the wheel again.

3

The face was astonishingly handsome. Garrett never grew tired of watching the strongly compelling eyes, the perfectly formed features. It was the kind of face that made someone look back to see if it really was as good as it first seemed, and then back again. Garrett stared greedily, reveling in its perfection. The ancient Greeks, he thought, must have stared this way when the master sculptor Praxiteles first unveiled a statue of a god. The facial lines superb, the hair rich and black, the cheeks glowing with health. And the dark eyes, lit from within like diamonds. . . .

"You won't feel this now, Matthew. You won't feel it at all. You will remain floating free, feeling relaxed and refreshed. Nothing can harm you. You are filled with goodness. Filled with power."

Matthew Garrett saw the face move to the side of the armless white leather couch on which he reclined. He heard the voice and felt at peace.

The handsome man with the jet-black hair moved easily to Garrett's right and lifted a large hypodermic syringe from a side table. The syringe was empty. He pressed the plunger completely into the chamber, expelling any trapped air. Then he withdrew a sterile needle from its sealed wrapper and twisted it into place.

"You still feel nothing from the outside, Matthew. You feel everything from within. Peace, Matthew, and warmth from within."

His fingertips traced a path from the lobe of Matthew Garrett's right ear down to the base of the neck, two inches above the clavicle, and pressed down. Matthew Garrett's external jugular vein began to distend slightly. Soon it was visible beneath the surface of the skin, a tube of grayish-blue against the strands of neck tendon and muscle.

"Now your right hand is beginning to grow light, Matthew. Lighter than your arm. Lighter than air. So light that it draws your entire arm up into the air with it. When I count to three, your arm will begin to rise. You will feel it rising. One . . . two . . ."

Garrett felt a tugging at his arm, looked over, and saw his own right fist, clenched, slowly starting to move. Impossible, he thought. Even the Leader's experiments have not gone beyond gravity. Then he realized he had been thinking incorrectly. The Leader was simply showing him the effect of his power on his, Matthew Garrett's, hand and arm, and by implication, on all his actions. The Leader's power.

". . . three. Now it is rising, Matthew. You see, it is already several inches from where it lay."

It was.

"Now it will continue to rise. But, Matthew, I want you to use all your strength to try to pull it down. You will use all the strength in your arm to try to pull it down, but you will find it impossible. Your hand will continue to rise until it is vertical. It is rising now. You are trying, but you cannot stop it."

Garrett's dark features tensed with the effort as the powerful muscles in his arm contracted, the flexors and the extensors opposing one another. The strain produced a heightening in his blood pressure. As he clenched his jaw, his neck muscles expanded, forcing the blue-gray jugular closer to the skin surface.

The needle and the syringe were ready. The point of the needle made a slight popping sound as it broke through Garrett's skin. The man with the perfect features watched Garrett's face carefully for a reaction.

There was none.

He guided the tip of the needle into the vein. The blood, under pressure from the tension in the surrounding muscle fibers, quickly filled the hollow core of the needle. It flowed red into the glass syringe, frothing slightly, lapping at the edges of the plunger, filling the chamber as the man drew it back. When the red liquid had reached the 125-cc. mark, the man quickly withdrew the needle and set the filled syringe aside.

"You may let go now, Matthew. Your arm will remain vertical for a moment, until I touch it. Then I shall gently lower your arm, and you will relax, letting the arm rest. Then you will begin to tell me things."

Garrett saw the face above him. He smiled slightly, feeling wonderfully calm as the warm fingers gripped his wrist and elbow. The arm was lowered gently, slowly, as though setting down a sleeping infant with infinite care. The face above him seemed radiant; the leather reclining couch seemed a cloud. The voice spoke to him, and he felt a surge of passionate loyalty to the truth and the boundless goodness of the Leader, who cared for him so. To serve the Leader he would do great deeds. He would do anything.

"Matthew, do you know that you are the first among my Guardians?"

A hushed whisper. Quiet pride. "Yes."

"Tuesday morning you made a delivery. Do you recall?"

Garrett looked momentarily confused. "I woke up at my home Tuesday morning. I dressed and went to work."

"Before that, Matthew. Before you woke up. Do you remember?"

"No . . . only Monday night. I remember receiving my assignment that night."

"What was the assignment?"

Garrett remembered clearly and told, in flawless detail, his instructions to withdraw one unit of packed red cells from a Mrs. Sharon Cranford, a patient traveling by ambulance from Madison Hospital to a resort spa, where she planned to recuperate from routine cosmetic surgery. Garrett was to board the ambulance at the corner of First and 125th, make certain that Mrs. Cranford's injection had taken effect, and then withdraw the blood, using the fractionalizing equipment in the van. Only one unit, unless a security risk was apparent. Garrett remembered parking his car on First Avenue, giving himself an injection, and waiting for the ambulance.

He remembered nothing more.

"I want you to try harder, Matthew. Try to remember who you saw."

Nothing.

The voice consoled him. "You have tried, Matthew, and it is very right that you should have no recollection. What you do not remember cannot harm you. Your soul is pure, Matthew. You have completed what was assigned.

Now I want you to try to recall something else for me."

Garrett stole another look at those wonderful eyes above him. If only he himself could have looked so . . . *beautiful*, there was no other word for the Leader's face; if only the boy Matthew Garrett could have grown up looking so splendid! His childhood would have been vastly different; so many things about him could have changed. . . .

"I want you to concentrate on your *feelings* that night, Matthew. Try to recall how you felt. You do not need to picture the ambulance. You do not need to imagine anything that you do not remember. But now, go back into the darkness between the time you waited in your car Monday night and the time you woke the next morning. Feel, Matthew. Listen to your feelings, and tell me. Now."

Signs of distress clouded Matthew Garrett's brown eyes. He compressed his lips and swallowed.

"Tell me, Matthew."

"I can't . . . tell . . ." Within him Garrett felt a hurt, a shameful hurt, a reflex·anger in response. He wanted to lash out. But he looked up. The Leader's face. God, he could never feel anger at that face!

"It's coming out now, Matthew. Let me know the feeling. It's all right."

"I . . . felt . . . someone betrayed me. I wanted to strike back."

"And you did?"

A sigh. "Yes."

"You did well, Matthew. You let the feelings come out. It is always good to let the feelings come out when you are on assignment, if that becomes necessary. By letting out the feelings, you have cleansed yourself."

Garrett relaxed. The man watched closely, then spoke again, his eyes on Garrett's.

"Why did you not bring us the medical records of Mrs. Cranford? Where did you leave them?"

An expression of bewilderment crossed Garrett's face, and the man who stood beside him gave a slight smile of satisfaction. The final test. Garrett had passed. He did not remember.

Now it was time for conditioning.

"It will be useful to us in the future, Matthew, if you bring us the medical records when it becomes necessary for you to terminate any subject you are assigned. You will remember this command, and add it to your conditioning."

Garrett nodded.

"We do this in your own interest, Matthew. For you are to share in the harvest. The records may be essential for your own protection. That is why we are renewing your conditioning at this time, to ensure that you bring back the records for your own protection. Do you understand, Matthew?"

"I understand." How wonderful that the Leader cared for him so! How good it was to serve him!

"You have done well, Matthew, and now you shall have your reward." The man withdrew the gauze pad he had been pressing to Garrett's neck vein, and examined the tiny puncture in the skin. It was not bleeding.

"We have pricked your neck a tiny bit to withdraw a few drops of blood for a crossmatch. You will know that when you awaken and see this small adhesive bandage." Quickly the bandage was unwrapped and pressed into place. "Now I am going to begin counting from one to ten. When I reach ten, you will awaken, feeling alert and ready to be made strong. You will remember nothing of our conversation, Matthew. You will remember only our conditioning revision. And you will be happy."

At ten, Garrett came awake. He saw Malcolm Lockwood standing at the foot of the couch, adjusting a clear plastic bag of red cells on the tall metal I.V. stand.

"You had a good rest," said Lockwood casually. "Now this will get you moving again."

"Was there a ceremony?" Garrett smiled, feeling a bit shy. "I don't remember."

"We had our own private ceremony today. You can come with the others next Monday night, if you like."

Garrett's muscular arms moved slightly. He shrugged. "Don't see the point." His eyes were on the red cells. "After today, I won't need any of that for another three weeks."

"As you wish. Some enjoy the Gatherings for themselves."

"Never saw the point, if you're not going to remember any of it."

"I've brought out some spansules. Thirty."

Thirty! Garrett pictured them immediately, a handful, more than a handful, and each good for a full twelve hours. To think of thirty made him feel like a man plunging his hands and arms into a large chest of gold coins.

He smiled. "Thank you."

"I shall have several small assignments during the next three weeks. You will be prepared to complete them."

Garrett nodded. He rolled up his sleeve and held out his right arm.

4

The woman flinched slightly as Phillip Bancroft came forward with the needle. She turned her head against the white fiber covering of the dental chair's neck support, and tried to speak clearly even though her lips were distended with plugs of cotton.

"I thought I was getting the gas again. I thought you were going to put me out completely."

The woman liked the way Dr. Bancroft smiled, an intelligent, professional smile that showed smooth, even white teeth with two first-quality gold inlays. His wavy light-brown hair remained in place as he tilted his head to look his patient directly in the eyes. When he spoke, his voice had a slight southern accent, and a trace of friendly amusement mingled with concern.

"You don't remember your injection when we took out the other tooth, Mrs. Eberhart?"

The woman did not.

Bancroft nodded, serious again. "Sometimes that happens when there is anesthesia. Let me explain once more. We use the local anesthetic as a prophylactic. In itself, it wouldn't be enough protection against the pain to enable me to work properly. But given in conjunction with the general anesthesia, it allows us to use a lesser amount. A lighter dose, if you will, so that you wake up more rapidly. The Xylocaine also continues to block the pain for several hours after you've left the office and gone home."

The woman looked at the handsome young oral surgeon as he waited with that bright stainless-steel hypodermic. He sounded as though he had given that explanation a hundred times before. But he had done good work on her last extraction; she had friends who hadn't slept well for three nights, whose jaws had swollen up in the back, where the wisdom tooth had been cut out. Not hers. And after one of those pills of his, she had even let her husband make love to her the night after.

She vaguely remembered the injection now but she didn't remember any explanation. She didn't even remember his giving her gas. "I suppose you know what you're doing," she said.

"I hope so," said Phillip Bancroft. "It worked before, at any rate. And according to the X rays, this one shouldn't be any more difficult than the other."

He pulled Mrs. Eberhart's upper lip away from the jawline and exposed the gum. She felt a hot, pinching pain as the needle went in. The heat spread as he depressed the plunger and forced the liquid in under her skin. She held rigid, afraid that if she moved the needle would scrape the bone.

He withdrew the needle and stood away. "All right, Mrs. Eberhart. Let's take out this cotton for the time being. You may rinse if you like. I'll be about fifteen minutes or so, getting the instruments and the dressings prepared, while we wait for the Xylocaine to take hold. Just relax in the chair and try to make yourself comfortable."

Mrs. Eberhart felt like making conversation. "Where's your assistant? Gone home early?"

"No, she's out front, straightening up. You're our last patient of the day." He turned away as he spoke, because it was coming over him again. The fear. The revulsion at what he was about to do.

The pills. He thought of them, as he usually did when he was under stress. But they would not be of use here. If he took another now, he would be feeling better within a half hour. But that would be too long after the time of need. In a half hour he would be fine, doing his work.

"Pretty girl, that little brunette of yours." The woman's voice sang the age-old message in its rising and falling cadences: "Why don't you marry her, Doctor?" it seemed to say. "A pretty girl like that can sure please a man."

"Thank you." He opened drawers, withdrew instruments, became active so as not to be interrupted. If you knew, he wanted to say, if you knew what that pretty girl is getting ready to do to you, you wouldn't be singing any praises for her. Then he stopped himself. There was no organic wrong done. He was performing a service for the Gathering. Those of the Gathering deserved it more than those to whom it would be given if she volunteered it tomorrow. She was healthy. She would not require termination, for she had been tested. She would recover quickly, and never know.

The old maxims.

He waited for the peace to come. As he breathed in, he felt it, like a soft wind. He closed his eyes.

But when he opened them again, it was wrong. He could still feel the woman's shock and horror.

Claire appeared in the doorway before him: statuesque, smiling, her blue eyes a subdued but unmistakable invitation. Her breasts magnificent. "All ready, Dr. Bancroft."

On the tray she held out to him were two syringes. One of them had been emptied. She had taken her scopolamine.

In the moment of hesitation before he picked up his syringe, he saw her watching him. Something else was in her eyes now. As though she knew his doubts; as though she had read them on his face when she had come upon him unawares, and had confirmed it in his reluctance to reach out for the syringe and adminster his own injection.

A tingle of fear constricted the base of his genitals. He took the syringe before his hand could begin to shake, and his mind worked swiftly to cover his error.

"Still awake, Mrs. Eberhart?" He turned toward the patient at the other end of the room, as if to indicate to Claire that he was reluctant to risk being seen injecting himself before the patient's injection of scopolamine took effect.

"Yep. Just starting to get numb over here on the side."

"All right. We'll test, before we begin work. A few minutes."

He nodded to Claire to move so that she would be blocking the patient's view of him. The strange look was gone from her face, and he thought, I've done it. He rolled up his sleeve.

It was humiliating, to be required to have her witness each injection. Yet she was a Guardian, and he was not.

Not yet.

He took the ethanol-soaked cotton ball from her tray and cleansed a spot on his arm midway between wrist and elbow, breathing in the cold vapor and resigning himself to what he was about to do. He felt her presence close to him, the force of her, willing him. Claire still exuded the confident energy that had so impressed him when she first came to work as his assistant. He had wondered at her then, her ability to work long hours without mental fatigue, her constant liveliness that sometimes made him feel old, even though he was only thirty-five. And she excited him sexually. He had felt vaguely threatened by the strength of her, the knowledge that she might prove him to be the weaker, even though she was the assistant and he the oral surgeon, the employer. So at first he had done nothing.

Then, one day after the last patient had put on his coat and left the office, she had touched him, her eyes promising miracles. Unable to restrain himself any longer, he had locked the door and they had made love right there on the soft cotton velvet of the new modular sofa in his waiting room. She had given him ecstasy.

And promised more, much more. There were secrets, she told him. If he would let her show him the Gathering, there would be so very much more. They would give him a strength he had never yet experienced—a strength that would set him above others—so that he could make his rightful place in the medical hierarchy and establish a practice substantially greater and more lucrative.

She had been right. And he still had the strength.

Yet each time from within came the doubts, and the strength was sapped from him.

As it was now. As she stood watching him, he could feel that her strength was greater. He thought fleetingly of challenging that strength, but the first code of the Gathering came instantly to his mind:

A member of the Gathering is a member for life.

Fear came to him again, and he took refuge in the sight of her wonderful breasts, so close to him now. What made him so obsessed with her body? When he cared so much more for Jill Weston—

He inserted the needle into his forearm and pressed the plunger home. Then he put the doubts aside.

"Mrs. Eberhart, we're going to put on a blood-pressure cuff now."

Claire nodded as she took the syringe from him and put it on the tray. She set the tray down on the work counter and opened the drawer where the sphygmoma-nometer was kept. She picked it up, and with it a roll of two-inch surgical adhesive tape. Together they walked to Mrs. Eberhart.

Bancroft explained that they were going to monitor Mrs. Eberhart's blood pressure periodically during the operation, the normal procedure when a general anesthesia was being administered. She asked what would be done if the blood pressure went down too far and he told her there was a medication that they used, a safe reliable medication that brought the level rapidly back up to normal.

"Did you use it the last time?"

He smiled. "No, but we explained about blood pressure, and we monitored during the extraction. I see that's something else that's still blurred in your memory."

"I guess it is. Hope I don't sound like a broken record, asking these questions over and over."

"Quite all right, Mrs. Eberhart." Bancroft looked at the clock. It had been five minutes since the injection in his forearm; eight minutes since Mrs. Eberhart had received her injection of scopolamine mingled with Xylo-caine. By now her injection, infusing from the mouth, so close to the brain, had already begun to take effect. After the last operation, when questioned after coming out of anesthesia, Mrs. Eberhart had had no recollection of instruments shown to her or explanations given nine minutes after the scopolamine had been administered.

She had passed the test. So on this visit she was now a candidate for donation.

And a very promising candidate, for she would have yet two more wisdom teeth when this one had been ex-tracted. As long as she stayed healthy, she would be useful to them at the time of both subsequent operations.

Claire was by her side with the blood-pressure cuff. Bancroft busied himself with his instruments, arranging the shining metal tools in the order he would be needing them. To carve a tooth out of a jawbone is never an easy task, especially when it was a molar impacted in the direction Mrs. Eberhart's was. He would have to be careful not to damage the root of the adjacent molar.

He concentrated on the X rays with Mrs. Eberhart's folder. You are going to do it, he told himself. You have skill and courage.

Claire's voice: "I think it's time for the adhesive, Doctor. Blood pressure is fine."

Claire smiled confidently as he turned and came toward the woman in the chair. He tried to think how fortunate he was to have Claire for his bed whenever he completed an obligation to the Gathering. He tried to tell himself he was not afraid of her. She was, after all, eight years younger than he. When he had been lifting weights and playing football as a thirteen-year-old, she had been only five. He tried to picture her as being less than half his size.

Mrs. Eberhart was speaking. "What does she mean about adhesive, Doctor?"

He explained that securing the patient's arms and legs during this kind of operation was another precautionary measure, a guard against any sudden involuntary movement. The type of anesthetic they would be using was not the sort where all movement stops and the patient is, to all intents and purposes, totally dependent on outside stimulus for breathing. This anesthetic was milder, to permit more rapid recovery. It was used in office procedures, whereas the anesthetic that would inhibit all movement would require hospitalization, which was really an unnecessary expense for an operation of this type.

Mrs. Eberhart nodded and said she guessed they knew what they were doing.

Bancroft congratulated himself on the way he had delivered the explanation under the gaze of his watchful assistant. He patted her on the buttocks as she leaned over to secure the patient's wrist to the arm of the chair. As she busied herself taping down the other wrist and the ankles, putting a gauze pad next to the skin to prevent marks from the adhesive, Bancroft went to the far end of the room and wheeled back the canister of anesthetic, a mixture of oxygen and nitrous oxide. He attached the tubing that led to the mask, and checked the pressure dial.

The catheter and empty blood pouch were in a bottom

drawer. When he saw that Mrs. Eberhart's arms and legs had been secured, he took them out.

Mrs. Eberhart was looking up at the ceiling. She said she guessed now that he had her trussed up like this, he could get down to work.

Behind her, Claire peeled off a long strip of the two-inch adhesive. She held the tape in the middle, with both hands.

"We'll get down to work right now, ma'am," she said. Swiftly she leaned forward over the woman and clapped the middle of the tape over the woman's mouth.

Mrs. Eberhart saw the inverted face above her as the tape descended. She tried to scream, but the sound was cut off. Her jaw was clamped shut, her mouth sealed by the tape. She tried to raise her head, but found she could not. The ends of the tape had been wrapped securely around the chair's neck support, pinning her down.

"She's ready," said Claire. "I'm going to apply stress."

Bending over the woman's middle, she lifted the buttocks and thighs away from the seat and hiked the woman's skirt up to the waist. Mrs. Eberhart appeared to be about twenty pounds overweight, so the task took a few moments. It took less time for Claire to draw down Mrs. Eberhart's panty hose.

Horrid gargling sounds came from beneath the tape on the woman's mouth.

Bancroft decided he would have to concentrate harder if he was going to get through this one without showing his fears. He forced himself to look only at the woman's arm, and at the catheter he held.

The drill. When Mrs. Eberhart saw Claire unhook it from the instrument console, the tremors shook her body. Tears of shame and horror spilled from under her eyelids. Bancroft did not see them; he was holding her elbow hard against the padded chair arm, positioning the catheter needle for insertion.

"Reacting nicely, I believe. Do you want a blood-pressure reading?"

Bancroft shook his head no. He managed to get the I.V. started and running without looking up.

The drill began to whir.

"Where shall we begin, Mrs. Eberhart?" Claire brought the whirling tip of the drill within six inches of the woman's face so that it could be seen clearly. "Where shall we start?"

She put her free hand between the woman's fleshy legs. "I like to drill down here, Mrs. Eberhart. Is there anything down here you wouldn't want to lose?"

Bancroft watched the blood slowly filling the plastic pouch. He concentrated on the sound of the drill as Claire stroked the back of the vibrating instrument slowly up and down the woman's bare thighs. If he could hear only the sound of the drill, the sound of the woman would not affect him anymore.

"It's half full," he said.

"I think we'll try for just a bit more," said Claire. She held the drill once more in the face of the terrified Mrs. Eberhart.

"You don't seem to like it down there," she said. "Maybe your husband doesn't like it down there either. Maybe he likes someone else. You'd probably never want to see him with someone else, would you?"

She brandished the drill, whirred the motor to high speed again and again.

"We can fix it so that you never see him with anyone else. We can put this drill into your eyes—"

Mrs. Eberhart lost consciousness.

Bancroft saw the trembling arm go limp, saw the legs suddenly relax. He was secretly relieved. An unconscious patient was one he could work with easily. But there was his role with Claire to consider.

"You've pushed her too far," he said. "We're not going to get more adrenaline from her when she's knocked out."

"I guess I did. Isn't it a pity I won't be able to remember this mistake for the next time?"

He looked up and she was smiling, beckoning him to her.

Eighteen minutes after the wisdom tooth had been removed and her incision packed and stitched, Mrs. Eberhart awoke. Her dress and panty hose were back in place. Her wrists and ankles were still taped, a precautionary measure in the unlikely event that the scopolamine had somehow proved ineffective. Bancroft and Claire were both watching her face very carefully as she opened her eyes.

She blinked as she saw them. "Am I all done?"

Bancroft looked at Claire and nodded. She moved to

Mrs. Eberhart's side. "Do you remember when we trussed you up here?" she asked pleasantly.

Mrs. Eberhart did not, and the three of them had a moment of laughter over the fact that she herself had used the phrase "trussed up." Claire removed the tape quickly with surgical scissors. Bancroft explained that during the course of the operation there had been a drop in her blood pressure and they had administered the medication he had earlier described to her, a solution of Dopamine HCl, and that she had responded well. There was a flesh-colored plastic Band-Aid over the crook of her right arm where, he said, they had given the Dopamine intravenously. Now they would like Mrs. Eberhart to drink this eight-ounce glass of orange juice. They asked her to be careful not to disturb the stitches on the right side of her mouth. The orange juice would raise her blood sugar and make her more alert for her bus ride home.

Mrs. Eberhart made an appointment to have the next wisdom tooth removed the second Tuesday in March, at the same time as today's visit. As she left the office she told both Dr. Bancroft and his assistant to have a nice weekend.

Claire locked the office door. She went behind the receptionist's counter and withdrew the pouch of Mrs. Eberhart's blood from the drawer in which she had locked it. She placed the pouch on the white formica counter, opened Mrs. Eberhart's file, and used a black Flair pen to enter the blood type on the pouch label. She also entered the date of collection. She left the file on the counter for the receptionist, who would be in on Monday to handle the accounting for Mrs. Eberhart's bill. As an afterthought, she opened the file once more to check the slip for today's extraction, making certain that the charge for 10-cc. intravenous Dopamine appeared. It did. She closed the file.

Opening her purse, a tan shoulder bag with the same French designer label as her shoes and gloves, she carefully inserted the pouch of blood.

Bancroft was in the small washroom with the door closed, being sick as quietly as he was able to under cover of the flushing toilet. When he had finished, he rinsed his mouth with the office mouthwash and splashed cold water on his face, keeping his eyes away from his reflection in the mirror. He dried himself with a fresh towel. Coming out of the washroom, he removed his white operating smock and rolled it up with the towel, putting both in the hamper for the laundry service.

He slipped on his sports jacket, a fitted British corduroy, and straightened his necktie. He would go home, he thought. Go home and have a drink, or maybe two, and sleep it off, and then wake up around midnight and get some good work done. That would make him feel better able to face Saturday night.

When he came out into the reception area Claire was waiting. She had taken off her nurse's clothing and stood before him clad only in her panties. She took his hand and cupped it against her breasts. "I thought we might finish what we started," she said.

Her voice was soft and inviting, but within it he heard the note of command. Courage drained from him as he realized this would be another test. He thought, *She won't remember either.* Yet there had been rumors that the Guardians could retain evidence of another member's failings during an assignment. And he didn't know what was in their injections. He knew his was more than scopolamine; had known that from the first. Anyone with any medical background would realize that people didn't do precision work like oral surgery after taking enough pure scopolamine to give an amnesiac effect. Scopolamine also produced drowsiness and euphoria, which, he knew, he was not feeling. Obviously the Gathering had added something else to counteract symptoms that would interfere with his work. The Leader was the world's pharmacological wonder, as anyone who took one of the white capsules would realize. It was not beyond the realm of possibility that he had developed, for the Guardians, a *selective* amnesiac. . . . He kissed Claire lightly. Then he took off his jacket, tie, and shirt, and folded them across the sofa. He slipped off his half boots and came to her.

Her mouth was on his, breathing passion. She guided his hand beneath the elastic of her waistband under her panties, to cover the soft hair. She pressed his fingers down into the wet folds, warming them with smooth moisture.

Bancroft drew in his breath and tried to relax, hoping that his passion would somehow be kindled. But he was unable to overlook her power. She made him afraid. He moved his fingers to stimulate her as she took her hand away.

"Do you still remember Mrs. Eberhart?" she whispered. She moved her hips with the rhythm of his hand.

"Yes."

"So do I. After this, we'll sleep."

5

Saturday morning at eight, when Dr. Jerry Chamberlain got to work, he found a good-looking young woman waiting outside the locked entrance to the Madison Hospital Blood Bank. She reminded him of a girl he had dated at Columbia, a whole *type* of a girl, actually, with the dark hair pulled back straight and the big round glasses and the skin that was smooth enough to look like she never smiled or frowned or anything-ed except to study and ask intelligent questions during lectures. He guessed they still made them that way.

"How ya doin'," he said. "I hope you're here to give blood. I'm Dr. Chamberlain."

"I'm Marcie Walsh. They sent me over from Personnel. I'm your new part-time receptionist."

"Oh. Good. Welcome aboard, Marcie." He had his keys ready and unlocked the door. "Come on in. We've got a lot to do this morning. I'm glad you're here."

She took in the outer office: white walls, with painted designs here and there, large bold orange circles and red arches over them. "It's cheerful," she said, taking off her coat.

"What else? We need every donor we can get, and the best way to keep 'em coming back is to make 'em feel cheery while they're in here. There's your desk. You can hang your coat over there. Then I'll show you around."

She thanked him and smiled a little. "I like your hat, by the way. That's an Irish tweed, isn't it? I've seen them advertised."

It was a favorite of Jerry's, a light-blue tweed rain hat, the kind you could wad up and put in your pocket. Jerry tossed it at the coat rack next to the door of his office. "You go to school, Marcie?"

"I'm premed at Barnard. I've been reading up on blood groups and lab procedures all week, ever since they told me I'd be working here."

"Be sure to ask when you have questions. I keep my door open." He hung up his coat, a blue parka, and waited while she fumbled in her purse for a note pad.

"All right," he said. "First, your sociology lesson for the day. Here's a lab coat for you. Notice it's short, and pink. That's because you're a clinician and not a medical student yet. When you get to medical school, you get one that's short and white. Then when you're an M.D., you sweep around in a long white coat like this one." He got his off the rack where the nurse's aide left it wrapped in brown paper, a clean one each day. "Protective coloration or status badge or whatever you want to call it. It'll keep you from being bothered with questions you don't need to know about yet."

"I want to do more than just clerical."

"Good. Now let me show you the collection rooms. In there's my office, by the way, when you have a problem. We'll keep the tour kind of brief and cursory this morning because there's a shortage on and we've got to get cracking to bring in some new blood."

He opened the doors to the two collection rooms, each with more white walls and geometric designs in blue and green. There were four blue naugahyde-covered reclining couches in each.

"Restful," said Marcie. "I was wondering, why do they keep this place locked up at night? What happens if they need blood for an accident or something?"

"Emergency has its own storage units. They come in evenings before I leave and pick up whatever they think they'll need. Which last night was a lot, and as it happened, they cleaned us out. So now we're short. We'll have to get on the phones and beg."

"What are those machines, behind the couches?"

"Fractionalizing units. We can centrifuge the blood from a donor while he's giving it. We push the button for what we need—red cells or plasma, or platelets or whatever component we're looking for, and the machine separates that out and returns the rest to the donor through another tube."

She was noticing his red hair and freckles, and the way his blue eyes seemed to look right at her, as though he really expected her to remember everything he said. "Are you Irish?" she asked.

"Brooklynese. Born and bred, like dey say." He gave a brief smile. "Now let's take a quick look in at the lab room, where we run the tests and store the units. There'll be a technician in at nine, when we open officially. Name's Alice. You'll like her. She'll handle the donors and the lab stuff unless we really get busy, which I hope we will, because we need the blood. If that happens we'll all pitch in. You'll learn quick that way."

He opened one of the stainless-steel refrigerator doors in the lab room. On one shelf were four clear vinyl bags filled with straw-colored fluid. On the shelf above was a single bag, with the dark-red color of whole blood. Only one.

"As you can see, the cupboard is pretty bare," he said.
"Those are one pint each?"

"Right. A pint is called a unit." He picked up the bag of whole blood and showed it to her. "See? This one's A-positive. If someone needs a unit of A-positive blood this morning, we're in good shape. Otherwise we're SOL."

"What's SOL?"

"Out of luck," he said. "The S is a vulgarism that we hematologists don't use unless it's called for."

"I can dig it. What's this test tube taped onto the bag?"

Jerry asked if she'd read about crossmatching, the process the lab used to make sure the blood they were sending out wouldn't react badly with the blood of the patient who was getting the transfusion. She said, oh how could she have forgotten, of course, that was the pilot tube, and started to run through the five procedures involved in crossmatching as though she were a student taking an oral exam. Jerry let her talk for a minute or so. He watched the way she used her hands for emphasis and the way her eyes lit up, even though she was only talking about mixing a couple of drops of donor blood with a couple of drops from the recipient and with various reagents to see that the mixture didn't clot. This Marcie was more of an eager beaver than most of the part-time people Personnel sent over, Jerry thought, but if she was premed that was to be expected. Everybody knew that premed types were overachievers.

He cut her monologue short by showing her where they kept the bromelin powder and the antiglobulin serum and the other crossmatch reagents. "You'll catch on fine," he said. "Alice will be glad you're prepared."

She was opening the other refrigerator. The shelves were stacked three-high with units of whole blood. "Isn't this blood too?" she asked. "Why can't we use this?"

Jerry shook his head. "We could, but I don't like to do it. That's commercial blood. We don't like to use it, because of the risk of disease. You know about commercial blood?"

She said she didn't.

"Look around at the storefronts when you're in the Bowery sometime, or over in the West Forties. That's where the commercial blood banks set up their intake clinics. People go in there and sell their blood for ten or fifteen dollars a unit. A lot of them are pretty desperate for the money. A lot of them are pretty sick, too. Plenty of viruses and bacteria floating around."

"But don't the clinics screen their donors?"

"Sure. With questions and sight examination. But people will lie about their health when they need the money. And you can't always see the kind of diseases they've got by checking for runny eyes and sniffles and hacking cough."

She made a face. "So this blood has *diseases* in it?"

"Probably not all of it. But here and there with commercial blood, you know you're going to get a 'bad unit.' And a bad unit can do some ugly things to whoever gets it. You've heard of complications after surgery, right? A lot of times that's a euphemism for hepatitis or some other damn thing picked up from a transfusion. We have tests for one kind of hepatitis, by the way, and we use them, but there are two other kinds that we can't screen. The basic thing we have to rely on is that a person doesn't volunteer to give his blood away for free unless he's feeling pretty good. And if he's feeling pretty good, the chances are that he's healthy. You'll have to keep that in mind when you call the people on our list today. Don't twist any arms. If they don't feel up to coming in, we're better off without their blood."

"Why do we get this commercial blood at all, if it's that bad?"

"One good reason. It's better than no blood at all. Now

let's go back out to the reception area, and I'll get you a pin."

The pin was shiny red, heart-shaped, about the size of a quarter. It said "Blood Donors Are Special People."

Jerry put it into the lapel of Marcie's coat. "You're now officially employed," he said. "Try to get in the habit of looking at the donors as they leave and making sure Alice or whoever's on duty hasn't forgotten to put on their pin. Offer it even if you don't think the donor wants it. Makes 'em feel good and it shows we appreciate what they've done. Which we do. Our patients would be in pretty bad shape without our donors."

He had her sit down at her desk and showed her the Rolodex with the standby donors. "Here's what I want you to get working on," he said. "Each card gives you the the name and number, the blood type, when they last gave blood, and what time is O.K. for us to call. You identify yourself, give your name and all, and say we've got a shortage and would it be convenient for them to come in. Got it? And you're the voice with a smile. Make 'em happy, O.K.? I'll be in the office over there, going through my own Rolodex list."

"Other people?"

"Nope. Hospitals. There are two hundred thirty-eight with blood banks, and if I'm lucky, maybe one or two will have a surplus of something. Probably type A-positive. During a shortage they tend to hoard supplies, so to get anywhere I've got to do the importuning myself. Great way to spend a Saturday, but that's what they pay us for."

"And all those other hospitals—they'll be calling their donor lists too?"

"Yep. And each other. So some calls may come in through you." He showed her on the phone where to push the buttons for his extensions.

Then he went into the office and got to work. In the drawer of his desk was a pack of Newport cigarettes but he left the drawer shut. He was trying to cut down.

Before doing the hospitals, Jerry tried calling the New York Area Blood Center, the largest blood-collection agency in the United States. That center distributed, at $34 a unit, the equivalent of 700,000 units of whole blood every year to New York hospitals. Most of it went to the big hospitals. Most of it also was type A, because the New York Area Center imported nearly half of its blood from European donor centers, from a population nearly 100 per cent white, who tended toward type A blood. Here in New York, the demand tended to be for type O during a shortage in the big hospitals, because that was the predominant blood type for non-whites, who tended to have more emergencies that required transfusion. Jerry had done his internship at Jacoby and seen them come in from the car crashes and the stabbings, and learned how to get the blood into them quick, doing the crossmatch after the I.V. was already running, but he was not thinking about that now. He was hoping that there were at least a few units of A blood available at the New York Center.

Then he could get an advance on next week's allocation. New York Area Center delivered eighty-four units once a week, on Mondays. Today was Saturday.

He reached the Area Center and talked them into eight units, average age fourteen days past collection. That meant the units would still be usable for another week. At that time, twenty-one days after they had been taken from their donor's veins, the disc-shaped walls of more than half the red cells would have worn thin and burst, spilling the red hemoglobin and the rest of their cellular material to mix uselessly with the plasma in the container pouch.

That made nine units of A. Jerry flipped up the Rolodex on his desk and started in on the hospitals.

He was on his fourth hospital when Marcie buzzed him on the intercom.

"Dr. Chamberlain, there's a Dr. Weston here to see you."

He looked up and saw Jill across the room. Grinned. "Tell her to come on in." Looking at her made him feel good; she always seemed so fresh and upbeat with those delicate features and wide blue eyes.

He cleared his throat for the hospital on the line and told the operator he'd call back later.

Jill had her lab coat on. "I thought you'd be out in the woods by now," she said as she came in. "It being a Saturday and all, you should at least be taking it easy. Have your feet up on the desk, reading your L. L. Bean catalogue . . ."

"I'll start taking it easy when you start taking it easy," he said. "Hey, look at this, though." He reached into the desk drawer that held the Newports and took out a colorful medium-sized booklet. "There you go," he said, handing it over. "The spring edition. If it's not in there, it's not worth having."

"I don't believe it. You really keep the L. L. Bean catalogue in your desk! I thought you were just kidding!"

"A man's got to dream, doesn't he? Besides, it's useful. Where do you think I got my hat?"

"That blue thing? All the woodsmen I ever knew would have laughed you out of the forest if you showed up wearing it. Or even carrying it. It looks like a bucket."

He sniffed, and made a show of taking back the catalogue.

"Upstate snob."

"Names will never hurt me."

"One of these days I'm going to show you. I'm going to get out of town and take a real camping trip. Backpacking, the works."

"You wouldn't last two miles."

"Hah. I've even started jogging lunch hours. Gonna get in shape. You wait and see."

"O.K. I'll believe it when I see it. Actually, I ought to be doing something like that myself."

He told her she was welcome to join his crowd of one anytime. Then he saw she was holding a pilot tube, rubber-capped, with blood in it. "But you didn't come in here to talk physical fitness, did you?"

She handed him the pilot tube. "This is from Mrs. Comfrey. She's a patient of mine. I'd like you to cross-match and hold about two units for her until about nine tomorrow morning."

In the middle of a shortage. "Is the woman in labor or something?"

"I won't lie to you. This woman is in for voluntary surgery. I'm going to try a fallopian dilation tomorrow at eight."

Elective surgery on a Saturday was rare; on Sunday it was almost unheard of. "We've got a shortage. If this was a Friday, they'd have had to postpone the whole morning's schedule. Better wait until Monday, when we get our good supplies in. Unless you want to go with a commercial unit."

"You're really that low?"

"You didn't hear about last night? A two-car collision

right over on Fifth and Eighty-first. Seven kids. Two of them died. Wiped us out of everything voluntary except one unit of A red cells. That's why I'm in here on the phone."

Jill looked at the jottings on his note pad. "She's a B-positive. Couldn't you just set aside those two units you're getting from Columbia? If they crossmatch?"

He covered the pad. "For an elective operation, that gets pretty shaky. What happens if we get another accident tonight? Or two?" He was holding firm, and hating himself for it. "We've got some B-positive from Herald Blood Bank in storage—"

"I can't risk commercial blood with this woman. This weekend is the only chance Mrs. Comfrey is going to get. She wants to have a child so badly she's willing to deceive her husband and violate her own religion by coming in here. Monday afternoon her husband will be back in New York, and if she's not in their apartment to meet him, he'll make her suffer for it the rest of her life. I'm only talking about two units. I'd give a unit myself, only I'm type A."

"You gave two weeks ago. I couldn't accept you as a donor anyway."

"It's only for twenty-four hours. And with this operation, we generally don't even use the blood. Couldn't you just put it aside?"

He thought maybe nobody would need B-positive tonight. Sometimes you had to bend the rules a little.

"O.K.," he said. "You'll have it. Unless we get another big emergency tonight."

"What if there *is* an emergency?"

"Well if our commercial supplies are gone, I won't let anybody die just to protect your two units, obviously. But I will make every effort to find you two more. And I'll be coming in early. If there's a problem, I'll try to have a staff donor lined up."

She nodded and smiled again. "I really do appreciate your help."

He heard himself saying it was O.K., just doing his job.

And asking her if she wasn't working tonight maybe she'd like to have dinner. She got a strange, kind of worried expression for a moment and he knew she would say no, just as she had said she was busy last October, the

second Friday in October, the only other time he'd asked
her out. Jerry didn't ask many women out, hadn't since
his wife and baby daughter had been killed by a hit-
and-run driver five years ago. So he remembered asking
Jill Weston out last October pretty clearly.

This time she looked like she wished she could go, he
thought. At least that was progress. But she was sorry, she
said; she'd already made plans.

"Too bad. You don't get a shot at the Fort Hamilton
woodsman every day. But I'll get back to you, don't
worry."

When Jill had gone, he picked up one of the red heart-
shaped donor pins from his desk top and chucked it at the
wastebasket. Then he flipped the next card on the
Rolodex and dialed quickly.

But when Marcie came in and asked if he'd show her
where people ate lunch around here, he said yes, he
would show her. And because it was her first day, he
would treat.

6

At 6:15 Saturday evening Mrs. Sarah Comfrey finished
dinner in her private hospital room. The food was the
standard insipid preop fare: a small portion of farina and
some gelatin, with fruit juice to drink. Mrs. Comfrey liked
the jello. It reminded her of childhood, when she had not
needed to worry about the laws of the church. Now her
very presence in this hospital was in violation of the laws.
Tomorrow would be a much greater violation, for she
would be allowing Dr. Weston to alter the body her God
had made. The body He had not seen fit to change in
accordance with her prayers. Or, as her husband would
be quick to point out, the body she had not prayed for
with sufficient sincerity and truth. For him, prayer was
the answer. Medical intervention was forbidden.

Mrs. Comfrey put her tray aside and reflected again

that her husband might be mistaken about several points of the law, which after all had been given years ago in an age when no one had heard of things like Dr. Weston's ultrasound and surgeons for a woman's birthing tubes. Especially a surgeon who was a woman. The hand of the High God was certainly greater than any book of writings, and she had had a strong feeling that His hand was directing her, from the moment she had spoken with the pregnant American woman at the UN reception and had learned of Dr. Weston's operation. Certainly His hand had guided her to that reception! And, after her first office visit to Dr. Weston, He assuredly had helped her to sell her gold bracelets and earrings in the shops on the West Side of Manhattan. Certainly His hand had given her the strength to convincingly describe the way a man had robbed her of those same bracelets and earrings, so that her husband did not realize she had obtained the dollars necessary for this surgery.

It was also possible, she reasoned, that His hand had taken the life of Lemuel, her husband's brother, in Texas last Wednesday. Her husband had left yesterday afternoon for the funeral, giving her more than two full days alone.

The first days they had been apart since her marriage eighteen years ago. She was now thirty-four. If she waited for him to leave again, she might grow too old and be left childless forever.

God's will, she thought, as she pushed away the feeding table. At any rate, He would certainly get all the credit if she did conceive a child. After eighteen barren years, a pregnancy for her would be called a miracle.

She pictured in her mind how warm the child would be to hold. The babies of the other women were so warm and soft it made her want to cry. She wondered if she would cry if the baby was her own.

She opened her eyes and saw there was a man in her room. And that the door was now shut.

"Mrs. Comfrey?" He was dark-haired and muscular, in a white coat.

"That's me. What is it?"

"Routine injection. Preoperative. You're getting surgery tomorrow morning?"

She nodded.

He took a thick pad of white cotton out of his pocket

and unfolded it. Inside was a glass syringe with a sharp-pointed needle. Mrs. Comfrey did not like injections.

"What's that for?"

"Routine. It will help you rest. Your doctor ordered it for you. It's ready now. Would you please bare your shoulder, Mrs. Comfrey?"

"Dr. Weston told me I would get a sleeping pill. She didn't say there would be any injection."

"It's hospital policy, Mrs. Comfrey. The sleeping pill makes you drowsy, but the injection helps you to relax. Now, please?"

He was at the head of the bed by now, looking down at her. For a moment she wished that her husband was in the room to make this man give her a better explanation, but then she immediately realized how absurd a wish that was. She drew down the sleeve of her coarse white cotton hospital gown.

He put his fingers on the place where her collarbone joined the shoulder and pressed, harder than she had expected. Then he placed the needle point at the base of her neck and pushed it in. The pain was sharper than she had prepared herself to accept, and she cried out softly. He did not appear to notice. She could not see the needle or the glass syringe as he injected the fluid, but she could feel it making a warm circle under the skin of her neck, the warmth spreading upward toward her face.

"I don't feel relaxed," she said.

"In a while. After the sleeping pill."

"Do you have that?"

"No. The nurse will bring it."

He drew out the needle, folded it and the syringe into his cotton padding, and put them back into his coat pocket. He opened her door and was gone before she had time to ask him any questions.

She wondered why he had not swabbed her neck with alcohol on cotton, as she had seen done with other injections. The bell cord was clipped to her pillow. She reached for it and pressed the button to call the nurse.

Nothing happened.

They must be busy, she thought, five minutes later. After ten minutes had gone by she climbed out of the bed and went to the door. The tile floor was cold on her bare feet and she reminded herself to ask for an extra blanket. The air had turned colder after the rain. The hospital kept the heat up, but her room felt chilly now that it was night.

A nurse was outside the door with a small tray. Wearing a net over her blond hair with her white cap, she looked younger than Mrs. Comfrey by several years, but much heavier. Mrs. Comfrey had a good figure and took pride in it. The white uniform of this woman showed rolls of fat where the waist should have been.

On the tray was cotton, a green plastic Phisoderm bottle, and a small throwaway safety razor.

"Hi, Mrs. Comfrey. Finished dinner? I'm Emily Francis. Come to give you your prep."

When Mrs. Comfrey learned that "prep" meant shaving off her pubic hair in preparation for her operation, she became very frightened. She forgot all about the man who had given her the injection. All she could think of was what her husband would say when he came home and discovered what had happened. It was inevitable that he would find out, especially if she was going to try again to have a child, and there was no possible way of explaining. None. For five minutes she tried to explain that she did not want them to do this to her; that it was against her religion. Then she told the nurse about her husband.

She at last convinced Miss Francis to try to reach Dr. Weston and ask for her approval to omit the shaving.

The nurse left the door open.

She was in the bed when Garrett came into her room again. When she saw him closing her door, she sat up straight.

"I will have no more injections."

"Of course not, Mrs. Comfrey. Only one was ordered. I only came in to see how you were feeling."

"I feel fine. It's the nurse I'm worried about. She said they were—" She stopped. This man was a doctor, after all, but she did not feel comfortable talking with him about this particular problem. And he did not look like the kind who would be willing to put the regulations aside.

"They were what, ma'am?"

"They weren't going to let me have anything more to eat. And I'm still hungry. The dinner was too small."

"I see. Well a good appetite is a sign that you're feeling well. Always glad to see a good appetite in a patient.

I'd like to just check that injection site for a moment, if you don't mind."

As he came closer she caught the odor of what she thought was the rubbing alcohol for injections.

Then he clapped something cold and wet over her nose and mouth, his big hands too quick and strong for her to get away. She drew a breath and screamed, but the hand muffled the noise. As she drew another breath the volatile anesthetic, drawn into her lungs and propelled swiftly by her excited heart, reached her brain. She lost consciousness.

When she awoke she found her mouth had been taped shut. She lay spread-eagled on the bed, wrists and ankles taped to the bars at each of its far corners. She felt pain. Something sharp was pricking the inside of her thigh, up near her groin.

The dark-haired man had a clear plastic tube, bent double. The tube looked thicker than others she had seen in the hospital.

When he saw she was awake he uncrimped the tube and the hollow plastic filled with dark, red blood.

It's my punishment, she thought. Oh God, you have given me my punishment. Only let me live, and I will remain faithful unto the Law until the end of my days.

The pouch filled rapidly. When it was nearly at capacity, Garrett unwrapped another injection kit. He stared directly into Mrs. Comfrey's fear-widened eyes as he found the artery in the neck again, trying to subdue her with his eyes the way a snake paralyzes a rodent. She did not flinch.

But when he injected a fractional dosage of Sodium Pentothal into the carotid artery, she became dead-weight. Her eyes closed. Clean, he thought. And the woman had shown no reaction symptoms. He carefully withdrew the catheter from Mrs. Comfrey's femoral artery. The ruptured vessel wall did not entirely close, so Garrett applied pressure to the area above the small puncture wound. Soon the bleeding stopped. He would have preferred to have drawn the blood from a vein, but the arterial flow was more rapid and the woman had mentioned that the nurse was coming back.

He let the blood drain from the catheter tube to fill the pouch to capacity, and then sealed the pouch. Opening a window, he cleared the air of ether. He wrapped the thick ether-soaked gauze in the plastic bag he had used to bring it into the hospital, and watched the bag fall into the night air, down to the iron basement grating. No one saw it. After quietly closing the window, he undid the woman's wrists and ankles and peeled the tape from her mouth. The tape had made red marks, so he got her under the covers and drew the blanket up almost to her nose.

Seventeen minutes later Emily Francis came through the open door to Mrs. Comfrey's room to tell her the good news. Dr. Weston had given approval; they could eliminate the "prep."

She found Mrs. Comfrey asleep under the blanket. I'll let her rest, Emily thought. She'll have her pill later, so she'll sleep through the rest of the night.

Because Nurse Francis did not disturb Mrs. Comfrey, neither of them was aware that the cut in the patient's femoral artery had reopened. The spreading pool of blood under Mrs. Comfrey's thighs also went unnoticed, hidden by the blanket.

7

Seen for the first time, the dark splendor of the Observation Gallery made a spectacular impression. The vastness of the room stopped Maryann Delvecchio at the upper entrance, on the ledge of the balcony. Even though the glass-walled elevator was open to take her down to the floor level, she waited, spellbound by the magnificence she saw. City lights glittered against the dark river skyline all along the balcony window wall, a spectacular row of plate-glass panes nearly a hundred feet long. On the mirrored opposite wall, perhaps fifty feet away, the same glittering skyline was duplicated along the upper portion of the huge reflecting surface. The darkness of the Gallery at its lower level, visible some thirty feet below, appeared softened, almost cloudlike, and was momentarily lit by

small red ellipses as first one, then another of a bank of
infrared spotlights glowed in random sequence.

For a few brief moments, two of the red spotlights illuminated glistening intertwined bodies.

A great darkened arch filled the lower half of the wall
across from where Maryann now stood. When the red
spotlights glowed near to the arch, Maryann could see
that it was really the mouth of a great cave, with en-
trances to smaller arched chambers built into the curves
of its interior walls. She thought of the time she had first
ventured under water in the Caribbean with snorkel
and mask and looked down to see the gradual darkening
of the sand and coral as the bottom sloped away into
the depths. Here, the faraway mouth of the cave held
her eyes transfixed. Something was in there.

She tried to think what could be waiting for her in
those small, darkened interior rooms. No answer came
to her. She stared again at the yawning expanse of shadows and warm flickering light. Fantastic, seeing it all
for the first time.

Maryann Delvecchio had come into the Observation
Gallery on five previous occasions since November.

Each time she entered, she saw the Gallery as if for
the first time.

With the exception of the Leader, she thought, so did
everyone else. None of them remembered coming here
before. None would remember being here tonight.

The red spotlight showed Maryann another pair of
bodies clasped to one another, undulating. So we really
are getting laid here every month, she thought. She had
guessed as much from morning-after examinations in the
privacy of her own bathroom. Well, she decided, it was
obviously O.K. O.K. before. It would be O.K. again.
She knew she would not remember who she saw here,
or what she did with them. Nor would they. She could
do anything she wanted that the others would allow.
No tongues would wag in the morning. There would be
no embarrassed blushes or dropped glances. Even if one
of the men who made love to her tonight happened to be
right there in the TV studio with her tomorrow, neither
of them would know.

That was their protection. A chemical bond of secrecy,
unbreakable. An injection wiped away all traces of memory.

You had to have faith coming here, she thought. In order to take that injection and wait for the required time until it took effect, you had to have a lot of faith. Because anything might happen, really, *anything*, and as long as there wasn't a mark or a scar on you when you woke up the next morning in your own bed, you wouldn't know whether to call the police or to call your best friend and give her the chance to join up.

But of course calling a best friend couldn't happen until you'd become a Guardian. Only Guardians were allowed to recruit. Ordinary members were not allowed to mention the Gathering to anyone unless they'd been specifically assigned.

Not that it would get you anywhere if you did. The person you told would have no use for anything you gave him. The pills were no good unless you had the special blood transfusion, and the location of this place was a mystery, except to the most senior Guardians. You didn't find the Gathering; it found you. After each meeting you were given a date, usually three weeks later. That morning someone would call with a place and a time. You arrived there alone. Then someone with a face you'd never seen before, a face that was heavy with make-up, found you. You both got into a taxi. When that someone was certain no one was following the cab, you got your injection. The cab was driven around until the injection took effect, and then the someone let you out of the cab and told you to wait for the limousine.

Tonight Maryann had been let out at Forty-ninth and Third, picked up by a black Cadillac limousine, and driven to this wonderful old apartment house on Riverside Drive, with its sparkling view of the Hudson. But she knew she would not remember that in the morning. All she would remember after the injection would be riding around in the back of a cab with a man or woman she had never seen before. Then there would be a gap. A blank space in her memory, as though a portion of a movie film had been cut out.

Then she would see the Leader.

Then another gap, until she woke in her own apartment on Park Avenue early the next morning.

Each time Maryann vowed to fill in the gaps. Each time she failed. The failure both pleased and frustrated her. She felt pleased because she knew that the system

protected her as well as the others. She felt frustrated
because she was a TV reporter and knew she was in the
middle of a story that could win her a show of her own.
Maybe even a network spot. Maybe the start of a series.
But there was no breaking a story that she could not remember.

Meanwhile, she worked hard. Harder than ever now,
because of the pills. She might get that show of her own
and go to the top even without learning the secret of
the Gathering. But she had a plan. The Leader had to
have an angle somewhere. It was true that Maryann
brought a hundred dollars to each meeting and left it
with her clothing and her purse in the small dressing
cubicle, but the Leader had to be getting more out of
the group than a hundred dollars each. You didn't buy an
apartment building and turn the top three floors into this
kind of a setup without more than a hundred dollars a
person.

She knew she would not remember the setup, but she
would remember the Leader. His face—just the memory
made her body feel warm inside. Someday he would show
that face to the public and she would see it. Then she
could use the resources of the station to follow him. Maybe even a helicopter tracking her when she went into the
cab for another of these meetings.

Or else she would figure out the angle. If she knew
what it was he was getting from them that made all this
worth his while, she could work from there. There had
to be something. For a hundred dollars, what she was
getting was way too one-sided in her favor. He was making her the wonder woman of "News Center Six," and
what was she doing for him?

The thought of doing something for him made her
warm as always.

She wrapped the red robe from her dressing cubicle
more tightly around her naked body and stepped into the
elevator. There were no buttons to press, only a clear
glass. Yet the elevator began its descent the moment she
stepped on.

As it carried her down, she saw a red glow above the
great archway on the far wall.

The red glow was suddenly transformed into a giant
image of Maryann's face. A television camera here inside the elevator was introducing her to those hidden in

the dark below, projecting her features onto a huge thirty-foot screen. A little surprised at first, Maryann smiled for the people the way she smiled for the unseen millions out there in TV land every weekday from 5 to 7 P.M., and when taping out on assignment. I'll bet they're all thinking they've seen me somewhere before, she thought. They'll say, where'd we see that cute little Italian girl with the frizzy black hair? Then her smile broadened.

She unloosened her robe and let it fall from her shoulders. She smiled at the gigantic replica of her naked shoulders and breasts.

Then she thought, I wonder if I take off my robe every time. The elevator reached the floor level and the giant red screen switched off. The curved glass partition swung away. Maryann Delvecchio picked up her robe and slipped it on again. In her bare feet, the surface outside the elevator felt soft, velvetlike. It buoyed her up, pulsating like an enormous water bed.

The angle, she reminded herself. Look for the angle. And some way to remember it.

Feeling like a jungle cat on a nocturnal mating quest, she walked into the red flashes and the darkness.

Another member of the Gathering had arrived.

8

The door of the elevator in Jill Weston's building opened at her floor. Phillip followed her out. He continued the conversation they had been having as they walked down the well-lit corridor to Jill's apartment.

"So, for example, there's a nice piece of residential property in Montreal that I'm thinking of picking up. If you wanted to go in with me, I could guarantee you a ten per cent yield within the year. Actually I expect to do better than double ten per cent—"

"You're looking for investment capital? Maybe you could rent out that boat."

"That's not the point, hon, and you know it. The point is *you*."

"I know. Outside interest for poor hospital-ridden Weston. You've been harping on that all evening."

"Well? Haven't some of the things I've said sounded interesting? Just here in the city, for example. Instead of living in this—"

"I happen to like my apartment. Maybe it's too new, too much noise, too much sheet rock—"

"Hold it right there, speaking of sheet rock. Do you know that if I wanted to get into your apartment I wouldn't need to use your door? I could just break right through the wall. I'm serious. I saw it done when I was looking at a property just under construction. Two of the workmen were drunk and fooling around, chasing each other in the hallway and the one reared back and heaved the other right through—"

"Excuse me. I think that's my phone ringing."

"Probably the hospital. You know they take advantage of you because you're only five minutes' walk away, don't you? If you bought into a nice condominium in one of the old buildings, a place with some real character—"

Another ring. She got the door open. "Come on in while I get the phone."

"Sure."

She caught a note of uncertainty in his voice. Of course he had been expecting to come in for longer than her phone conversation. Probably she ought to have said good-night to him downstairs.

She left her coat on. If it was the hospital and she was needed, that would save time.

An emergency at the hospital would also solve the problem of tactfully saying good-bye to Phillip. Jill did not want to hurt him, but who could break off with a lover without hurting? She had come close to it at dinner tonight, when he had started to become serious. "It's not any one thing I'm trying to push," he had said, leaning forward across the table and covering her hand. "I wouldn't care whether you decided on shares in COM-SAT or a ranch in Wyoming. I just want you to get a little more out of life."

"I already do twice as much as most of the people I know," she had said, feeling defensive again.

"If you really wanted to, I could show you how to accomplish three times as much as you're doing right now. And you wouldn't be knocking yourself out anymore, either."

"That sounds like bragging." Was it indignation or jealousy that had made her forget how tired she was?

"It's simple fact. And there's medical foundation to it."

"Such as?"

"I can tell you only that it works. If you want to make the decision to get involved, you'll have to do it on trust. That's the way I had to do it."

That was the point at which she had nearly told him she didn't love him anymore. She had seen him their past two dates only because Dr. Polder had practically ordered her to take some time off.

But he had looked so earnest in the candlelight of their table. It was no place to hurt someone. She had let the moment pass.

And now if this was the hospital, she would be saying a rushed good-bye, and again putting off the moment of telling Phillip they couldn't go on—

The phone was in her bedroom, where she could get to it quickly in the middle of the night. She reached it in the middle of its fourth ring.

"Dr. Weston." She sat down on the edge of the bed.

Open and listening for a voice, she waited.

And in that vulnerable moment of uncertainty and expectation, she felt it come to her.

The terror.

The voices.

The faraway humming along distant wires—or was it in her mind? The voices were coming—

"Dr. Weston? Madison switchboard. Please hold one moment for Obstetrics."

It *was* a call! Not the voices—

But the humming grew louder as the line clicked on to hold, and then trailed away, taking Jill with it as she strained to hear despite her growing dread, strained to follow the humming sound as it diminished.

The whisper leaped onto her like a hissing cat. *Got you, dearie.*

She choked, and the voice became a hideous cackle. *Please hold one moment for a BIG surprise.*

A click. Then a woman's voice. Emily Francis, one of

the night nurses. "Dr. Weston, it's Emily at the hospital. We've been trying to get you."

Get you. Get you. GET YOU. The crone's cackle broke in like a reverberating echo. No, Jill thought. It's not happening. I don't really hear it. No.

"Hello? Dr. Weston?"

She drew in her breath, tried to speak. "Hello?"

SURPRISE! And then without a moment's pause, the penetrating malice became her father's voice. *This thing, it's in my bones and in my veins.*

"Dr. Weston? Are you there?"

She covered the mouthpiece. "No," she whispered; the trembling started with her hands and spread up until she shook uncontrollably. "No! I don't HEAR you!"

I hear YOU though, dearie.

Shut it off. Now. Shut it off. Shut it OFF!

She dropped the receiver as though it were a snake and pulled the base of the phone to her, clawing at the hard beige plastic, her hands shaking violently. The buttons. She pressed both of them down at once with her open hand and tightened her grip, holding on as though the phone itself contained the horrid unseen presence that had to be kept bottled up tightly so that it would not explode in her face—

Silence.

Still trembling, without taking her hand from the switch hook buttons, she replaced the receiver, pushed down, took her hand from underneath.

She was alone in the bedroom.

The presence had gone. The voices were silent.

She forced herself to think. The call had been real. She had recognized Emily's voice.

But the other voices—

God*damn* the other voices, she whispered to herself. What it came down to was that she had to pick up the phone again and dial the hospital.

She would say that it had been a bad connection.

She sat up straight on the bed, placed the phone squarely in the center of her lap, lifted the receiver, and dialed.

9

Ted Sanford's desk clock said five minutes to eleven when his receptionist buzzed him on the intercom. The hospital staff coordinators had started to arrive. A good sign, he told himself, and got up to greet each one of them at the door as they came in.

Ted liked to have the difficult meetings here in his office. He felt at home here, with his own oriental rug over the already-plush carpet, his polished ebony furniture, and his gilt-framed oil paintings on the walls. He could think of himself as a host, inviting those he worked with in to share a few minutes of comfort. Ted's office was large enough to accommodate the long conference table, two leather sofas, and the executive's desk he had paid for himself. As the hospital's administrator, a non-M.D., a former corporate executive, Ted was aware that some of the staff physicians looked on him as being incompetent and insensitive. So he had been careful not to use any hospital funds when he had his office redecorated. Above all, Ted wanted the hospital staff to see that he believed in fair dealing. Maybe he couldn't stop the rumors that he didn't know what was going on in his own hospital, or the snide jokes about the on-the-job training program Ted had created for himself. But he could at least convince people that he was honest, and trying his best to run things.

"Got some tough ones this morning," he said to each one as he shook hands. "Hope you've brought your thinking cap."

When they were all seated, he began. "We have two problems just added to our list this morning. I propose we take them up before our regular agenda items, since both require some kind of immediate action. Is that all right with everyone? One is a budget item; the other concerns security."

From his position at the head of the table he saw them nodding. They were a good group. After almost a year he had been able, through one means or another, to move to the positions of leadership those people who he thought liked to work and inspired the same attitude in others. Not all of them were medical, which he viewed as an advantage: his predecessor had held staff meetings too, but with only the house physicians and surgeons. The way Ted felt, the medical people were entitled to run their own show when it came to questions of medicine, but the other departments also had a stake in the success of Madison and should be contributing to decisions that might affect them and their work.

A case in point had been their recent decision to form a joint purchasing co-operative with five of the other medium-size hospitals in Manhattan to buy supplies in quantity, at reduced rates. Taken on face value, that decision could have been made by Ted alone, or by anyone who knew that discounts were available for large purchases of many items, from trash-can liners to soft drinks and laundry supplies. Yet the savings would be lost if the people directly concerned were made unhappy and unproductive by that decision. For example, if buying trashcan liners in bulk meant that Elwood Johnson, the chief custodian, had to act as a shipping clerk to send the liners to four other hospitals, or if his men had to double-bag each of the cans because the kind of liner purchased at the discount wasn't strong enough, there wasn't any real savings.

So Elwood sat at the table this morning, all 220 pounds of him, in his gray work chino shirt and pants. His black hands, nearly as dark as the ebony table, toyed steadily with his pipe.

Beside Elwood Johnson, Sally Tomlinson, representing the nurses' aides, folded and unfolded the frames of her glasses as she waited. If Sally's co-workers had not been able to make do with the delivery schedule of the group laundry service or the packaging, then it would have been foolish to switch from the private firm who ran the "linen room" in the basement and turned out clean sheets and autoclaved surgical gowns and all the other washables right there on the premises. But Sally had gone back and talked the idea over with the other aides and they had agreed to give the proposed new system a try.

Blood 61

So when the hospital had saved $148,000 in laundry expenses during the past seven months, they had all known that those savings had not been eaten up in extra employee work time.

And because John Spielberg, head of the hospital pharmacy, had sat in on the meetings that had produced these group savings, he had gotten the idea to try the same thing with the purchase of drugs. With the other four pharmacy heads, the group now bought generic drugs in bulk, and put the larger orders out for bids. So far, the past four months they had been using the system, the hospital pharmacy had saved $236,000. It didn't make the salesmen from the name-brand companies happy, but the patient and his insurance company and the government also saved money.

And Ted hoped still better innovations would be coming out of this group. The key was to cut not only existing expenses but also to bring in new revenues. . . .

But right now, dreams had to be put aside and real problems settled. A big loss of funds, and what could be a serious security matter.

Around the table, the staff looked at him expectantly, ready to proceed. Gelson Todd, white-haired chief of surgery and by seniority the unofficial spokesman on some occasions, chose to act in that role now, probably because several patients were involved. "It's all yours, Ted. Do you want to take our security problem first?" Gelson was a friend, one of those who had suggested Ted's name to the Madison board of directors. He was also the man who had suggested that Ted's wife, Rachel, should consult with a young female surgeon about a new technique for repairing blocked fallopian tubes.

Todd related how night nurse Emily Francis had found a patient bleeding from a puncture wound in the groin. If she had not learned from the patient's physician, Dr. Weston, the patient's blood had already been crossmatched, if two new units of blood had not been waiting for her in the blood bank, and if nurse Francis had not called down there immediately and gotten it sent up, the patient, a Mrs. Comfrey, probably would not have lived.

Some of them had heard the story through the hospital grapevine, either yesterday or this morning. But they all looked worried. Security for patients was too important for anyone to remain undisturbed by an event like this.

The hospital's survival depended on an ever-increasing flow of surgical patients, as well as those who came because of some chronic condition or sudden infection. The slightest hint of danger associated with a hospital's reputation could have a disastrous effect. Both potential patients and, eventually, physicians would very rapidly switch their allegiance to one of the other hospitals. If this incident were publicized, Ted was certain that the number of empty beds would triple or quadruple within the month.

"Did this Mrs. Comfrey see her attacker?" The speaker was Roger Avery, the chief resident this year. Handsome and well muscled, with blue eyes and thick curls of blond hair, Roger was a hard worker and full of energy. It was like him to try to get right to the main issue, Ted thought.

"She saw someone," said Gelson Todd. "And there were two other incidents." He paused and surveyed the others. "Both patients were healthy, awake, in private rooms. Both of them say they raised an objection when a man came in with a needle and told them to roll up their sleeves and take their medicine. But in both cases the man reassured them. He gave them the name of their physician and told them the injection had been ordered as part of their preop routine."

"So it must have been someone familiar with the hospital. Someone with access to patient charts," said Roger Avery.

"What *was* the injection?" asked Sally. "What did it do to them?"

"We don't exactly know. Both report feeling slightly drowsy, but that was at the end of the day. They say they accepted the injection as a matter of routine and stayed in bed. When the nurse came in to give them their preop sedative, she found both of them sleeping."

"The same pattern as with the third patient, Mrs. Comfrey," said Gelson Todd. "A man gave her an injection as well. The injection seems to have put her to sleep."

Ted asked if the first two were injured in any way. He was fairly certain of the reply, but it was possible that some new information had been uncovered. Besides, he felt it was better not to sit back and appear as if he had all the answers.

"Apparently not. Both patients went up for surgery

the next morning and recovered quite nicely. Not that the surgery was anything major in either case. They were both basically in good health, as I said. On the third, Mrs. Comfrey, it was decided not to operate. She was rather upset about it."

Will she talk? No one raised the question aloud, but it was in the mind of everyone in the room.

"The other two apparently thought everything was in order until they remembered that injection and thought to ask their physicians about it. It was when they learned that their doctors hadn't called for anything of the sort that they lodged their complaints. They grew quite emotional."

"I'd be emotional too," said Sally. "Imagine if it was you in the room alone. There could have been anything at all in that injection!"

"We're just fortunate none of them want to press charges or go to the police," Mary returned. "I'd hate to have the police in here!"

"I'll raise my question again," said Roger Avery with a polite nod at Mary. "Rephrased a bit. You said it was a man who gave the injections. Did they tell you what he looked like?"

"They said they could recognize him again. Well-built, heavy beard, dark-brown eyes. They both said he wasn't one with a warm bedside manner, though that may be hindsight on their parts. After all, he did con them into accepting the injection."

"It don't make sense," put in Elwood Johnson. "To stick a needle in three women—"

"One of the patients was a man, actually," interrupted Mary. "I'm afraid I didn't make that clear."

"—and then to *cut* one of them," the black man went on patiently, refusing to be silenced. "To leave her cut and bleeding. I think we're talking about somebody *mental.*"

"Does security have photos of all our employees?" Avery asked.

Ted told them. All three patients had been shown the photo books from personnel, all 124 pictures of the male employees. No one had come close to making an identification.

"I'm just trying to recall," said Gelson Todd. "Maybe

this is someone who worked here before. He might be using an old I. D., without the guard's noticing."

Ted thought that was a good point. He made a note to himself to order a search of the old personnel files.

"You think it's someone trying to give the hospital a bad name? Someone trying to frighten patients away?" asked Sally Tomlinson.

"Lot worse ways to scare patients than that," said Elwood.

"But why should he pick on *our* hospital?"

Elwood shook his head. "Mental. Maybe he's trying to pretend he's a doctor. Maybe that's why he cut that woman."

"Maybe a lot of things," put in Avery. "But I guess the point is how are we going to proceed, now that we know there's a problem."

That Avery was a comer, thought Ted. Getting them all to stop trying to solve the mystery with speculation and going directly to the heart of the matter: how to proceed. He uncapped his pen and wrote PROCEDURES across the top of his note pad. "Okay, let's have suggestions," he said. "We've got other problems to tackle when we're through with this one."

10

At about 12:30 Jill Weston came down to the Madison Hospital Blood Bank after a hectic morning. A seven-pound two-ounce infant had come into the world at half-past six by emergency Caesarian section after the mother had fallen down a flight of stairs in the middle of the night. Jill had been called in as attendant surgeon. At eight an operation was begun to determine the source of chronic cramps in a forty-five-year-old newspaper-woman; nearly an hour later, Jill had removed what she hoped was all of a seventeen-ounce ovarian tumor that had looked just as malignant as it could be. And the microscopic examination, done within minutes of the operation by freezing part of the tumor and slicing off a transparent-thin wafer, had confirmed the malignancy. Jill dreaded going in to let the woman know, but that was part of the job. Birth and death; the endless cycle. In forty years perhaps she would be able to accept it. The newspaperwoman's cancer had made Jill late for a tubal dilation she had scheduled. And then still later for Mrs. Comfrey.

She found Jerry Chamberlain back in the lab room, making room in the refrigerator for several one-pint glass bottles of blood.

"I thought we never used glass anymore," she said.

The bottle Jerry was putting onto the shelf slipped from his hand and rolled into the refrigerator on its side. Unbroken.

"Oh, hi." He grinned as he set the bottle upright and shut the refrigerator door. "Actually, *we* don't use glass. But some of our counterparts in the other hospitals aren't quite so progressive. I wish they were; bottles are a pain, especially in the summer with the humidity. They get slick and slippery, like they're just waiting to be dropped."

"These are on loan?"

"Yep. From little St. Jude Hospital over on Thirty-third, of all places. They still believe in glass. And when we're short as many units as we were last weekend, I'm not inclined to be choosy." He bent down as he spoke, picked up the carrying container marked HUMAN BLOOD: FRAGILE, and set it on the lab table in front of the refrigerator. "But with plastic I don't have to be nervous. Did you know the guy who invented the plastic blood bags used to be a pathologist? Now he's a millionaire and spends all his time buying and selling high-quality oil paintings. That's the truth. Gave up his practice altogether."

"I guess for some people it's another job. I've never felt that way."

"Never would have guessed it." Jerry put the last of the glass bottles into the refrigerator and shut the door. "I thought you were like me, just waiting for five o'clock to come around every day."

"So you can go camping?"

"Just you wait. When I'm out there in the wilderness, with nobody but the squirrels and the chickens, and the sunset shining red across the deep lagoon—"

She raised an eyebrow. "Doesn't sound like any wilderness to me."

"Oh now here it comes. The voice of experience. Come in here to spoil my simple pleasures—"

"Actually I came in to thank you. For Mrs. Comfrey."

Jerry nodded. "I just sent up another two units for her this morning. How's she doing?"

"She responded well to the procedure. We had to postpone a day because of an accident she had—"

The beeper in Jill's coat pocket interrupted her. "Excuse me," she said. "Can I use your phone?"

As he watched, Jerry thought briefly of asking her out to lunch. Then he remembered. Marcie. He had promised to show her the procedure for screening type-A hepatitis from a blood sample using the radio immunoassay technique developed by his old mentor, Barbara Thorwald. In return, Marcie had brought in a picnic hamper of goodies she'd made herself. The kid was really working out well, taking an interest in everything; learning the laboratory methods, making public relations posters. She seemed to have energy to burn.

Jill put down the phone. "Upstairs," she said, smiling. "Got to go. But thanks again for helping Saturday."

"It's okay. Stop in anytime. Saturday night was a breeze. Maybe you brought us good luck."

On the way out Jill noticed the poster set up on an easel facing the hallway traffic. A big red Valentine's Day heart, with one of the little red "Special People" buttons pinned to it. Stenciled in was the message TODAY IS FEBRUARY 12. GIVE BLOOD AND HAVE A HEART.

11

When Otto Lindstrom walked among the Wall Street lunch-hour crowds, people were inclined to turn their heads. To begin with, he was unusually tall: nearly six feet nine. He was also distinguishable from most others by his well-trimmed silver hair and goatee, and by the not-quite-concealed strawberry birthmark at the right-hand corner of his mouth. Beyond that, however, Lindstrom's was a face familiar to many on the Street as a financial wizard. His sharp black eyes glittered at several thousand opulent investors every week from the lead page of the *Lindstrom Letter,* and at several dozen even more opulent investors who paid even more handsomely to hear Lindstrom's shrewd and conclusive advice from his own lips. Even when Otto Lindstrom walked uptown to the theater or to some of the midtown banking offices, he was conspicuous. And on Wall Street he was a celebrity, lunch hour or no lunch hour.

This time Otto Lindstrom was trying to avoid being seen. He was on a particularly sensitive errand, one that he could not entrust to an assistant, and he did not want the wrong people to notice where he was going.

Unfortunately, Lindstrom did not know whether or not the wrong people were watching. Still worse, he knew that he would not have recognized one of their people had he seen the man or woman staring at him through binoculars.

He could not remember who they were. Any of them. Except the Leader.

And the Leader's words. *A member of the Gathering is a member for life. Those who betray the Gathering shall be members no more.*

He spotted a passing taxi and hailed it; pushed through the crowd, maintaining eye contact with the waiting driver above their hats and bare heads. A smaller man could not have done it. Here he was using his conspicuous stature to advantage, he reflected wryly, when at the same time it might be the death of him.

Once in the cab, he turned to see if anyone was watching closely. No one. He gave the driver an address two miles across town from where he wanted to go. There was no point in trusting any of them, not even this taxi driver. For all he knew, this same man had driven him to last month's Gathering.

As he rode he went over his plan again, probing to see if it had any flaws. The thought of taking action against the Leader excited him, for Otto Lindstrom was a man who enjoyed high stakes and high risks. They were part of his business. Men whose instincts were excited by aggression came to him to find those instincts whetted, sharp-

ened, and, more times than not, satisfied, whether the
victim was another firm, a particular group of other investors, or the United States Government. Otto Lindstrom
provided the sharp weapon of his intellect and strong
energies to help the powerful grow stronger. It was a game
he played with zest and vigor, and without mercy or regret. The world, he knew, had followed the same pattern
since living forms had evolved millions of years ago and
begun to prey upon each other. The process was relentless
and inexorable.

It was an equally inexorable process that had led him
to the Gathering: the process of aging. He had sensed
the quickness going; refused to settle for slowing down to
a life outside the world he had built for himself. He would
never give up willingly, but his world made terrible demands. To draw in each day's hard information from the
world's markets was challenge enough for most analysts,
but then to keep up with the complex web of informants he
had put together over the years; to keep their highly intelligent minds assigned to the most profitable areas; to
judge their worth accurately; to reward and punish in
ways that touched the inner man, not merely the man's
bankbook; to synthesize the whole ceaselessly changing
picture daily; to condense enough of his analysis to be of
some value to the subscribers; to determine the better
clients, their needs, and how much to offer each of them;
to act on the best information for himself, in ways discreet enough not to call the attention of the crowd or the
regulatory bodies. . . .

Not a pace for an old man. Especially in a world where
Otto was called upon to live up to his legend, to frequently
demonstrate that he could stay with a crowd of younger
men and match their intake of food and drink and women
until the hours just before dawn, and then dazzle them with
insightful intelligence at the breakfast table.

The Gathering had given him back his old strength.
Each morning when he woke, he now reached automatically for the silver bedside box where he kept his capsules.
The white capsules and the blood injections had driven
away the years.

But the Gathering had also taken something from him.

He stopped the cab a half mile from the address he
had given, paid the man well, and got out. He walked
through the Lexington Avenue entrance to the American

Brands Building, took an elevator up to the fourth floor, alone, then walked down the fire stairs to the entrance on Park Avenue where he caught another cab uptown.

Two cabs later, he looked out his window at a small electronics equipment store near Rockefeller Center, told the driver to stop, looked behind him at the rest of the traffic on Sixth Avenue to see if any other vehicles did the same. When none did, Otto Lindstrom stuffed three dollar bills into the driver's pay slot, opened the door, and walked directly into the electronics store without looking right or left.

The young clerk was well dressed. The middle-aged manager in the back of the store was even better dressed. His manicured fingers reached out to take Otto's hand and arm in greeting. Otto avoided the gesture. "You recall a telephone conversation eighteen days ago with a man named Brandt?"

The manager did. He was pleased that Mr. Brandt had come, and happy to tell him that his order had been filled.

Otto went with the manager into the back room that served as an office. There the manager opened his desk drawer and produced a small white plastic sphere about the size of a robin's egg.

"I should like a demonstration," said Otto.

"Of course." The manager rotated one half of the sphere with his fingertips, holding the other half in place. "A demonstration is perfectly in order." He reached into his desk drawer and pulled out a plastic glass, and a bottle labeled MURIATIC ACID, .004 m.

He poured three fingers of acid into the plastic tumbler.

Then he dropped in the small plastic sphere.

Nothing happened.

"Would you care to say something else, sir?" he asked Otto.

"Yes. We'll see if it picks up a phrase I remember from my childhood. *Chevalier sans peur et sans reproche.* A fearless and stainless knight." He smiled inwardly at the appropriateness of the phrase. The Leader had seemed a *chevalier* to him at first, during those wonderful seven months following the night he had entered the Gathering. He had waited for the effect of the capsules to diminish, fully expecting one day to need two capsules instead of

one, then three; he had even made a resolution to stop at
three per day—but one capsule daily continued to be
fully satisfactory. He noticed a very slight weakening as
each twenty-one-day cycle drew to a close—this afternoon, for example—but by the morning following each
blood injection the feeling of superabundant energy had
returned. He fully expected to feel wonderful tomorrow
morning.

Unless he was no longer alive. *Those who betray the
Gathering—*

A residual anger made him banish the thought. He
watched with interest as the electronics shop manager
carried the plastic tumbler with its acid and the small
white sphere to the washroom at the back of his office
and rather unceremoniously dumped the contents of the
tumbler into the sink.

"I'm quite certain it's waterproof, Mr. Brandt, as
you'll notice." The man turned on the cold-water tap
and rinsed the tumbler several times, pouring water over
the sphere. "And it's too large to worry about having it
slip down the drain."

Despite a reputation for icy calm at the moment of
truth in the most speculative of ventures, from high-
stakes *baccarat* to the final counting of critical proxy
votes, Otto Lindstrom watched the manager's action with
rising excitement. This was a minor investment of his, in
financial terms—less than eight thousand dollars. Yet,
measured in personal satisfaction, the small plastic sphere
could give value far greater. With the shpere, if it worked
properly, Otto Lindstrom could learn whether or not his
suspicions about the Gathering and the Leader were
really justified. He could learn if he had indeed been
exploited.

The thought made anger surge through him again, as
it had surged through him two days after his last visit to
the Gathering and learned that he had been robbed of
one small piece of information. Small, but extremely
costly. Information gathered from three sources, one in
Hong Kong, one in Tokyo, the third in Johannesburg.
All sworn to secrecy and paid well. None aware of the
others. None aware of the importance of their information, which became significant only when compared with
the thousands of other bits of data that passed through
Otto's brain that day. Otto himself had not realized the

meaning of what he knew until Monday evening, January 14, when he was putting on his coat to leave for the Gathering. The realization had warmed his heart, for he knew that if he acted the next morning promptly, he could realize a very substantial profit within the following twenty-four hours. If he acted alone.

. He had made his move at precisely the right time Tuesday.

On Wednesday, he learned that someone else had made the same move, at the same time.

Otto's profit had been diminished by half.

But it was not losing that sum of money that enraged him. It was losing the *information*, the product of his intelligence and his experience; the source of his livelihood and prosperity. People paid, and paid well, for Otto's information. If someone was stealing it from him, that someone would have to be stopped.

Even if that someone was the Leader. Otto could not risk attending meetings of the Gathering if his ideas were somehow being tapped during those two intervals each evening for which he had no memory.

The small white sphere was visible between the fingertips of the manager's two hands. He rotated one half of the sphere against the other and held it in position for a moment. Then he reversed the rotation and handed the miniature globe to Otto.

"You'll have to bring it close," the manager said. "But of course it can be amplified."

Otto held the white ball to his ear. And heard: ". . . is perfectly in order." A tiny voice. "Would you care to say something else, sir?"

Scarcely a drop in fidelity, though the tiny recording apparatus had been submerged in acid.

Otto smiled again as he heard his own voice: " . . . *chevalier sans peur* . . ." He took the little sphere between his fingertips and rotated it as he had seen the manager do, and the voice was silent.

"The small indentation is to mark the top," the manager said. "Keep that on your right. Clockwise one position is to play, two positions is to record. To rewind, go back to stop and counterclockwise one position."

My *chevalier*, thought Otto. My impure, thieving *chevalier*. Tonight the information will be stolen from *you*.

12

Alone in the elevator on the way up to Ted Sanford's office, Jill tried to close her eyes, take some deep breaths, and analyze the feelings of fatigue and dread that had been plaguing her. She had scheduled another appointment with Virginia Polder for tomorrow's lunch hour, and Dr. Polder would be expecting Jill to have done something to help herself over the weekend besides simply going out on the town. Analyze, she had said. Your past three months. Your past six months, and before. When you were feeling right, and now. What things have changed. Behaviorally. Emotionally. Changes in sleeping habits, in your diet—

The elevator stopped and Jill's eyes blinked open. She could see that it had only reached nine; Sanford's office was on twelve. If someone was getting on, she could hardly be found standing there with her eyes shut, or people would really begin to talk. The past few weeks she had caught both patients and staff looking at her with more concern than necessary, as if to say you look tired, dear, why don't you get some rest.

Tired, dearie?

Dear God, she thought. And shut her eyes against the voice.

Mercifully, it did not return.

But the elevator doors opened.

"You look tired, hon," said a wide-faced Jamaican nurse as she got on.

Jill straightened up. "On all weekend," she said. Glancing away from the woman to the elevator buttons beside her, she added, "Where to?"

Nice touch, dearie, take the lead, assume control.

"Twelve, please." Twelve was Obstetrics: delivery rooms, labor rooms, after-care rooms where the mothers rested, and the nursery. Jill was on twelve every day. Why didn't she recognize this woman?

"How do you like it on twelve?" Jill asked.

A broad smile, teeth widely spaced. "Oh, they my babies, hon. I'm *myself* when I'm up there with my babies."

She leaned across. "Better push twelve. We almost there."

Embarrassed, Jill stepped back as the woman's thick brown finger jabbed the proper button and lit it. "I'm sorry. I was just trying to place you. I'm up on twelve all the time and I'm sure I must have seen you before. I'm Dr. Weston."

And now you'll ask her to dinner, won't you, won't you, WON'T YOU.

The elevator was stopping. It's my ears, Jill thought quickly. We're going up in the elevator and it's the air pressure in my ears with the altitude—

"I'm Sheila Russel," the woman said. "I generally work four to twelve, and you're in early mornings. Guess we notice each other more now." She nodded politely and stepped out of the elevator; then she turned back, her face registering concern. "Hope you're feeling better tomorrow."

She saw Dr. Weston nod absently as the elevator doors closed. "I don't know, mon," she said to no one in particular. "They just workin' 'em too hard."

"Who's working too hard, Sheila?" The voice belonged to Harriet Pierce, a diminutive brunette whose slender frame seemed capable of perpetual activity. Harriet worked two part-time jobs at Madison. Mornings she was in the O.R. with the O.R. nurses; afternoons, when there was less activity in surgery, she worked on the obstetrics-gynecology floor. A full-time position would have paid better for the same hours, but the hospital was not hiring full-time nursing staff. To cut costs, the administration had shifted to the use of part-time workers wherever possible.

Dr. Jill, hon." Sheila used the more familiar first name when talking about Jill Weston with another nurse, not as an indication of disrespect, but rather because Jill was a woman, and young. In the hospital hierarchy, youth and femininity were not conveyors of status. And though it was not often acknowledged, a woman physician had more difficulty than a man in getting prompt efforts from most staff members, whether nurses or orderlies, female or male. A male doctor could generate some sex appeal with the female nursing staff; he could inspire respect in the males. The same staff could sometimes view a woman physician's attempts to inspire productivity with jealousy and resentment. Female interns new to a hospital quickly discovered, or at least suspected, that their male counterparts had an easier time of it. Most often they were right. Though the physicians at the top, nearly 100 per cent of them male, would be quick to point out that the number of women was on the increase, the medical world still tended to view the young woman doctors as temporary, without real futures in the profession, as though each would inevitably decide to drop out of practice and raise a family.

Because of the unspoken judgment on young women, Dr. Jill Weston was "Dr. Jill" when the staff spoke behind her back. Here and there a male first-year resident would be known for a time as "Dr. Freddie," or "Dr. Mike," but soon, after a year or so, the last name would be used. If the man stayed on and moved up the ladder, his name might one day become a word to conjure with. A nurse could get her patient's test results from the lab at Madison Hospital fully a half day sooner just by making it plain that Dr. Gelson Todd, the chief of surgery, was interested in her patient's case.

"Oh, Dr. Jill," Harriet echoed. "I know what you mean. I was in surgery with her this morning and she about took Katie Keiser's head off because we were short six clamps."

"Well, she didn't even recognize me. Only been sayin' hello for two years, but today she didn't even recognize me. Had to ask me who I was."

"I guess she had things on her mind," said Harriet. "It was her patient got stabbed Saturday night, you know."

"I just hope that's the worst that's gonna happen. That's all I hope."

"What are you talking about?"

"She look like she was goin' to pass out any minute now. Leanin' back in the elevator with her eyes close—I thought she might faint or somethin'. I told her to get some rest, but she didn't let on she heard me."

Harriet shook her head. "I wouldn't worry." Harriet had only been at Madison for six months, but she had worked through some very difficult cases with Jill Weston. As a member of the surgical team Jill had assembled she felt more than enough loyalty to try to stop destructive gossip. Besides that, Jill had said she appreciated Harriet's talents and gone out of her way to become a friend. "I've seen her tireder," Harriet said. "She can take care of herself."

Harriet hoped her voice carried more conviction than she felt.

13

At his station inside the front entrance to Madison Hospital, security guard Jeremiah Walker shifted his feet against the cold wind from the continually opening glass doors and wished that he had taken time to put on his long underwear that morning. The uniform required by Doyle Security, the service he worked for at $3.75 per hour, was a heavy gray gabardine that just didn't do the job when the temperature outside was nine degrees Fahrenheit and twenty-four below when you counted the wind-chill factor.

Jeremiah hated wintertime duty at the front entrance. His post was only ten feet from the inside doors, and people came in and went out all the time, opening both the inside and outside doors at the same time, which made a draft that was not to be believed. Or worse, one of the outside doors would swing open and get caught in the wind and people wouldn't bother to come back and close it. So when any of the inner doors got opened the wind just howled right on in.

Unless he, Jeremiah Walker, left his post and went out and closed the outside door. Which meant he got even colder.

He looked at the clock: 4:15. Only forty-five minutes

till his relief man came. Then he would be done with
front-entrance duty until another two weeks had gone
by. That would make it almost the end of February, and
maybe it would have warmed up some. He guessed it
was fair that everyone took a turn at this post, and he
knew he should have remembered the long johns this
morning. But damn. It was *cold!* Even his coffee had
gone cold! He sipped at it anyway, to pass the time, and
watched the people as they went by, checking I.D.
badges of the faces he had not seen before around the
hospital. Jeremiah wasn't one of those guards who got
on an ego trip by making people wait in line and dig the
I.D.s out of their bags and wallets. If he knew someone,
he didn't hassle. And if someone he knew was bringing
in someone else he didn't recognize, he still didn't hassle.
If people had business here in the hospital, Jeremiah
thought, his job was to let 'em get to their business. If
they were visitors, his job was to check the patient list
to see if the name they gave was on the visiting list. It
was the ones who didn't have business here that Jeremiah
was paid to keep out. And most times that kind turned
around and went anyway when you asked 'em to sign
the book and say who they wanted to see.

But this afternoon there was a little more action going
on. Somebody to watch out for. White male, dark hair
and eyes, maybe 210 and six feet, looks like he needs a
shave but doesn't. If he came through instructions were to
call whoever he wanted to see and give the guy's name
while he waited there, like always, but instead of ringing
the line the guy wanted you rang the Administration
office and said "This is Doyle down at front-desk security.
You have a man to see you." Then he would give the
guy's name, while Administration called two other security stations and got them to come to his aid and make
the collar. The guy was supposed to believe the office
was "checking on the appointment," and wait nice and
quiet while Jeremiah listened to nothing on the phone
and hoped the other guards were awake.

The plan was a bunch of crap if you asked Jeremiah.
What you needed was two guys in plainclothes in the
lobby waiting, and when the guy came in Jeremiah could
give a sign and they'd be on the case. But O'Donnell, the
young Mick grinner from Administration who had
briefed Jeremiah on the plan, said the hospital couldn't

afford that kind of coverage. Like they *could* afford to have this guy in the wards. Jeremiah could be standing there with the phone in one hand and his dick in the other, and this guy could see something was going on. Then the guy could just walk away and try another entrance.

But maybe it wouldn't happen on Jeremiah's shift.

He jammed his big hands into his pockets and squeezed his thumbs to get them warm. One of the nurses said good-bye to him as she went out, but then she left the outside door swinging in that cold breeze coming down from Harlem and points north. Jeremiah scanned the lobby for potential outgoing traffic and saw a nurse getting a little boy buttoned up in a coat and scarf. When they opened the inside door to go out—

Damn, he said under his breath. He might as well shut the door now, before some more cold air got in.

As he left his station, he saw the crippled man outside, struggling to get out of one of those Checker cabs. The cabby had unfolded the man's wheelchair beside the door and was trying to drag him over to it without much success. What the hell, thought Jeremiah as he reached the doorway. I'm out here already.

Moving quickly, the wind penetrating his jacket and trousers, Jeremiah came around behind the crippled man and told the cabby to just hold the wheelchair. Then he worked his hands under the man's arms and hoisted him up. He weighed more than Jeremiah had expected and had both hands clutching a small suitcase, but Jeremiah managed to flop him over the wheelchair arm. Then he lowered the cripple into the seat. The man's arms and shoulders were wide and muscular, the way they get on cripples who have to move around a lot on just arm power.

The cabby was back behind the wheel by then, out of the cold, driving off without a good-bye. The cripple looked up at Jeremiah.

"Thanks, friend." Jeremiah couldn't see him too well, because he had one of those Russian-style round fur hats pulled down over his forehead and ears, and a red wool scarf wrapped around his neck and up to his chin.

"It's O.K.," said Jeremiah. Feeling the cold start to numb his face, he got behind the wheelchair and pushed. "Where you headed?"

"Outpatient clinic. My hydrotherapy."

"Outpatient? That's clear around the other side. You go through Emergency."

"But I always come through this way. The cabbies all say they don't want to get stuck waiting in the parking lot."

They were on the sidewalk. The wind came through Jeremiah's coat like cold needles. There was no way he was going to wheel this cripple around the block, and it seemed like doing him dirt to make him wheel himself, just because of regulations that said no outpatients were supposed to come through the main entrance until this mental they were looking for got caught.

He pushed the cripple through the open outside door. Two departing nurses stood aside to let him pass. He wheeled the cripple over near his station. "Wait here a minute, please, sir," he said. "May I have your name to check with Outpatient?"

"It's Matthews. Is something wrong? They never asked me my name before."

"New procedure," Jeremiah said. As he dialed, he looked around again to see if any newcomers had arrived. He didn't see any, and had been watching the entrance while he had been outside, off and on, without seeing anyone go in, but it never hurt to check. Security work was one damn check after another. The only one you didn't get enough of was the paycheck.

As he looked around he felt the cold air coming in again. Two men who looked like salesmen.

The phone in his hand gave a busy signal from Outpatient.

"They're busy," he said. "Just hold on, please." Jeremiah tried to remember the man's name as the two salesmen came over and introduced themselves as representatives of Pfizer Drug Laboratories. Each gave Jeremiah a card. Jeremiah called through to Clinical Services and confirmed that both of them did have appointments. The men smiled at each other and signed the book.

"Now I can get back to you," said Jeremiah, turning—

The man was gone.

Quickly Jeremiah's eyes swept the lobby. Without the man's name, he couldn't call Outpatient, and if the man showed up coming at Outpatient from the inside and if

Jeremiah had not called ahead, that would be a foul-up Jeremiah would hear about from his supervisor.

The round Russian hat and the wheelchair were over by the elevators. He's screwed up his directions, thought Jeremiah. That's not the way to Outpatient. He checked the entrance doors to be sure no one else was coming in at the moment; then he took out the stenciled sign that said WAIT HERE PLEASE FOR SECURITY CHECK and put it on top of his stand so that any newcomers would see it.

He reached the elevator just as the doors were closing on the man in the wheelchair. He got a hand on the button and popped them open again.

Alone in the elevator, the cripple looked up at him as if he didn't understand what was going on.

"Pardon me, sir," said Jeremiah. "I need to have your name again, so I can call ahead and announce you to Outpatient." He leaned against the rubberized edge of the elevator door, keeping it open.

"I thought you did that," said the man. "I'm Matthews. I told you before." The man fingered his red wool scarf and seemed annoyed.

"You did, Mr. Matthews. I forgot. Would you mind coming back to the entrance area with me while I call?"

"Not at all, officer." The cripple tried to get his chair moving again, but something seemed to be stuck. He reached over the side and fumbled with the brake lever. "I think it's jammed," he said. "Could you take a look at it?"

Jeremiah got into the elevator and bent over the brake. The metal appeared to have been twisted. Behind him he heard the doors close. "Hit the Open Door button, would you?" he said. "I don't want to take any rides this afternoon."

The doors remained closed.

"Hey," he said. "Didn't you hear me ask—"

The words died in his throat as he looked up. The cripple was standing over him, the red scarf now in his hands.

White male, 210 pounds, six-two, looks like he needs a shave—

The man's knee exploded under Jeremiah's chin, snapping his head back with terrible force. He had one fleeting moment of agonizing pain as his jaw snapped and his teeth bit through the flesh of his tongue.

Then the hard edge of the man's hand caught him across the throat. His windpipe crumpled.

Wide eyes staring at nothing, Jeremiah Walker fell back across the wheelchair, dead of a broken neck.

The other man dug into his pocket for a key. He inserted it into the elevator control panel and turned it quickly to the right. The elevator stopped.

A short while later the elevator doors opened on the basement level across from the entrance to X Ray. The line of waiting patients saw a dark-haired man in a white laboratory coat wheel out a man still dressed for the outdoors in overcoat, hat and scarf. The man in the chair was slumped forward. The man in white wheeled the chair toward the end of the patient line.

"What's his trouble, Doc?" asked one of the patients.

"That's what they're supposed to find out down here," replied Matthew Garrett.

14

Ted Sanford met Jill at the door to his office and escorted her to one of the sofas. He drew over one of the conference-table chairs and sat down across from her, but not directly across: at about a forty-five-degree angle. Normally Ted had people come over to the desk and sit either at the side or in front, depending on the occasion, but Jill, after all, was Rachel's doctor as well as an employee.

"Well, Doc," he said, "like the man says, I've got some good news for you and some bad news." He sat up very straight in his chair, a habit he had cultivated after learning from a book on acupuncture that the body's energy flow can be blocked by slouching. Ted did not quite know whether or not he believed in acupuncture, but he enjoyed following some parts of the theory, simply because it was something for which the house physicians had no explanation. One of the things Ted liked to guard against was becoming intimidated by the physicians' vast array of medical terms and descriptions. To know that he, Ted, had studied in an area where most physicians knew little made him feel more confident. "I'll give you the bad news first. Then I want to have Nick O'Donnell, our grants man, come in to talk over the rest and bat some ideas around."

As Ted talked, Jill watched him, trying to concentrate but not terribly interested in what he was saying once it became clear that the "bad news" had nothing to do with her individually but rather with a budget shortage, caused by the state's reduction of Madison's daily reimbursement rate for Medicaid patients, that would affect the hospital as a whole for a time until Ted could make his influence felt in Albany. Administrators, she thought, tended to assume that staff were equally enthusiastic about the bureaucratic battles fought in their behalf. When she looked at Ted Sanford, she did not see Madison Hospital's breadwinner. She saw a slightly obese white male of perhaps six feet whose general demeanor seemed healthy. An exception she could note was some evidence of irritation in the scalp, probably from scratching, to judge from the way Ted's dark-brown hair was no longer neatly parted. There was also evidence of overwork. Like Jill's, Ted's eyes showed traces of redness in the corners, and the skin around them had that shadowy, partially dehydrated look, as though some of the facial cells had gone flaccid.

If he tells me I ought to get some rest, Jill thought, I'll tell him how he looks.

". . . so to get to the bottom line," he was saying, "everyone was just super in today's staff meeting. We're converting to a call-in system for the part-timers. You'll be asked to make do with one less nurse for most surgical procedures—"

"You're laying people off?"

"But if it's a special case, you're authorized to call in more help. Naturally we'll be keeping a close watch on the number of requests for extra help so that costs don't get out of hand."

"So what's minimally acceptable today will be 'extra help' tomorrow?"

Ted gave a wry smile. *"Touché.* Unfortunately, we

can't spend money we don't have. So we're spreading the misery around."

"Across-the-board layoffs?"

"Oh, c'mon, Doc. You guys in Surgery won't feel it as much. Don't you always say you can make do with a piece of string and a lid from a tin can? The ones who'll really have trouble are the folks down in the labs."

She thought of Jerry, and had the image of him greeting a donor at the reception desk, then getting up and taking the donor to the couch, taking the pulse and blood pressure himself, hooking up the I.V. while other donors waited. Jerry would probably put up with all that before he came up and complained.

"Everybody's getting cut?"

"Everywhere but Security. Even I'm giving up my part-time typist, except for emergencies. We decided not to touch Security because of what happened to your patient on Saturday. Incidentally, I found out who her husband is. Staff assistant to our UN ambassador himself. I hope you managed to smooth her over."

"I gave her what she wanted," said Jill. "We made a deal, more or less. I'm going to tell Mr. Comfrey his wife came in here for emergency treatment after a bad fall, and she won't tell him she was attacked by a dark-haired man and nearly bled to death into her own leg. By the way, if the attack had happened next week, and the blood bank had been too short-handed on staff to have had her blood crossmatched and ready the night before—"

"I know, I know. That's the trouble with staff cuts in a hospital. Practically every damn place you look at can turn into a life-or-death situation. We'll just have to play it by ear."

"I gave her the operation, too," Jill said. "She really wasn't in such bad shape, considering. And it's hardly a stressful operation compared with something like a gall-bladder. But of course you know that. It's the same operation Rachel had."

"I thought Mrs. Comfrey had to go home today."

Jill nodded. "By now she's probably explaining to her husband how she fell when she was uptown here shopping and how the nice people at the hospital took care of her. She has a mighty convincing hematoma to show for her fall. The reason I mention it is that I don't want the bill to reflect the surgical procedure. Her husband would go through the roof if he knew what she'd really done. It's forbidden by their religion."

"Well . . ." Reluctance was in Ted's voice.

"She's helping us, remember."

"It's just that I hate to be deceptive."

"I'm sure she does too. But do you want her to tell the truth about Saturday night?"

Saturday night? Tell HIM the truth about Saturday night—

She held her breath in her throat and sat motionless. No. Not when she was up here. Ted Sanford might be a friend because of Rachel, but he was also known to be very critical of people who showed signs of weakness. Such people tended, to use the current phrase, to "create vacancies."

She realized that she did not know what he had said. *Quick thinking now, dearie.*

"Well it's up to you, anyway," she said, hoping that he had agreed. "Now didn't you say you also had good news?"

During the next half hour Jill learned that Ted had agreed to take care of itemizing Mrs. Comfrey's medical bill. She also learned that three potential funding sources, the National Science Foundation, NIH, and the Marcus Foundation, had all expressed interest in funding her continued research and development of the tubal dilation procedure she had developed.

Then Ted called in Nick O'Donnell. The balding young hospital grants officer and assistant comptroller came in smiling, both arms loaded with a stack of preliminary application forms. "Oh come on, Nick," said Ted. "She doesn't have to fill in *that* many."

In his shirt sleeves, Nick set the stack down on Ted's desk and grinned. "There's a lot of duplication. And about half this stack are copies of other people's entries that got funded. I thought you might want to have a look."

The forms and instructions Nick O'Donnell had for Jill to use totaled some two hundred pages, for the three foundations. If the chances of getting funded grew stronger, of course, there would be many more forms to complete later, and probably provisional studies on former patients to run and tabulate.

"Normally we'd be glad to help you filling out all

these," Nick said. "The problem is we're losing our part-time help because of the budget reduction." He gave a glance at Ted as he spoke, as if to ask whether this instance, because of the promise of acquiring additional funds for the hospital, might qualify for an exception.

"It's just paper work. Jill can handle it. You've got two full weeks till the deadline. And it's an opportunity that doesn't come along too often, I can tell you that."

Jill grimaced inwardly. With fallopian blockage the problem in fully 80 per cent of female infertility cases, she had known her surgical procedure had the potential to attract foundation interest. She would have preferred to have waited until the technique had progressed further before making any applications, but Ted Sanford, full of enthusiasm after Rachel's pregnancy seemed to be coming along so well, had spread the word among his many contacts. Now the interest was all coming at once. If her response to that interest was mediocre because of her fatigue—

"I think I could use some help with all this, Ted. I really do."

"We all could use more help. I'm going to make that case as strongly as I can to Albany, first thing next week. That's the earliest I could get an appointment with Secretary Weisbrod himself."

"The deadline is in two weeks."

Ted shrugged. "We can't spend money we don't have. Look, do me a favor and give it a try. Let me know how it's going. Then next week when we see where we're at maybe we can get somebody in to type up all the final drafts."

Not telling you to take a rest, is he? And you'll LIKE filling out every little line of every little form.

Then she thought, Why am I being so self-destructive? What is wrong with me?

Dr. Polder was tomorrow. Tonight she would stay here and work on the forms. She would make herself some coffee, and she would concentrate, and the voice would go away.

15

Matthew Garrett left the body of the security guard and continued walking along the corridor past the point where it turned left and he could no longer be seen. He put his small bag down beside him and drew a deep breath, letting it out slowly to drain away the tension. He had to think clearly, plan his next moves with great care, and he could waste none of his concentration dwelling on how nearly he had come to being caught.

Avery had told him the new security precautions would make operations more difficult, but he had shrugged that off. The description they had—it was too vague, he had said. Too general. Once they began looking for a dark-haired man with a cleft between the chin and lips rather too big and a nose that turned up slightly, showing too much nostril opening to be attractive—then Garrett would be in trouble. And when they started a search for a man of that description and added that his brown eyes held none of the Leader's charm; that his smile, compared with the Leader's, appeared sour; and that his body, though useful, possessed none of the Leader's grace—then, he felt, he would be too easily recognizable and would have to begin operations at another hospital.

Now, however, it seemed that he had shown bad judgment. The expression on the security guard's face the moment he had dropped his scarf plainly showed he had been recognized. What if someone outside Avery's committee had brought in an artist and worked up a composite from the three who had complained? What if the composite had been circulated through the hospital?

It might be too risky to go upstairs and keep his meeting with Avery.

But meeting or no, Garrett still had to produce. There was a Gathering tonight. Eight units—exactly four liters of type O blood—had to be delivered.

And Garrett had no charts. No medical records to examine to determine those donors in the best of health: those who would make the best risks. Unless he could get to Avery, he would have to think of something else.

The blood bank, of course, was out of the question. He had once done that, months ago: called ahead and said he was director of St. Boniface Hospital Blood Bank and needed four units O-positive for an emergency and would send someone over to pick them up. Then he had gone in himself and walked out with the four units, priding himself on the speed and ease with which he had accomplished his mission.

The Leader had soon rid him of his pride. He had told Garrett what a "bad unit" was, and in a very painful process had altered Matthew's conditioning to preclude any more visits to hospital blood banks. The people who came to the Gathering could not be exposed to the risk of blood whose donor was not known to a Guardian as being in complete good health. The Leader said he knew this made Matthew's job more difficult. They were working on a long-range plan to develop an ongoing source of large amounts of healthy blood. Someday Matthew would not have to leave hospitals and ambulances like a thief in the night.

But now, eight units. And he dared not risk going upstairs.

An idea came to him.

Freddie Donlin lay prone on the wheeled litter, unable to believe his good luck. He twisted around under the canvas straps, trying to see the attendant who was wheeling him toward the exit of Radiology. "I still can't get over it," he said. "I could have sworn I heard it break!"

"Just a bad sprain, pal. You heard the man. Camera don't lie."

"I might not miss the play-offs, then."

"Up to your doctor."

"But if it's just a sprain, if I tape it up—"

"I seen 'em take six weeks. Whirlpools, ice, heat treatments, all that stuff. And still six weeks. What team you play for?"

"St. Francis Academy. We're second in our league. Today was my best game all season till the third quarter. I took a pass goin' down court and tried to turn the corner, and their guy was all over me—"

The attendant brought the cart to a stop in the hallway, just outside the exit.

Freddie tried to look around. "What happens now?"

"You wait here for the orderly. He'll take you back up to Emergency and they'll wrap up that ankle for you."

"Where's he coming from?"

"Elevator down the hall and around the corner. Same one you rode down on. You take it easy, now."

"I want to sit up. Can't you take these straps off?"

"I'd get in trouble. That's the rules. I'd take 'em off if I could, but I'd get in trouble." He slid a four-copy work order and insurance statement form a bit farther under the thin vinyl-covered foam pad that served as a mattress for the litter. "Now your papers are right up here behind your head, pal," he said. "I've got to get back. You take it easy, now."

Alone in the hallway Freddie squirmed under the straps that ran across his chest, his hips, and his shins. Like they expected him to get up and run out of here or something, with his sprained ankle. He wondered if they did the number with the straps if you were in college or over eighteen or something like that. Or maybe if you didn't have insurance—

He was looking at the asbestos-covered steam pipes above him when the cart moved. Backward.

"Hey!" he said, and tried to see who was behind him.

"Relax, son," came the voice of a man. "You're all done here now."

The man had a white coat on and a white shirt and tie, just like some of the doctors Freddie had seen in Radiology. Instead of pushing him down the hall to the elevator, he was pulling Freddie's cart backward.

"Hey, where we goin'?" Freddie asked.

The man pulled out the papers from beneath the vinyl mattress.

"You're Frederick Donlin, isn't that right?"

"Yeah, sure. I sprained my ankle playing basketball. They said an orderly was gonna take me back up to Emergency."

"I know that. Do they call you Freddie? . . . Good. Then I'll call you Freddie. They sent me down to get you, because they'd forgotten to take a history. Do you know what that is? It's just questions. We don't have to do a complete history, because you're only an outpatient, but we want the records complete for the insurance."

He stopped the cart and pivoted it around smoothly so that now Freddie was moving down the hall feet first. Then he asked if Freddie had had any colds recently, any flu, stomach upset, infection, anything like that. Freddie said no, he'd been in very good health.

"I've been playing ball since November. Got me in good shape. Today was my best game this season, till the third quarter."

"It says here your blood group is O-positive. Is that right?"

"I guess. Coach filled in all the stuff on the form. He's upstairs waiting."

"How much do you weigh, Freddie?"

"About one twenty-five. I'm almost five-seven. The guy in Radiology said my sprain might take six weeks to heal. Do you think it'll take six weeks?"

They stopped in front of an elevator. Not a new one like the one Freddie had come down in. This one had old painted doors and you had to open it with a green metal handle. The man pushed the Down button.

"It might take six weeks," he said. "Maybe less if you stay off it."

"Why did you push Down? Emergency Room is up-stairs."

"This way's quicker. If we go back to the other eleva-tor we'll get tied up with all those people waiting to get into Radiology. How long did you have to wait before they took you?" The man glanced at the elevator and pushed the Down button again.

"About half an hour. My ankle was hurting something awful. Then a nurse came out and gave me a shot. I can't feel the hurt at all now."

The man consulted Freddie's papers again. "Xylo-caine," he said. "Right. It'll take a while before that wears off. Then it'll be sore for a few days after that."

"If it takes six weeks, I'm gonna miss the play-offs. And I just worked my way onto the starting five this month."

"Can't be helped," said the man. Behind the wire-reinforced glass window in the painted metal door the lit elevator cab was now visible. The man waited until it had completely descended before opening the door.

The inside of the elevator smelled of stale food and dirt, like a closed hallway in a crowded apartment building.

"What do they do," asked Freddie, "bring down the garbage in this thing?"

"It's the service elevator," said the man. "We're taking the short cut."

He closed the door.

"Well if I miss the play-offs, I guess there's always baseball. The coach said I might be starting pitcher this year."

There was a clank of machinery as the cables moved again. The elevator bumped once and then started to descend.

"Last year I played right field mostly, but he said I had a good arm if I can just get my control down."

A whir behind him. To Freddie it sounded like adhesive tape being pulled off a metal spool. He looked around.

The man was holding an arm's-length section of two-inch adhesive tape stretched out between his hands like it was a roll of film he was looking at.

"Hey," said Freddie. "What are you doing now?"

Garrett brought the boy out of the service elevator at the sub-basement level and went straight across the dimly lit corridor, pushing through the swinging doors of the now-vacant laundry room as though he were taking the boy into the O.R. for surgery. The room was dark and smelled of detergent and chlorine bleach. Garrett left the lights off. It was more difficult to work in the dark, but he could manage by feel. Especially since he would have to be tapping the big arteries.

He put a hand on the boy's forehead, a warning signal he had told him about in the elevator, but the boy kept moaning through his nose and struggling. Though two yards of tape bound his head securely to the litter and his hands and knees were also tightly taped, he was still managing to put pressure on the canvas straps. It was good in a way, Garrett thought, because it showed good health. But he could not afford to have the boy wriggling when it was time to put in the catheters. Also, someone might hear the noise.

He pinched the boy's nostrils together. The high-pitched nasal moans of the boy suddenly stopped. The tape across the boy's mouth still held tight, even though the little jaw was working frantically to dislodge it.

"Remember what I said, Freddie." Garrett kept his voice low and heard no echo in the large and empty room. "If you want air, you'll have to be quiet."

The boy renewed his struggles for what Garrett estimated as a minute and a half. Then his body went limp.

It was a difficult dilemma to resolve. Garrett knew he needed the boy alive if he was going to get a quantity even approaching eight units out of him.

He settled for taping one nostril shut.

While the boy was still unconscious, Garrett quickly got out the catheters and collection bags. There was some light coming in from windows to the hallway and his eyes were growing accustomed to the shadows. He found the carotid artery on the first try and hooked up the catheter, going in with the needle from above to take advantage of the flow pressure as the blood spurted up the neck toward the boy's head.

The first bag began filling nicely.

He opened the boy's shirt and exposed the chest at the clavicle. From his bag he took a large-bore needle and broke the skin above the bone over the right side, probing for the subclavian artery. The pain brought the boy back to consciousness. He tried to hunch up his shoulders but Garrett put his weight on his chest and forced him to lie flat. The top catheter was keeping most of the blood away from the boy's brain by now, so his struggles were weaker.

Finally Garrettt found the subclavian artery. The blood came through the hollow stem of the needle with a gush, and he wasted some of it before he could screw in the catheter tube. He also got his hands wet. He wiped them on the boy's trousers and then pulled them down to get at the femoral arteries.

By the time he got both those catheters implanted and going, it was time to change the collection bag on the first one.

The boy's heart quit when Garrett was putting the new

bag onto the fourth catheter. He could tell, because the blood just stopped flowing.

He only had five units. The other three were nowhere near full. The one he had just put on, in fact, was still empty.

He needed eight units.

Quickly he took the tape off the boy's mouth and started resuscitation. As Garrett breathed air into the boy's lungs, he put the heel of his hand over the exposed sternum and pressed down hard. Closed-chest massage was a two-handed operation normally, but not under these circumstances.

After about a minute's steady work, he got a heartbeat going again. The catheter bags started to fill once more. To speed up the return of venous blood to the heart, Garrett began rhythmically elevating the boy's arms and legs.

Then he caught the scent of pipe smoke in the room. Someone else was here.

He whirled, and saw a shadowy figure in front of the entrance doors.

"Thought I heard someone in here." The voice was a rich baritone, the inflection American Negro. He could not remember having heard the voice before. It certainly was not Avery.

"I can't see you," Garrett replied. Another one, he thought. I'll have to kill another one.

"I can see *you* pretty good, though. Your white face shows up pretty good in here."

"Well I'm having a bit of trouble. Do you suppose you could give me a hand?"

"Sure thing. Looks to me like you're goin' to need all the help you can get."

With that, the man flicked on the lights.

Garrett saw a large black man in gray work coveralls, waiting by the light switch, not moving, just looking at him. Garrett's right hand went to the pocket of his white lab coat. His fingers curled around the surgical probe.

"Aren't you going to help me?" he asked.

"I've heard about you," the black man said, still not moving. "Heard about you in a meeting this morning. And before. And they tell me a security man is missing from the front entrance."

He was about twenty feet away. Too far. At that dis-

tance the probe would tumble in the air and strike with
the handle instead of the point.

Garrett started to wheel the cart closer. "This boy's
in trouble," he said. "He's hurt pretty badly."

"I think you're the one's in trouble. I think you gonna
need some help gettin' yourself out of here."

Fifteen feet. Twelve. "Why would you want to say
that?"

"You're wonderin' why I'd want to help you, when I
can see you got that boy's blood all over your hands? I
think you oughta know."

His grip tightened on the probe and he stopped to set
himself. His target was the black man's left eye. He had
hit smaller from this distance with the probe. "What
should I know?" he asked.

"That a member of the Gathering is a member for
life," said Elwood Johnson.

16

Phillip held out his hand across the table to Jill, and
opened it suddenly. Two white capsules were in his
palm. Perhaps it was the suddenness of the gesture, or
perhaps it was Jill's fatigue that made her recoil.

"Hey," said Phillip. "They're not snake eggs, for God's
sake."

"Will you put them away? I don't want people to think
you're some kind of pusher!"

"You're overreacting. This is a hospital cafeteria. Nobody notices capsules in a hospital. Look around and see
for yourself."

He was right. The men and women in hospital greens
and whites were intent on their own dinners, not even
glancing at Jill's table.

"Here," Phillip said. "Look at them."

They resembled oversized Contac time-release capsules,

except for the coloring. Inside the gelatin coating, the assorted sizes of granules were all pure white.

"What's in them?"

"I've never had one analyzed. I meant what I said the other night. You have to go into this thing on trust. All I know is that they work."

"I think you're very foolish. To take something when you don't even know—"

"Wait a minute." He eyed her, a half-smile on his lips. "You're saying I'm foolish. But look at yourself and then look at me. Which one of us would you say was in better health?"

"I don't put much stock in a superficial examination."

"But your patients do, don't they? If one of your patients were to walk into this cafeteria right now and sit down with us, which doctor do you think would seem healthier to her?"

"You're bigger. You're a man. She'd probably be taken by your southern conviviality."

"Not to mention the fact that my color is better, that I don't have fatigue circles—"

"Is this what was so important that you had to come here to meet me tonight?" Jill cut in. She felt herself growing angry. "You had to tell me about my looks?"

"Well they're important. A patient likes to see a healthy doctor. It builds confidence."

"No one's forcing you to stay at this table."

"Don't be so vain. You're pretty, Jill, even the way you've let yourself get overworked. But you don't look as though you feel well. Is that the truth, or isn't it?"

"I'm not so badly off that I need to take medication I know nothing about."

"Neither am I. I take one of these only when I want to do more than usual. The rest of the time I'm perfectly good on my own. They're nonaddictive."

"How many do you take in a week?"

"Maybe two or three. If I take one, I can work flat out on whatever I'm doing. For twelve hours. Fast, efficient, concentrating—the best I've ever done. Then I fall into bed and sleep like a baby."

"What is it, some sort of amphetamine?"

"No. I took those when I was in college. There's no comparison. Amphetamines just mask fatigue. These *eliminate* fatigue. And you don't get nervous, you don't get insomnia—"

"I don't want your capsules, Phil. I—"

"I wouldn't give you one of my capsules. I just wanted to show you part of what I have that you don't. Because I have a hunch you're going to be needing it soon."

"What are you talking about?"

"Face the truth, Jill. You're overworked now. And you're about to take on more work, all for the good of the hospital. The Marcus Foundation—"

"How do you know about the Marcus Foundation?"

He shrugged. Again came that hint of a smile. "Don't forget I have surgical privileges here at dear old Madison. And the grapevine is rather efficient among surgeons. Especially when a foundation starts talking about putting three million dollars into the hands of one of their number who happens to be female."

Three million dollars?

"Who told you? Who?"

"Hey. Don't get upset. You know I was in to operate this morning. It was just another bit of gossip in the locker room."

"But *I* didn't hear about it until just this afternoon! And Ted Sanford is a personal friend of mine!"

"You think he was holding out on you?"

She thought for a moment. "Probably he wanted to check with Gelson Todd or someone like that. Someone senior. Ted's pretty new at hospital work, and he probably didn't know all the implications of what they've written us to do. Or maybe he wanted to check with Nick O'Donnell about the budget or about facilities. Three million dollars is a lot of money."

And she would never tell Phillip that Ted Sanford had not mentioned an amount that *any* of the three foundations was willing to commit. Was it because Ted didn't think she could handle that kind of responsibility?

"A lot of money and a lot of work. For the greater glory of Madison Hospital, of course, but it won't exactly make life easier for you. You'll drive yourself crazy trying to fill out all those forms. And who is that paper work really *for?*"

"It's an excellent research opportunity. An operation that could have wide applications. It could bring a lot of children into homes of parents that really want them—"

"Have you ever thought about having children? A child of your own?"

Thirty-four years old. In her mind's eye she saw the graph that correlated Down's Syndrome with maternal age. Every year the odds went up that a child she bore would be Mongoloid.

"I didn't come here to discuss children, Phil." She said it as kindly as she could, because of the way he was looking at her. Break off with him, she thought. It doesn't give him any hold over you, just because he wants to—

"Of course you didn't. You came here because I said I wanted to talk to you about something important, and you didn't have time to leave the hospital to have dinner out. So let me say what I came to say. Then I won't take up your time any further."

"Okay, Phil. Go ahead."

"I came here because I knew you'd be adding to your work load even though we both know you're overtired. I thought you might be worried and upset about where the extra time and energy were going to come from. I thought that you'd want some help, and so I came to offer it."

"In the form of pills?"

"That's only part of it. Only a small part."

"What, then?"

"There's a meeting I attend once every three weeks. There's one tonight. If you'd like me to, I'd be willing to take you with me."

The two capsules were still on the table where he had placed them. She still did not like the way they looked. Black coffee, she thought. I'll make myself a pot of strong black coffee.

"I don't think so, Phil. Thank you anyway."

"There's not another one for three weeks. You'll have a lot of pressures on you in the next three weeks, if you're going to get through all that paper work."

"How long does the meeting last?"

"Most of the night. But tomorrow you'd get twice as much accomplished in half the time. I'm serious."

She shook her head. "I still don't think so."

17

The red light swirled warm around Otto Lindstrom.

The woman whose head was buried in his lap did not notice. Her tongue worked busily, exploring, tasting, making him harder. Passion warmed him. In the momentary redness he saw her long, tousled hair spilling dark over his loins. As the light moved away he reached down and fondled her, letting the strands of hair flow between his fingers, touching her forehead and her eyes. Her cheeks were soft, unfamiliar. He traced two fingers lightly around the wet O of her lips.

"Mmm," she said. "You like?"

"Very much." He reached farther down and cupped her naked breast in his palm. The skin was warm and smooth, the nipple erect. With a nudge of his hand he urged her upward. Her mouth made wet kisses along his abdomen, his chest, his neck. She brought her cheek to his, hesitating only a moment as she felt his beard.

"Touch me," she whispered, her lips soft against his ear. He put his hand between her thighs and felt moisture.

"You're ready," he said softly.

"Mmm. I know. I love it. Don't you love it?"

"I keep coming back," Otto said. Speaking coolly, with understatements, served to heighten his pleasure of anticipation.

"Mmm. You're witty. Are you witty outside? In what you do?"

"In a way. I'm Otto Lindstrom."

"I've heard of you." Her tongue opened his lips and touched his. A stranger's tongue. Otto found it the more erotic for its unfamiliarity. It made him feel he could lose himself with this woman and be as bold and reckless as she was.

And so he could, he reminded himself. He could stop

thinking. The sphere was going to do the work for him. The sphere that was now inside his belly. He wondered if it would record the sound of the woman's kisses.

"Look," she whispered. "The screen. Someone new."

The great red screen glowed faintly above them at first, then more brightly. A faint image appeared.

"I'll bet it's nothing more than an oversized Advent projector back there, and they turn the hue control all the way red," she said softly as they waited for the image to clear. "The governor's office has one. We have the same trouble getting it to focus."

"The governor?" Otto's interest quickened as she whispered a name he instantly recognized.

"Between you and me, he's a little pansy. And he works us to death. If I didn't think he'd make President someday I'd—hey, he's cute. Do you recognize him?"

The screen had cleared. A ten-times-magnified image of Phillip Bancroft was offered to the members of the Gathering for their inspection.

"Never saw him before," said Otto. Then he added, "At least not that I recall."

She laughed softly. "Same with me. For all I know, he may have been humping me right here on this very spot three weeks ago." She began to fondle Otto again, cooing at his size and hardness. "Mmm. You're big all over, aren't you?"

"Big enough."

The red of the screen faded away as they watched. "Do you think he's blackmailing people with that thing?" she asked.

"Who?"

"The Leader, silly. Do you suppose he's videotaping what that TV camera sees?"

"Wouldn't be worth his while, I'd imagine. Would you get upset if he threatened to expose a videotape of you in a red robe?"

"Some of the women take off their robes when they see the screen come on."

"But the camera only takes a waist-high shot. I wouldn't find that threatening if I were a woman."

"What about down here?" She patted Otto's naked bottom and then resumed her caresses. "What if he's got a

camera that can see in the dark? A camera with a tele-
photo lens—"

"How long have you been coming here?" Otto interrupted.

"About a year and a half. Why?"

"It seems to me that if you were going to be black-
mailed, the Leader's had more than enough time to do it
already. If he hasn't, it follows that what he wants from
you is something else. Isn't that logical?"

"I suppose it is. When you're in politics you tend to get
a little paranoid about screwing around. I wonder . . ."
Her voice trailed off.

"Wonder what?"

"I was just thinking, maybe I do this every time I come
here. Maybe I have to get convinced that nothing bad is
going to happen before I—you know, get really unin-
hibited."

Otto put his hand over hers. "You're not doing so badly
now, you know."

"Oh, but there are things I want to *do* to you. I mean,
so many *things*. When we're just so *free*—" She buried
her face in his neck and he wrapped his arms around her
protectively, pulling her onto his chest. Her breathing
began to quicken. She just needs reassurance, he thought,
and then she'd really be something special. A pity that
there won't be any memory.

Then he remembered the little white recording sphere
he had swallowed before leaving his town house that
evening.

He smiled inwardly. His little investment in electronics
was earning an unexpected dividend.

Farther across the large room Phillip Bancroft had
found Claire in the half-darkness.

"When I saw you on the screen," she murmured, "just
the sight of you, up there, looking so enormous—" She
reached for him. With her other hand she guided his fingers to her *mons*. She was wet with a warm, slippery fluid.

"Just watching *me,* were you?"

She moaned. "Oh Phillip—"

"How many were there?" He would be hard on her, he
decided. It would be a pleasant release after curbing his
temper all day.

"What does it matter, darling?"

"How *many?*" He dug fingertips into her hair and began to exert pressure.

"Oh, four perhaps. None as big as this. Does the thought excite you?"

"You're the one we're talking about, not me."

"But I'm in the position to tell, aren't I? And I do think you're getting more excited."

"No man under two hundred years old could come within ten feet of you and stay the same," he whispered, marveling at the fever her lust aroused in him. Was it like this every time? he wondered.

"Do you realize," he said, "that if we always take our injections beforehand we'll never grow tired of each other?"

She breathed warmth into his ear. Then she put her hand on his wrist and moved him up and down on her in a slow rhythm. "So you'll forgive me my . . . others?"

"Never. I want you all for myself."

"Not fair." Her hand continued to move.

"Why not fair?"

"I forgive you your . . . assignment, don't I?"

"Let's not talk of her."

"I'm looking forward to seeing her when you finally bring her, you know. Do you think she'd like me?"

"She's not that kind."

"What kind is she?"

"Different. Let's talk about someone else."

"Are you still sleeping with her?"

"Not at the moment. At the moment I'm with you."

"I was just thinking. When you're with me, you can remember her. But when you're with her, you can't remember me."

"I can only remember you from our first time."

"Is she as good as me?"

"She's different."

"Better?"

"I didn't say that." And I never would, he thought. Even though Jill *was* better, in her way. Or had been. She had shut him out now; he had recognized the signs. But that was to be expected. It was inevitable. He had to accept that she would not want him, not want anyone, until he brought her to the Gathering.

Claire quickened her movements, bringing his thoughts back to her warmth and desire. "I guess you couldn't know how good I really am, could you?" she whispered, "when all we remember is our first time."

He repeated the thought like a litany. "And that way we'll never grow tired. We'll always anticipate what it will be like."

She giggled. "Maybe it's awful."

18

In a brightly lit workroom within the same building, Diana Falke pressed the switch to rewind the videotape. She shifted around in her chair, which was covered in a smooth synthetic fabric of pure white, and looked across the room at Malcolm Lockwood, the Leader.

Wearing a one-piece fitted jumpsuit of the same smooth pure white material as the chair, Lockwood was studying one of the files spread out on the shining white worktable before him. His wonderfully handsome features showed an absolute concentration as he turned the pages.

Diana decided to replay the segment for herself first, before saying anything. She turned back to watch the numbers on the indicator dial. Lockwood's peripheral vision noticed movement: the shimmering gold of her lustrous long blond hair.

'What did you find?" he said.

"I don't know yet. Something on Lindstrom."

"Lindstrom?" He put down the file he had been studying and found Lindstrom's. "Tell me when you've got it clearly."

She bent over the hazy blue screen and adjusted the control knobs. Unlike Lockwood, Diana Falke was wearing the garb of the other members: a red robe and nothing else, for soon she would be mingling among them, before the ceremony began, to see what she could learn. Hoping to attract praise from the Leader, she had tied her robe loosely, the front opened top and bottom to reveal a well-proportioned bosom and shapely legs.

"Look here." She stopped the tape. On the screen, a bluish male outline suddenly halted its undressing movements, frozen in profile.

Lockwood joined her. "Where?"

"You have to look closely. In the abdominal area, in front of the spine."

He saw. "A circle. Two tiny circles."

The circles were outlined in red, which indicated metal.

"And I think they're moving. Watch as I start the tape again."

They watched. "Only one is moving. You can see the spokes. The other must be a battery."

"A transmitter?"

Lockwood shook his head. "A recording device." He tapped the file on Otto Lindstrom that he was holding. "I believe I aroused Otto's indignation last month by making that little investment. He seems to be trying to find out how I did it."

"A member no more," said Diana with a satisfied smile.

"Not until the time comes, I think." He tilted Diana's chin and brushed the golden hair away from the high, arrogant cheekbones, the narrow, highly arched eyebrows. He framed her face in his hands and searched the cool blue eyes. When he looked long enough he could always see what she wanted waiting beneath the blue surface. He loved to watch it in the same way he had loved to stare at the killer animals in their cages when he was a child. Or at the giant squid at the sea aquarium, with its writhing tentacles and sharp beak.

His to control.

"When the time is right, you shall be the one to make the example for the others. For you are the first of all my Guardians."

She lowered her eyes, grasped his hand and kissed it softly. "Leader," she breathed. "Leader."

PART TWO

FIRE

19

Harriet Pierce came over to the scrub sink as soon as she saw Jill Weston. She was about the same size as Jill, and also with attractive features; in their surgical greens, with the shapeless green caps hiding their hair, there were no distinctions of rank visible to separate the nurse and the surgeon as they stood together. Someone who did not know either of the two women, however, would very likely have made the correct identification immediately. Harriet's skin was the color of *café au lait*.

"Happy Ash Wednesday," said Harriet. "And thanks for asking for me. This new call-in policy's been driving me craz*ee!*"

Jill greeted her with a smile. "I know. They're such hypocrites in Administration. They've kept us cut back for more than two weeks now, and do you know why we can afford the full team today?"

"I saw the schedule. We're on display this morning."

"And they don't have the guts to put us in the amphitheater and on the closed-circuit TV and let outsiders see we're understaffed. But wait till tomorrow when I ask for you again. Then I'll hear about economics and priorities and all their weasel words—"

"I'm just glad for today. Even if I did have to fly back before the Mardi Gras got over with last night."

"Mardi Gras?"

"Have to spend my money somewhere, don't I?"

"Come on. You didn't."

"Well, it was kind of my private local celebration, to tell you the truth. Here. Let me get you." She held a green towel to catch the water running down Jill's elbows as she finished scrubbing.

"Still celebrating with Nick?"

Harriet smiled happily and nodded. "But keep it quiet, okay? You're still the only one who knows."

"Oh, I don't gossip that way. But I still don't see why you have to keep it secret. This is New York. Nobody's going to——"

"Oh, yes they would. When there's money anywhere in the picture, you can just bet they would. That's why I won't let Nick say a word about moving me up the preferential list, even though he wants to. It'd be bad for his career if people started talking, and then *both* of us would be in trouble. No sense in that."

No sense in arguing, either, Jill thought. If Harriet wanted to be overly protective of Nick O'Donnell's reputation for integrity in personal decisions, that was not something for Jill to question.

"He'll be in the amphitheater this morning, you know," she said.

"Really? He didn't tell me. Must have thought it would make me nervous."

"That's good, Harriet. I have yet to see you nervous."

Harriet held up a surgical gown for Jill to work her arms into. "Must be some pretty big brass comin' if they're getting the money man to do the escort work."

"Somebody from the Marcus Foundation. If they like what they see on this preliminary visit, they send the full-dress team for evaluation. Surgeons, administrators, all of them. Supposedly they'll even scrub in with us. That's when we'll see the real pressure build up."

Harriet moved behind Jill, tying the strings of the surgical gown in the back. "I never heard of the Marcus Foundation."

"They're private. They fund mostly in health areas, that's all I know. Aside from the fact that they love to read impossible amounts of paper work. I was at my desk staring at charts and numbers and descriptions and files . . ."

"I don't see how you do it, hon. And they tell me you even started jogging and got yourself a new boy friend!"

"Gossip, gossip. Jerry Chamberlain and I are strictly jogging partners. A half hour a day, in the open air. Nothing more."

The exercise had been Dr. Polder's idea. So had been moving out of the apartment temporarily, setting up a cot in Jill's small office at the hospital. When Jill had gathered her courage and told Dr. Polder about the terrifying voices, she had been met with sympathy and understanding. If Jill heard the voices most vividly when she was alone in her apartment at night, the doctor reasoned, then Jill should simply stay away from her apartment for a while. And the exercise would help to counteract the feeling of depression.

Bless Dr. Polder. She had been right. Jill's exhaustion had grown less and less debilitating with each passing day. And the voices . . .

"You run for a half hour?" Harriet finished scrubbing and broke open a packet of sterile gloves.

"I wouldn't call it running. We hardly get out of breath. Most of the time, we're talking about one thing and another."

"He's a talker?"

"Not really. Not much more than I am. Neither of us says anything important."

"Well now!" Harriet smiled as she held up a glove for Jill to work her fingers into. "Sounds like romance to me. A man you can talk to—"

"He's just doing it to keep his weight down. Just for his health. And so am I." A special kind of health, she thought. But it was working, that was the important thing. The terrible attacking malice of the voices had not returned. Now and then would come memories, some vivid, some not, but they were only pale echoes of the originals. For two weeks now, Jill had been feeling stronger each day.

Soon, she would be strong enough to move back to her apartment.

"Well a lot can happen in a half hour," said Harriet knowingly. "Here's your other glove."

20

The surgical amphitheater at Madison Hospital was newly decorated, and Ted Sanford was especially proud of the results. He beamed with satisfaction as he opened the door to the observation gallery for the woman accompanying him. A strikingly attractive blonde, she was the representative of the Marcus Foundation.

"I feel three times lucky today," he said, genially. "Not only do I get to show off our new setup, but I also get to escort a beautiful lady, and I get to say it's all in the line of duty!"

"That's very flattering," said Diana Falke.

Ted pointed to the front row of seats, molded blue plastic shells of the sort found in buses or subways. "We'll go all the way down to the front. Just in front of the plexiglass. You'll get a better view down there and we'll also be closer to the front TV monitor."

"It's quite—brightly lit," said Diana as they took their seats. She looked through the newly cleaned plexiglass at the white-tiled room below them. Centrally positioned was the large chromed-steel operating table, shining under the ceiling lights. Except for the table and the TV camera apparatus suspended from the ceiling directly above, the room was empty.

Behind them, Nick O'Donnell spoke up. "You'll see. They'll bring in more lights. The don't want any shadows interfering."

"Not with this operation, Nick," Ted corrected. "They don't need so many lights. She's flying on instruments."

"Are we early?" Diana Falke checked her watch against the large clock on the opposite wall. The time was 9:58.

"Only two minutes. They'll be wheeling the patient in soon. What do you think of our setup? You haven't been here before, have you?"

"No, I haven't."

"You should have seen it before we remodeled. Incredible what a difference it makes. You know, where you're sitting now was about five rows from the top of the most depressing room you ever saw. You remember your high school chemistry lab, with those old wooden seats and you'd walk up these creaky wooden steps—"

"Our lab didn't look that way," said Diana.

"Well take my word, then, this was really gloomy. Old black stone-topped laboratory tables and sinks down there, and the first row of those old wooden chairs not two feet away from the table—"

"They'd let people sit that close during surgery?"

"Oh well of course it couldn't be used that way back then. They'd use it for grand rounds, mostly. That's when they bring in a patient or make reports on different cases and take questions and observations from each other."

"I'm familiar with the term," she said.

"It's good practice, I think. Good for morale on the staff, to have them thrash things out in a group like that. But to get to the point, Miss Falke—or do you prefer *Ms.* Falke? It's really hard to know, these days, with the old-fashioned things becoming more fashionable—"

"Mrs. Falke."

"Oh? My congratulations to the lucky man."

"Mr. Falke died two years ago."

"Oh, well I'm sorry to hear that. I—"

"I wasn't sorry. I rather hated him."

Ted blinked. Then he grinned. "Are you putting me on?"

"No."

He felt there was nothing to do but laugh at his own discomfort, so he did. "I just can't win with you today, can I? No, don't answer that. I just hope I have better luck explaining what we want for Madison Hospital than I do talking about your personal life."

She smiled sweetly, not joining in the laughter. "That's what I came to hear. And, of course, to see this operation. Whenever it begins."

"Find out if there's some delay, would you, Nick?" He continued as O'Donnell left. "You see, Mrs. Falke, what we're trying to do at Madison is to take the high ground. We feel that Madison has a natural constituency, a client base that the big teaching hospitals these days have more and more difficulty attracting."

"You mean the affluent."

"Precisely. And the adequately insured middle-class patients as well, of course. We're not going to let Madison go downhill the way others have, chasing Medicaid patients. They can't pay their bills. And what's worse, they drive the adequately insured patients away!"

Diana kept her eyes on the operating forum, where the green-clad nurses were wheeling in various tables with instruments and equipment. "How do you intend to attract affluent patients, Mr. Sanford?"

"Oh, we're a natural. We have a prime location, in a low-crime East Side neighborhood, so patients and visitors don't have to worry about being mugged or attacked when they come in and go out. And, of course, that means staff people don't have that problem either. Also, we're beginning an outreach program with the staff at some of the larger hospitals. Several already have found it to their advantage to bring their patients here."

"I've heard of hospitals competing for patients. But you're the first I've heard from who openly admits to organized pirating of physicians."

Was that admiration in those blue eyes of hers? Or mockery? Ted wondered why he was having such a difficult time with Diana Falke.

"We prefer to call it recruiting. It's a free-enterprise system we live in, after all." He thought that sounded lame, so he pressed on. "Too much of medicine still harks back too strongly to the medieval traditions, in my opinion. Doctors are businessmen nowadays, and we might as well recognize that as a fact. That's why I get so incensed with our government, trying to impose more and more socialism and more and more mediocrity—"

"You don't believe in the selfless, dedicated hard-working—oh, look. They're wheeling in the patient. And she's awake!"

The woman, slightly overweight, was lifted by three nurses, who hefted a folded sheet, a "drop cloth," beneath the patient and slid her from the litter onto the operating table.

"She's awake, but I'm sure she's been sedated," Ted said. "Dr. Weston will tell us when she comes in. They generally wait until the patient's fully prepared before they make their entrance."

"Will she describe those instruments?"

"I don't know what she plans to say. But I'm sure the equipment is all covered very thoroughly in the application materials."

"I don't read the applications. We have other people who are interested in the technical details. What I concern myself with on these initial visits are general impressions of the personnel. How they cooperate. How they react to one another."

Ted nodded. "Yes, I quite agree. The interpersonal relationships are critical. I emphasize that a good deal when I work with the staff."

"Leadership ability," said Diana Falke, leaning forward to watch two other nurses as they entered.

"Oh, yes. Leadership—"

"It's what I expect to see in any applicant for a project as large as this one we're considering now. I'm talking about strength, Mr. Sanford. Strength of will, strength of character—"

"Well you'll find it in Jill Weston, I'm sure. Look, there she comes. That's her, talking with the nurse, next to that piece of equipment that looks like a TV screen. It's our new ultrasound scanner—"

"She looks rather frail, to me. Small and frail."

"Oh, I wouldn't be deceived by that. Any woman who becomes a surgeon has to have unusual strength. Strength and determination—"

"I'm not talking about working as a surgeon. *You're* paying her for surgery. The Marcus Foundation is concidering Dr. Weston for something considerably more demanding."

"Oh, she has what it takes, believe me. She puts in a work day here that makes me tired just to think about it. All the nurses respect her—"

"What kind of hours is she accustomed to?"

"She begins at seven in the morning, and it's not uncommon to find her at the hospital at midnight. Phenomenal endurance, in my opinion."

"I tend to doubt the organizational abilities of people like that. If all they have time for is the job they're doing, it doesn't seem reasonable that they have time to take on new commitments."

Beside the patient on the table, Jill Weston looked up at them. Ted waved, hesitantly, feeling himself unaccountably more and more uncertain of Diana Falke's intentions. Maybe she's made up her mind against us already, he thought. Catching Jill's eye, he sent her a silent message of support: *You just go ahead and don't worry. I'll do my best for you up here.*

"She'll have time for this," he assured Diana Falke. "Why, she personally prepared all those materials last week without any slackening at all from her regular duties—"

Jill's voice came through to them from the TV monitors. Following tradition, she wasted no time with introductory material. Instead, she began immediately with the description of the surgical procedure that was to come.

"The patient has been sedated with intravenous diazepam solution and her pelvic area will now be immobilized with thirty milliliters of 1.5 per cent lidocaine in isotonic sodium chloride solution, introduced into the sacral canal through the sacral hiatus. For this procedure we have added a weak epinephrine solution of one part per hundred thousand, to delay systemic absorption . . ."

Diana Falke turned to Ted. "You're telling me that she added two hundred pages of paper work to a seventeen-hour day? That's difficult to imagine."

"Perhaps. Nonetheless, she did it."

"I don't see that she'd have had time to go home. What did she do—sleep here at the hospital?"

"Dr. Adriani will now be administering the caudal block. He will use a fifteen-gauge spinal needle to introduce a fine catheter. Analgesia will be maintained by intermittent injection of the lidocaine and epinephrine through the catheter."

They watched as nurses rolled the woman onto her side and helped her draw her knees up to her chest, exposing the bony ridges of spinal column. The area to be penetrated had previously been marked in red with a Mercurochrome solution. A tall man, gowned and masked, bent over the woman with the needle.

"That's John Adriani. One of our top anesthesiologists," said Ted.

"We were talking about Dr. Weston, I believe. You

were telling me about her extraordinary time at work. Does she actually sleep here at the hospital?"

"I'd have to check on that. But it's not uncommon. Our residents are accustomed to it, when they're on weekend call."

He turned around to see if Nick O'Donnell knew, but Nick had not returned to the observation gallery. Funny, thought Ted. Wonder what's holding him up.

"The catheter has been positioned," said Jill Weston's voice from the monitor. The TV screen showed a close-up of the woman's lower back. Just above the cleft of her buttocks from the red-stained patch of skin, a thin catheter tube now protruded. "We will now proceed with the lidocaine."

"I should think it would be bad for Dr. Weston's health, staying inside the hospital all day," commented Diana Falke.

"Oh, she's in fine health. In fact, I'd wager she is in better shape than either of us."

"What makes you say that?"

"Well, perhaps I shouldn't speak for you. I suppose I should only speak for myself. But I happen to know she's a jogger. One of the nurses was telling me just the other day. She and another of our physicians have a regular route."

"Really? How interesting. Is it another surgeon she goes out with?"

"It's our Blood Bank director, actually. Fine young chap. You might like to meet him."

They had rolled the patient onto her back and had wheeled a black box beside her, above the level of the operating table. Wired to the black box was the scanner "paddle," thick-chromed steel, shaped like an inverted mushroom. A nurse held the paddle extended over the woman's abdomen again. Jill Weston picked up another catheter.

"We will now infuse a disclosing solution through this catheter into the uterus. The solution has a specfic gravity and some permeability different from the surrounding tissue, so we are better able to see the outline of the uterus on the ultrasound scanner."

The TV monitor focused on the ultrasound picture tube, where a faint white outline was beginning to take shape. On either side of the rounded shape, a small white nodule began to form.

"Ultrasound, as you probably know, is preferable to scanning techniques that involve radiation when we are working so near to the ovary," Jill went on. "Watch the screen. You can see the outline of the fallopian tubes appearing as we infuse more fluid."

The white nodules on the screen began to extend themselves in opposite directions, like thin branches slowly growing from a large round seed.

"We're using a low-intensity transducer adjusted for this particular disclosing fluid. Soon you will see the blockage in each of the fallopian tubes. It shows up rather dramatically on the cathode-ray screen. Watch. The progress of the white pathways will be abruptly halted when the solution reaches the obstruction."

Ted's eyes were on the screen, fascinated.

"Where does she go jogging?" asked Diana Falke. "Central Park?"

On the TV monitor, the right-hand branch of white stopped moving. "Look," said Ted. "There it is.'"

"We have illuminated the obstruction in the left fallopian tube," said Jill. "As you can see, the blockage occurs approximately five centimeters from the entrance to the uterus, or about halfway along the tube. An ovum would take nearly four days to travel this distance. Of course in this patient, the ovum cannot get through, which is what we are attempting to correct."

"I said, does she go jogging in Central Park?" repeated Diana Falke.

"Oh. Beg your pardon. I was completely absorbed. Central Park? I suppose she might—oh, no, wait, I'm remembering now. I think they said she goes farther east. Where they run the marathon race, you know."

"Using the laparoscope, the dilating catheter will now be inserted through the cervical mouth into the uterus, and positioned in the left fallopian tube. We will work on the left tube first."

Ted leaned forward again. "They did this procedure for my wife, you know. Jill and her team. Just about a year ago."

"Has your wife had a baby?"

"Not yet. But we're expecting one within the month. In fact, she's coming in for an examination today."

"With Dr. Weston? She takes time for obstetrical cases?"

"This time she did. Look. That catheter's coming into focus on the screen."

A thin line, whiter than the area around it, appeared within the image of the obstructed tube.

"When we reach the point of obstruction, we will inflate the tiny balloon at the tip of the catheter," said Jill. "This applies a gentle pressure to expand the fallopian walls and loosen the obstruction. Then we work our way through the blockage with the catheter and expand the balloon again. If we are fortunate, we can 'hook' the obstruction in this manner, and draw it out. If it remains immovable—"

"They run the marathon over on the FDR Drive, don't they?" asked Diana. "Why would she want to go all the way over there?"

"Maybe it's not as crowded. I'm told Central Park fills up with joggers during lunchtime."

"Really? I should think it would be too noisy, with all the cars. Oh, well. Her preference, I suppose. This seems to be a fairly routine operation, wouldn't you say?"

"I think that's the point. It's a tamer procedure. They don't cut into the body, so there's less risk of infection or loss of blood—"

"Yes," said Diana Falke, abruptly. "Yes, I'm aware of that."

21

Maryann Delvecchio crouched down beside the weeping little girl and looked directly into the camera. "And so, coming to you from Bayside, Queens, this is Maryann Delvecchio, 'News Center Six.'" The last part was the most important: repeat the station name at the end of the story where it lingers in the ear. Constant repetition breeds familiarity and thus establishes authority. That was Scott Hummell's theory, anyway. Scott Hummell was Channel Six's station manager, so his theory carried weight enough for Maryann to follow it. Even though she would just as soon have had the name of Maryann Delvecchio in people's ears if there was going to be any lingering going on. She had even tried it once. And gotten her ass chewed.

She gave the little girl a kiss. "You be brave, honey," she whispered. "Maybe somebody out there watching tonight will know where you big brother is." Then she stood up and thanked the parents. Maryann always made a special point of thanking the people she interviewed. Not only was it good press relations for the station, but it also made her feel good. She felt low enough putting other people's misery on the air without treating them as if she'd done them a favor. Nobody got famous on News Center Six.

Except Maryann.

She hoped.

She gave the parents her card and got them to promise to call her if another anonymous note came about their son's ransom.

By then the crew had the equipment back in the truck. "All right, let's hit it," she said, and climbed in. As she shut the door, she was already checking her clipboard for the next location. One thing about TV news work, it kept you busy.

"Where to, boss?" Jamie, her driver, shaggy-haired and lovable, with a grin under his wispy mustache, always called her "boss." She still got a charge out of it.

"Manhattan. Madison and Seventy-fourth. Madison Hospital."

"We going inside?" asked one of the cameramen behind her in the van.

"Probably not. They probably won't want us within ten miles of the place. They're going to be embarrassed as hell."

"Yeah?"

"We're titling this story 'The Case of the Disappearing Patients.' The hospital's going to go crazy when it gets on the air."

"You've got the goods?"

"Hey. Don't I always?" She gave the cameraman a grin that told him not to worry, and looked back over the schedule, setting up the story angles. After Madison Hospital they had two more locations to cover before lunch. If they worked quickly and didn't get stuck in traffic, they would have time to get to maybe three more before bringing it all in to be edited at the station. If Maryann was lucky, two of the eight stories she had covered today would see air time. Maryann would not be watching. When Gary Greenspan, host of "News Center Six at Six," went on the air, she would still be on the phone with hot-line callers, reading her mail, and wrangling with Carolyn Rhoaded, her assignment editor, over which stories she would get to cover tomorrow. None of the other reporters worked as hard as Maryann, but then none of them had Maryann's ambition.

Or if one of them did, he didn't have Maryann's other advantage.

The white capsules.

She fingered the capsule in her jacket pocket as if it were a talisman.

The dashboard clock said 10:30. At noon she would drop the capsule. Then she would be good until midnight. While the others were slowing down after lunch and sneaking in drinks around four or five o'clock, Maryann would be just hitting her stride. After they had gone home and were drowsing in their living rooms after dinner and trying to get the kids into bed, Maryann would be working her contacts for new stories. She might be at Sardi's or Elaine's buying drinks for an expert on her expense account so that she would be armed with the right questions when she went out the next morning. She might be at a new play or a new film, working up an imaginary sixty-second review so she would be ready to fill in if Barry Boyce, "News Center Six's" critic-in-residence, called in sick again. That had happened once before and Maryann had been ready, gone on live at the studio and been terrific, and come away with three fan letters plus a compliment from Scott Hummell on her versatility. Real stage presence, he had said. Maybe sometime soon she would like to try anchoring the weekend edition?

Maybe. She hadn't jumped at him, because she knew about anchoring. You couldn't come on pushy. The reporters got out in the field and were pushy. The anchors stayed in the studio and showed people that whatever it was, no matter how bad it was, they could live with it.

At least one story every night had to be really bad. Otherwise people weren't interested. Maryann's job now was to make sure her stories made them stay tuned to "News Center Six." She would be ready when the time came to act mature and calm about it all, but for now she had to get out there and sweat and cry with the people.

"So who do you have us set up to see outside the hospital, boss?" asked Marvin, her cameraman. "Do we interview the window washer?"

She didn't like his tone. "You don't have to concern yourself with the schedule, Marvin."

"Aw, c'mon. I didn't mean it that way. I just like to have some idea where I'm going, like anybody else, you know?"

She heard the note of apology in his voice and told him it was O.K. You had to be careful, or they'd take advantage. "If it'll help you plan ahead, we've got two interviews set up for the hospital. One is a nineteen-year-old college boy, and the other is a prep-school basketball coach, probably in his fifties." And both of them could be lying, she thought, though that would be an unlikely coincidence. The trouble was, just having them talking outside the hospital wasn't visual enough. What you needed for a real news story was on-the-scene *action*.

"I think we'll set up at the Emergency entrance," she went on. "That's where the coach last saw one of his players. We've got a good angle with that one, because the kid's an orphan. Some bank in town is his guardian; the coach doesn't know which one. And the school thinks he might have just run away, because he wasn't doing well in anything but basketball."

"So why would that make the kid want to run away?" asked Marvin.

Jamie spoke up. "He had to go to the hospital 'cause he was hurt, right? He couldn't play if he was hurt. Right, boss?"

"He couldn't run away, either," said Marvin.

"That's the point," said Maryann. "It's a mystery. You can't figure it out right away. And it's got the good angle. The lonely kid, on his own in the big city, against the system—"

But it still wasn't *the* story, she thought. Not the one that they'd remember Maryann Delvecchio for. Probably it was a missing piece of paper somewhere that made it look bad for the hospital, and the kid had just taken off.

Freddie, her sound man, was interested now too. "Did the kid have a girl friend? Maybe we could get a shot of her, asking him to come back. What do you think?"

The three men started arguing about whether the story was about the missing kid or about the school or about the system the kid was floating around lost in. None of them seemed to remember that the story was the hospital. When they quieted down, Maryann decided, she would tell them about the talk she had had last night with the hospital administrator. They were on the Queensboro Bridge by now, and Maryann was looking ahead at the great big beautiful skyline she never got tired of. There was so much to find out in the city; so many things nobody but a few people knew about, and when you put them on the air people thought you were terrific. What a great job she had. And somewhere in that skyline was the story that was going to give her the big break to an even better job.

She fingered the capsule again. Maybe she would take it a little early today. Tonight was free so far, so probably between eleven and midnight whatever she was doing wouldn't be as important as this story at the hospital. And if it was, she still had three more capsules. She could take part of Saturday's tonight if she had to; there wouldn't be much going on Saturday.

Unless they asked her to anchor the "Weekend Edition." . . .

But she'd still have enough in the capsule to get her through. Then at seven-thirty or eight or whenever the voice on the phone told her, she'd be in the taxicab on her way to the Leader and twenty-one more capsules.

God. Now there was her breakthough story. If she could only figure out how to *get* it! If she could only make the Leader show himself somewhere, and then follow him—

"What's the story on the other one, Maryann?"

Pleased at Marvin's respectful tone, she smiled. "Other one?"

"Yeah. You said there was a nineteen-year-old college boy?"

She looked at her clipboard. "Did indeed. David Cranford. Actually, he's the one who got me started on Madison Hospital. His mother had a face-lift there, and then she disappeared."

They loved it. "Wow," said Jamie. "A missing orphan and a boy who's lost his mother. You sure can pick 'em."

"That's why she's the boss, kid."

"Yeah, she homes in on trouble like she's got radar—"

Maryann smiled. With the feeling she always got, relief mixed in with excitement, she slipped the capsule into her mouth without any of them noticing.

She was swallowing the capsule when the idea came to her.

"Hey. Marvin," she asked, "do you know what kind of radar equipment we have at the station?"

22

Alone in the examination room down the hall from Jill Weston's office, Rachel Sanford climbed up onto the padded table. She was waiting for Alexis, Jill's assistant, to come back. Rachel had already undressed herself and put on the disposable light wrapper, a synthetic cellulose sheet with holes cut in for the arms. The paper covering the table crackled as she sat down. It felt cool on her bare legs, but not uncomfortable. She was glad that Jill kept the heater in the room going. Being cold would be a final indignity when you had to take off all your clothes and pad around in a ridiculously flimsy paper sheet that left your arms and legs bare. And when you already felt so awkward about your belly sticking out, this thirty-pound belly you had to haul around in front of you—

She reminded herself that this was her child, and pictured a soft, fragile infant with a high forehead and the closed eyes big and rounded, like the ones in the book of intrauterine pictures Ted had brought home. In her mind's eye she saw the tiny hands, no longer webbed now, the little fingers wiggling as they went into the baby's mouth. She called up feelings of love for her unborn baby. Rachel went through the mental pictures a lot, and especially every time she found herself thinking a negative thought about the little one. He or she didn't ask to be born, she reminded herself. You went through a lot of trouble to create this child, and you're not going to complain about something you went into with your eyes open. Just because of Mother—

She did not want to think about Mother. Rachel's mother had been a complainer. Whatever she did for Rachel had to be asked for two or three times, with complaints every time. And then when Mother finally mended the dress or filled out the application form or paid the camp or whatever it was, Rachel heard about it for at least a week afterward. Along with comments on how ungrateful and selfish young girls were and how they never wanted to help anyone. On her eighteenth birthday, when her uncle had asked if Rachel wanted to come down to the shore and take a job waitressing in one of the hotels, Rachel had been more than willing. She had made enough that summer to pay tuition, room, and board at the state university, for that was back in 1960, when the costs hadn't yet become impossible. At State she had majored in art, and discovered that she had courage enough to tell her instructors that she hated the abstractionists, the cubists, the expressionists, the surrealists, and all the rest of the twentieth-century moderns then in favor. What Rachel liked to do was paint the kind of pictures she saw in magazines. Pictures of people you could tell were real people.

Her second summer at the shore, she had discovered that she could sell some of her paintings. At the end of that summer, she had enough money for tuition, room, board, and three hundred dollars left over. She had bought paints. And canvases and brushes.

And, the following spring, new waitress uniforms and a new swimsuit. Even though Rachel was convinced that her bottom was a little too big and her breasts a little too small.

As it turned out, the uniform and the swimsuit were what counted, for that summer at the hotel she attracted the attention of Ted Sanford. He had come down for a week with his family. He was twenty-seven years old, shy, and still dressing in Weejuns and Bermudas like a college kid, even though he was already middle management in Bancroft Manufacturing, the people who made more steel office furniture and files than any other American com-

pany. The second night of their visit she had finished her
tables early and gone walking on the beach to watch the
sunset. He followed. Tousle-haired, a little chubby, his
eyes brown and wide, and, unaccountably, very shy, he
waited while she walked down to the end of the beach
where the waves came in to the land on three sides. She
knew he was waiting, even though she hadn't turned
around she knew, and she stood watching the sun drop
down red and glittering across the water, thinking I'm
twenty years old and it doesn't matter if I haven't been
introduced to him on his level, doesn't matter that I'll be
waiting on him at breakfast and his parents will be looking at me. I'm twenty years old and I've been on my own
for nearly eighteen months now and I can take care of
myself. She gave the sun a last look and picked up a
shell and skipped it against one of the dark-blue waves,
and felt somewhere inside that she was saying good-bye
to something. "Hi," she said brightly when she turned
and saw him. "Do you like the beach? I love the colors
this time of the evening."

He had stayed on a week after his parents had gone,
and then another. They had names for each other. He was
"Bear." They used to race in the surf, splashing out to
where it was over their heads and then back, and sometimes she could beat him, sometimes not. In one of their
races her swim cap came off and her sandy brown hair
turned wet and wiry like an Airedale's coat, and when
they came in he had looked at her, touched the rounded,
freckled tip of her nose with his, and christened her
"Dale."

That fall, her senior year, he surprised all the girls in
her dorm by coming up to see her on weekends. He would
take a room in a motel and drive her there, and
they would talk. He wanted her to become an artist, because that was what she really wanted to do. He confessed
he had always wanted to be a doctor, but discovered he
just couldn't pass organic chemistry and biology even
though he tried, so there he was in Bancroft middle management. He cried, and so did she, and held him very close
for a long time and told him it was all right.

Before the next weekend she had endured the scorn
and admonitions of three local doctors before she found
a fourth who would fit her with a diaphragm. She kept it
with her weekends after that, but Ted never took advan-

tage of their opportunities and they never went beyond what they called "heavy petting." Rachel wondered what Ted was doing during the week. And told herself that he might be saving her for something special. They hadn't talked of the future.

She lined up a job in the spring on the strength of her ad sketch for the school paper and the recommendation of a personnel man who had bought one of her paintings at the shore. The job was in New York. Ted's company—his father's company—was in Pittsburgh. He said he would come to see her after graduation and help her get settled. He didn't. She spent July and August drawing fall fashion ads for A & S and wondering if Ted was on the beach somewhere, waiting for another girl to finish looking at the sunset.

On a Friday evening late in September she had come out of the office building with everybody else in the world and stopped to buy a hot pretzel from the man on the corner because the air was cool with fall and she wanted to walk awhile before going home to dinner. She had her purse open to pay him when she saw a hand with a dollar bill and heard Ted's voice. "My treat this time, O.K., Dale?"

He had his car and they drove down the Garden State Parkway to the beach and lay under the stars on blankets watching the path of the moon on the water. He had brought a ring. Trouble with his family, he said, but it was past now and he wanted her to marry him. The diamond was two carats raised up in a Tiffany setting, glowing cold in the moonlight. Looking at it, she hesitated, and he took a deep breath and blurted out the truth of where he'd been that summer. Medical school. He had wiped out the small trust fund his parents had established for him and bought his way in on a provisional acceptance. During the last three months he had worn himself out with studying and made a lot of friends, but had managed to pass only one of the five midterm examinations. So now you know, he said. The dean had told him not to waste any more of his time. His parents had agreed to let him work in the new sales office they had started in New York. He was facing facts. Would she still want him? She kissed him and told him to put the ring back in the box for three months; that she wasn't going to pick him up on the rebound from medical school.

Then to show him how she felt she kissed him again. They made love under the stars, even though she hadn't brought her diaphragm, and then in his hotel room overlooking the surf they had made love again.

After they had been married two years, he was running the New York sales office and she was drawing TV story-boards in the ad agency that handled the Bancroft Manu-facturing account. She liked the work, but he wanted a baby, so the next year she stopped using her diaphragm. The following year she was told by her gynecologist that she couldn't have children.

They had been happy enough together for thirteen years. Always there was something new to work with or go to see in Manhattan. They bought a beach house for weekends in the summer and both worked hard. Then last year came Ted's chance to get closer to medicine again with the hospital job, and she had Jill Weston's op-eration and got pregnant, and they both realized that it might be possible to be even happier. Both of them had started to hope.

Rachel shifted her position on the table to ease the pressure on her bladder. What was keeping Jill's assis-tant? The wall clock said it had been almost five minutes since Alexis had shown her in here and told her to wait. Rachel was due back at work by one-fifteen. She would have to pick up something at the deli and have lunch at her desk. These were her last weeks in the studio before she went on maternity leave and she had too many ends to tie up to be taking long lunch hours. Besides, she was now management, a shareowner in the agency, even, and she wanted to set a good example for the artists who worked under her supervision.

Two minutes later, the examination-room door opened. A man looked in. a doctor with curly blond hair, almost like Rachel's but lighter.

"Where's Dr. Weston?" Rachel asked as soon as she saw him. "Where's Alexis?"

He glanced behind him in the hall. "Beg your pardon," he said. "I think I've got the wrong room."

Jill Weston came in only a few moments later.

After she greeted Rachel, Jill picked up the file where Alexis had left it, beside the centrifuge. "That was Roger Avery who just popped in on you," she said. "Somebody paged him to the right room on the wrong floor. Terrific hospital your husband's running here. How're you feeling?"

"Pregnant. Very, very pregnant."

"Sounds accurate." She was looking at the chart in Rachel's file. "Now what's happened here? Alexis didn't enter your hematocrit, or the baby's heart rate."

"She didn't *take* my hematocrit. I haven't seen her since she showed me in and told me she'd be right back."

"Probably in the little girls' room. She wasn't feeling well this morning. Never mind, I can manage." She opened a drawer and broke off a foil lancet packet and picked up three pipettes for the centrifuge. "Here comes the hard part. Hold out your little finger."

"You're cheerful today."

"I'm even going jogging." She pricked Rachel's finger and drew the bright red droplet up into the first pipette.

"Ted says you're making the hospital rich and famous."

"Maybe. Somebody from a foundation was over this morning to see the operation. Supposedly she liked what she saw. I didn't have a chance to meet her." She put the full pipettes into the centrifuge and turned it on. "Now let's check the little one's heartbeat."

She helped Rachel lie back on the examination table and got the Doppler apparatus and the gel. Her fingers palpated Rachel's abdomen, feeling for the baby's head and shoulders. "Still kicking?"

"Yes. Especially at night."

"When you lie down, they tend to wake up. Gravity pulls on them differently when you're lying down. Makes them want to wriggle. How are your ankles?"

"Fine. Not swollen anymore."

"Still taking the kelp?" She squeezed the gel onto Rachel's lower abdomen, on the right side. "The iron? All that stuff? Drinking your milk?"

She always asked these questions when she was sliding the Doppler mike around in the gel, searching for the baby's heartbeat. Silence only added to the mother's natural tensions as she lay there wondering where the heartbeat was and if the baby had suddenly gone dead. "That whooshing there is the placenta; I'm sure you know that by now from Alexis—" Then there it was, the baby heart, like someone tapping the mike, loud, at about twice the speed of an adult pulse. She timed it for fifteen seconds: "One hundred and thirty beats per minute. I guess she's sleeping. Even though you're lying down."

"When do I get my first pelvic examination?"

"This is your thirty-sixth week. If I give you pelvic today and induce labor, then the baby's premature. If that happens the thirty-seventh week, it's not premature. So we wait till next week."

"Induce labor? You mean I could have the baby this soon?"

"Been known to happen. You haven't been smoking and you've been eating right, though, so the odds of premature delivery go down." She helped Rachel pull herself upright to a sitting position on the table.

"I guess I hadn't quite got it into my head that the baby could come this soon. I mean, I feel as if I could just go on being pregnant."

Jill made the entry in Rachel's chart. "Not much chance of that happening. Now let's do your blood pressure."

"I'm wondering about Ted. When do we have to stop —stop making love?"

"Intercourse is fine right up until the end. After the amniotic membrane ruptures you have to be careful of bacterial infection, but not until then. When that happens, you call me right away."

Rachel nodded.

"We were both wondering, too, about a Caesarian. Is there any way you can tell whether I'll need one?"

"I don't think you'll breech. The head's down, and it usually stays down. And you're a big girl—five foot, what, eight?"

"Five-nine."

"And you've got good wide hips. If I ever have a baby, I think I'll be wishing I had your hips. Of course we'll watch you closely during labor. If it seems the head isn't moving too well we can take pelvic measurements with ultrasound. But the baby feels about average size and you've only gained thirty pounds. I'd say you're likely to have plenty of room."

She unclipped the blood-pressure cuff from Rachel's arm and recorded the reading in the chart. The centrifuge had switched off automatically. As they talked, she removed the pipettes and looked at the separated red cells.

"Well your hematocrit's still good. You must really be taking that iron."

"Six tablets a day. God I hate the stuff."

"You can taper off after next month. But we want your blood count up before delivery."

"We're hoping to get through without any anesthetic."

"Fine. Ted's going to be there with you?"

"Oh, yes. We've been taking the classes together."

"Good. Just be sure neither of you thinks that you have to be a hero. If you need help, you *can* ask for it, you know. It's not going to hurt the baby if we give you a caudal block."

"But they said there were studies that showed babies born without anesthetic are more alert. They said so at the class."

"I'm sure they did. The problem with those studies is they can't factor out the influence of the mother after the baby's born. Mothers who are motivated to give birth without anesthetic may be motivated to work more with their babies later on so they score better on an infant-alertness test—"

She saw the door opening. "Yes?"

It was Alexis, her round face flushed, her dark hair more tangled than when Rachel had last seen her.

She apologized for being late. Something had gone wrong. The door of the staff women's room. When she went in it had locked behind her, and she couldn't get out. They had to call the custodian to come with a special key and remove the whole lock apparatus.

"Gee," said Rachel. "I wonder how that could have happened."

23

They started across town on Seventy-fourth at about five past one. At this hour most of the lunchtime traffic had already gotten to where it was going and hadn't yet left to go back to work, so the street wasn't too crowded.

Jerry ran ahead just slightly, in his bright-red warm-up suit and his blue wool hat, with the little heart-shaped pin in the front that said blood donors were special people. "Public relations," he had told Jill when she first noticed it pinned to his chest.

"Then you should pin it on your hat," she told him. "If you want people to see it. And the hat could certainly stand some decoration."

He felt good with her. The sun was out, and the thermometer had hit forty the first time in the two weeks they'd been jogging together. This was the best half hour of his day. Other groups of the staff loved running, too, but the ones Jerry knew had families to go home to at night, so they jogged in the morning. Nobody else jogged at lunch. Around Madison, as with most hospitals, lunchtime was scarcely recognized as a break in the workday by physicians. That was fine with Jerry. He was in early and out late, and everyone knew it. No one would accuse him of goofing off during the noon hour. And if no one else wanted to jog with Jill Weston, so much the better.

He turned slightly and got another look at the way her chin tilted up when she ran, at the way her eyes shone.

She caught him looking, but he had a question ready. "How do they feel?"

"The Nikes? They're fantastic!"

"But are they worth the fifty bucks?"

"You know how it feels when you just put a marshmallow in your mouth? That's what these shoes feel like, every time I take a step."

"Sounds like a sales talk to me." The light was turning at Lexington so they sprinted to get across. Then they slowed down to their usual pace, about twelve minutes a mile. Their rule was never to run fast enough to hinder them from talking.

"Actually the price was what convinced me," said Jill. "If I've got fifty dollars invested in running shoes, that's a good incentive for me to keep running."

"I still say you bought 'em because they match your velvet warm-up suit. 'Ol Silver Shoes,' we'll call you."

"You could do with a bit of cushioning yourself. You've got a lot of weight coming down on those sneakers of yours."

"Hey. Don't you recognize Captain Marvel when you

see him?" He took a leap as they ran, came down on both feet, and jumped. *"Sha-zam!"*

"Ever hear of stress fractures?"

"Hey." He plucked the pin from his cap and waved it at her. "Have a heart. We hematologists are sensitive about our weight."

"You're not fat. Your shoes just don't have enough cushioning for pavement. If we're going to work on increasing our speed or extending the distance, you could start showing some wear and tear."

She's just kidding around, Jerry told himself. It's not as though she's really telling you she's interested.

"Maybe I'll try on a pair," he said.

"The store's between Lexington and Park, on Eighty-sixth. They're open till eight. I walked up there after dinner last night, and do you know when I wore them back I started running? There I was in my slacks and my ski jacket, carrying my purse, running down Park Avenue just because these shoes felt so good. People looked at me as if they couldn't believe it!"

"They probably thought you'd stolen the purse. I can see it now, underpaid physician turns to life of street crime—hey, speaking of street crime, did you see the TV crew out front this morning?"

"TV crew?"

"Yep. And did you know two detectives from the missing persons bureau were in the Blood Bank this morning?"

"Really?"

"Oh, yeah. We people on the ground floor get in on things."

He told her about the two missing patients. And about how Ted Sanford had come out to the TV cameras with the discharge papers for one of them, just to prove that the hospital was in the clear.

"Of course then the sharp lady reporter asked him what kind of proof he had for the other case. She really put him in a bind. That's what Marcie said, anyway. She was on her way in and stopped to watch."

"I don't think I'll be tuning in for that one," said Jill. "We've got enough real problems at the hospital without worrying about imaginary runaways."

"What bothers me is the hospital's reputation. If it

goes out on TV that people come to Madison Hospital and disappear—"

"Not good for the image," Jill agreed. They were coming to York Avenue now, where they would cross and run on the sidewalk down to Seventy-first, the entrance to the river walkway along FDR Drive. That was the part Jill was becoming most fond of. They could stop watching for traffic and just ramble on.

"Definitely not good." *C'mon, Chamberlain,* Jerry thought. *Now's the time. Ask her.* They jogged in place as a white ambulance van passed slowly before them, probably on its way to New York Hospital. Jerry could see some of the buildings of its vast complex from where they stood. Then he chickened out. "Now *there's* a place with an image," he said. "Sloan-Kettering, Rockefeller U, all that endowment money—why can't the TV people pick on them instead of us?"

"Maybe it's politics. You know Ted hasn't made many friends in Albany with his talk about getting the government out of medicine."

Ask her. Why did it have to seem so important? "Did you ever think of working at a place like New York Hospital?"

"Sometimes. But in the really big places a female surgeon tends to fade into the background. Ted's giving me a good opportunity."

Ask her. "He should. I hear the Weston Procedure is bringing us a lot of foundation interest."

She waved the compliment aside, but found herself blushing nonetheless. "Oh, c'mon. Nobody calls it 'the Weston Procedure.' "

"Ted does. Marcie said he was playing your operation up with the TV interviewer this morning, telling her she ought to report on some good news for a change."

"Well, that's kind of nice of him, don't you think?"

"He was saving his own neck with it, but yeah, I see what you mean. At least he was thinking about it."

"He watched the whole procedure in the amphitheater this morning. Do you think that would happen if I worked in a big hospital?"

"If it was you, maybe yes. Who knows?"

"Oh, c'mon," she said again.

He bit his lip. All right, here goes nothing. "I was wondering if—"

The noise from his pocket beeper cut him off. Flustered, he pulled the beeper from his warm-up suit and fumbled for the switch as they ran. He dropped it. Jill waited while he bent to pick it up.

"There's a phone over there," she said, pointing across the street from the FDR pathway. "I've got a dime if you need one."

He shut off the beeping and straightened up, red-faced. "Thanks, I've got a dime, too. I'll just be a minute."

He came away from the phone looking worried. "They want me back," he said. "Somehow a fire got started in my office and they're pretty upset. I can't think what the hell happened, I wasn't even smoking in there this morning."

"Maybe it was the wiring," Jill offered. "C'mon, I'll go back with you."

"Oh, no, finish your run. You got your new shoes, and I'm going to have to take a cab. Finish your run. It's too nice a day."

Jill glanced up at the sun, sensing that he wanted to handle his own problem. "O.K.," she said, "but let me know what happens, will you?"

Halfway across the street, he turned and sprinted to catch up with her.

"I was just thinking," he began. "How about if I take you out to dinner tonight? We could celebrate your new shoes."

Her surprised look turned to a smile. "I'd like that, Jerry. Thank you."

He was crossing the street again when he heard her say, "Call me!"

He raised a fist and waved back. A taxi honked at him and he dodged, hearing the screech of brakes behind him as he gained the curb. Don't get yourself killed now, for God's sake, Chamberlain, he thought. Then he realized that the cab had been empty, that he had to get back to the hospital in a hurry, that she was probably watching him make a fool of himself. The cab was stopping at a red light on Seventy-third. He sprinted.

24

Matthew Garrett raised the dark-blue hood of his sweat shirt, covering his hair and forehead. He could see the woman on the curb, waving good-bye to the man in the red suit. If she was coming across, it would be soon. She would come through the small park, up the steps, and over the concrete walkway and the traffic below on the FDR Drive, and then down another flight of concrete steps to the jogging trail that ran along the river. The question was which direction she would take from there. Would she go north, upriver, or south? Garrett had watched other joggers come down the flight of steps and counted four in the past fifteen minutes who had gone north. Only one had come south, toward the spot where Garrett now stood. He decided to remain where he was. As two runners went by him on the narrow path Garrett bent over, stretching his calf muscles as though warming up. Neither one noticed him.

Jill smiled inwardly as she descended the concrete steps to the FDR path. Wind from the river was cold on her cheeks, but the sun was warm, and she felt as though she could run for miles. An illusion of course. After only two weeks jogging she was not yet a distance runner, but she was coming along. What counted were regular workouts and not going too fast or too far on any one day, so that the body had enough time for anabolism. She remembered her physiology courses from medical school on the anabolic process about how tissue rebuilds directly in proportion to the amount of activity, food, and oxygen it gets, and wondered why all these years since then she had not thought of giving her body the activity that it obviously had needed. Live and learn. She could see the faded blue line on the jogging trail, the guiding path left from the big marathon race last October. Fifteen thousand runners Jerry had said. Five thousand of them women. It took an hour's running a day and two hours on weekends to be able to finish a marathon. She wondered if Jerry would really want to commit that much time.

At the bottom of the steps she turned north. The sun and the wind were at her back, and she eased into a steady lope, enjoying the feel of the new shoes along the trail. She wondered if Jerry was thinking of changing jobs, or if he had just been asking about her, wondering how long she would be staying. She realized she was looking forward to dinner with him tonight. Jerry didn't make her feel the same way Phillip did. With Jerry, there wasn't the tension, the need to prove herself. When she was with Phillip, she had moments when she remembered her father's house in East Aurora, and his car, the old Packard much admired by the people in town, and thought to herself that Phillip, even if he tried to understand, wouldn't be able to feel the same way as she about a small-town life-style. Or about her, the way she was when she got away from the hospital and the physician's frame of mind. To Phillip, life outside medicine was something very different from East Aurora, New York. He assumed that Jill shared his point of view, and when she was with him, she found it easy to go along. But when she was with Jerry . . .

Jill checked her watch. Sixteen minutes had gone by since she had left the hospital. She was feeling good; maybe another four minutes. Then back the same route for a total of forty.

Behind her, Garrett saw Jill raise her wrist to see the time. He also knew she had been running for sixteen minutes. The fact that she was only a recent convert to exercise indicated that she would soon be turning around to go back to the hospital. Unless, of course, she planned to run as far north as she could, and then walk away from the drive to where she could get a cab. Not knowing her plan, he kept a distance between them of about fifteen yards, far enough back so as not to be noticed. He ran easily, at about half his normal workout speed.

Jill decided that what Jerry did was make her comfortable with her own point of view. It was strange, she thought, how little Phillip knew about her, even though she had been to bed with him. But with Jerry, in only two weeks of jogging, she had felt secure enough to talk

about her background, her childhood, her opinions of
people at the hospital—things she would not feel safe at
all telling Phillip. She wondered if that meant she was
taking Jerry too seriously. If Jerry were to disappear
tomorrow, she asked herself, what would I do? Answer:
Come down here and run and think what to do next. But
did that mean she would miss him? She didn't want to
think about that. He wasn't going to disappear tomorrow.
He was going to have dinner with her tonight. She wondered how that would change their relationship, and decided that she wouldn't try to plan ahead.

Her watch said twenty minutes had passed. Time to
turn around. How far had she come? Here it was almost
Ninety-sixth Street. A pretty good pace, faster than they
usually ran. When she turned around into the wind, she
realized why. Now the air was holding her back instead
of helping her along. And the sun was in her eyes. She
leaned forward a little, into the wind, and watched the
blue line as she ran. A man passed her going the other
way, but she scarcely noticed.

Garrett looked up and down the walkway as he turned
to follow her. Two women were coming at a good pace
from the north; they would probably catch up within a
few minutes. Squinting into the sun, he looked past Jill
to see who was coming from the south. Along the edge,
across the bend of the East River, he noticed several
dark shapes. He decided to use them, rather than the
two women, because he could see them as he ran without having to turn around. Either group might turn off
before the right moment came, of course, but if that
happened he had an alternative plan.

He leaned into the wind, closing rapidly on Jill Weston.

When she first heard the footsteps behind her Jill barely
noticed. Other joggers had passed her on the way up,
and she assumed this was just another. She knew she
was not fast; many of the people along the walkway
were serious runners. When she and Jerry jogged this
stretch, they regularly saw women and men who ran
seven, maybe even six, minutes to the mile. Jill's speed
now was not much below ten-minute pace, if that, with
the wind against her. She kept her chin up as she ran and
resumed her thoughts, debating whether her own admiration for Mrs. Comfrey was possibly an indication of an
urge to have children. At some point she would have to

make a difficult decision about having a child. She told herself that the main thing, the first thing, would be to find the man she wanted to be the father. But then there was the question of time, it really came down to time, whether you were married or single, children took time. . . .

Behind her Garrett moved up to within two yards, close enough to be intrusive. He waited for the right moment. As he ran, effortlessly, he remembered nothing of the woman he had killed a few miles north on the Harlem River Drive, nor did he remember any of the others. But he did know that somehow, on the last assignment at the hospital, he had placed himself in danger. The Leader had told him he would be working away from the hospital for a while. He accepted that, but at the back of his mind was the nagging fear of another mistake. If he did not perform satisfactorily, he would no longer be the first of the Guardians. What would the Leader do if Matthew Garrett began to make more and more mistakes? He did not want to be punished because of his errors. So he waited carefully, watching the pair of joggers coming from perhaps a quarter mile ahead of them, judging their speed before he made his move.

Jill was picturing in her mind one of the little soft-skinned newborns that she cuddled, very briefly, while clearing the air passages with the syringe. She wondered what it would be like to be the mother instead of the physician. Rachel, for instance, would be in the hospital within the month, probably, and Jill would be handing her the baby, and instead of waking up the next morning to go to work, Rachel Sanford would wake up with a little warm baby to hold and snuggle and care for. . . .

She was aware of the footsteps behind her again. They were closer. She moved over to the right to let the person pass, but he did not pass. He continued, practically on her heels by now, and she could hear the breathing too, intermixed with her own. Annoyed at the interruption to her concentration, she slowed down. When the person still did not pass, she looked around.

At her shoulder. A dark, hooded face, cold brown eyes deliberately staring. The lips curled back. "You're runnin', aren't ya?"

Her fear at the sudden interruption caught in her

throat and kept her from speaking. She tried to think of what to say that would make him leave her alone. Nothing. She turned her head away. Up ahead some runners were coming. When they reached her she would turn around, she decided, and run with them. She wished she had not come out here alone.

The voice was close to her ear now. "How fast ya think you could run with a knife in your back? How fast ya think if you were dead?"

She heard a metallic click and felt something sharp jab through her warm-up jacket, touching her bare ribs. Unbelieving, she turned and saw the wide, leering grin, the tip of the long blade raised up, flashing in the sun. For a moment fear overcame her with weakness. The sky seemed to move above her and she stumbled. She pitched forward, nearly falling, and when she regained her balance she was running as hard as she could, desperate to reach the joggers coming toward her. She could not think what he would do, whether he would attack them first, whether either of them could somehow stop him. She only ran. Scream, she thought, they won't know he's chasing you, you're supposed to scream, but her breath came too hard now and the wind hurt her throat and the scream was more a whisper, scarcely audible even to her.

They were a man and a woman, young, both of them black, she could see them clearly now, see the surprised looks on their faces as she came at them full speed, arms upraised. "Help!" she called weakly. "Look out, he's got a knife!"

The woman shied away but the man reached out his arms for her as she stumbled into them, gasping now, "Help me, please, he's got a knife—"

The black man pulled her to a stop. "Knife?" he said. "What knife?"

She tried to get her breath as he held her. There are three of us now, she thought. He won't attack three at once.

"Hey. Little lady. Somebody try to hurt you?"

She caught the kindliness in his tone, the lack of urgency, the focus on her, as if she were the only one there —Then she saw that the pathway around them was empty. About three hundred yards away, two more joggers came toward them at a steady pace. The man in the blue-hooded sweat shirt was not there.

"He had a knife," she said. "He came up behind me with a knife, and I ran." The tears were blurring her vision but she looked up at her rescuers and tried to thank them. They told her it was all right. The woman asked if Jill wanted them to stay with her until they found a policeman. Jill said no, it would be O.K. now.

"He had on a dark-colored sweat shirt with a hood," she said. "Didn't you see him?"

"I don't think we were looking up that far," said the man. The woman nodded. "We just saw you, coming at us like you were gonna fly. Guess you outran him."

"Probably he saw you up ahead and backed off." Jill was beginning to get her strength back. "Oh, but he frightened me," she said. "I wouldn't go back up there alone for a million dollars!"

"We'll keep an eye out for him," said the man. "You're sure you'll be all right alone now?"

"I can manage. It's just a few more blocks till I turn off. Just—be careful up there, okay?"

"Nobody's bothering those others," said the woman. "I expect we'll be safe enough."

Jill thanked them again. When they left, she was still shaking. She wanted to bend double and cry, to find someone's warm arms and curl up and be protected. Instead, she took a few steps, walking, and then moved faster. Her warm-up suit felt cold now, too fragile for the wind. She had to get back to the hospital. When she reached York Avenue, she decided, she would take a cab. She had only a few blocks to go, she was sure of that, because this was Seventy-ninth and she had come in on Seventy-fifth.

The clatter of a helicopter coming in to land startled her and she spurted ahead faster. She looked back over her shoulder. No one was following her. Two men just up ahead, chatting, not noticing as she went by. Only a few blocks. She could see the concrete steps now, and she increased her speed. God, she thought, what am I running from? He's gone. He's like an obscene phone caller, picking on anyone at random. He wants to hurt someone who can't defend herself.

The concrete steps. She took them two at a time, catching her breath for a moment at the top before cross-

ing the walkway. Just beyond the little park she could
see the cars cruising up and down York Avenue, the
pedestrians on the sidewalk. The traffic on FDR Drive
roared beneath her, but she did not look down from the
walkway. There was a cab, she could see a cab on York,
stopping to discharge a passenger. She tried to hurry,
but her adrenaline had dissipated by now, no longer
masking the pain in her leg muscles from the sudden
sprint. As she breathed, the air was cold in her throat,
harsh in her chest. She reached under her warm-up
jacket for the spot where the knife had gone through,
but she could find no tear in the fabric, and no blood.
It must have just been the pointed tip that had touched
her flesh. She could see the knife in her mind as she held
the rail and stumbled weak-legged down the steps to the
park. The cab was still there. She would pay the driver
with money from her office when they got to the hospital,
she thought, and hurried into the park, along the path
between the tall, barren trees.

Garrett was waiting for her behind the second tree.
When she had gone past him about three yards he
stepped out and took her from behind. A silent blow
to the neck. She barely realized she had been hit before
she fell.

25

Otto Lindstrom's private office was on the thirty-fourth
floor of Number One Battery Park, a corner office, two
large windows, each with a view of New York Harbor.
Looking outside, a visitor that clear afternoon could have
seen the oil-storage tanks in New Jersey, the red-brick
Coast Guard barracks on Governors Island, the Brooklyn
dockyards, the Statue of Liberty, and the shipping traffic,
the smaller tugs and ferries, the barges, and the big
freighters, liners, and tankers that cruised majestically

past the tip of Manhattan on their way to and from the ports of the world.

But Otto was not looking out the window. He was at his desk, a huge old rolltop desk built of unstained oak and trimmed with gold and leather.

On one side of the desk was a call director phone with thirty-four buttons, seventeen of which were lit. On the other side of the desk was a single gold-colored telephone without a dial, connected to Otto's private line. The gold phone was ringing softly. Otto did not look at it. He kept his eyes on the center of his desk, staring at the small white capsule.

He was not seeing the capsule.

In his mind Otto was reliving the morning two weeks and one day earlier when he had awakened at 4 A.M., his usual time, and reached for the heavy silver box he kept on the table by his bed. Under the lid of the box, his half-asleep memory told him, were the capsules. When he came home from a Gathering meeting he always put the new supply of capsules in the silver box, so that he could reach out and swallow one of them without having to get up.

That morning fifteen days ago he had reached out as before, eyes shut, unremembering, expecting to find the capsules that would comfort him and make his strength return.

His fingers had touched the small white recording sphere. The touch produced a tightening in his belly, a sudden knot of pain that spread up to his chest and made him gasp. He drew himself up on his knees, suddenly afraid of something dreadfully wrong that had happened the night before, something he could not remember. His mind raced as the pain intensified. My God, he thought, I must have hurt myself getting the thing out last night, but no, why in the world would I do that instead of waiting? The pain was making him tremble now, the sweat tingling on his forehead and under his arms, trickling down into his silk pajamas, and he fell over on the bed doubled up, bringing his knees hard against his chest, shutting his eyes as the tears squeezed out. A coronary, he thought, it's happening, a massive coronary and I can't move to reach the phone and call for help. He tried to cry out, but the waves of pain turned the cry into a gasp that no one could have heard. He began to cough and retch, mucus and saliva mingling on the silken pillowcase and smearing his cheeks. Dear God, he thought, what have I done to die like this alone, and then he remembered the little white sphere. The recorder. He had to switch it on, had to make it play back last night so he would know what he had done. Blind with his tears in the still-dark room, he managed to get it out of the silver box and pressed it to his mouth, his tongue searching out the indentation that would tell him which way to turn it to make it play. At last he clicked it on. Held it to his ear, hands shaking uncontrollably.

The Leader's voice: "A member of the Gathering is a member for life."

And silence.

Astonished, Otto sat up in bed. Then he realized that the pain had vanished.

He turned on his bedside light and stared at the little plastic recorder for a full minute before he realized what the Leader had done to him. He shuddered. The skin on the back of his neck went cold. He has reached my mind, Otto thought. He has gotten inside somehow, into the lower centers, and switched on these terrible convulsions. There can be no worse a fate than to lose the mind to another—

Weeping in terror, Otto stared at the silver box. Opened it again, afraid of what he might find.

And saw forty-two capsules.

Each morning the pain had returned.

Until Otto switched on the Leader's voice, he was helpless. He had taken to sleeping with the recorder in the breast pocket of his pajamas, which was sometimes uncomfortable but which spared him moments of agony. He reached for the recorder upon waking and fumbled with it desperately, finding the indentation with his tongue and rotating the top half as the fireball spread within him, shuddering with relief and hatred intermixed as the Leader's voice finally ended the torment.

Now, at his desk, he was trying to undo the process, trying to reverse whatever conditioning method the Leader had used to turn his mornings into hell. A man who believed in orderly timetables, Otto had taken five minutes of every waking hour for his own deconditioning process. The capsule was his focal point, his talisman, his source of strength. He would stare at it and mentally call up the suffering of the morning, willing himself to stand above the pain, to let it flow beneath him like a turbulent river beneath an arched stone bridge. He pursued this exercise in mind control with a tenacity he normally reserved for the most complex and hazardous dealings of his profession, because the thought of the Leader's having reached him so completely aroused a hatred greater than the lust provoked by any business or political challenge. The Leader had caught him, somehow, and was exacting punishment, that much was clear and understandable. Even, in some perverse way, Otto supposed, justifiable, for he knew the codes of the Gathering to which he had sworn his loyalty. But to invade his *mind*—

Otto shook his head and was aware of the clock. The hour was 4 P.M. He would be working late tonight, so it was time for another capsule. He picked up the one on his desk and swallowed it without water.

At least the Leader had been generous with his capsules after the last meeting.

But some way, Otto vowed, as he vowed once every hour as he resumed his work, some way he would rid himself of the Leader's influence. He would soon have the means at hand to exist without the Leader's help. Then before he left the next meeting of the Gathering, Otto would take his revenge.

And the Gathering would be no more.

26

By the time Jerry got back to the blood bank the office fire had long since been put out. It had only been a small one, in a stack of papers in the corner near the wastebasket, or perhaps starting in the wastebasket and spreading to the papers. Both were charred now, and covered with the sticky remains of the foam from the wall extinguisher.

"I guess I panicked," said Marcie as Jerry surveyed the damage. "Dr. Avery was passing by and heard me screaming, and he came in with the extinguisher. I'm just glad there weren't any donors here when it happened. I was so frightened!"

"Lucky all around," said Jerry.

Cleaning up, he double-checked the pack of Salems in his lab coat. Unopened. At least it wasn't me, he thought. It couldn't have been me.

When it came time to leave at the end of the afternoon Jerry picked up the phone to call Jill's office upstairs. Then he realized he didn't know her extension number and got out the hospital directory from his desk drawer. There was her name with the "W's." He looked at it for a long moment, smiling to himself at the way that one name seemed to stand out from the others even though the print was exactly the same. God, Chamberlain, he said to himself, you've got it bad haven't you, and a line of verse from college came to his memory: *Oh, when I was in love with you/Then I was clean and brave.* He said, "Crap," softly, to himself, and then dialed.

The nurse on Jill's floor said she'd gone home for the day.

The home number was listed beside the office extension.

He dialed "9" first to get an outside line and then the number, wondering if she had gone home to get dressed in something special. Of course he wouldn't ask her that. He'd wear a coat and tie, or his good suit, the one he had bought at Brooks Brothers last October. If she was dressed up at all, he'd take her somewhere expensive. Maybe Moriarty's over on Fifty-fourth. He had the credit cards; he might as well get some use out of the service charges he was paying every month. He smiled as the phone began to ring, for he had thought of what to do about reservations. Once they had set the time, he would simply call two restaurants. One formal and the other casual. That way, whatever she was wearing, he'd be prepared.

27

The first thing Jill saw when she awoke was a half-empty water glass in front of her own clock radio. The clock's digital display read 5:09. She stared, not comprehending, and tried to understand the meaning of the three numbers before her: 5:09. She generally did not wake until the alarm went off at six, though frequently she had been awake at three when fatigue and tension kept her from needed sleep. But she had not before wakened at five. . . .

Then she saw the letters in the corner of the "9." The clock was telling her it was 5:09 P.M.

She blinked and sat up so quickly in her bed that the blood drained from her eyes and she could see only darkness. What she saw when her vision cleared bewildered her further. She could see sunlight behind her bedroom curtains. So it *was* day. But here she was in bed, in her nightgown—

Her mouth tasted of salt and she had a headache. On the bench before her dressing table was her warm-up suit, neatly folded. Beneath the bench were her new jogging shoes.

It came back to her in a rush that made her weak with terror. The pathway along the East River. The hooded man. His knife. The taxicab she had been running toward, the sudden impact at the base of her neck—

She felt the spot, gingerly. It hurt. There was probably a bruise.

But what had happened then? How had she managed to get home? And *why?* My God, she thought, as she remembered the afternoon schedule she had planned. My God, what if I've missed it all? Where will I say I was—home sleeping?

She drank the water from the glass on her bedside table. Then she heard a noise in the kitchen. Silverware. She saw in her mind's eye the drawer, the knives. The drawer closed. Unmistakable. Someone was in the apartment with her.

Trembling, she reached for the phone, picked it up as quietly as she could. Dialed "9." The clicking of the dial as it spun back seemed unbearably loud. She heard footsteps coming from the kitchen. Dialed one, one again. Police emergency.

The line was still ringing when she saw the figure in her bedroom doorway. And screamed.

"What the hell?" he said.

Phillip's voice.

He came farther into the room, and she saw that it *was* Phillip. In sports coat and slacks, looking concerned.

"Hey," he said. "A bad dream? What are you doing with that phone?"

"How did you get in here?"

He stared at her. "What are you talking about?"

The voice in the telephone receiver said, "This is the police. Where are you?"

"I'm sorry," she whispered into the phone, and put the receiver back. "Phillip," she said, as clearly as she could, "I asked you a question. Tell me how you got in here?"

"Well, I stayed," he said, looking at her as though she had hurt his feelings. "After you fell asleep, I stayed. I wanted to be sure you were all right. And now that I recollect, you asked me to. You said, 'Don't leave me, Phillip.' Whispered it to me, just as you were drifting off. Like a little girl with her daddy. Made me feel kind of proud."

"I did that?"

"You were falling asleep. I was still holding you, right there, and you whispered it, your lips just brushing my cheek and then you drifted off. So I waited a bit and then I got up and dressed, made myself some coffee in the kitchen—"

"Phillip, I don't remember that at all!"

"Well, you were falling asleep—"

"No, Phillip." She struggled to keep her voice from breaking, struggled not to cry, not to scream at him that she never wanted him in her bed, had never wanted him in her bed again—

She tried to focus on his face, tried desperately to remember. There was nothing. He did not even quite look the same, as she stared at him, her intensity making her question whether his nose had always been quite so pointed, his lips as thin, his cheeks so ruddy.

"What is it, hon?" he said. "What do you see?"

For a moment she thought of hiding it, saying "nothing," admitting nothing, simply getting up and seeing him out of her apartment and telling him that this really would be the last time. But she had to know.

And if he did care for her, he would not tell her secret to others.

"Phillip," she said. "I don't remember being in bed with you. I don't remember letting you into this apartment. I don't remember seeing you for the past two weeks!"

He shook his head as though he did not understand. "Hey, you're kidding. I guess you're kidding."

Then when he saw that she was not, his expression changed. He seemed to understand. "You've got amnesia, hon," he said. "You know that? You've really got it."

He sat down on the bed with her and explained. She had come to his office in her jogging clothes and asked him—practically demanded, in fact—to drive her back to her apartment. Now, she had said. He had just finished with a patient and two others were waiting, but he canceled them both and went to the garage with her and got the Ferrari—

"Phillip, I don't remember *any* of this!"

"You said you'd been attacked. You kept saying over and over, 'I nearly died today. Someone nearly killed me, just this afternoon.' You said it as if you were trying to convince yourself. As though you felt dissociation. I hadn't noticed anything really unusual about your manner when you first came into the office—except for the way you were dressed, which certainly isn't all that unusual for my patients. I just hadn't seen you in running gear before. But when we were in the car, and I saw how you were repeating yourself, I got the penlight out of my bag and checked your oculomotor reflex. It was normal. You said you hadn't been hit in the head, so I ruled out any concussion."

"Did I describe the attack?"

"You said a man chased you with a knife when you were running and then waited for you after you ran away from him. Then he hit you in the neck and pulled you down, but you twisted away from him, and kicked him in the face, and ran. I was proud of you, do you know that?"

She shook her head. "I just don't believe it. I can't believe it could have happened."

"Poor kid. Did you block out the whole incident? How much can you remember?"

She saw it again in her mind: the taxi. Then the swift impact. The shadowy figure. Then—

Then nothing.

"I just don't remember anything. From the time I was a hundred feet or so away from York Avenue, and something hit me from behind one of the trees. Just a blank. Until I woke up here a few minutes ago."

He turned up a palm. "I guess you repressed it, then. You certainly wouldn't be the first woman who's done that. If I got attacked on the street, I don't imagine it's something I'd want to remember either."

"But I want to, don't you see? I don't understand what happened to me and I want to *know*."

"What happens when you visualize?"

She tried. "Nothing. Just nothing."

"You don't remember telling me to take you home?"

"No. I don't. I don't understand why I went to your office at all. It's nearly as far away from FDR as the hospital. Or my apartment! If I wanted to come home, I don't see why I didn't just—"

She was talking in a rush now and Phillip interrupted. "Hey. Slow down. You don't have to justify what you did. You were attacked, for God's sake. Don't criticize yourself. Just take it easy. Do you want to know what you said to me?"

"What?" She was feeling the old weakness now, the depression. No, she thought. No. It's not coming back. No.

He spoke tenderly. "You were telling me in the car. You said you wanted me to come home with you. That you'd nearly been killed this afternoon—"

"I just don't understand it. Why in the world would I have gone to your office? I hadn't even *seen* you in two weeks!"

He gave her a smile. "You want to know what you said?"

"What did I say?"

"You leaned against me as I was parking the car, and you asked me to come up with you. You said you'd been working so hard, and you hadn't even kissed me in two weeks. You took my arm and you explained to the doorman that you'd left your key at the office, so he came up in the elevator and let us in with his pass-key . . ."

"I still don't believe it."

". . . and then we came in here. And you got un-dressed . . ."

She turned her face away. What in the world could have made her go to Phillip Bancroft? It made no sense. She tried to smile to herself as she thought, *Repressing it certainly makes sense. I think I'd rather remember being attacked.* But it wasn't funny. Of course there had been stress associated with the attack, but she was a surgeon. If she couldn't stand up to stress without running to someone like Phillip, running home to bed—

And then not admitting it to herself afterward—

"Are you trying to remember?" he asked. "I must say, you didn't act as though you'd been seriously hurt. You were frightened at first, but when we came in here and got into bed—"

"I don't want to talk about it anymore, Phillip."

"What do you mean?"

It's now or never, she thought. If she let this go on any further, he would think she was becoming dependent, getting more and more serious. She would be lying to him and soon she would have to start lying to herself.

"I might as well be truthful. I don't understand why I would have gone to you in the first place, much less asked you to come home with me. I hadn't seen you in two weeks. To be perfectly honest, I had been seriously thinking of calling off our—relationship. These last two weeks have been difficult, but I've felt better than I've felt in months. I just don't think it's working out. That may be hard to understand here and now, after what you say just happened, but it's true."

He took it hard. He tried to sound confident when he interrupted, but he could barely keep his voice from breaking. "You're just not yourself, that's all. You did come to me when the chips were down. Even if it's our last time I've got that to remember—"

He got up from the bed and stood with his back to her, hands in pockets, shoulders hunched.

"I'm sorry, Phillip. It was going to hurt whenever it happened, there's no way to avoid it—"

"Yes? Is that right?" He sounded as though he scarcely heard her.

She wanted to get up and touch him, the way she would comfort a troublesome patient. But that would mislead him. Instead she got up and took her robe from her closet and put it on over her nightgown.

He saw her. "You want me to go now, is that it? Just —go?"

"Thank you for bringing me home, Phillip. For canceling your appointments, for taking time—"

"And the next time. When you call up and want to talk to me, want me to come to you, when you're in trouble—"

"Phillip—"

"—the next time what am I supposed to do? Ask you whether you're in your right mind or not?"

She held her temper. "That was uncalled for. As I told you a few moments ago, I hope there won't be a next time. I'm sorry, Phillip."

Behind her, the phone began to ring.

"I'll wait in the living room," he said.

It was Jerry Chamberlain. "Hi. I just realized that I hadn't set a time or place for us to meet tonight."

And overriding his voice, the faraway echo.

The whisper of malignancy was coming.

She could feel the tightening in her throat, the weakness growing. "No," she whispered, scarcely aware that Jerry was listening.

"Jill? I don't think I heard you. About tonight?"

Hello, dearie. The suddenness of the foul hiss made Jill freeze.

"Jill, are you there?"

Tonight, tonight, won't be just any night.

Oh, God, what was *happening* to her!

She managed to get the receiver a few inches away to keep the sound at a distance. "Jerry," she said. "I'm sorry. It's just that tonight—"

You belong to ME.

A wave of dizziness overcame her and she dropped the

phone. She bent to retrieve it, her breath coming in shallow gasps. Then Phillip was at her side.

"Jill, are you all right? Who *is* that on the phone?"

She got her hand around the receiver and picked it up, put it against her ear. "Jerry, something happened this afternoon—"

I'm back. I'm back. I'm back.

"I can tell you're busy," he said.

Phillip Bancroft watched her trying to explain, saw the tears, saw her tremble and close her eyes and try to fight against what she was hearing on the phone. He turned away and covered his eyes. It was his own stupidity, he thought, trying to keep her when she didn't want him. She was an assignment; not someone he was supposed to love. But there was something he did love in her, something he wished he had, even though he spent half his time with her foolishly trying to persuade her that she needed him instead of the other way around. If he could get away, he thought. If he could get away with her. Maybe on the boat. In his mind he visualized the coastal waterway map, and saw the line down the Hudson and past Staten Island, off Atlantic Highlands, and then inside the long stretches of beach islands, the calm bay waters where they could just drop anchor and go below and have a drink and hold each other.

Someway he would have to keep her with him. Even if it meant continuing with the Gathering. He would have to be sure he stayed away from her enough so that she didn't grow dangerously self-destructive, but on the other hand, he needed her to need him. A fine balance to try to achieve, but wasn't that the art of medicine, keeping systems in balance?

What worried him most was not taking an injection first before bringing her here. It was sentiment he could ill afford, but he had known there would be the lovemaking and he had wanted to remember. The negative payoff was that he would have to remember her this way too.

She had hung up the phone and was huddled on the floor trying to get her breath.

"Are you all right? I don't want to leave you like this, even if we're not—"

"I'll be all right. I just want to be alone for a while."

"I could bring you back some food. You said you hadn't eaten since breakfast."

"No. Thank you. Good-bye, Phillip."

"Call me if you need me," he said.

28

The interior of the limousine was perfectly ordinary gray velvet or velour or whatever it was they called it, thought Maryann Delvecchio. She smiled as she got in and closed the door. You'd better start getting used to limousines, she thought. When you break this story and they give you your own show, you'll have a limousine coming for you in the morning to take you to work and another to take you home at night. Or somewhere else. You'll probably get another apartment, a triplex, maybe, a little farther east.

She wondered if the Gathering always used this limousine to pick her up. Did they always drop her off at Fifty-third and Fifth in the taxi and tell her to wait for the limousine, or another cab, or whatever it was they used for the pickup? She noticed that the windows back here had gray plastic shades drawn across, like airplane windows. Probably so no one would happen to look in when they were stopped at an intersection and say, hey there's Maryann, and then call tomorrow and ask what she was doing in a limousine at the corner of whatever and whatever. They were a smart organization, this Gathering.

But tomorrow morning she would know about them. Tomorrow she would get up early and before she went to work go to the garage where she had parked the van with the special radio tracking equipment—

The driver's voice crackled over the intercom speaker, interrupting her thoughts.

"Miss Delvecchio. You have a transmitting device with you. Give it to me."

Maryann froze, looking through the plexiglass barrier at the face in the limousine's rearview mirror. When she tried to speak her mouth was dry.

"Transmitting device?"

"Give it to me, Miss Delvecchio."

On either side of her, the rear-door lock buttons glided down.

"I'm sorry," she said. "I must have forgotten. I was wearing this electronic thing on an assignment this afternoon—"

The voice cut in. "Give it to me now." The eyes in the narrow mirror flicked up from the street ahead to make contact with Maryann's, and she felt cold in the pit of her stomach.

"I should have turned it in at the studio hours ago," she said nervously. "I can't think why nobody noticed it was missing."

To her right, below the plexiglass barrier, a metal drawer like the kind on a sidewalk bank-teller machine tilted down and waited, empty.

Maryann took off her necklace and removed the silver pendant from its chain. She put the pendant into the drawer. As the drawer tilted back to the driver's seat the metallic rattling seemed to reverbrate.

Through the plexiglass she saw the front window opening across from the driver, saw the flash of silver as the pendant arced into the night.

The window closed again.

"If it's still functioning tomorrow," the voice from the speaker said conversationally, "your device will lead you to the Natural History Museum."

She forced herself to show bravado. "I wish there was some way you could have given that back to me. I'm going to have to pay the station for it. I'm sure it's expensive."

"Maybe you'll get it back tomorrow. If you find it."

"I hope you don't think I planned to bring that thing along with me tonight," she went on. "I hope you don't think there's anyone trailing us. It was a mistake, that's all."

"The Leader allows for an honest mistake, Miss Delvecchio," said the voice. "One mistake." He paused, and, in the mirror, the dead brown eyes found hers. "You have now had your one mistake."

29

Thick-lined blue drapes were drawn over the three tall windows in Malcolm Lockwood's high-ceilinged bedroom, cutting off most of the daylight. Normally at this time of year the drapes would be open, and the rays from the late-afternoon sun across the Hudson would spill through the narrow openings in the four pairs of shutters that maintained the privacy of the room. Malcolm Lockwood enjoyed the light from the sunsets, the golden red warmth it cast over the bedroom's chilly blue and silver furnishings.

However, Diana Falke liked firelight.

So this afternoon, three logs burned in the blue-tiled fireplace opposite the tall canopy bed. The flames danced high, suffusing a cheerful glow onto the silver sheets and pillows, flickering light across the underside of the wide blue canopy above the Leader.

"I love the way your face looks in this room," said Diana as she entered. She closed the door. "When you turn your profile to the fire, the shadows fall across your cheek, and around your eyes—"

The Leader touched his finger gently to his lips to silence her. He was sitting cross-legged on the center of the bed, fully dressed, his white cashmere sweater taking on an amber hue from the fire.

She came over to the bed and cradled her head on his lap, blond hair framing her upturned face in gold. She let her robe fall open. The light from the fire accentuated the smooth skin of her thighs, the shadowy tuft below her softly rounded abdomen, the reduced contours of her breasts, their nipples erect.

"I think we'd better talk of something else, Diana."

"Do you want me?"

He smiled. "You know, Diana, I can always tell when you aren't quite certain that you've done the right thing.

You know that, don't you? You start asking for what you think you're sure of first, and hope that something will happen in the meantime to show that you hadn't made a mistake after all.'"

She sat up. "I suppose I'll have to think of something else, then, darling. But I still want you."

"If you ever want to begin a Gathering of your own, you'll have to want more than that. You'll be in sad need of good judgment, I'm afraid, until you understand our limitations and come to terms with them."

"I don't think I follow you."

His finger traced the high-arched outline of her eyebrows. "Jill Weston," he said.

"We're working on her together—Bancroft and Avery and Garrett and I. We're increasing the stress."

"Was that necessary?"

"She was avoiding her apartment, not seeing Phillip, developing a steady relationship with another man—"

"But she would have returned to her apartment eventually."

"I don't like to wait. Each time we send Garrett out it seems that—"

"I don't want to hear about Garrett. Garrett is safe. Even it he is captured, he is safe."

"But then how do we replace him? If we have Jill Weston here, if we have her center organized and staffed—"

"I want you to see what I'm talking about, Diana," he interrupted, patiently. "You have found a candidate that would solve our supply problem, and you have a fixed idea in your mind that you must pursue that particular person because her circumstances fit our needs so very well. But has it occurred to you that the person *herself* may—not fit?"

"We tested her for scopolamine yesterday. She remembered nothing after Garrett gave the injection and carried her to the ambulance. Phillip met her a block away from her apartment and forced her to take him home with her. At gunpoint. Then he gave her a sedative. When she awoke she remembered nothing."

Lockwood shook his head slowly. "Diana, Diana. All this activity, and what does it get you?"

"She's back in her apartment, she's under stress again—"

"And you think she will break? You think she will let Phillip bring her here when her fears become too difficult for her to bear?"

"Her fears, her work——"

"So she will come to us because she has nowhere else to go. Is that your reasoning?"

"Avery was in her office yesterday morning while she was with a patient. She had set up a cot in her office, did you know that? But now her sleep there will not be so pleasant either."

"You have to grow, Diana." The Leader lifted her head with his hands and gently kissed her forehead. "You're so infatuated with what we can do that you fail to see our limitations clearly enough. If you drive this woman to us against her will, do you know what will happen?"

"People have doubts when they come at first. It's normal. But they convert."

"Not all of them. You don't hear the confessions, Diana. You don't know the insatiable curiosity of some of them, the resentments others harbor against *anyone* who holds power over them. With all our precautions, a few still try to circumvent our secrecy every time they come to us."

"None have succeeded."

"None have yet become truly, passionately committed to finding us out. Or to destroying us. I have seen to that in the confessionals. Those who might do us serious harm are selected out."

"Members no more," she murmured.

"As you say, it has worked until now. But until now, we have always taken people who wanted very much what we have to offer them. People like Bancroft, or that young woman, Delvecchio. Their ambition leads them to come to us. We don't have to coerce them."

"Jill Weston is ambitious. Look at the hours she works. She is the star of that hospital, and she loves every minute of it——"

"Does she love Phillip Bancroft?"

Diana's blue eyes flickered. Malcolm saw.

"It's not working, is it, Diana?"

"We just need a bit more time. Phillip says she'll come Monday night, because we've scheduled the foundation inspection team for Tuesday morning. She'll be under too much pressure not to want to come."

"I'm quite serious now, Diana. I want her to come of her own choice, or I don't want her to come at all."

"She'll choose to come. I'm sure she'll choose to come."

"You remember Otto Lindstrom, don't you?"

She nodded.

"At his confessional last month, I asked him to think of a way to destroy us. He thought of a way. Almost immediately."

"Would it have worked?"

"Yes. It would have destroyed Otto Lindstrom in the process, but it would have worked, if properly carried out. Otto said he had associates who could make a concealed bomb, one that the metal detector in the limousine would not pick up. Otto would write a note explaining to the police, or to a friend, or whoever he wanted to act for him that an explosion would take place on such and such a night somewhere in New York. That place, he would tell them, should be the object of serious investigation. Then, just as Otto entered our building, he would detonate his bomb. The sound would attract attention, damage would be done, people would come to investigate—"

She looked fascinated. "Do you think he would actually attempt that?"

"Not at this point. He didn't seem enraged enough to give up his own life. The real danger is that he may think of something else, some other way to reach us. I mention him as a warning of what our people might be capable of if they are dissatisfied. If they resent us, despite what we are giving them, we could be in serious difficulty."

"Without pure blood, we are also in serious difficulty," she countered.

"We can always get blood. We have done it without Jill Weston before, and we can continue without her. What I will not have is someone intelligent and determined spending twenty-one days and twenty nights away from our direct control, scheming ways to free herself from a master she never chose to follow."

"She will choose to come on Monday."

"I want you to begin looking for someone else, Diana. I want you to begin today. There are other physicians in

the city with the potential of Jill Weston. Find some of
them. There must be several who would be quite willing
to join us, without coercion. I'm still convinced you became fixated on Jill Weston only because she was so
conveniently placed at Madison Hospital. You need to
widen your scope. Examine fresh alternatives."

The blue eyes smoldered with a light of their own,
colder than the reflection from the fireplace. "I will."

"By Monday night I want three names besides Jill
Weston's. You understand?"

"I'll get them for you. But may I also have until
Monday evening with Jill Weston?"

"No coercion."

"We'll just continue the same stress pattern. Nothing
new."

"What happens," said Lockwood, "if she does come?
And you set up her operational center. You invest three
million dollars of foundation money. And after all that,
we find that she has begun to hate us. We can control
her while she is here, but for twenty-one days and twenty
nights she is out of our hands. What do we do then?"

"By then we'll have the institution she's developed.
The delivery patterns will be set. It won't matter who's
controlling the center. The moment she appears a risk, in
any way, she will become a member no more."

"You would see to it?"

Diana smiled. "Of course. Why should she be any
different from the others?"

The hint of satisfaction played across the Leader's face.
"All right," he said. Turning away from her, he reached
behind the blue bed curtain and pressed a switch built
into the canopy post. Above them, a ceiling projector
glowed brightly, and the underside of the canopy became translucent, a giant viewing screen over their heads.
At the touch of another switch, a videotape began to roll.
The canopy shone red. The languorous forms of a naked
man and woman became visible on the screen. The red
light moved, and found two others that were coupling.

When the Leader looked at her again Diana Falke had
taken off her robe. Her hands went quickly beneath his
white sweater, her fingertips passing lightly over his
smooth, heavily muscled chest, tracing a circular pattern
over his nipples. He closed his eyes for a moment, until he
felt her hands on his belt.

"No," he said quietly.

She paused, completely motionless, waiting.

"You," he said.

She nodded and lay back naked against the pillows, parting her legs, closing her eyes. Slowly her hand began to move downward from her breast. When she spoke, her voice was oddly childlike. "Will you come to me?"

The Leader waited until both her hands were moving. "If you're good, Diana," he said. "If you do exactly as I tell you."

30

Dr. Polder looked tired. She glanced up from the notes on her desk as Jill came in; her face showed a strain, even though her voice was steady.

"I'm not a psychiatrist," she said, "but I think we might consider emotional matters in our discussion of what's been happening to you. I made some notes after your visit yesterday evening, when you were still feeling so disturbed. Why don't you pull your chair a little closer so we can examine the possibilities and perhaps look for a particular pattern."

Jill sat, feeling upset over Dr. Polder's abrupt beginning. The greeting, the handshake, the welcoming to her seat, these were part of the ritual between doctor and patient during an office visit. Jill knew it and so did Virginia Polder, and what was more, Dr. Polder had shown Jill the utmost concern last night when Jill had called and disrupted her Sunday evening. Now, it seemed, she was reluctant to have Jill in the office.

Or was that just Jill's perception, her fear and distress, worrying about being abandoned and rejected—

She forced herself to concentrate on the notes. In a well-ordered diagnostic manner, Dr. Polder had created a chart of the possibilities. As Dr. Polder saw it, Jill's difficulty might fall within four broad categories: (1) neurological; (2) allergenic; (3) tumor- or cancer-related, and (4) psychosocial.

"We can try to eliminate the least likely of these candidates as we relate your symptoms," she said. "To begin with, the amnesia at the period of stress. If you had a chronic neurological difficulty, I doubt that you would have experienced memory loss only on that particular occasion. And why do you remember part of the attack and not the rest? It seems to me that your nervous system would be under at least as much strain during the run from the man and his knife as it was when you finally escaped. Of course it's true you've been having the headaches and the weakness, and that neurological difficulty is aggravated by stress, but you've been under stress for a long time. With your family history, we have to be concerned with something cancer-related, but again . . ."

Jill tried to concentrate as she went on, but she was picking up a definite impression that Dr. Polder was very much worried about what she was saying. That she wasn't convinced in her own mind that her diagnosis was correct. She was talking more rapidly than usual.

". . . and even though a tumor might account for the headaches and weakness, how do we explain your two weeks of remission? By the way, how did you feel this morning?"

"I felt better again. I appreciate your letting me spend the night here. I just couldn't face staying in my apartment alone. And then when I got to my office and had the same—"

"Auditory hallucination, yes. That's the problem. If you have a tumor, it's conceivable that you might be getting pressure and perhaps a bit of an aura where you hear voices or become aware of a certain taste or odor. That would be if you were about to go into epileptic seizure. But we don't see any evidence for that, do we? After you hear these voices, what generally do you do?"

"I try to pick up where I was. I call the person back, if I heard the voice on the phone, or if it's just something that woke me up in the night I try to get back to sleep just the way I would after a bad dream. Except for last night. When I heard the voice as I was working at my desk, I just couldn't stand it, couldn't stand to be there any longer. So I came to you."

She nodded. "All right then. Clearly you're not having

seizures. I have one question regarding the third category. Did you alter your diet in any way during the two-week period in which you were free from the symptoms?"

Jill considered briefly. "No. Nothing changed, really. Nothing I was aware of."

"Well then, we are left without a strong allergenic possibility. That puts us in the fourth category. Psychosocial. These difficulties began during a period of emotional strain, with your father. Agreed?"

"I just don't see how it can be something *like* that! I've been through my mother's death, and medical school, and the intern year, and I'm not *under* that much stress anymore. I'm very busy, that's true, but I don't have the emotional stresses I had back then. I have friends, I'm accepted at Madison—"

"But you wouldn't want anyone there to learn you were having difficulty. Isn't that why you came to me?"

"It's hard for a woman," she said finally. "I'm not arguing with you, but people in medicine are always being evaluated, and women more so than men. Especially in surgery. I don't think there's a surgeon anywhere in the country who would want his hospital to learn about it if he had psychological problems. That's only common self-preservation."

"But surgeons can have psychological problems, then." Jill nodded.

"Well as we said before, you had a loss, you had a depression that might be considered perfectly normal, and when it started to lift, you suffered a relapse. I might insert parenthetically at this point that jogging is considered a positive form of therapy for depression."

"So you're saying that I'm trying to stop myself from working too hard by torturing myself when I'm in my apartment? I don't see the logic there."

As she thought, Dr. Polder seemed to be looking through Jill, at something beyond her. After a few moments she spoke again. "You have the surgeon's personality, Jill. I think you're wonderfully suited for what you're doing. You like to be able to locate a problem and do something immediately with it—and you're certainly doing wonderfully well from what I can see from here."

"But I'm uncomfortable with uncertainty in my own case. Is that what you're telling me?"

Dr. Polder stared down at her notes. "I think you want

to be working hard and doing as much as you can. I think that when you find something interfering with your ability to work, you resist it. You'd like to locate the problem and put a stop to it."

"And so would anyone else in my position, wouldn't she? I don't think I see the point you're trying to make. Are you saying that what I have is just something self-limiting, that I'll have to wait for time to heal—"

"That may be what it is," Virginia Polder said, her gray eyes now holding Jill's attention. "That may be a possibility you will have to live with. You were doing well for two weeks until the sudden attack. If you get back to your routine again, you may do well again."

"For another two weeks? Until some new stress comes? There's an evaluation team coming tomorrow to go over my surgical procedure, to ask all sorts of questions, and I'm backed up again with my paper work—"

"I understand. That's what I'm telling you. What you'd like, what I'd like to give you, would be a specific therapeutic measure that would keep you happy and healthy, whatever came your way. I wish I could do that. But it may not be possible."

"Do you think I should continue to stay away from my apartment?"

She leaned forward and nodded slightly. "You have to do what seems to work. The same goes for your office. If you continue having the hallucinations there, perhaps you could try to relocate." She pressed her lips together and drew a sudden breath as if in pain. "Pardon me," she went on. "I might add that the same applies to your jogging. You might want to change your route, or avoid going out alone, but if it's working to alleviate your symptoms, by all means continue. Have you been jogging since the—attack?"

"No, the person I've been running with has been—busy the past few days. He went away for the weekend. And I haven't wanted to go by myself."

"Well, see what happens there. Now what's left to us? I can schedule you for an EMI scan if the headaches continue for any appreciable amount of time. I certainly don't want you on any kind of antidepressants or sedatives that might interfere with your work. If you're looking for some other form of therapy—"

"I'm not interested in psychiatric counseling."

"I wasn't going to suggest that," she said, tapping the large circle she had drawn around "psychosocial" on her note card. "I had in mind something a bit less traditional, if you're really determined to give some other form of treatment a try."

"I just want to be able to function at my best again. Whether the treatment is traditional or not doesn't matter."

"All right. I haven't had direct experience with what I'm about to recommend to you. But I have been told that it's extremely effective. Evidently the man behind it is very secretive since it's still in the experimental stage. I'm told he doesn't want to have competition from the big pharmaceutical houses until all the patents have been granted. So I can't even tell you the man's name."

"What kind of treatment is it?"

"I know only two things. One, that endorphins are involved."

"Brain proteins? I know they've been used for depression in experimental groups—"

"—and two, that he administers erythrocytes. The patient's red cell count is elevated almost to the limits of ciculatory tolerance."

"I've heard of that too. In the Olympics. Jerry was telling me about the scandals, with the distance runners having the red cells injected before the races to increase their oxygen capacity—"

"Yes." Dr. Polder interrupted. "So you are interested?"

"It sounds as if it has possibilities. But I must say you don't seem terribly enthusiastic."

"Oh, don't mind me. It's just gastric distress this afternoon. I'll be quite my old self tomorrow."

"You have confidence in this procedure?"

"I don't want to sound as if I'm evading the issue, Jill, but I'm really not at all familiar with it. I only mention the procedure because there's nothing else that seems to be appropriate in your situation." Her eyes flickered away from Jill and then returned. "Except for the measures I outlined previously. Relocating, running if possible, watching your diet—they really may be all that you need. Then again they may not be enough. Perhaps you will be very pleased if you try this new treatment, or perhaps not. It's really up to you."

"That's a left-handed referral if I ever heard one," Jill

said lightly. "Don't you know about building patient confidence in the specialist you're recommending?"

"It's up to you," she repeated. She looked uncomfortable again. "If I had the direct experience—"

"Oh, don't worry, I'm not demanding a miracle of you. I'm really grateful you've taken so much time to try to help me. How do I get in touch with this experimentalist?"

"All I have is a phone number. I can't even tell you where I got it."

Looking down at her notes, she read the number aloud. Jill took the desk pen and wrote down the number on the prescription pad.

After Jill had gone, Dr. Polder looked steadily at the door to the examination room, behind where Jill had been sitting. The door stood partially open. Several moments passed before a man came out.

In his right hand was a hypodermic syringe. In his left was a large black pistol with a silencing tube screwed into the barrel.

"You almost let her get away," said Matthew Garrett. "That wasn't very intelligent of you."

"I'm not interested in your opinion," she said. "And if you're going to shoot me now, get it over with. I'm sure you realize that as soon as you're gone I'll be calling her."

"You'd like to warn her off, wouldn't you? I could see you trying while she was here. It's only fortunate for you that you weren't successful. That's why both of you are alive now." He advanced toward her desk. "Now I'll have a look at those notes of yours. If I see something that looks like a warning, you'll be smearing those notes with your own brains."

She glared at him as he put the pistol to her temple. "I've held brains in my hands, and before you were born," she said. "You don't frighten me with that kind of talk. I've seen death all my life."

Placing the hypodermic on the desk, Garrett spread the note cards apart from one another. He saw nothing that seemed out of the ordinary. He turned the cards over and examined the blotter beneath them, slowly, enjoying the feel of the gun and the anxiety of the old woman. There was still nothing that could have alerted the Weston woman to be on her guard. And certainly she had appeared convinced as Garrett had watched her leave. He did not like this old one and would have enjoyed killing her, but he had been given orders on how to proceed.

"I guess it's your lucky day, granny," he said. "You don't get the bullet after all. You get another needle."

31

Walking down Fifth Avenue to Seventy-fourth, Jill tried to keep her hopes from running away with her. Dr. Polder had obviously intended for her to reserve judgment on the new treatment she had recommended. She was well aware of the placebo effect of *any* treatment in which the patient has confidence. As a physician, she respected Dr. Polder's attitude of skepticism, her refusal to try to persuade Jill that a quick and easy cure was readily available. After all, Jill had spent four years in medical school and six in surgical residency being trained against overcredulity. The people who did not have results published, who "could not take time" to put together a proper research study, who complained that the "medical establishment" was trying to "suppress" their discoveries out of professional envy and jealousy—these were the ones who relied on faith from their patients. If they were really onto something that could be replicated, they would have the numbers to back up their claims.

Even with her own surgical procedure, she was reluctant to push ahead too rapidly in asking for development grant money until she had more long-term longitudinal data. As of now she had eight healthy babies, all less than one year old, and nine pregnancies in varying stages of what appeared to be normal progress, but she would have liked to continue with her own patients for another year or two before expanding to a center even half the size of the one Ted Sanford was talking about. With only word-of-mouth contacts from previous patients, Jill already had more requests for treatment than she could keep up with;

more, even, than she could properly evaluate. And when
the news of a large grant appeared in the media, the
letters and calls would begin to pour in. There were so
many women who wanted so badly to have a baby.

Of course, as Ted had told her, a high volume of surgical patients was exactly what Madison was counting on
during the next few years, and favorable publicity was
what the hospital desperately needed now, to offset the
TV scare. The story had been seen by two of the patients
who had been "attacked" with unauthorized injections,
and they had gone to the papers, and now even patients
from several months back were starting to call in with
stories. How much of it was due to a real mix-up somewhere along the line and how much to a yen for getting
their names in the news was impossible to say. Ted and
his committee were going over the records of each patient as the names came out, but finding nothing unusual.
None of them had even been in for anything serious.

And they still hadn't found either of the two supposedly missing patients. They were looking for a security
guard, too, and the reporters had made some wild specu-
lations about his being part of a conspiracy, and running
when the investigation had begun—

Ridiculous, of course. But it was hurting the hospital.
The patients were talking about it, and the rumors were
beginning to feed on each other.

The telephone booth on the next corner drew Jill's
attention away from problems of the hospital and to her
own. Ought she to call the number Dr. Polder had given
her?

She stopped in front of the booth, making up her mind.
The day was sunny and mild and she opened her ski
jacket. March was coming in like a lamb. She was feeling
good. Better than yesterday, she decided. That was certain. Today was Monday. How would she feel tomorrow
when the examination team was in the amphitheater
with her, asking the questions, looking over her data and
her files. More important, how would she feel after that,
when the real work came to be done? The final applications, setting up the center if it really was funded, in-
terviewing, hiring, supervising, screening, recording all
the preliminary and follow-up data that would be required. . . .

The traffic went by on Fifth, the cars and buses and

taxis heading downtown, each with its occupants, all with their own problems and decisions to make. "It's up to you," Dr. Polder had said. Perhaps she ought to let well enough alone. Tomorrow she could try once again to get the jogging started with Jerry. She wondered how busy he really had been. Of course his feelings had been hurt when he heard Phillip's voice. That was only natural. But with time, he could certainly understand that she was not committed to Phillip any longer. Or a least, she and Jerry should be able to simply run together, without thinking of a deeper relationship.

But perhaps it would also be wise to begin the new treatment. It could have its possibilities. Endorphins were brain proteins. The natural triggers of various emotions and attitudes; matter over mind. Could endorphins drive away the voices? And erythrocyte infusion, or "blood-doping," as the sports world called it. She thought about what she knew of each method as she idly watched a cab coming toward her booth. New, experimental, not enough real work published for anyone to be exactly certain of all the possible applications. Perhaps the combination would work as a prophylactic against stress. She wondered about the research methods being used, the screening procedures. It was possible after all that she might not be accepted for treatment.

As the cab drew closer she saw him. In the passenger's seat, looking directly at her.

The same swarthy chin, the pouting fleshy lips, the lifeless brown eyes—

The man with the knife.

The scream rose within her as she stared back, trembling now, pushing the door of the booth shut behind her. If he slows down, she thought, I'll call the police. If he so much as slows down, but how could he dare to try right out here in the open—

The cab cruised by without changing speed. The man did not turn to watch as it passed. He seemed uninterested.

Jill tried to catch her breath, to get heart to stop racing. He was following her! Or was it only a coincidence? Was it really the same man? He had been wearing a hood then and here he was at a greater distance, seen through the glass of the phone booth and the cab window. Perhaps her imagination had been at work. Perhaps—

The rapping on the glass behind her. She whirled.

A small boy, tapping with his dime to use the phone.

She took a deep breath and steadied herself. No, she thought, I can't be going around on pins and needles this way.

"I'll be through in a minute," she told the boy.

And dialed.

A woman's voice answered. "Doctor's office."

"This is Dr. Jill Weston," she said. "I was referred to this number for treatment."

"Your referring physician, Dr. Weston?"

She gave the name of Virginia Polder.

"One moment please, while I put you through."

A man's voice came on. "Dr. Weston?" She thought it sounded familiar.

"Yes. I was referred for treatment—"

Then he interrupted to tell her she was talking to Phillip Brancroft. And that he was happy she had called. She overcame her surprise. "Phillip! You're not doing endorphin research—"

He laughed. "Of course not, hon. I'm just the middle man here. One of many, I might add. I'm glad Virginia Polder sent you our way. We've got a lot of respect for her."

Jill spoke rapidly, not wanting to show embarrassment at having Phillip know she had seen a physician. "She didn't seem to know much about what you're doing, Phillip. Just exactly what is involved with this treatment?"

"I can't tell you over the phone. But I can take you where you can get it. And you can see for yourself."

"When?"

"Tonight."

"I don't know. I have to get started early tomorrow morning. I have a lot of preparations to attend to—"

"It's like I told you before," he interrupted. "Either tonight or we have to wait another three weeks. Really, it's up to you. I don't want to pressure you into going anywhere you don't feel you have time for."

After making it clear that she was interested only in a professional consultation, that she had been surprised to hear Phillip's voice and was not intending to get involved again on a personal level, Jill agreed. She would meet him at 7:30 that evening in front of the Metropolitan Museum.

32

Otto Lindstrom crawled to the back of his little dark cave to wait for the Leader. The cave was warm, the carpeting soft and quite comfortable, and whatever it was that they had all drunk from the ruby chalice was making him drowsy. He smiled to himself. As a precaution against falling asleep he had taken one of the white capsules just before coming. Not the last of the capsules the Leader had given him; Otto still had fifteen of those left. But now he had white capsules of his own. Duplicated in Switzerland from one Otto had sent by courier. A most interesting formula. Otto's contact at the Swiss pharmaceutical house had assured him that it had been duplicated precisely, and thirty-six hours of clear-headed work on three of the new capsules had convinced Otto that they were correct. There was nothing that could not be bought, not even genius.

Light streamed into the cave as the door behind Otto opened. Otto looked up and saw the face of the Leader. His hatred nearly overcame him. He wanted to break that beautifully sculptured jaw, smash his fist into those perfect teeth, drive the heel of his hand into the tip of that finely sculptured nose, sending fragments of bone up into that malicious, scheming brain—

"Otto," said the Leader. "You're awake."

He nodded, and followed where the Leader beckoned, to a reclining armless couch covered in white synthetic leather that was positioned immediately outside the door to Otto's cave. Standing by the couch, he could see others on either side, empty, forming a curved line behind other small doors.

"This room is like a doughnut," he said. "Like a doughnut hollowed out and painted white and lit up and furnished—" He realized he was talking more freely than he meant to and he stopped.

167

The Leader smiled. "That's what you always say, Otto. Why don't you lie down here on your couch and we'll start your confessional. When we're through, you can have your red cells and get dressed."

Otto nodded, warmed at the memory of what he knew was waiting for him in the dressing room. He lay down on the couch. It was smooth and comfortable. He drew his robe around him and relaxed, confident. "Okay, Dr. Freud," he said happily, "what do you want to know?"

The Leader brought over a medium-height padded stool and sat on it, facing him. He reached out and took Otto's hand. Otto relaxed some more and let him inter-lock fingers, even though he generally avoided the touch of other men. More conditioning, Otto thought.

"What do you think you should tell me, Otto?" The Leader's voice was casual, friendly, as though they were about to have a good-natured, man-to-man talk. "I think you have something in mind that I ought to know."

Otto was ready with the truth. Some of the truth. What the Leader would be expecting. "I was mad as hell at you for a while. After the last time."

"Your punishment."

"I know. Every morning I've had to take my punish-ment. Sometimes I get the recording on quickly, though, so it doesn't hurt more than a few seconds."

"We learn. We adapt. Man is a learning creature, wouldn't you agree? What did you learn from your pun-ishment, Otto?"

"That it was fair. I tried to take back the secrets of the Gathering. I broke my oath. And I paid."

"You told me last month why you tried to record our talk together. Do you remember what you said?"

"No. But I remember why. Should I tell you again?"

"If you like."

Otto told him. The black market for gold in Zurich. How he had shorted 10,000 ounces in gold futures pre-cisely a half hour before the surprise announcement of the enormous new Russian offering began to drive the price down. How Otto had tried to get $860 an ounce at the fixing, but had to settle for $850 because some-one else was making the same offer at the same time and the dealers were becoming wary. How he had been an-gered at the Leader's interference.

"Do you remember what I said, Otto?"

"No. But I know that I was wrong. The punishment was fair, and so I must have been in the wrong."

He nodded. "You see, you came in to confession six weeks ago full of pride in your discovery. You thanked me for what I had done for you, and said that you were pleased now to have a means to repay me. Then you told me what to do, the numbers to dial, the exact time, everything. The pity of it was that you didn't remember your generous impulse the next morning. But of course that couldn't be helped. Many of my people have the same difficulty. They are grateful and share their resources with me when they come here, and then later they wonder how it was that they could have done such a thing, and they feel resentment at me. Instead of a divine, I become a demon. You understand, Otto?"

"Yes. Yes I think so."

"I would imagine you thought of me more as a demon during the past three weeks. Because of your punishment."

"Well, to be fair about it, you did give me an extra dozen capsules in return. That compensated somewhat."

"Did you have thoughts of vengeance, Otto? Did you investigate other recording devices?"

"No. I think the punishment turned me away from recording devices forever."

"What about other things? Hidden cameras, perhaps? Homing devices? Professional surveillance? I can tell you all of those methods have been tried. Many of our members are very resourceful, with influential connections along those lines. That is one of the reasons they have been chosen for membership. But their potential power must also make us aware of their potential harm. So we try to be alert. Why should we be alert with you this week, Otto?"

Otto smiled, letting the question pass beneath him. He was the stone bridge; the Leader and his questions were the torrent that flowed underneath, unable to reach up to disturb him. In his mind he lifted one of the uppermost stones; took his two wonderful, forbidden secrets, parchment scrolls, and dropped them into the opening; mortared the stone and replaced it on top of the scrolls where neither river current nor anything else could find it.

"I'm all right this week," he said.

"Good. Then you won't mind the small injection I'm about to give you."

"Depends on what's in it."

"It's a natural substance. A brain protein. Its name is omicron-endorphin, but you won't find it in a pharmaceutical house, Otto. Not even in Switzerland."

Probably he knows of my contact from before, thought Otto. He can't know about the pills.

Then it struck him that his contact in Switzerland might also be a member of the Gathering. Though highly unlikely, it was possible; a member from Europe would need only a day's travel every three weeks, and perhaps it could be combined with a regular business trip.

"Your hand is growing moist, Otto. Why?"

He willed the sudden fear of betrayal into the waters he envisioned beneath him. Let it flow away. "I don't like injections."

"This is only a very small one. Regrettably, I don't have very much at present. Someday I'll be able to synthesize omicron-endorphin, though, and then my work here will become considerably easier."

"This is something you invented?"

"Extracted, Otto. Before I give you your red-cell injection each month, I take twenty-five cc.'s of blood from your jugular vein. A few drops are for next month's crossmatch. At the time and place where I extract it, your blood is coming directly from your brain. Omicron-endorphin is present in the blood at that time. When small amounts from many members are isolated and combined they accumulate into usable quantities. Do you know about brain proteins, Otto?"

As he spoke, he withdrew something from one of the white cabinet drawers that looked like a jewel case, the kind of thing one would use to carry an expensive watch or necklace. "The published research in that area since the mid-seventies has been very promising. They've done far-reaching work at the Salk Institute, at Johns Hopkins, in Montreal and Germany . . ."

When he opened the case Otto saw the syringe and the needle.

"I can't recall," said Otto. "Medicine isn't my field."

"Well, to put it simply, the brain is a vast chemical and electrical complex. What you refer to as your mind, Otto, may be spiritual in scope and quite unique, apart from any of the mechanisms we can control by injecting various substances into your system. But you'll have to admit your mind does respond to those substances—whether they are something as mundane as the alcohol in a cocktail or as exotic as the preparation in the white capsules you've been taking."

"And these brain proteins affect the mind?" Otto eyed the needle as the Leader traced his fingers along the line of Otto's jaw, stopping below the corner, resting on Otto's neck. Otto could feel his own pulse thumping against the Leader's fingertips.

"They're produced by the mind. By the brain. They're part of the means the brain uses to communicate with itself. In a sense, one could say they *are* the mind."

He kept his fingertips on Otto's carotid artery while he positioned the needle. "Hold still now, Otto. We want this to go straight up the carotid to the brain, so we don't waste any. If this were beta-endorphin I were injecting, you'd soon find relief from any depression or anxiety you perhaps might be experiencing. If it were enkephalin, you'd find relief from pain. If it were scotophobin, you might suddenly be afflicted with fear of the dark."

Otto could feel the point of the needle pricking beneath the surface of his skin as the Leader guided the tip into the wall of the artery. "What does this one do?" he whispered.

The Leader's eyes remained focused on the needle, absorbed in the task at hand. At last he felt the arterial wall give way. He smiled with satisfaction as the red arterial blood seeped up into the syringe, proving that the needle was properly positioned. He pointed the tip up, in the direction with the flow of blood in the artery, and pressed the plunger home, sending the contents of the syringe up to Otto's brain.

"Obedience," he said, "omicron-endorphin is the brain protein associated with obedience. It's produced in greater quantities when the brain has entered a state of deep hypnosis. I'm explaining all this to you because you're an intelligent man and would doubtless be wondering how I could get such truthful answers from you in such a short time, and your wondering might prove a distraction during the rest of our confessional."

He withdrew the syringe and put it back into its case. "Now, Otto, you're going to tell me more about your feelings of anger against me because of your punishment. You're going to tell me exactly what you did during the last three weeks that was motivated by your anger."

In thirty seconds Otto had told the Leader about his mental conditioning exercises. About the stone bridge. That there were secrets locked way in the stone.

"Well now, Otto, that's to be expected. Now I want you to take the secrets out and tell me about them. All of them."

Within the next minute Otto had told of the Swiss pharmaceutical house. About his satisfaction when he learned of the contents of the white capsules.

"Really? Tell me what they found. Tell me what you thought."

"It was cocaine," he said, wondering if it would be possible to somehow keep the conversation going on the capsules so that he would not have to tell his other secret. Perhaps after a certain time the effect of the damnable injection would wear off. ". . . cocaine and a gelatin, and another protein of some sort. You're nothing but a pusher, Lockwood!"

The Leader smiled. "You're being truthful, Otto. Yet you should understand. What you have in those capsules is hardly the same cocaine you would buy from a dealer. Even the most reputable. To create the spansule effect by creating the varying sizes of granules, to encase them in the tiny pinpoints of gelatin so that the intestinal lining is not irritated—this sort of thing requires complex equipment and expertise. When you add to that the synthetic beta-endorphin—that 'other protein' you mentioned—you vastly reduce the addictive effect of long-term usage, and avoid altogether the danger of psychotic episode. So you see, Otto, you're getting more than your money's worth from my capsules. Despite what Keppler Pharmaceutica might have implied in their report."

"Well, they sent me capsules. I tried them and it seemed to be the same thing," said Otto. He clenched his fists, wishing somehow he could stop himself.

"They gave you a supply I had sent them, as a matter of fact. Does that surprise you? You should understand that psychopharmacologists in my field are few, and tend to be clannish. Even the Swiss."

"They know about you and cocaine, do they?"

"That's good, Otto. Keep on letting your true feelings

come out. That's the benefit of confession, to release the floodgates and let the torrents run their course."

"I think you're damnable. Filthy drug-dealing swine."

"Dear Otto. I'm sure those are part of your feelings, but clearly as a reasonable man you also have others more complimentary. When you learned of the cocaine in your capsules, what then? Did you stop taking them? No, instead you ordered more. And yet you're blaming me. Look deeper, Otto. Tell me how you really felt about the cocaine in the capsules."

"I—didn't care what it was, really. So long as the capsules had their effect, I didn't care."

"Yet part of you feels guilty and wants to blame me. It might ease your conscience to know that we are now working on a replacement for the cocaine. A synthesized protein hormone identical to those produced by the pituitary gland, but in slightly more concentrated form. We can improve concentration and memory with what we now produce, but have yet to find the duplicate for cocaine's metabolic stimulus. When we do, of course, we'll make the transition."

Stall him, Otto thought. You really do want to stall him, and he hasn't told you not to. "So someday you'll be 'going legitimate.'" The contempt in his tone caused the Leader to smile slightly.

"We'll be legitimate soon. For the time being, we're vulnerable."

"Where do you get your cocaine?"

"Otto, I wish I had time to tell you everything. But I'm sure you realize that there are others here. Before I turn to them, I need to know. You mentioned two actions you had taken against me. You have told me one. What is the other? Tell me completely, along with your feelings about it."

Otto strained to invent a lie, but relentlessly, the parchment hidden in the stone unrolled itself before him and he read aloud. Within two minutes he had told it all. His belongings in his dressing room. The watch that was more than an electric watch. The metal watchband that hid the conducting wires. The two innersoles of his shoes, which together made a twenty-four-ounce *plastique* bomb to be detonated by the wristwatch. He would leave the bomb behind in his dressing room after tonight's meeting.

The leader considered for only a moment. "It sounds

like a good plan, Otto. An explosion at a time you knew beforehand, and of course it would be large enough so I would not be able to keep the papers from reporting the disturbance. You would either have killed me, or fixed my location so that I could be killed later."

"I wanted to beat you," Otto said simply. "I am not used to being controlled. I—perhaps overreacted."

"I'm glad you've apologized. The only problem with your plan was something you couldn't have remembered —that during these visits you tell me everything I want to know. We can't blame you for not wanting to be controlled. That's part of your personal make-up. Part of what has made you so independently successful. All we can do is try to condition you against a similar attempt in the future."

"Punishment," Otto said.

"Don't worry, Otto. You won't be waking up with the abdominal pain anymore. Clearly that method was not effective. We'll try another method, one that involves other people. We'll have you say an oath as they're watching you. We'll take you back to the rotunda and they'll all gather around. You'll tell them you tried to betray the Gathering. But you're sorry, and you want to give your life to the Gathering in the future."

"How can I say that if I don't believe it?"

"A natural question. But remember the brain protein we gave to you. It should still be effective for another half hour or so."

"Punishment," Otto said again. He could scarcely believe that he was getting off this easily. An oath repeated before the others—people he would never recognize again, people who would not recognize him again! But he wondered about the omicron-endorphin, and its effect. Perhaps there was something about an obedience protein that aided conditioning and made one's promises difficult to break.

"We'd rather call it conditioning, Otto, but it's a matter of semantics, really. If you'll just lie back, I'll go and prepare the others. You remember your oath?"

Otto nodded, and settled back on the couch.

"I'm going to adjust these ankle clamps, Otto. Don't be alarmed; they're part of the procedure. We elevate your feet to increase the blood flow to your head during conditioning. If we didn't have the clamps around your ankles, you'd slide right off the couch. You understand?"

Otto nodded again. He watched as the Leader bent down and unfolded the metal clamps from the base of the couch. The brackets that fastened around his ankles were padded and not uncomfortable.

33

Around the sunken stone circle they came, each of them, out of their smaller caves, blinking a little at the shaft of light from the high-vaulted roof of the great cave. The light was pure white, unlike the red they had seen during the ceremony of the chalice. It filled the sunken circle, illuminating the round floor and side walls, making the white tiles sparkle. A little of its light spilled over onto the dark-red carpeting of the cave, but not enough for the Gathering to see beyond the mouth of the cave into the huge observation room where they had been earlier.

They watched the Leader emerge from one of the smaller caves, still dressed in white. Behind the Leader, a white armless couch, with someone on it. In a red robe. The couch appeared to be motorized, for the strikingly attractive blond woman who walked behind it appeared to be guiding it without effort.

As the couch and its occupant came toward them, several of the Gathering members recognized the face of Otto Lindstrom. Some of them, who had only seen Otto while under the influence of the scopolamine injection, did not. They saw only a tall, gray-bearded man with a rather serene expression on his face and padded white clamps around his bare ankles.

Diana Falke guided the couch to the mouth of the cave. She turned it so that Otto's feet were pointed out toward the darkness of the observation room. Then she moved the couch forward. Otto's face was now under the white light of the ceremonial circle.

He blinked. It was hard for him to see because of the

light. He supposed it was part of the conditioning business. But he did not like it. Someday, he thought, he would make the Leader pay for this.

Beside him, at his shoulder, he saw a lovely blond woman in a red robe. She touched his robe lightly with her hand. He wondered if he had ever made love to her. Reward and punishment, he thought. I'm supposed to be good and come back, and maybe she'll be here for me one of these fine evenings.

He watched her, because it was easier to turn his head to look at her than to stare directly up at the light. She sat down on the edge of the sunken circle, and slid down into it as though she were getting into the shallow end of a swimming pool. As she stood next to him, her face was only inches from his, her blue eyes sparkling. She kissed him on the mouth, her lips warm and moist, and he felt the stirrings of excitement.

Then the lower end of the couch began to rise. Otto's feet and legs went up and his chest and head tilted back and down. Soon his eyes were at the level of the woman's breasts rather than her face. Her hand caressed his cheek.

As the couch tilted still farther backward, the front of Otto's robe began to fall away from his thighs. Instinctively he put his hands down and held it in place before his nakedness was exposed to the group under the light. It was one thing to let one of those red flashes show your skin for a second or two, but quite another to have everyone staring while you were helpless here on the couch, hanging by the ankles.

He looked up to the blonde. "How long does this take?"

She smiled. "Quiet, now. Only a few moments."

He heard the Leader's voice.

"All of you remember the codes," the Leader said. "They are a part of your conditioning process. To violate the codes is to risk losing membership in the Gathering. Rather than have you become members no more, from time to time we provide a conditioning ceremony during our meetings. You will have no intellectual memory of what happens here, but as with all of your activity here, you will retain an *emotional* impression."

He paused. "Otto, would you tilt your head back a bit more? Straight back, so that people on both sides can see your face clearly."

"I'm practically upside down," Otto said, feeling a bit nervous. I'll show them I'm not afraid to speak, he thought. I may say that foolishness that the Leader told me to say, but they'll not think that I'm ashamed of myself.

"So you are, Otto. Beloved of the Gathering, this man has attempted to violate our codes. His action might have threatened each of us with exposure. Yet his action is harmless to us now, because of our precautions. He has confessed his error and wants each of you to know his feelings at this time. Diana, would you move away from Otto's shoulder just a bit, so that everyone can see him?"

Otto looked at her as she moved, his hands still pinning the robe to his sides to keep it from falling away. "You wouldn't want to hold my robe for me, would you?" he whispered.

She bent down and kissed him again, silent.

"Now, Otto. You will look directly behind you and try to make eye contact with at least one member of the Gathering as you speak. And then you will tell the Gathering how you feel about your attempt to break the codes."

Damnably foolish, he thought, but he knew that was not the oath he had promised to speak. The words seemed to come automatically to his lips. As he spoke, he saw a shadowy row of people seated in a circle behind him, only dark shapes. He tried to see their eyes but the light above him made it impossible to focus properly.

"I made an attempt to betray the Gathering," he said. "What it was that I did really does not matter, I suppose. The Leader has told you that the attempt did not succeed. What matters is that I am sorry for what I have done."

He felt the woman's hand resting lightly on his shoulder, and he paused.

"And, Otto?"

He remembered the phrase. "Yes. There is more. And for the future, I want to give my life to the Gathering."

"That is good, Otto. Diana, he is yours."

He was just starting to raise his head to look at her when she brought the blade down hard across his exposed throat. He felt a terrible impact just below his larynx as the blade severed his windpipe. A hundred thoughts flashed through his mind. She had hidden it in her robe. It was all a trick. To get his blood. And he lay here offering up his throat like a damnable sacrificial lamb!

He filled his lungs and tried to scream, and the air whistled out of his open trachea, making red bubbles in the blood that spurted from the surface vessels. He tried to reach out for her with his hands, to break her cursed body, tear her robe, but she was bearing down hard with the blade and the pain exploded within him and his hands fell away.

Then the pain stopped.

Having severed the cervical vertebrae, Diana Falke continued to exert pressure with the heavy razor-sharp blade, cutting through the remaining muscles at the back of the neck.

The lifeless head of Otto Lindstrom fell away, splashing into the blood that now covered the white tiles of the sunken circle. The head rolled over several times and came to rest, blood streaking the forehead and the silver beard.

From the perimeter of the sunken circle the members stared as blood continued to pour from the brightly lit headless neck. There would be nearly two gallons, drawn out by gravity, collected within the shining tiles.

Diana Falke folded the blade into its handle and put it in the pocket of her robe. She lifted herself up to sit on the edge of the circle. When she swung her legs around to stand up, the members could see her feet and ankles glittering crimson.

She stood and faced them. Spoke. "A member no more."

My God, thought Maryann Delvecchio. Now she understood why they had brought her here tonight, even though she had come to a Gathering only last week. A warning. Somehow they had found her little electronic tracking device the last time, and they wanted to show what would happen if she tried it again. She wondered if this was a special meeting, just for people who needed to be warned. Then she thought, My God, what a story. He was on the tiles, still bleeding. If she could only have managed to bring a camera.

At the edge of the circle, Phillip Bancroft silently began to weep. He looked at the shadowed faces around him, trying again to find Jill Weston. But she was not there.

34

Jill walked beyond the last of the white couches, to the end of the wide, curving tunnel that Malcolm Lockwood had called the treatment room. The white-tiled floor was cool under her bare feet, but the room was comfortably warm and very brightly lit. She wondered why everything in here was white, if this was the room Lockwood used for research. The linens and gowns in any hospital surgery were green, to provide some relief from the glare. If she worked in here for any appreciable length of time, she would have to wear dark glasses.

She sat down on the end couch and wondered how much more of an explanation she would be getting from Lockwood. And whether erythrocyte treatment would begin tonight. Lockwood had been pleasant enough, but not very informative about his methods, even though she had made it clear that she was looking for medical justification before she seriously embarked on any therapeutic program. He had been vague about what actually would take place this evening, saying only that behavioral conditioning was part of the procedure and that as she came in for further visits the conditioning would enable her to accept more of the treatment given to the other members. What sort of treatment that was, Jill had no idea. They had separated her from Phillip at the entrance to the building. She had spent most of the time so far, about an hour, according to her watch, telling Malcolm Lockwood about her symptoms of depression. He had been particularly interested in the voices she was hearing. In his consulting room, a high-ceilinged book-lined parlor furnished with antiques, green and gold, he had even tried to get her to imitate their tone, and to describe precisely what about them made her most frightened.

She had asked him about the injection they had given her after the taxicab had taken her to Phillip's office. He had made the same reply as Phillip; that it was a mild tranquilizer, given to make her more at ease when she discussed her symptoms. The relaxation was barely noticeable, but she supposed it might have made the initial interview go more smoothly.

Then he had left her, and after a few minutes a woman in a red robe had brought her to this large, curved room and told her to wait. The woman's long blond hair was very familiar, and yet when Jill had asked where they had met before, the woman denied knowing her. All very friendly, but still it was odd. Jill was certain she had seen the blond-haired woman before. Perhaps later on she would remember.

"May I ask about the robe?" Jill had said.

"Later on you'll have one, if you decide to continue treatment. It's part of the therapeutic process. You'll enjoy it."

Footsteps sounded on the tiles. Jill turned and saw Lockwood coming toward her. His smile was cordial, professional, attractive. Jill theorized that most of his patients would be women.

"Sorry to keep you waiting, Dr. Weston," he said. "We have a number of other patients here this evening and they took a bit longer than I expected. Would you like to lie down on the couch, please?"

Jill remained seated.

"What are you planning to do?"

"Of course. Please forgive me. I don't want to move you along too quickly. I do have some other patients waiting, but you're the only one here for the first time tonight. I'll try to give you as complete an explanation as possible, and if what I'm proposing sounds reasonable, we'll go ahead. If not, we'll see if we can arrive at some alternative. Or if you like, we can simply forget the whole thing."

His smile was congenial, the kind that inspired trust and confidence. "I hope we can agree on something," Jill said.

"Well, what I'm proposing is this. For tonight, we limit

ourselves to taking a small sample of blood for a future crossmatch and administering a trial dosage of one of the endorphins. As you probably know, several have been found useful in treatment of depression. MIF, TRH, beta-endorphin . . . but which one would be the most effective in your case remains for us to determine."

"Which one do you intend to use tonight?"

"The beta. It seems to be a broad-range agent without any appreciable side effects. Among my patients, at any rate. We find that it's most helpful if you're lying down when the injection is given, so that the cerebral circulation is enhanced. We also try to have you relax as it begins to work, even to the point of going to sleep for a brief period."

Jill sat up straighter on the couch.

"For how long?"

"Only ten, perhaps fifteen minutes. The light dosage of diazepam you received earlier this evening should make it easier for you to relax. The sleeping isn't really essential; it's just that many people do drift off. I wouldn't want you to be surprised if that happened."

"I'd like to know the exact dosage. And the after-effects that you anticipate."

"I can show you here." Lockwood took a flat metal case from the pocket of his white suit and opened it. There was a syringe inside, partially filled with a clear liquid. Lockwood held the case vertically so Jill could see the measurement gradations on the side of the syringe. "It's a .04 solution, and as you can see there are six milliliters here. That's a slightly lower dosage than the one used by Bauer and Ackermann at Montreal, but we tend to be a bit more conservative in starting out. Have you read their work?"

Jill nodded. "I looked it up this afternoon. In the *Lancet*."

"So then you know what we're dealing with. When we've completed the injection we should see some results within five or ten minutes, and they may continue for anywhere from one to ten days after. We'd want to bring you back in a week for another visit."

"Phillip comes every three weeks," she said.

"He's further along, of course. In fact, he no longer has injections. On our maintenance program, we use capsules. And the erythrocyte supplements, of course."

"What kind of improvement ought I to expect?"

"Probably just a general lessening of anxiety. I wouldn't look for any kind of euphoric state. I'm not here as a Dr. Feelgood type, you know. We're just looking to move people to their optimal performance level."

Jill made up her mind. "All right. I suppose we'd best begin." She lay back on the couch.

"Just make yourself comfortable," he said as he moved over to the counter. "If you would, please unbutton the top buttons of your blouse. We use the carotid artery as the injection site."

She turned her head to the side as he swabbed a patch of skin on her neck with a puff of cotton soaked in alcohol. The odor stung her nostrils and she realized her nasal passages were dry. Then she heard his voice, quiet and resonant.

"All right now, Dr. Weston, if you'll just relax. You'll find yourself quite comfortable on this couch, I think, if you'll just relax."

She could feel the point of the needle against her skin as he spoke. There was only a slight pricking as it entered the artery.

"That's good," he continued. "Very good. Now you'll find yourself relaxing a bit more deeply. Very relaxed, even getting sleepy . . ."

How right he was. She felt her hands unloosen as though automatically controlled. Her knees felt like they were being lowered on strings as her feet slid down, her legs now fully reclining. Her eyelids were getting heavy. Why fight it, she thought. And drifted with his voice.

"Now, Jill," said Malcolm Lockwood. "Now we are going to make you a member of the Gathering. You are going to feel very good about becoming one of us . . ."

Later, in the workroom that contained the video scanner, Malcolm Lockwood spoke to Diana Falke.

"She's about to leave. I think we need to talk about Phillip Bancroft."

She nodded. "I just finished listening to that tape of his confessional you gave me. It's too bad. I don't see why he's so attracted to her. She's not all that appealing."

"I don't think it's sexual attraction so much as his own upbringing. Remember, he's had thirty-eight years of conditioning by the dominant culture before he came to us. If he loves a woman he wants to protect her. He only brought her to us because he'd convinced himself she'd be closer to him. Now that it's time to give her to the group, he feels the conflict."

She twined a wisp of golden hair around a fingertip and looked thoughtful. "It's a pity you don't have the obedience hormone synthesized. If we had enough, we could add it to his capsules and tell him to stay away from her."

"If. But we don't. And it wouldn't work."

"Why not? You could add it in spansule form, for continuous action—"

"You're overestimating its power, I think. Even though we don't really have enough data to say conclusively, just now, I don't expect the omicron-endorphin to be any more effective than a deep hypnotic suggestion. After all, that's where it originates. And you can't hypnotize a man out of love."

"What do you think he'll do?"

Lockwood shrugged. "You heard the tape."

"I suppose," she said, "that I'd better tell Garrett to watch for him."

35

It was past midnight and Madison Avenue was cold. Jill buttoned the collar of her ski jacket and walked faster. The car had let her out on Sixty-eighth Street, even though she had asked to be taken to the hospital. For security reasons, the driver had said, politely opening the door for her. She wasn't quite certain what he meant. Or even that he had said anything at all. Her memory of the entire evening had begun to fade, leaving only fragments here and there, momentary images from a dream. She could recall the face of an extremely handsome man looking directly into her eyes, telling her that it was all right for her to forget what had happened now that she was a member of the Gathering. The Gathering would sustain her and protect her and give her new life.

The streetlamp bathed the sidewalk and the locked storefronts in sickly yellow. Jill caught sight of her own reflection in the plate-glass window of a fur shop. *I look ghastly in this light*, she thought, and wondered why she did not feel tired. She tried to remember if they had given her anything at the place they called the Gathering, but could not recall anything except the injection at Phillip's office. Part of her felt alarmed, and worried that the memory loss from last week, after the man with the knife had attacked her, might be recurring. But, curiously, another part of her accepted the gap in her recollection. She was not to worry. They had said the injection was diazepam, and she herself had seen intravenous diazepam produce amnesia in patients. Frequently when she used it during an exploratory procedure the patient would remain wide awake and observant as she worked, and then afterward, when she stopped by to discuss the findings, would have no memory whatsoever of what had taken place.

So she was not to worry.

The street sign up ahead said Seventy-second, even though the buildings looked dark and unfamiliar at this hour. She wondered why she was here, on Madison, instead of farther east and closer to her apartment. Then she realized that she did not remember how she had gotten here. The thought that she might have appeared here on Madison Avenue in the middle of the night without being able to account for her past movements struck her as faintly amusing at first. She envisioned a police interrogation unit, stern questions under a glaring incandescent bulb, asking where she had been the night of March 5 and her replying with great sincerity that she didn't know.

The lights of Madison Hospital were visible two blocks away. She would go to her office and try to sleep on her cot. If the voices returned, she would move to another bed, perhaps the one in the nurses' lounge. If they didn't return, perhaps that meant that the treatment, whatever it was, had been successful. She felt guarded optimism.

Behind her she heard footsteps, and walked faster. The footsteps quickened. At Seventy-third she turned in the middle of the intersection to look. There were two of them. Dirty faces, jackets, sneakers, but one was female.

Jill had the embarrassed impulse to look up and down the empty streets, pretending to search for a cab. Instead she turned and continued to walk, crossing to the other side of the street.

Phillip's red Ferrari was parked in front of the hospital. As she approached he opened the door on the passenger's side and called for her to get in.

She stood outside. "What are you doing here at this time of night?"

He didn't laugh. "I just filled up with gas," he said. "I'd like for us to take a ride."

She looked beyond him and saw the security guard on duty in the hospital lobby. And remembered. The site visit from the Marcus Foundation. The evaluation team.

"I've got a hard day ahead of me tomorrow, Phillip. I'm going to need all the sleep I can get."

"Please get in." She saw fear in his brown eyes.

"Phillip, I thought we understood each other about—"

"No. That's not it. I don't want to talk to you about us. I want to talk about them."

"Them?"

"It's important. Please get in."

"Who's them?"

"The Gathering. There are things you've got to know. Things I did. What happened tonight—it's not the way you think it is. Now will you please get in!"

She lowered herself into the leather bucket seat and stretched out her legs. "All right," she said as she closed the door. "What is it I have to know."

"We've got to get out of here." He shoved the gearbox stick into first and gunned the engine. They were away quickly in a squeal of tires, heading up Madison, a string of green traffic lights opening up before them.

She raised her voice over the roar of the engine. "I've got to get back."

He shifted into third at about forty-five and held the speed steady. "I'm driving," he said, "because I can't look you in the eye when I tell you this. But you've got to know. I can't live with myself until I tell you, even though I'm ashamed."

She waited. "Whatever you're going to say, don't connect it with your driving, all right? Whatever you've got to tell me won't do any good if you get us into an accident."

Obediently, he slowed down. "You're right. You've been right all along. I've been stupid. I didn't realize what I was doing until tonight. Now I feel terrible. I wish I hadn't made you go."

"I didn't go because of you, Phillip. It was Dr. Polder who referred me—"

He cut in, impatient to clear his conscience now that he had begun. "Forget all that, will you? We set you up. You wouldn't have gone to her if you hadn't thought you were sick, would you? Well, we're the ones who made you sick."

She stared at him. The night seemed suddenly colder. The lights of the car coming up in the far left lane seemed glaring; the sound of the Ferrari transmission a disconcerting whine.

"What did you do?" she asked.

Ahead of him at Ninety-sixth the light changed red and he slowed, pulling over to the right lane. "I want to turn here and get on the drive."

"No. Back to the hospital. What did you do?"

"Don't go back to the hospital. Your office isn't safe. Neither is your apartment. I got in there with a passkey and did things."

He stopped and waited for the light to change. Three lanes across, a tan Chevrolet Monte Carlo stopped one car length back and cut its wheels to the right.

"When did you get in there? What did you do?"

"Months ago." He turned to face her.

And saw in the mirror the glare of headlights coming at them full speed.

Before he could scream, the front end of the Chevrolet burst through the thin steel door at an angle and caught the driver's seat from behind, crushing Phillip Bancroft instantly. The steering column of the Ferrari penetrated Bancroft's chest at the collar bone. The front bumper of the Chevrolet shattered his pelvis, smashing his intestines, his liver, and the rest of his lower abdominal cavity into red-brown pulp. He tried to draw breath before he lost consciousness, and failed.

The impact knocked Jill Weston against the door assembly on the passenger's side with an overwhelming force. She was not wearing a seat belt. Her skull hit the window beside her with a blow that caused her momentarily to black out. When her door opened, she did not realize that flames had begun to issue from the front end of the Ferrari. She felt strong hands under her, lifting her away, dragging her to the sidewalk.

She opened her eyes in time to see the white flare of the explosion, and the raging fire. By the time the authorities arrived, both vehicles were charred beyond recognition. So also was the body of Phillip Bancroft.

PART THREE

ASHES

36

They had drawn the white curtains around Jill's hospital bed. Virginia Polder parted them. She came close enough to make certain that Jill was breathing properly before she sat down on the wooden-armed easy chair at Jill's bedside.

Fifteen minutes later Jill awoke, her eyes widening when she saw Dr. Polder. She stared for a moment at the hospital curtain. Then she sat up in bed. I'm in the hospital, she thought, and I can move, and my head hurts. "What time is it?" she asked.

Virginia Polder got to her feet a bit slowly, for she was not accustomed to hospital visits at five in the morning. "I'll tell you everything I know, dear. But first I'd better take a look at you. I'm afraid you're going to have a fairly visible bruise on your forehead."

She had her penlight ready. Jill blinked as Dr. Polder shone the tiny beam first into one eye and then the other. Not quite awake, Jill had the vague impression that in a moment or two she would understand clearly what was happening to her. She put her fingers to her right temple, where the pain was coming from, and probed gently. With relief she decided that whatever had happened to her had not included skull fracture.

Dr. Polder had her sitting on the edge of the bed and was testing neural reflexes. "Are you worried about a concussion?" Jill asked.

"Not anymore. Stand up now, would you please, and try to take a few steps."

Jill got out of bed and did as she was told. "Now close your eyes and come back to me. Good."

"How did I get here?"

"In an ambulance, they tell me. Now. Close your eyes again, and stretch out your arms. Now bring the tips of your index fingers together."

"You *are* worried about a concussion. What was I doing in an ambulance?"

Dr. Polder watched as Jill's fingertips met. "All right," she said. "You can get into bed. I think you're still all in one piece."

"That's good to know. Now I'm starting to think you're afraid to tell me, so would you just please—"

"Right away," she interrupted, "as soon as you tell me something. Think back to this evening. What is the *last* thing you can remember? Describe it as completely as you can."

The recollection came back to Jill, dimly. "I was coming out of Phillip's office. With Phillip. And a woman. The woman had a veil, and I couldn't see her face clearly." She tried to picture the scene. "And then I don't remember anything else. Did the cab have an accident?"

"No," said Virginia Polder. "What time was it?"

"I met them at seven-thirty. In front of the Metropolitan Museum. This would have been eight-fifteen at the latest."

"Well now it's five in the morning, dear. And you came in here at about one. They said you were talking rationally about all you had scheduled for this morning; how you were worried that you wouldn't be able to perform surgery. Then they gave you a sedative—"

"In Phillip's office!" Jill interrupted. "I remember now. The woman gave me a sedative. An injection of diazepam, she said it was. She gave one to Phillip too."

"And you remember nothing after the injection?"

Jill shook her head again. "I've had that happen with patients of mine when I was doing a procedure and using diazepam. But never for that long a period." She bit her lip in frustration, trying to fight away the fear, the sense of futility. "We're talking about—it's five hours, and I can't remember, just like the last time—"

"Well I don't know what happened during those five hours, dear. But I suspect that it has nothing to do with any organic or psychological difficulty on your part. You see, I had a bit of an extended memory lapse myself."

Jill listened in astonishment as Dr. Polder explained. Yesterday afternoon. At a restaurant for lunch, an hour before Jill was scheduled to come in for her afternoon appointment. A man had been watching her, and followed her out to the sidewalk. Before she could hail a cab, he had put a gun to her ribs, made her take his arm, walked her back to the office. There had been no patients; her receptionist had not yet returned. They went back to her consulting room.

"And there he gave me an injection," she said. "He held the gun where I could see it all the while, and very neatly emptied a hypodermic into a vein on my wrist. He told me if I did not cooperate he would turn the gun on my patients and my receptionist after he had killed me. There wasn't anything else I could do. I remember him sitting there, holding the gun on me, looking at his watch. An ugly man. I remember watching his ugly brown eyes, and thinking that something had damaged them. They were clouded over, even while they stared at me."

"What did you do?"

"I don't remember. That's the point. One minute I was in the office with that—*thing*—and the next, Carol, my receptionist, was waking me. I was asleep at my desk, and if was after four o'clock."

"The man with the knife." Jill said the words slowly, as though not wanting to accept what they meant. "He had eyes like that."

"I remembered your saying so. And I tried to call you at once, but you were away from the hospital. I left instructions with the switchboard that they were to phone me the moment you returned. I must say I didn't expect you to be coming in through Emergency admissions."

"I didn't either." Jill began to feel a growing dread. "So you don't remember seeing me? You don't remember what you told me to do?"

"My receptionist assures me you came in for your consultation and left in quite the usual manner. But I really can't tell you a thing. Even the notes I made have disappeared."

"You gave me a phone number. You told me about a treatment. Endorphins. Erythrocytes—"

She thought for a long moment. "I'm afraid I don't know anyone who works with endorphins." She seemed to be making up her mind. "And your erythrocyte level was normal on your last series of tests."

Jill tried to keep her voice under control. "It was Phillip Bancroft's number. That's why I went to his of-

fice. They said the injection was part of the treatment.
You don't remember telling me *anything?*"

"Nothing. Evidently I was forced to tell you whatever
I said about endorphins or red blood cells. Did I give
you any names?"

"You said the man was secretive. You couldn't even
give his office location because of his concern over keeping the big drug companies from learning what he had
discovered before he could get it patented."

She nodded. "You'll forgive me, but I'm trying to understand. It seems as though someone went to quite a
considerable effort to force me to tell you something I
didn't know yesterday. It was Bancroft's telephone number?"

"It was his office."

"And had he been expecting your phone call?"

"No. He sounded surprised. Surprised and pleased.
He'd been trying to talk to me into this same sort of
treatment for weeks."

Virginia Polder looked thoughtful. "Then I *don't* understand. If this is what he wanted, and what the other
man wanted, to take you in for this treatment of
theirs—"

"And they succeeded! But I can't remember what in
the world it was they *did* to me!" The fear and the
frustration nearly made her cry like a schoolgirl. "I think
we should go to the police! I think we should have them
arrest Phillip!"

"You don't remember the accident, do you, dear,"
Virginia Polder said quietly.

"No! I don't remember . . ." Her voice died away as
she saw the look on Dr. Polder's face. "Tell me," she
said. "Tell me what happened."

"You were in a small car with Phillip Bancroft. You
survived the crash. He did not. Someone driving a stolen
car collided with him. Two witnesses said it appeared to
have been done deliberately."

She explained how she had read the police report before coming in. How Jill had been brought in by the
ambulance, and been able to tell the police nothing beyond what they already knew: that the driver of the
small car was Phillip Bancroft, and that he was surely
dead.

The tears formed in Jill's eyes and she shuddered. She

felt suddenly alone and vulnerable, and for a moment it seemed she would never be able to trust anyone again, never even go outside, without being afraid. "Poor Phillip,"she whispered at last. "He was trying so hard—he was so happy with this—whatever it was—so sure it was just the right thing for me—"

"Here." Virginia Polder handed Jill a box of tissues from the bedside table. "Take your time. Then we'll try to think about what to do next."

On the other side of the white curtain surrounding Jill's bed, Roger Avery stood quietly. As chief resident, he had assumed control of Jill's case as soon as she had been brought into the Emergency Room, and had continued with questions and treatment until he had decided to sedate her. Now that Virginia Polder, Jill's personal physician, had arrived, Roger Avery had withdrawn from active participation.

He listened carefully.

37

Harriet Pierce told herself for the fifth time that evening that she didn't really mind working late, that it didn't hurt to double up with an eight-to-four and then a four-to-midnight, that the hours of sleep you lost when you worked late didn't compare to the hours of sleep you lost when you didn't have a job and lay awake wondering how you were going to pay the bills. She considered herself lucky; because she was cross-trained, she could handle a surgical post in the O.R., private duty, or, like this morning and tonight, a fill-in spot on regular floor coverage when two of the more senior nurses had gotten sick.

Only trouble was, Harriet didn't feel like she was getting any younger either. And it was hard, burning the midnight oil as a part-timer, trying to be where the job was when the work was available. She guessed it wasn't much harder than Nick's job, though, because Nick *always* had it with him, in his head, trying to make those hospital budgets balance out. Well, he wasn't *always* thinking about work, she had to take that back. They had their moments, that was for sure. But he was working late tonight, same as she was.

The room where the call light had come from was 318. The patient was sitting up in bed. Middle-aged white woman.

"Hi," said Harriet. "May I help you?"

"No, it's not me," said the woman. "I heard a noise through my wall. The room next door. I was leaning back against the headboard of the bed, you see, and the sound carried. I know that's the way I was able to hear it, because when I heard it I got out of bed and looked outside in the corridor, and the door to that room is shut tightly."

She could see she was pretty worried. Harriet had the impression that the woman had rehearsed her speech, saying it over several times while she was in here alone. She thought it was always better to have a semiprivate room, because even if you couldn't stand your roommate, at least it kept your mind occupied. But then, Harriet had never been a patient in a hospital and she supposed she saw things from a different point of view.

"I'm not sure that room's occupied just now," said Harriet. "What kind of a noise was it?"

"A man's voice. He said, 'No,' quite distinctly, and several times. The last time it sounded as if his voice— as if he was choking. It may be that I'm overreacting, but with the TV news about those missing persons the other day—"

"Quite all right, ma'am," said Harriet. "I'll check it out."

From the corridor, Harriet could see that the door to 320 was shut tightly, just the way the lady had said. For a moment she thought of going back to the station and checking to see the name of the patient, and for another moment she thought of bringing back one of the other nurses with her, and after that she thought of maybe just calling the room and asking if everything was all right in there. Then she decided she was really turning into a chicken heart in her old age, and opened the door.

A man in surgical greens was at the patient's bedside,

performing a procedure of some sort. He saw Harriet, and spoke, his voice from behind his surgical mask sounding deep and authoritative, as though he were accustomed to command.

"Come in here, nurse," he said. "I could use some help with this catheter."

Harriet couldn't place the voice. But she decided that as long as she was down here she might as well help. She came to the bedside. And saw a dark-red tube coming from the patient's neck. Then something exploded at the back of her head, and she saw nothing else.

38

Lockwood sat down at the window table and turned his chair slightly away from the general's. He wanted to face the plate glass at the proper angle so that he could catch the reflection of people coming into the VIP lounge. Too many of the Gathering flew in and out of Washington. The Leader was not about to become careless of being recognized here at National Airport.

He kept talking as they ordered drinks, summing up his report as the general's per-diem consultant for an army drug problem. Later he would return to New York and the general would fly to Seattle.

"All right," said the general. The drinks had come. He lifted his martini glass to his lips without ceremony and drained it. Small droplets of gin clung to the white stubble of afternoon beard at the corners of the general's mouth, but he appeared not to notice. Already he had caught the waiter's attention and signaled for another round. Then he turned his bright gray eyes on Lockwood. "That's enough about rehabilitation for now. What do you think of this mess we've got in Washington?"

Lockwood kept his voice casual. Long before the general's office had asked him to help, Lockwood had known that this man was different. He had a future *outside* the

Pentagon. Though no less right-wing than others of his rank and only slightly better-looking, the general had a smoothly colorful way of simplifying issues that made him a quotable favorite of the media. "I'm flattered," Lockwood said. "They're calling you the next Eisenhower, and you're asking me for a political opinion?"

"No bullshit, soldier." The general grinned. Lockwood grinned right back.

"Everyone knows. It's a question of leadership. Whenever there's weakness at the top, there's chaos."

Lockwood watched his man. Age was attacking the general's face in places the cameras did not show. Just above the star-studded collar the flesh around the jowls and neck had begun to pucker into folds. The collagen around the cheekbones was no longer firm. Perhaps, Lockwood speculated, the general's energy level had also started to decline.

"Our friend on the Coast told me you'd say that," said the general. From behind fleshy lids, the gray eyes glittered.

"The governor?" Lockwood concealed mild surprise.

"None other."

"I talked with him several months ago. At the time he seemed interested in running."

"Oh he's still interested. But I think he's aware by now that second on the ticket might be more realistic."

"You're at the top, then."

"That's right."

"I like that."

"Do you?" The eyes glittered once again. "Our friend the senator tells me you liked *him*."

"I did," Lockwood said easily. "But at that time you weren't in the race."

"I'm still not in. Not for publication. Don't go spreading any tales."

"Physicians know how to keep a confidence."

"I hope they also know about loyalty."

"They do." Lockwood held the general's eyes with his own for only a moment; not long enough to be coercive.

"Then we understand each other. Both our friends tell me you have some influential contacts."

"That's accurate." Lockwood had told the two other potential candidates, also after his consultant work had paved the way for a private meeting. He was making his plans for the future. The Gathernig could not remain forever a collection of divided individuals completely unknown to one another. When the time was right, when the synthesizing processes had been tested and the blood was no longer a problem, the activity of group members could be directed into other channels. That would be the next phase of his Leadership.

"And you're prepared to deliver some well-placed help."

Lockwood nodded, wiating to see if the general would be curious about how that "help" would be "delivered." The other two candidates hadn't been. To them such details were irrelevant.

The general picked up his second martini and looked at it. "I suppose they're people who share our beliefs."

"Some do. Some don't." Lockwood kept his tone offhand. "But they'll all do what I tell them."

It got a laugh. "That's good. Just like the Army!" The drink wet the general's lips again.

"When did you plan to get started?"

"Six months, maybe a shade less. You'll help?"

"Yes."

"Good. What for?"

Lockwood blinked. "Well, as we said, they're well-placed people. They can work with—"

"No." The general leaned forward. "Not them. You. What do you work for? And don't tell me it's for our shared beliefs."

A modest shrug hid Lockwood's distaste at bargaining. "Oh, there are certain political appointments in the medical field. As you know, I do research. I'd leave it up to you."

"I could give you the V.A. hospitals. Hell of a lot of research subjects put away in there. And I might even be able to do better."

"Fine," said Lockwood. "But you don't have to be definite. We can wait until you've seen what I can do. I'm sure I'll be pleased with whatever you think is right."

39

Ted thought the view tonight was spectacular. A clear sky and a seventy-five-mile visibility range, so you could see the landing lights of the jet liners coming in to Kennedy Airport and even the flame from the Statue of Liberty. Faced with a view like that, Ted supposed a man could find it a bit difficult to concentrate, and maybe that was why it was taking Dr. Harold Daniels, a key member of the Marcus Foundation evaluation team, so long to order. Probably the doctor was also wondering how Ted had managed to get their party a table so close to the window. They did a fabulous amount of business at this restaurant here at the top of the World Trade Center, so getting such good tables had been something of a coup.

Possibly Dr. Daniels was also distracted from the menu because he was wondering why Diana Falke had not yet arrived. For that matter, so was Ted.

The waiter smiled graciously as Daniels, a thin, graying fellow whose pasty complexion looked as though he could benefit from some of his own vascular surgery, finally decided on the filet mignon, well done. A waste of good beef, thought Ted, and gave an approving nod.

"They do it up well here," he said. "Would you like to have another drink while we're waiting?"

The doctor drummed thin fingers on his napkin and said that he would be driving back to Tenafly, New Jersey, as soon as they were through. Ted gave the same nod of approval and said they were glad he had found the time to have dinner with them and meet the Madison team.

"I just want to be sure you get a chance to ask Jill Weston about any problems you might find in the application," said Ted.

Daniels' voice was thin and sour. "I haven't seen the

application. The Marcus people handle that end of the proceedings. I only come in to evaluate the surgery, as far as I know. I assume you *are* planning to have us look at an operation at some point before a decision is reached."

"Oh, yes. I can't tell you how unhappy we were that we had to postpone. But under the circumstances—"

"I know. My secretary pointed out the story on Dr. Weston's accident in the paper after you called this morning. I'm not saying I was inconvenienced, not at all. A man can always use a few hours' free time, especially in the morning. She doesn't appear to be seriously injured."

"Oh, it's just a precaution. I'm sure she'll be doing surgery in another day or so. Then we'll reschedule your visit."

They both looked over to the adjoining table, where Jill was explaining a point about her operation to Joseph Bross, another surgeon, and to Maryann Delvecchio, the young television reporter who was doing a "day in the life" feature on Ted Sanford for her news show. Ted had talked Maryann into doing the story nearly a week ago. Now he felt rather pleased with his success in showing the good side of Madison Hospital so far, and the day was nearly over. Of course she didn't have her film crew in here this evening—she was just making occasional notes, gathering "background," as she called it, and helping herself to a sixty-five-dollar dinner on the hospital's expense account.

But sixty-five dollars was nothing compared to the effect favorable—or unfavorable—publicity would have on Madison's flow of incoming patients. Since the story on the "missing persons" last week, the number of elective surgical entries had fallen by nearly 18 per cent. Thank God the publicity seemed to have died down this week. And with this one bold stroke—opening up his office, showing the surgical amphitheater he had helped to design, the equipment, the happy children in the pediatrics ward—getting all that out to the public, Ted could very well have turned the trend around. At least he hoped so.

"Oh, yes," he said, gesturing in Jill's direction. "A very strong little lady. You know, we buy the equipment for these procedures, but it's really the hand behind the knife that matters. I go with the old adage, myself, that a real surgeon could make do with just a piece of string—"

"Yes, and the lid of an old tin can," interrupted Daniels. "I've heard that adage many times. Most often when the administration of a hospital doesn't want to buy equipment."

"Well now here, of course, it's a bit different." Ted groped for something diplomatic to say, something that would show this surgeon that Ted really considered physicians and administrators all part of the same team. "In Jill's case, we'd be happy to buy anything she recommended that we thought we could afford. That's how much confidence we have in her. And we're a pretty thoroughgoing budget-conscious office, too, believe me."

"Isn't everybody? Practically everything I hear these days at Mount Sinai is about money. Cut the capital outlays. Recruit new patients. Get involved with the community to spruce up the image. It's as though we were marketing breakfast food and trying to get ahead of the competition."

Ted winced inwardly at the idea that Mount Sinai might see Madison Hosiptal as competition. "Well I'm glad you could take time to come over and meet a group from a smaller place."

"I'm adequately compensated. When I agreed to serve on the Marcus advisory panel I knew I'd need to allow for these getting-acquainted dinners. I know the fund-raising game."

Ted sipped at the ice left from his bourbon, wondering how he could get across the barrier this cold, gray man seemed to be putting up. "Well naturally we're not intending to compete with you people," he said. "Ours is a different region of the city, a much smaller group of people—"

"Of course. Though why you should want to expand into a specialized surgical area in such a major way as the foundation says you're contemplating—I must admit I'm curious." His gray eyes regarded Ted with an interest Ted would have expected to see reserved for a laboratory specimen of some rare disease.

Ted decided to be frank. "Well, it's the baby market, you see. You know there are at least fifteen thousand women in the United States that could benefit from Jill Weston's operation. And—"

"Her figures? The fifteen thousand women."

"Government statistics." Ted wished he had remembered to make a mental note of the source Jill had appended to the grant application. "With that many women, and New York so easily accessible, we can expect large numbers of patients. And after the operation is successful, the women from the metropolitan area are likely to come to us for their perinatal and obstetical care."

"Possible, I suppose." He was drumming those long fingers on the napkin again, and looking over at the third table of the Madison party, where Nick O'Donnell was making conversation with a female epidemiologist specializing in birth disorders. Ted had taken special pains to get to know her well during the time they had spent at the bar, waiting for the others to arrive. She was not bad, Ted reflected, trying to remember her name. He hoped Nick was having better luck with her than he was with this cold turkey beside him.

"Actually, we're pretty encouraged by the pattern so far. Nearly all the women Jill has operated on have come back to her when they've gotten pregnant. Including my wife, Rachel. We'll be having our first baby in less than a month now."

"Congratulations," Daniels said. "I assume you've had amniocentesis."

At Jill's table, the conversation was going more smoothly. Bross had done electron microphotography of fallopian tubes during his residency, and he well appreciated the advantages of Jill's technique over traditional surgical methods that cut into the tube from the outside. He was explaining to Maryann Delvecchio how scar tissue from a traditional operation to unblock a fallopian tube could interfere with the thousands of tiny folds of the mucous membrane lining.

"The egg is cradled in those tiny folds," he said. "It's carried along to the uterus inside them, like a little ball rolling in a groove. If something blocks that tiny protective pathway, the egg may never reach the uterus. So it can't properly implant even if sperm manages to get through and start fertilization. Do you understand?"

"Gee," said Maryann. "Maybe we ought to do a feature on this new technique. It sounds exciting. We could take three women, you know, and follow them through the examination and all, and then when they got pregnant we could maybe get some footage in the delivery room—"

She stopped talking as a strikingly attractive blond woman entered the room and came toward them. .

"Who *is* that blonde?" asked Maryann. "I'd bet a thousand dollars I've seen her somewhere before."

"Isn't that odd," said Jill. "I just had the same feeling. I don't know who she is either."

Bross, a bachelor in his early forties, gave a friendly grin. "You won't forget her after tonight. She's the one who's holding the purse strings for this project of yours. That's Diana Falke."

Ted was on his feet, smiling, to welcome Diana to their table. Before she arrived, however, a waiter appeared at Ted's side with a telephone. An urgent call, the switchboard had said. The waiter quickly connected the instrument to its jack beneath the table.

Shortly after Ted picked up the receiver, his smile vanished.

40

The seven-foot TV wall screen showed Maryann Delvecchio standing with her microphone, motionless, her dark-eyed Italian features rendered in full color and with striking clarity. In the Leader's projection room, Lockwood himself was watching her. He sat in a comfortably upholstered leather chair, his right hand resting lightly on the controls. When he pressed the switch marked Forward, the Maryann on the screen began to move and speak.

"—stunned by this terrifying new tragedy at New York's Madison Hospital. Where before the whispers among patients and relatives were quiet, many of them not seeming to be worried about the allegations of missing persons, the discovery of what the police laboratory has

confirmed to be the remains of human skeletons in ashes
of the hospital's incinerator—"

The Leader's finger pressed firmly on the button marked
Pause and Maryann's image froze, her strident voice
abruptly silenced.

The Leader stared at her face.

Diana Falke entered the room behind him. "Aren't you
sitting awfully close to that thing?" she asked.

"Sit down, Diana." The Leader spoke pleasantly. "Perhaps your powers of observation can be of some help."

"I didn't come in here to stare at *that*." She took the
chair beside the Leader's and curled up, leaning toward
the control box between them as though impatient to
reach out and press the Off switch. "I wanted to speak
with you."

"It can wait." The voice lost only a little of its pleas-
antness. "I want you to watch her face. I want you to
tell me if she's made the connection."

"Connection?"

"She's covering the Madison Hospital incident. I need
to know if she's connected Garrett's mistake with the infusion of red cells she receives every three weeks. Something should show up in her face if she's worried about
it; she's a very superficial woman and a bad liar."

His hand moved at the controls again and Maryann
began to speak.

"—has brought patient fears into the open. And the
incident last night has *fanned* those fears. I have with
me Marion Goldman, who today elected to *leave* Madison Hospital rather than risk another night in the building where the 'vampire killer' has already killed one
patient and bludgeoned an innocent nurse into what may
be an irreversible coma. Mrs. Goldman, would you tell us
how you *felt* last night, knowing you were in the room
just beside the vampire killer's victims?"

They watched in silence as Mrs. Goldman recounted
the events of the evening. She was telling how she had
been afraid to take the sedative her doctor had pre-
scribed. Diana Falke spoke again.

"I told you not to send Garrett back there. He's a
clumsy and incompetent—"

"One thing at a time," said the Leader. "Watch this
part closely. It was taped earlier."

Maryann was on camera alone again, the collar of her

trench coat up against the wind, microphone just below her chin.

"To learn what measures are being taken to *protect* the patients and staff at Madison Hospital, 'News Center Six' cameras were on hand earlier this afternoon when Ted Sanford, hospital administrator, read a statement concerning safety at Madison and answered questions from the press."

Ted appeared on screen, looking awkward and worried. Rachel Sanford was at his side. The camera lingered a moment on the curve of Rachel's abdomen under her maternity blouse, and then cut to a close-up of Maryann. Maryann was standing in a crowd of reporters, calling out a question.

"Mr. Sanford, you talk of the hospital's budget problems. Are you saying that Madison Hospital cannot *afford* to keep its patients protected from killers who would bleed them to death and burn their bodies—"

"See here now!" Ted cut in. "You're not being fair at all!"

"All the same, you've told us that you're doubling the security force, and yet there's a persistent rumor that you've had to take the money to pay the additional guards out of your own bank account. Is that true? And if so, how long can you continue subsidizing a hospital that can't pay its own bills?"

"I—don't have any comment on that," said Ted. "Hospital funding comes out of many sources."

Another reporter, a sandy-haired young man, got Ted's attention. "Mr. Sanford, how many people last year *died* in Madison Hospital?"

Ted stood groping for the correct figure. "How many— well, you'd have to compare that with the number who are discharged and sent home well for the numbers to have any meaning."

He looked up in surprise at Rachel, who was reaching for one of the microphones in front of him.

"May I say something, Ted?" Rachel's mouth was set in a determined line. She barely waited for Ted's "Of course, dear" before continuing. "I think it's terrible what's happened last night, and I think it's almost as bad to see what you people are doing with it today. You're not being fair, and you're putting everything in the worst possible way just to attract attention, and I've got only this one thing more to say to you. My husband is committed to safety at Madison Hospital, and I *believe* in him. As everybody can see, I'm going to have a baby soon. I want everybody to know that when the time comes, I'm going to have the baby right here at Madison Hospital!"

The camera lingered for a moment on Ted and Rachel as they looked at one another. Then Maryann Delvecchio was alone on screen once more, standing on the sidewalk in front of the hospital. "And so, while the vampire killer remains at large, Rachel Sanford is making plans to have her baby in her husband's hospital. The future of Madison may depend on how many others share her confidence. This is Maryann Delvecchio, at Madison Hospital, for 'News Center Six.' "

The screen went dark as the Leader turned to Diana Falke. "What do you think?"

"I don't see why you're wasting time with her," said Falke. "She knows nothing. But there are others at Madison—"

"You don't have to see everything, Diana. Tell me why you think that Miss Delvecchio is safe."

A moment passed. Diana Falke looked as though she were about to say something disrespectful and then brought herself under control. "She has only one thing on her mind when she's talking," said Diana. "She's making love to the camera. If she were worried about being connected with this vampire killer, she would never be so flamboyant."

Lockwood considered. "Possibly. Then again, she may be indulging her exhibitionistic nature in order to conceal her fears. She may even be concealing her fears from herself."

"I thought you said she was shallow."

"It's not unheard of for people to deceive themselves," said the Leader. "Whether they are shallow or infinitely complex, it still happens with great frequency."

Falke sat up straighter. "But why *bother* with her? What does she have that the other people at Madison don't have? It seems to me they'd be just as likely to connect—"

"She has a *motive*, Diana. Maryann Delvecchio is the only person connected with our Madison difficulties who also wants to expose the Gathering. It's been her dream— the big story that would set her apart from the others.

I've tried to take steps to dissuade her from that dream, but you know the limitations we have. Until we've come a bit further, we can't be really confident that we've succeeded in dissuading her. Particularly when the motivation is so strong to begin with."

"Weston may be a problem also," said Falke. "I have a report from Avery. She knows that she was manipulated into coming here, but she doesn't seem completely certain what to do about it."

"Is that what you came in to talk to me about?"

Falke nodded.

"I suppose she'll bear watching, then. But nothing overt. Don't try to influence her in any way."

"It may be necessary. She may—"

The Leader turned his face to Diana, and she grew silent.

"No contact with *anyone* at Madison," he said gently. "We aren't going to take risks. You'll concentrate on the other locations."

"I'd like to begin using Avery for collections," she continued, as though she was unaware of the growing intensity in the Leader's eyes. "I think it's time to retire Garrett completely. I think last night made that obvious."

He watched her for a moment. "No contact with *anyone* at Madison," he repeated. "The people there are not worth the risk of exposing what we have. As long as we don't call them, they'll appear perfectly innocent. More important, they themselves think they're innocent. Did you see the tape of Elwood Johnson? He remembers nothing of what he did; only that Garrett gave him an injection one afternoon several weeks ago. I want to keep him feeling innocent, and I particularly do not want someone from the police who may be watching him or anyone else at Madison to pick up a conversation he might have with you. Or to follow him here. Is that understood?"

"I understand," said Falke. "And I think you're making a mistake. We're making valuable contacts at Madison, and we should move them toward permanent membership."

41

Jerry Chamberlain was at his desk, bent over, completing a chart. Jill stood in his office doorway for a moment or two before he noticed she was there.

"Long time no see, Silver Shoes," he said, keeping his voice casual. "Have a seat. You here on business or what?"

"Partly business," Jill said. She took the single chair opposite his. "And partly what. I think I should probably tell you the business part first."

Jerry gestured expansively. "Be my guest."

That battered blue walking hat still hung on his coat rack. Jill thought of the way he had laughed when they had talked about camping, and then about the way he had sounded, hurt and distant, when he had called her apartment and heard Phillip's voice. He doesn't know how lucky he is, she thought bitterly. If he had gotten involved with me, he might have been held at gunpoint and shot full of drugs.

Business first, she had said. The trouble with being tired was that you weren't able to concentrate on one thing at a time without having your mind wander.

"You remember the Marcus Foundation," she began.

"Sure thing. They're still interested in us, during these troubled times?"

She shook her head. "Don't remind me. Harriet Pierce is the best O.R. nurse I've ever worked with. And a friend, too. The whole thing makes me—"

Jerry was looking beyond her, at the doorway. "Hold on just one second." He raised his voice slightly. "Yes, Marcie? You have something?"

His dark-eyed assistant smiled as she came in. "Just these forms for you to sign, Doctor. The mail pickup's just about due. If it's not too much trouble." She added the last with a pointed glance at Jill.

Jerry ignored the comment and reached for the papers. The old story, Jill thought. There was jealousy in the look that Marcie had given her. The young assistant, the good-looking eligible doctor.

Jerry breezed through the forms, signing with his ball-point. "Close the door on your way out, would you please, Marcie?"

After she had gone he said, "Nice kid, but she tends to get underfoot like that. Now where were we? The Marcus Foundation, right?"

"I had dinner with them last night. At Windows on the World."

"Impressive."

"Ted was paying. But their representative talked to me about this fertility center they're thinking of funding for us. They want to modify the proposal slightly in a way that involves the blood bank.

"They'd want us to do collection, storage, and shipping of blood from these patientts who'd be coming in for the operation. They'd come in here roughly two weeks before surgery and you'd take a unit and store it separately. If it was needed for any reason during surgery, we'd have it ready. But it probably wouldn't be."

"I know," said Jerry. "You hardly ever need any of the units we hold for you with that operation. We people on the first floor are pretty observant that way."

"The point is, the Marcus Foundation has a connection with a blood bank. They didn't say which one, but it's here in the city. What they want is the blood we don't use."

Jerry shrugged. "It'd be a week away from its discard date at that point. But I guess they'd have no problem using it quickly, if they've got a rapid turnover. You don't know what outfit they're connected with?"

"She didn't say. I guess we'd know when it all got set up, though. We'd have to know where to ship it."

"So how many units are we talking about?"

"If the center gets going well, maybe as many as seven or ten a day."

"Then there's nothing to it. A veritable breeze. We'll handle it. Where do you want me to sign?"

She smiled. "Thanks. I've got some forms upstairs. If you could just fill in the specifications of the blood bank, the equipment we'd be using for collection and storage, that's all we'll need."

"You send it down here, you'll have it the next day." He clasped his hands behind his neck and leaned back in his chair. "We in the running fraternity have to stick together."

"Thanks," she said again. Now here came the hard part. She tried to think how to begin, but no matter how she tried to work it around in her mind it came out sounding either hopelessly forward or hopelessly distant or hopelessly confused. But she had promised herself that she would say *something*. She owed it to him.

"About the other thing," she said.

"You brought your running shoes?"

"No, actually, I've been a little off schedule lately. Not feeling too well. I think I'm going to have to pass on the running till I get settled and get some proper sleep."

"How soon do you figure that's going to be?"

When I find out who killed Phillip, she thought. When I find out what they did to me. When I know they can't do it anymore. Then I can sleep. Not until!

But suppose she never found out? The car had been stolen; the police said they had no clues about where the driver had disappeared; she couldn't remember a single thing, except for Phillip's phone number and an anonymous taxi and a woman with a hypodermic syringe and a veil—

She had to admit it. It was conceivable that she could stay in this limbo of uncertainty forever.

"Hey, Silver Shoes.'" Jerry's voice broke into her thoughts. "You look like you've got a problem. We hematologists have a sixth sense about that kind of thing. You think there's anything I can help you with?"

That was the difference, she thought. If it had been Phillip, he would have been all over her with advice. For her own good. She realized now, that was why her feelings about Phillip had changed. *He* had changed. He had started trying to convert her, to bring her into his way of life, with his investment portfolios and his capsules.

That was why she now, knowing he was dead, she felt only the sadness she would feel at the passing of a casual friend, perhaps, or a distant relative, or a patient one had known a few years back and then lost touch with. She felt no loss of someone close to her, because Phillip, during these past months, *hadn't* been close. Not really. He had been pressing her, and she had been keeping him away out of an instinct to defend herself, and as it turned out she had been absolutely right to do that, because all the while Phillip had been working with those people.

She didn't want to involve Jerry with them too.

"I think it's something I'll have to work out for myself," she said. "But thank you anyway."

His expression did not change. "Anytime. I'm still hitting the pavement around noon these days, whenever you feel like starting up again."

There was the one other thing, really the hardest of all, and she felt her cheeks redden as she forced herself to continue.

"The last time we went, you remember. We were going to dinner. You called the apartment. Someone else was there."

Jerry nodded.

"I don't know how clearly I explained—"

"C'mon. It was just dinner. No big deal."

He's not interested anymore, she thought. He's not. Well, she couldn't go chasing him. Maybe some things just weren't meant to be.

"Okay," she said. She nodded, stood up, put on a smile. "I'll get those forms down to your office."

"All for the cause."

When she opened the door, she saw Marcie across the room at her desk, listening on the phone. Their eyes met. Marcie looked slightly surprised. She turned away and began talking into the mouthpiece.

42

Maryann Delvecchio got down from the examining-room table where she had been waiting and came forward to meet Jill. Even with the powder-blue paper examination robe wrapped around her, she still managed to look as though she were on camera. She held out her hand. Jill took it and said hello.

"I should call you Dr. Weston, I guess," said Maryann, "since now I'm your patient. It's really good of you to see me. After yesterday's broadcast, I wasn't sure they'd let me in the hospital!"

"We're all being professional," Jill said. "If you'd like to just get back on the table and lie down, we can begin your examination." Jill walked to the other side of the table, feeling the tension that Maryann seemed to generate. Slow and easy, she told herself. Yet it was difficult to stay calm. Ever since she had awakened in the hospital with Dr. Polder, Jill knew her own adrenaline had been up; her system working overtime. Because she was angry. People she did not know had manipulated her. Had attacked her. Had threatened and drugged her, and done the same to Dr. Polder, the woman she respected more than any other, and to Phillip Bancroft, so much worse. . . .

Stop it, she thought. She couldn't afford to let emotionalism divert her attention and keep her from her work. Besides, whoever had killed Phillip might *not* have been connected with those who had attacked her.

She realized that Maryann Delvecchio was still sitting up. And giving her an uncertain look. "If you like," said Jill, "we can go a bit more deeply into your medical history before we do the physical examination. I generally combine the two procedures to save time, but if you'd be more comfortable sitting up for a while—"

Maryann fingered her tight, black curls in a nervous gesture, as though touching a balloon. "You're making me feel guilty, Doctor," she said after a moment's hesitation. "I guess I'd just better come right out front with this and you can decide how you want to deal with it. Maybe you'll want to kick me right out on my can, and if that's the way you see it, it's O.K. with me. The fact is, I *am* interested in having your operation, and I *do* intend to try very hard to have children someday . . ." She hesitated again.

"You were saying it was urgent at the restaurant. Is it something else?"

"No, it really is urgent. It's just that it doesn't have to do with my needing to get pregnant right away. You see, I'm not really married."

Jill could see genuine distress in Maryann's eyes, so she simply nodded. Let her talk.

"The fact is, I'm concerned about my health in a different way. And I'm on the trail of a story."

Jill stiffened. "There's nothing I can tell you about Madison Hospital—"

"Oh, no! It doesn't have anything to do with Madison. I'm looking for something else. And you're the only person I've run into who seems like someone who could help me."

Flattery. "At the dinner table Tuesday night, you decided I was the only one who could help you?"

"Yes. I might be wrong, but I just had a strong feeling. Actually what I guess I should have done is to offer to take you out to dinner somewhere for a private talk. But coming in here as your patient seemed just as private. And if I'm your patient, there's the doctor-patient relationship of confidentiality, isn't there?"

She looks frightened, Jill thought, and her own mistrust lessened, even as she felt some of Maryann's obvious anxiety. "Of course I can keep a confidence. But I don't see how that would relate to a television story if you're using me as a source. I think you'd better come to the point."

Maryann drew the paper robe more tightly around her body and looked down at her purse. "All right," she said. "I'm trusting you, because you're a doctor. You swore an oath when you were in medical school to protect your patients and never to do them harm, isn't that right? So even if you've sworn any other oath—"

"I told you I'd keep your problem confidential."

"O.K. I'm just worried, that's all, because I have the feeling that what I'm trying to do could get me killed. I hope you understand that."

Jill simply waited. There was nothing to be gained by pressing someone who was this frightened.

"It goes back to what you said at dinner Tuesday night. When Diana Falke came in. I said I'd seen her somewhere before, and you said the same thing. But neither of us could remember where we'd seen her. Isn't that right?"

Jill nodded.

"Well, I got this really strong emotional hunch that I wasn't *supposed* to remember where I'd seen her. When she came over and sat down and started talking to us, I was practically dying to get away from her, I felt so frightened. I hope I didn't let it show. Did you feel anything like that?"

"Not really. Just that I'd seen her somewhere recently. Nothing terribly unusual."

"All right. Now I want to ask you if you remember something else. I want to know if you've ever heard before what I'm about to say to you now."

"Go ahead."

Her dark eyes watched Jill intently as she spoke. "A member of the Gathering is a member for life."

Jill drew in her breath. Something inside her seemed to suddenly turn cold.

"You've heard it before, haven't you?" asked Maryann.

"Yes. But I don't know where. I can't remember—"

"That's it! You're not *supposed* to remember!" A fierce triumph radiated from Maryann's face. "How long have you been in?"

In her mind's eye Jill saw fire. A white-hot ball of flame, its heat parching her lungs, making her gasp. "In . . . the Gathering?" she asked, not quite comprehending what that meant. She had gone to a doctor. For treatment. But to a member. . . . And the words were there. . . .

What had they *done* to her!

"Are you taking the capsules?" Maryann reached down for her purse and got out a white capsule, held it out to her between her fingertips. "Is this what he gives you?"

The clear coating. The tiny white granules. Phillip had shown her the same thing.

There could be no doubt. Wherever Jill had been Monday night, Phillip had taken her. And the capsules were the link to Phillip. The Gathering—

Her mind spun. They had tricked her before. Was this another trick? A loyalty test? Now she could remember that she was always to keep the Gathering secret. That was the reason for the injection. And now had they sent Maryann Delvecchio to her to try to trick her into a betrayal?

What came back to her was Phillip's smoothness. His easy confidence while he had drawn her to people who threatened and attacked, who had drugged an innocent old woman like Virginia Polder. Maryann Delvecchio had none of that smoothness this afternoon. She was showing fear. As though she knew she was putting herself in danger.

Or she might be a consummate actress—

"I've never taken one of those capsules before," Jill said. "But someone once showed me one. And the same person took me to a place I can't remember."

"How many times have you gone?"

"Only once."

"Let me tell you how it went. I'll bet you got into a cab, right? And there was someone in the cab who took you someplace you already knew about and gave you an injection. Isn't that what happened? And that someone watched all the time to be certain no one was following. . . ."

Jill nodded.

"And that's all you can remember. Right?"

"That's all. The next thing I knew it was five in the morning and I was back here at the hospital."

"Why'd you go in the first place?"

"I'd been feeling sick. This friend recommended a new kind of treatment."

Maryann turned the white capsule in her palm. "Did he mention blood?"

"Erythrocytes. Red cells."

"Same thing with me. Now I'm afraid I'm hooked on this stuff. I don't know what it is, but I've been taking one every day for months now. Don't start taking it."

"My friend told me it was non-addictive."

"Famous last words, right? Let me tell you something else. I think they're screwing around with my mind in there. You see, all the time I've been going in there, I've been telling myself I could quit whenever I wanted to. And that someday I was going to do an investigative reporter number on the whole setup, whatever it is, and make myself famous forever. Daring lady reporter infiltrates secret blood cult, you know? I kept holding on to this dream, that someday I was going to put the Gathering story on the air. It was really part of me, that dream. I'd stay awake nights trying to figure out how I could somehow locate where they were. You know the feeling? I *really* wanted it."

Jill could feel Maryann's urgency. This couldn't be acting. She said she understood, and found herself trying to think how the two of them could somehow expose these people who called themselves the Gathering.

"Now here's the kicker," Maryann went on. "They had me come in Monday night. An extra time, because I think they caught on to something I was trying to use to find out where they were. And when I woke up Tuesday morning, and I thought what I always did, you know, that someday I was going to figure it out and do my big number on them, do you know what happened? I started getting these cold chills. I couldn't stop shaking. It felt like I was about to die, you know? I mean *really* about to open up the old window and sail out headfirst and no turning back, no way, really end it all. I nearly wet myself, I was so scared, and crying—"

Jill filled a paper cup with water and put it into Maryann's hand. "Just take it easy," she said. "No one here's going to hurt you."

She sipped at the water and sat up a little straighter. "Thanks. I guess you can see why I'm a little nervous about telling you all this without being sure you'll keep a secret. And if you're really into being one of the Gathering—"

"I'm not," Jill said quietly. "They tricked me into going there."

"You're for real," Maryann said after a few moments. "I can tell. I really feel like I can trust you. I mean, I had a strong hunch right from the start, but it's like now I know it's not just that you're an O.K. person. You've really got a reason to want to help me. If they tricked you."

Jill nodded. And probably a better reason than Maryann could imagine, she thought, remembering the agonizing days she had spent being afraid for her sanity.

"Anyway, that's why I think they've been screwing up my head. Somehow they found out about my dream, and now they're trying to take it away from me. Make me so scared I won't be able to do anything more to bring them out into the open. And if they can do *that* to me, if they can make me afraid of the thing I've wanted to do practically the most in my whole life—God! Just think what else they can do! I'd been wondering this whole time, ever since I started, what they got out of it, why they'd go to all this secrecy stuff just for my one hundred dollars every three weeks. And it hit me. They could be *using* me! Here

I've got a pretty good position, I mean, it's not the White House or anything, but I do influence a pretty fair number of people with what I do, and if they're controlling my head, and the heads of a lot of other people—"

"Endorphins," Jill said quietly.

"What?"

"Brain proteins. I was told that this treatment of theirs involved brain proteins. It's a new medical field. Psychopharmacology."

"You mean you know about this stuff? What they really can do to someone?"

"It's too new. Too experimental. I don't think anyone could say what the limitations are, or what the possibilities are. But there have been published reports in the medical literature. Various changes in behavior have been made." She shuddered a little as she spoke. It had sounded so promising when she had talked about it with Dr. Polder. And now, it seemed so threatening. But she couldn't allow herself to be afraid, any more than she could allow herself to make decisions on the basis of her anger at what they had done to her—

"So maybe they used those—whatever they are—on me, or maybe they gave me electric shocks or something else. The point is, I know they did something. And I know it worked. And that scares me more than anything else. To know that someone got inside my mind and made me afraid of what I've always wanted to do—I just can't take it, that's all. The thing it tells me is, I can't ever go back there. And I've got to hurry up and find out what they're doing and where they are and all the rest of it, or I'm never going to. That's why I was in such a hurry to have this talk, you see?"

"Jill nodded. "Tell me how I can help."

"All right. Here's what I did. When I had that big hunch about Diana Falke up in the restaurant Tuesday night, I decided I must have picked it up from the Gathering. So I took a big chance, and decided I was going to do it. Now or never. I got this kid who drives for me out of bed to come down to the restaurant and follow her when she came out. He's good at that; looks like a real nobody. You don't notice him when he's after you. The next day he called in sick to work and stayed on her trail. He told me she went three places. One was her apartment. Another was an office in midtown, which I checked and found out was the headquarters of that Marcus Foundation. The third place she went to, she used two cabs to get there, and got off a block away. A big building on Riverside Drive. I'd tell you the address, but I don't want you to get in trouble. In case anything happens to me and you go back there, it's better that you don't know. 'Cause if they find out that you *do* know . . ."

Jill's mouth felt dry. "I think we'd better call in the police."

Maryann shook her head. "I knew you'd say that. But think about it again. What would you say to them? And can you picture them *listening?*" Maryann struck a pose and deepened her voice. "Let me get this straight, ma'am. You went to a place, you don't know where, and something happened but you don't know what—"

"I think I could convince them they ought to investigate."

"Suppose you did. What would happen to the hospital's reputation when people found out? What would happen to that grant of yours? The minute people know you're mixed up in this—"

"The police would keep it confidential."

"Don't kid yourself. With this kind of a story, the *Daily News* would have you in the headlines two days after you talked. There are *ways* to get to police records."

"I agree it's a risk, but I think we can't hide this any longer. For all we know, the Gathering might be mixed up with these killings here at Madison—"

Maryann put a hand on Jill's wrist. "Not to worry," she said. "Of course we're going to tell the police. But not when all they have to investigate is *you*. We bring them in later, just as soon as we know where the Gathering meets. Then your name won't have to be connected. I'll take the story myself."

Jill was silent for a long moment. "How do we find out for certain?"

"If you're with me, I can prove that the place on Riverside Drive is really the Gathering." She paused. "But it means you'd have to go back there."

Jill nodded, feeling the fear crawl up the back of her neck again. You're not promising anything, she told herself. Not yet.

"The way they do it, to take you to the meetings, is they call you. They tell you to be on the corner of whatever at a certain time, and then someone meets you there and you get into a cab. Right?"

"I guess so. My friend arranged the meeting the time I went."

"O.K. This next time, will you be working with your friend?"

Jill shook her head no.

She handed Jill a card. "So they'll call you. When that happens, I want you to call this number. Don't use your own phone. I think they've got all our home phones and office phones tapped. Go to a pay phone and call this number and just say one word. 'Tonight.' Got it?"

"Tonight."

"That way I'll know that you're coming to a meeting. And I'll be somewhere across from this place on Riverside waiting for you. If I see you arrive there, or even if I miss you going in and see you coming out, we've got our proof."

Jill nodded. That *would* prove the location of their meeting place. Then, she supposed, all sorts of monitoring devices could be used. Someone from a television station would know what kind of electronics would be required.

"And one more thing. When you get inside. Like I said before, I think they had a way to find out what was in my head. And what's in your head now isn't so good for them to know. So if I were you, I'd try to get the hell away from there, and fast."

43

It was past midnight when Jill opened her eyes and heard the voice. She was on a cot in her office. Her door was closed. She had left the little reading light on when she had gone to bed, she was sure of that, but now the room was dark. And she had heard it. Down into her sleep it had come.

The whisper.

A knot of acid burned her stomach and her forehead prickled with the cold sweat of fear.

I'm back, dearie. You know I'm back.

She tried to see and could not. Her eyes hurt with the strain of staring hard into the blackness. The reading lamp, she thought, how had they turned out the lamp? How had they come in here—

In here with you.

Her body went rigid and her thoughts raced. The door was on her right. She could reach it quickly; there was nothing between her cot and the door. Outside would be the light from the hallway. If she held rigid and kept her breathing regular, whoever was in here could not know she was yet awake, and as soon as she could determine where the voice was coming from she could throw the blanket into his face and make a run for it—

Inside you, dearie.

No. It wasn't. It was *out* there in the darkness somewhere. Not inside. She could tell. It couldn't be inside.

And you know now I can cause you pain.

Behind her. Somewhere behind her.

You need them, dearie. They can help you.

Behind and to the left. The voice was back there in the darkness. In her mind's eye she saw him, the man with the dead brown eyes, playing with his knife as he sat there on her desk and whispered—

Go to them. To the Gathering. They will give you new life. The Leader can keep ME away, dearie...

Breathe. Just as though you're asleep. Her head tightened on the blanket.

You'll remember me when you wake up. You'll hear me everywhere, just like you did before. . . . Unless you go to the Leader. . . .

The bastards, she thought. I'll go to him all right, and before I go I'll call Maryann—

The phone.

Maryann had told her. They had the phones tapped. The phone was on her desk.

The voice was coming from the phone—

Had to be. No one could have walked in here, turned out the light, and then found his way across the room behind her without waking her up. God, she had woken up when the *whisper* had started, that's how lightly she'd been sleeping and no one could have gotten in here—

You don't want to die with ME, do you, do you, do you.

The light switch was to the right of the door. She stared at where it had to be. If I'm wrong, she thought, I'll be at the door anyway, and I'll scream and run like hell.

Breathe.

Off with the blanket. Lean over. Feet out.

And she was moving, two quick silent steps, three, and the wall. The switch, right where she knew it would be.

The room flooded with light.

The desk. The papers as she had left them. No one else.

New life, dearie. The Leader gives you new life. You'll hear me when you wake up, just like you did before. . . .

The phone hissed at her.

The bastards, she thought. The goddamned rotten little bastards! They were *conditioning* her! A voice in her sleep, programming her to hear voices the next day.

To make her believe that she had lost her mind.

To make her believe that only the Leader could save her.

She sat down on the edge of the cot and tried to get her breath. She would fight back. By God, she and Mary-ann *would* fight back!

The phone stayed silent.

Then she remembered. The reading light. Someone had known she was in here, or they wouldn't have started up the voice. Someone had looked in here and seen she was sleeping and turned off the reading light and told them—

Her father's voice came from the phone, rasping with pain: "It's inside me, this thing, and I can't seem to get away—"

She reached out suddenly for the phone and tore the cord from the wall socket. *Bastards!*

Into her pillow, muffling the sound, she screamed.

44

The New York City policeman stood six foot four and weighed close to 240. Nick O'Donnell tucked his shirt into his belt as he approached the man. At five foot seven, 143 pounds, Nick felt the urge to compensate for his smaller size by taking an aggressive approach. He reminded himself not to be childish. He was a reasonable man, in a reasonable position.

"I'd like to visit with Miss Pierce," he said.

"Yeah, so would I," the cop said. "But she's still unconscious."

He moved to the side as he spoke, blocking the entrance to the room. Nick could see Harriet in there, on her back, her head bandaged, eyes shut, plastic tubes inserted into her nostrils.

"I'd like to go in anyway," said Nick. "I'd like to sit beside her for a while. It may be that she can hear what's going on, you never know."

"I've got orders," said the cop. "Nobody gets in. Not until she wakes up and says who it was fractured her skull. She's an important witness."

"I'm not just anybody. I'm the budget director and assistant administrator of this hospital."

"Sounds like a good job." The cop stood where he was.

"I can write pretty well. I once wrote a letter to Commissioner Callahan, who's a personal friend of mine. The letter was about a patrolman who'd done well. He's now a captain."

"Probably he's grateful to you," said the cop.

"On the night Harriet Pierce was attacked, I was with several physicians and administrator Sanford—"

"—at a restaurant downtown, right?" The cop went on, with slightly exaggerated courtesy. "It was the Trade Center, if I'm not mistaken. The restaurant at the top of

the Trade Center. I don't recall the name, but I do remember hearing about you from two other patrolmen.
They each said a guy who said he was a hospital official
came and tried to get in here. The past two nights. With
a story about a restaurant at the top of the Trade Center.
They couldn't figure out why the guy wanted to be alone
with this unconscious nurse."

Nick kept his temper. "It's not what you think," he
said.

"I don't think anything. I just do my job."

"It might help her wake up," Nick said. "You never
know." He hesitated a moment, and then went on, "I
didn't tell the others, but it's a personal reason, why I
want to sit by her. I want to give her something."

He reached into his pocket. The cop's muscles tensed
for a moment. Then Nick produced a small box, and
opened it to reveal a diamond ring larger than the one
the cop had given his wife.

"She's my fiancée," Nick said. "I was going to give
her this when we both got off work two nights ago. I
still want her to have it."

The cop examined the ring. He looked at Nick, and
then at the sleeping figure inside the room. "Hey," he
said, giving the ring back. "I wish you'd told me before.
Go ahead on in, and let me know if she wakes up."

When Nick had gone inside, the cop used the pay
phone across the hall to make his report to Diana Falke.

45

"Just stay relaxed now," Jill said to Rachel Sanford as
she began to perform Rachel's pelvic examination. "The
thing about any internal exam is to not tighten up."

"Like labor pains," Rachel said.

"Contractions," Jill corrected. "You just try to stay
loose. You can practice your breathing now if you want."

Moments later she withdrew her hand and peeled off
the surgical glove.

"It's over?"

"All through. You're moving a bit faster than I'd anticipated. Three centimeters dilated and I'd have to say seventy-five per cent effaced. The baby's head is right down there."

The surprise showed on Rachel's face. "Is that normal?"

"Normal enough. Our 'due date' is only a statistical average. About fifty per cent of all normal babies are born before the end of forty weeks. About fifteen per cent come where you are now, at the thirty-seventh week."

"So you're saying—the baby could come any day now?"

"That's right. I've done internal exams on women in the labor room who were no further along than you. On the other hand, you could go on to the fortieth week or even two weeks beyond. I've seen that happen, too."

Rachel hesitated. "I was wondering. You know, when we established the due date. We did it on the basis of my last period, isn't that right?"

Jill said it was.

"Well I've been thinking. My last period wasn't a very big one. It was really just spotting. I've always been kind of irregular that way. Do you suppose I was already pregnant then?"

Jill held out her hand and helped Rachel get herself upright. "That's an interesting question, about your real date of conception, and it is possible to have a small amount of bleeding at the start of a completely normal pregnancy. But at this point, it's really completely a theoretical question. You've got a nice big baby in there, and your uterus is getting very well prepared to push that baby out. That's the important thing. A week from now, two weeks from now, we'll see how you're doing. Then if it looks like we ought to try to hurry things along, there are procedures we can talk about. But for now, just relax. Clean out your desk at work, get the curtains up in the baby's room and the sheets on the crib—"

"It's just so—*amazing,* you know, to think it could be happening this soon!"

"The last month is the hardest. You'll be glad to stop being pregnant, believe me."

"It's kind of scary, though. Having it all of a sudden right here, that it could happen any minute."

"You'll do just fine. You know, the staff is still talking about what a brave wife Ted has. They really were impressed, when you stood up to those reporters. They really appreciate what you did."

"Oh, that was just publicity for the hospital. And I *am* loyal to Ted. It was easy to speak up then. But this is different. I just so much want to get through it without having to be knocked out. I feel like I've—I don't know. Gone soft or something. Fresh out of courage."

"Everybody's that way. Especially with the first baby. Don't worry, we'll keep a close watch on you. You'll have lots of support."

"You're going to be here, aren't you? Not going away to some conference or anything—"

"Staying right here," said Jill. "I wouldn't miss it for all the conferences in China."

46

Blood in the eight 25-ml flasks shone softly under the fluorescent "nature" bulbs in the ceiling lamps of Malcolm Lockwood's personal laboratory. The red surface of each flask seemed to Lockwood to glow with promise, as if he could already see the thinly distributed protein molecules he would extract from the remainder of the blood. Lockwood would spend the next two hours on concentrated work, a well-established routine of centrifuging away the red cells, washing the serum, filtering the serum, dissolving the filtrate in Ringer's solution and washing again, and so on through the fourteen steps necessary to separate omicron-endorphin from the rest of the blood Lockwood had taken out of the Gathering members.

Then it would be time to meet the evening's Gathering, and take more blood from them.

It was a necessity for Lockwood to work alone. To allow another to work with him would mean making another person aware of the amount of blood extracted from each member during the "confessional" period—an amount very nearly equal to that infused at the end, during the "conditioning" period of the visit when the first scopolamine derivative had worn off and the second had not yet been administered. During conditioning some memory was desirable, according to the needs of the individual. It was good for them to remember receiving the extra blood, for so many of them really believed that the additional red cells protected them from any ill effects of the white capsules and made them strong again.

For someone to know that the net gain of red cells to any one member was relatively insignificant would undermine that someone's faith in the Gathering. And that someone could undermine the faith of others, producing an untenable situation.

So the Leader had to do his laboratory work unassisted. The sacrifices he had to make were considerable, but the rewards, when he had fully developed the synthesizing process for the omicron-endorphin, would justify his efforts. To attain those rewards, he needed to keep the blood coming in—from the outside, to give to the Gathering members, and from the Gathering members themselves, when they were under hypnosis, to provide him with yet more omicron-endorphin. He was analyzing that material to determine it's components and molecular configuration. Preliminary efforts to learn the composition of omicron had looked promising.

Then he would synthesize the compound.

The process took time, especially working alone, but that time was completely justifiable. Synthetic omicron was not essential to the help he had promised the general; it would only make that help easier to guarantee. Lockwood had other ways to influence his people. Far better to use another month or two, even longer, than to risk letting a laboratory or a colleague understand the nature of the material Lockwood was working with.

The centrifuge tubes each held 25 cc. Lockwood poured the blood from each of the flasks into the matching centrifuge tubes, balancing the load of the machine by placing the filled tubes opposite one another. Then he covered the machine and switched it on. It hummed quietly as it whirled the tubes at 2,000 rpm, separating the components of the blood by forcing the more dense elements to the bottom of the tube. Lockwood checked his watch and thought again of the difficulties he was having with his two primary Guardians, Garrett and Falke.

As he was shutting off the centrifuge the telephone buzzer sounded. Lockwood disliked being interrupted when he was in the lab, but he was wise enough not to isolate himself completely. He knew well how essential he was to the organization he had created; the more so because of the need for secrecy. To nearly four hundred people, the face and voice of Malcolm Lockwood were all they remembered of the Gathering beyond a vague impression of a blood infusion and a white capsule that they took each morning. He, Lockwood, *was* the Gathering. If he did not function, literally nothing would happen. Nothing *could* happen. The Gathering would cease to exist, its members not knowing why, or how, or even if it would ever begin again. All they would know would be that three weeks had gone by, and that the phone call they had been expecting had not come. None but Falke and Garrett even knew the location of their meeting place.

Of course, Lockwood had no intention of leaving the members uncalled until he had synthesized omicron-endorphin. And probably not even then, for most of them. Because most of the Gathering members were very well-placed people, and their positions and influence would then be of steadily increasing value to Malcolm Lockwood. And to the general if Lockwood continued to support him, or to someone else in the political system who could be made to share Lockwood's vision of a new social order. So much could be done. . . .

He picked up the phone. He heard the voice of Diana Falke. "I'm just outside," she said. "I'd like to talk with you about Garrett. I want to replace him with Avery today."

Lockwood's handsome features showed his distaste for both the idea and the interruption. But his voice did not. "Wait," he said. "I'll come to you."

She was standing beside the videotape screen in the workroom. When she saw him she came forward, holding out a leaflet. On the leaflet was a crude sketch of a face that slightly resembled Matthew Garrett's.

"I picked this up at Madison Hospital today," she said. "From the desk of a team of security guards. They were distributing them to anyone who cared to pick one up."

Lockwood's eyes were on her. "Why were you at Madison Hospital?"

"To see people." She smiled, watching him. "Are you wondering *which* people?"

"You're like a child, Diana. You want to assert yourself, so you pretend to disobey and hope that I'll become upset enough to repeat my order that our Madison people are not to be contacted. Then you can say that you think that order is foolish, that it is much more of a risk to allow Garrett outside when these leaflets are in the hands of the police. When you have made your childish points, you plan to say that you have not disobeyed after all and make me feel foolish for imagining that my authority had been challenged. When are you going to grow up?"

She made a face at him and took back the leaflet. Then she opened her purse and took out a cigarette and lit it. "I went to Madison for the Marcus Foundation," she said. "As a concerned official, wanting to see for myself whether the media hysteria has any foundation in fact. I can tell you that it does. When I met with the foundation board this afternoon, I told them that the reports of the media had greatly exaggerated the problem."

She paused, drew smoke into her lungs, and exhaled, slowly. Lockwood sat on one of the white plastic swivel chairs and watched her.

"The foundation *will* be giving the grant to Dr. Jill Weston for her obstetrical center," she went on. "The final arrangements with the consultants will be made over the weekend. Monday night there will be a meeting at which I will not be present, and the board will vote unanimously in favor of a grant of two hundred thousand dollars. Formal notification will be made the following morning."

The leader seemed amused. "Two hundred thousand. I'd been wondering about that figure of three million."

"We're calling it 'seed money.' And they'll take it. They're desperate."

"And you won't have parted with nearly as much if Dr. Weston doesn't choose to cooperate. Very prudent."

"It's my money," she said, and looked at him.

"It is indeed."

"I've given you enough of it."

"Indeed you have. You've given me enough so that I now have my own, enough to continue here for as long as I need to without any more assistance from you. So if you're about to try to persuade me that your money should be buying you more influence here, spare yourself the effort."

She held her ground. "You know very well that Garrett is incompetent. And if that nurse wakes up when one of our own people isn't around, he could be identified. You're only being stubborn. And you also know that I fully deserve to have more say in operations. You yourself said I would begin my own Gathering someday."

"But there can be only one Leader, Diana."

She looked at him, silent.

"I wonder if you remember a wealthy young girl, Diana. A very unhappy young girl, who had run away to a small seacoast resort because she was very unhappy—"

"Stop it," said Diana Falke.

"—very unhappy over something she had done to her parents when everyone thought she was in her school dormitory, forty miles away from where they were sleeping—"

"I asked you to *stop!*"

"—very unhappy, but also very proud, and very frightened, too frightened to come out of her room, too frightened even to keep herself clean—"

Diana Falke closed her eyes, and bowed her head. Her posture reminded the Leader of Matthew Garrett, the morning he had first come across him in a Maryland Veteran's Administration hospital. After three years of electric shock and Thorazine the hospital staff had given up on Garrett and told Lockwood he was welcome to perform whatever procedures he wanted to test out. After four days of testing and a week of Lockwood's chemicals, Garrett had been well enough to escape. He, too, would never leave his Leader.

"Garrett will drive the limousine tonight, as usual," Lockwood said. "We'll have him wear the mirrored glasses. No one will recognize him. And you'll stay away from the young Dr. Avery so you don't become unhappy anymore."

47

Jill had kept the door to her office open all day Thursday and Friday when she was working there. When it was time to sleep, she headed for the south wing of the eighth floor, Obstetrics, where there were three empty labor rooms, each with two beds. Thursday night had been fine, the most rest she'd had in weeks, it seemed, but Friday a nineteen-year-old with narrow hips and no training in breathing exercises had come in at 10 P.M. Jill wasn't her obstetrician, but she heard every scream until 3:17 A.M., when she finally gave up and decided to move upstairs to the surgeons' lounge.

She woke up on the couch Saturday morning at 7:35 with her back aching in three places, and decided she was being foolish to stay away from her own apartment.

Downstairs in her office she changed to street clothes.

Coming out the front entrance, she met Jerry Chamberlain.

"I don't believe it!" he said. "Here I thought I was getting in early on a Saturday, and you've already come in and finished up!"

He had on his blue hat and the morning sunshine was in his face under the narrow brim, making him squint. The wind was coming in off the East River, cold. Jill zippered her ski jacket. Her hands were shaking as she jammed them into her pockets. She felt tired and chilled and not like going to her apartment alone at all.

"Are you in a big rush just now?" she asked him.

He shook his head no. Coming in out of habit, he told her.

"I wonder, then. I need to change the lock on my apartment. Or maybe just put on an extra one. Do you know anything about locks?"

"Do I? Hey, you're talking to an expert."

"They're in the L. L. Bean catalogue?"

"They're in Toro's Hardware, Bay Ridge, Brooklyn. Where I did my apprentice and journeyman work, I'll have you know."

"You used to be a locksmith?"

"Summers, sixth and seventh grade. Best delivery boy Toro ever had. Come on with me, kid, I'll fix you right up."

The hardware store on her block wasn't open until 8:30, so Jerry bought her coffee.

That was when she told him why she needed the new lock. She didn't tell him everything; just that somebody had broken in and tapped her office phone with a two-way bug that woke her up at night, and she was sure they'd done the same thing at her apartment.

He decided they should take the phone apart first thing when they came in, disconnecting it at the jack before either of them spoke.

He sat on her bed. With the screwdriver set he had bought along with the drill set and lock at the hardware store, he unscrewed the metal plate from the bottom of the phone. Then he rummaged around inside, and finally pulled out a black metal box about half the size of a pack of cigarettes. The box had two wires protruding from one end.

"Power pack," he said. "With this thing, someone could have a receiver not too far away and hear everything that was going on in your room, even when you weren't using the phone. Handy little gadget."

Then he unscrewed the mouthpiece and the earpiece from the receiver. From behind each of the phone-company speakers he removed a small silver-plated disc. One of the discs had wires; the other did not.

"They had you hooked up pretty thoroughly," he said. "They could pipe sound in and out of *both* ends. Give a more realistic effect. Like a miniature stereo."

Jill stood beside the bed, feeling sick with anger and frustration. "They can't hear us now?" she asked.

"Nope." Jerry reached for the message pad and pencil Jill kept on her bedside table. "Nope, we've cleaned it right out. They can't hear a thing." He scribbled on the pad as he talked. Then he showed her what he had written.

MAYBE. I'M GOING TO LOOK AROUND SOME MORE, IF YOU DON'T MIND.

"That's good," Jill said. "It'll be such a relief to be able to *sleep* for a change."

She lay down on the bed as he reassembled the phone and plugged it back into the socket.

"Have a listen," he said, handing her the receiver. "Hear that dial tone? Works just fine without the extra parts."

"Thanks," she said. "You know, this really is a help. I just wish I'd done it sooner."

He took the phone back. "Let's have some radio music. Celebrate, you know?" He pushed the button on her Sony and the voice of the all-news station she used as her alarm in the mornings came into the room.

"Just as good," he said, quietly. "It'll serve the same purpose. Why don't you just take it easy there while I have a look around?"

She closed her eyes.

When she awoke, the radio was off. He was sitting at the foot of her bed, holding something in each hand.

"Hi," he said. "Don't worry. You don't talk in your sleep, and you don't snore, and it's only one-fifteen. You've got a whole afternoon ahead of you if you need to get some work done."

She sat up in bed. He had covered her with a blanket. "Hi," she said, getting her bearings. "How long have you been sitting there?"

"About five minutes. I just got finished putting on the lock. I think what woke you up was the quiet all of a sudden."

She saw his hands were full. "What are those?"

He held up another of the black boxes, this one larger, and connected with wires to a thick black metal disc about the size of a silver dollar. The disc had holes in it. Looking closer, she saw that the wires now were cut.

"Another little sender-receiver package," he said. "Did you ever hear voices when you were in the living room? This was taped to the frame of your couch."

She shuddered, remembering. Months ago. She had run screaming from her bedroom and curled up on the sofa

with a blanket, and the whispers had begun again. . . .
"I'm glad you found that," she said. Her voice felt weak.

"If you think that's nasty, take a look at this." He
handed her a small cylinder, clear plastic tinted blue,
about the size of a fruit-juice glass. The label said Insta-
pure. She recognized it. The filter element from the water purifier she had put onto the tap in the kitchen.

"My water filter," she said. She looked at the paper in
the bottom half. Not dirty yet. "Is there something wrong
with it? It looks clean."

"Remember when we first started jogging? You told me
you used to feel weak all the time, couldn't get your
breath, headaches and so on?"

She stared at the filter. "I remember."

"Take a look at the top half of that filter."

She did. The white crystals looked fairly clean, except
for a few traces of sediment—

Then she knew. She remembered first putting in the
new filter. Turning on the tap and letting it run for a
half minute, so the black charcoal filings that had come
loose inside could be washed away.

"My God," she whispered. "There's supposed to be
activated *charcoal* in here. And these are *white* crystals—"

She was trembling now, trying to control the fear that
was flooding through her. She had let Phillip come in
here, and they had deliberately, systematically set out
to drive her *insane,* to give her *poison*—

She bit her lip and gave the filter back. Phillip was
dead. She made herself stop shaking. "What do you think
is in here?" she asked.

"We can take it into the lab and have it analyzed,
if you like," he said. "But I remember from my pharmacology text. If we look at your symptoms and generalize,
we're really talking about cytotoxic hypoxia. So I'd guess
we're looking at crystals of sodium cyanide. The water
comes through the filter element and dissolves a little bit
each time, and you're drinking a dilute solution of hydro-
cyanic acid. Not enough to kill you or send you into convulsions, unless you're drinking really a large quantity,
but enough to make you feel generally pretty rotten. Whoever it was that got in here and did this didn't have your
best interests at heart."

She shuddered again. Then she got up from the bed and came over and sat down next to him.

"Jerry," she said. "I really thought I was going crazy in here. I really did. How can I ever thank you?"

He blushed. Covered up with a shrug. "No sweat, Silver Shoes. Seriously, if you'd have just called in the police, they'd have found the same things. Probably quicker too. I'm just glad to help."

"I mean it. I want to thank you."

"Wellll . . ." He looked up to the ceiling. "Maybe one of these weekends you might want to show me how the camping's really done up there in the upstate territory. I'd appreciate a little guidance."

"You've got it. Name your weekend."

"I think you better wait a bit before we set any dates, to tell you the truth," he said. "And you'll figure it out for yourself in a minute. We ought to wait until this thing clears up. Until they catch whoever it is that's been after you with these things."

"I think I know the one who did this to my apartment," she said. "He was in a car accident Monday night. Somebody killed him."

"Nice people."

She nodded. "I trusted him."

"Now you're trusting me," he said.

"I am."

"But you wait awhile, O.K.? You said someone was still around the hospital. Someone got into your office the other night. Right?"

"Right."

"O.K., now use your New York paranoia and you'll see what I'm getting at."

She saw. And was afraid again. "You're in the hospital too," she managed to say. "But that's ridiculous. You wouldn't be helping me—"

"That's what you say now. But later, you're going to remember how the other guy probably helped you. And you're going to wonder how I knew to look around for this stuff. And no matter what I say you're never going to be sure until they find whoever it is that's after you and put him away. So we'll just take it easy for a while, all right? And then, if it's going anywhere between the two of us, it'll be able to go the way it ought to. And you can look back on this afternoon and know for sure that old Jerry wasn't giving you the best double-reverse con-number you've heard all year."

For a long moment she stared at him. A feeling came to her from way back, from the first time she'd ever flown, up in a little Piper Cub two-seater at five thousand feet with the wind in her face, screaming at the pilot how terrific it was to be flying, screaming because she was only ten and the pilot was her father. The feeling had come when she looked down at the clear blue lake beneath them and the pointed green tops of the pine trees around the shoreline and heard the motor cough, felt the bottom start to drop out as the plane stalled and her father struggled to get the engine going again. For a moment fear emptied the pit of her stomach and she wanted to cry, but then something else filled her and she had two simultaneous thoughts: one, that if she was going to die she would damn well do it as well as anyone; and, two, that she had never felt quite so grown up before. When the engine caught and her father turned around she had been grinning, reaching up to pat him on the back.

Now she felt the same. Maybe it was fatalism, maybe it was fatigue and despair and foolishness masquerading as courage, but she knew what she felt.

"To hell with it," she heard herself saying. "You've got to trust somebody."

She reached out and took his hand. He felt warm. His clear blue eyes waited, questioning, for only a moment before he kissed her.

"Silver Shoes," he whispered.

She clung to him, savoring the delicious urgency that began to fill her, comforted at the thought that she hadn't lost her feelings for love, that this would all be waiting for her sometime soon when she was free of the Gathering, that she could let go and lose herself. . . .

Then she held him away, studying his face. "Listen to this, for a minute," she said. "A member of the Gathering is a member for life."

The blue eyes blinked, looked puzzled. "What kind of talk is that?"

"Just testing," she said. "The Gathering are the people who tapped my phones and poisoned my water."

"Sounds like a slimy bunch." He drew her close.

She took another look at his face, and then kissed him again. "But there are so many other things to think about," she whispered after a while. "So many better things."

Several hours later Jerry Chamberlain walked into the Madison Hospital Blood Bank.

Marcie was behind her desk. When she saw him she came around and closed the door. Her pink lab smock was open, revealing a low-cut denim blouse, with an attractive curve of breasts underneath.

"There's no one else here," she said, and came closer, looking up with an I-want-to-be-kissed innocence in her brown eyes.

Jerry held her chin while his lips brushed hers, lightly at first, and then with passion.

Then he spoke. "I was with Jill Weston," he said. "I took the electronics out of her apartment this morning."

"She trusts you?"

Jerry nodded. "And you'd better pass the word along. She's got some plan that she thinks is going to turn the tables on the Leader."

"You found out what it was?"

"No. Maybe I will later."

"Fantastic," she said.

And kissed him again.

48

Diana Falke switched off the tape recorder, and the voices of Jill Weston and Jerry Chamberlain were silenced. She looked across the workroom at the Leader. "It's only love sounds from here on," she said. "Meaningless, until at the end before he leaves. I'll move it forward."

"Not necessary," said Malcolm Lockwood. "I've already heard it."

Surprised, Diana Falke stood up. "How did you know to listen?"

"I didn't. But when I came into the workroom this

afternoon I saw the tape connected to her apartment was moving. I knew it was a voice-activated microphone we had put in, so the conclusion that she had returned and was talking to someone was obvious. I didn't expect that someone to be your other star recruit, though I suppose I should have. She'd mentioned him when she was here. Rather too bad. They both turn out to be disloyal."

"You just know everything, don't you," she said.

"They were your recruits. Yours and Marcie's, anyway. I suppose you have a right to feel resentful that they failed. But don't turn your resentment toward me."

"So sure of yourself, but in this case you're wrong. Do you want to know why I know you're wrong?"

Lockwood leaned forward, resting his elbows on the control panel across from her. "Of course, Diana," he said. "Tell me."

"Because I know that Dr. Chamberlain is *not* disloyal. After this conversation with Weston, he went directly to Marcie and reported to her. He told her what he'd done, and he also told her what Weston had said about having a plan to identify us. More than that, he offered to try to learn more about her plan, and to pass the information along to us."

Lockwood appeared interested. "That's quite impressive," he said.

"I think it is. And I hope it makes you think again about some other opinions I've tried to get across to you."

He nodded. "Marcie told you all that, did she?"

"No. She told Avery."

"And Avery told you."

She met his gaze without faltering. "Yes, he did. I know that you told me I was to have no contact with Avery. But I had a very strong feeling that I should have his report for this week."

"So you saw him."

"I saw him. And the information I got from him proves that I was *right* to see him. Otherwise both of us would think that Dr. Chamberlain was a traitor, and we'd lose a man who is in a very good position to help us. Particularly now, with Weston obviously disloyal."

"I assume you were careful after you saw Avery. I assume you took the usual precautions to see that no one followed you here."

"Of course I did." There was triumph in her eyes. "And

no one followed me. So there's no harm done, and a great deal gained."

"We'll have to bring Weston in." The Leader's voice was softer, musing, as though thinking aloud rather than giving orders. "We'll have to examine her and find out what plan she has."

"I agree," said Diana Falke.

"Monday night."

"Yes. And I think Avery should be the one to bring her in."

The Leader shifted his weight slightly in his chair. As he moved, his right hand brushed against one of the switches on the control panel and moved it to the On position. "Yes," he said. "You've expressed that opinion before. Can you tell me as fully as possible now why you recommend Avery?"

She sat up a bit straighter, pleased at the note of respect in his voice. "I can put it very simply," she said. "Roger Avery represents what the Gathering stands for so much better than Garrett. He is intelligent, and Garrett is scarcely capable of a conversation. Avery has a position of his own, a good position considering he's only beginning his medical career, and Garrett is a recluse, totally dependent on what he gets from us. There's even the matter of physical appearance. When the members see Garrett, I'm certain they recoil inside, as I do. Avery is much better-looking. At least he looks like an intelligent human being."

"I thought the only objection you had to Matthew Garrett was because of the security problem at Madison. I had no idea you felt *that* strongly."

"You never let me tell you."

The Leader nodded in acknowledgment that she was correct, and Diana Falke felt the pleasure of victory more keenly.

"What would you like to do with Matthew Garrett?" the Leader asked.

"He's of no use to us anymore," she said. "When you consider the security question, he's a definite liability. Yet he has eight quarts of blood in him that our members might profit from."

"Interesting suggestion," the Leader said quietly. Then a bit louder: "I wonder how it makes you feel, Matthew?"

Diana Falke stepped back and stared at him. "Mat-

thew," she whispered. She looked down at the panel, at
the open switch. "You didn't . . ." she began, but the
Leader's voice overrode hers.

"Why don't you come down here, Matthew, and show
Diana just how you feel about her suggestion."

Diana Falke turned, and fled.

As she was almost to the front entrance of the building,
Garrett met her.

He had his knife with him.

He felt bad afterward, because he had not had specific
instructions to kill her. As they were disposing of Falke's
body in the dissection room, he told the Leader how bad
he felt.

The Leader assured him that he would make Garrett
feel better again.

49

It *was* Riverside Drive. They had the side windows of the
limousine blocked off with pleated gray plastic, but Jill
could see out the front, through the windshield, and there
was no mistaking it, the Hudson on the right, and closer,
the rolling hills and hollows of the Riverside Park land.
They were heading south. Jill recognized the silhouette of
the monument to the World War dead, the tight circle of
stone columns that looked like a Greek temple the last
time she had seen it. Tonight it looked like a shadowed
ruin, because someone had broken the streetlamps on that
block. Probably the temple was full of broken glass by
now. Jill felt the limousine slowing, and thought how
ironic it was that the Gathering should be down here on
Riverside Drive somewhere in the Eighties, only a few
blocks away from where Phillip had parked his Ferrari
the day he had taken her to the Seventy-ninth Street Boat
Basin to see his new yacht. Or cruiser, or whatever one
was supposed to call it. She wondered if Phillip had even
suspected what else was in the neighborhood as he told

her what a great life it was for him and how much fun she could have if only she'd loosen up and quit being such an idealist.

She shook her head at the memory, her hands on her purse, with the keys and the papers that had come in the package when she had opened her mail on Saturday. She winced, recalling the letter. Phillip had been so . . . she did not quite know the word. Maudlin, maybe. Pathetic, certainly. So convinced that he was going to be killed soon, so determined to locate her and explain, so eager to try to make things right with this last, foolish gesture. As though Jill had wanted the boat. As though the keys and ownership papers to a forty-eight-foot yacht could make up for trying to *poison* her, for trying to drive her *insane.* . . .

Her nails were digging into her palms. She took a deep breath, tried to relax. That was over. What Phillip had done to her was over. And he had tried to do the right thing, at the end. Tried to explain, she supposed; that was probably why she had been in the car with him at the time of the accident. Also, to give Phillip his due, he probably loved that boat more than anything else that he possessed. So to sign it over to her as a token of his sincerity . . .

Crap, she thought. Knowing Phillip, there were probably installment payments due on the boat, and docking charges, and insurance, and whatever else people paid for to keep the things afloat. He was probably unloading it onto her. Or maybe he was, and maybe he wasn't, but she had no time now for charitable thoughts for Phillip, or for any other member of the Gathering. She had a job to do. Stay with the limousine without making the driver at all suspicious, and then when they were going in to whatever place it was, make certain she was visible enough for Maryann Delvecchio to spot her.

Really, she thought, sitting up to look out through the windshield again, really they couldn't have asked for a better place. On the right the cars were parked in a solid line, giving plenty of cover for Maryann to wait, and then beyond the cars, on the other side of the sidewalk, was the blackened stone wall at the edge of the park. Maryann could be waiting crouched behind the wall until she saw a car approach, and then she could get up and look through the windows of one of the parked cars as Jill

got out. The site was perfect. Things were really in her
favor now. Ever since Saturday, when she had met Jerry
and changed her luck. No, she thought, that was wrong,
what she'd done before that on Saturday was to decide to
go to her apartment. To take some action. That was what
had changed her luck. If she hadn't done that, she might
still be hiding out in the hospital, or riding here in the
limousine scared stiff instead of confident, knowing that
she had friends she could trust, and that she had resources.

She hefted the purse again. That, she supposed, was
the final irony: that she had brought along Phillip's keys
to the boat basin docks and the yacht. Just a hunch, but
Maryann *had* said Riverside Drive, and there was the
distinct possibility that if she was right, it would be very
useful to have somewhere nearby to run to, somewhere
safe, somewhere that could be locked and even, if it came
to that, driven away, or piloted, or whatever it was that
boating people called it when you roared off into the
night. Jill felt oddly calm about the prospect of steering
the big thing on the cold river, but after all she had driven
it—*steered* it—once before without cracking up. To try
the same thing in the dark wouldn't be much harder, and
even maybe, now that she thought about it, kind of fun,
kind of an adventure—

No.

She would have to watch it. The injection they had
given her was making her loosen up, feel relaxed, and
overconfident. Euphoric, even. Diazepam, they had said,
but that was crap, because diazepam didn't produce euphoria like this, and anyway what she knew, and what
Maryann Delvecchio had known too, was that the business of calling the injection a mild tranquilizer was all
lies, that it wasn't sedation the Gathering was after, it
was amnesia, so whatever had been in that hypodermic
back in the taxi had been an amnesiac, probably scopolamine, that old standby from the belladonna alkaloid
group, known to every obstetrician since 1910, but more
likely than not compounded with something else, some
sort of CNS stimulant, to cut the sense of drowsiness
usually accompanying a therapeutic dosage. With a start
Jill realized that her mouth was dry and her vision
slightly blurred—just what to expect with scopolamine—
and her mind was clearly racing because it had seemed

like forever and yet here they still were, cruising slowly down the drive and she could see the chauffeur had his left-turn blinker on now so it would be any minute, and then, up ahead on the right, she saw a woman standing on the sidewalk, fumbling with her keys at the door handle of one of the parked cars.

A woman with curly hair. Black curly hair, plainly visible under the streetlamp.

Maryann Delvecchio.

What in the world was she doing? Why was she *showing* herself like this?

Then Jill saw the chauffeur, a big man with broad shoulders that stretched the fabric of his gray uniform, and mirrored sunglasses under his chauffeur's cap, saw him pick up a little plastic box from on top of the dash and press the button, and start to cut the wheel, and when she looked left, where they were about to turn, she saw a big building with a garage, and the garage door was starting to rise.

They were going to drive in. Then the door would close behind them.

Maryann would never see a thing, never know Jill had been here—

The window.

Jill moved to her right, and slid back the plastic curtain, moved her face right up against the glass as the limousine swung around, looked straight at Maryann, but the light from the streetlamp was in her eyes and she was blurring a little still from the scopolamine and it happened so quickly that she wasn't at all certain Maryann had seen.

"Hey," said the driver. "You're not to touch the side curtain. You were told that."

"I thought I saw someone." Jill stared hard at the mirror-eyes in the chauffeur's rearview mirror, a huge thing nearly a foot wide, the better to see her with, she supposed, trying to convince both of them that she wasn't afraid. "Someone in the park. It looked to me like they were hurt."

"It's not your concern," he said.

"But I'm a doctor. Didn't you know that? When someone's hurt, it *is* my concern."

She got a good look at the number on the front of the house as they nosed into the garage. Two big eights.

Eighty-eight. If she could remember Oldsmobile, or eating, or anything else like that the next time she saw Maryann . . .

But she wouldn't. She knew that. No more would come to her when she tried to remember the next time than had come back before, which was exactly nothing unless you counted the slogan about members of the Gathering and the face of the man who called himself the Leader. The injection had worked on her once, and it would work again. If it was scopolamine, it would be blocking the memory formation right there at the synapse level, interfering with the basic electrical impulse, with the conductivity of the acetylcholine—

". . . when you are here, the Gathering takes precedence," he was saying. "I'll have to report the incident."

And she knew what she had to do. She put it on, the attitude of the outraged New York consumer. "Report?" She made her voice shrill. " 'Report the incident'? What do you think this is, some sort of prison camp? I've come here for *treatment* tonight, and you're talking to me as though you were the Gestapo. No way, buster! You don't talk to a patient like that and get away with it!"

"I have my orders," he said, and brought the limousine to a stop inside the garage. He pressed two more buttons on his little plastic control bar. The lights in the garage came on. And behind her, Jill could hear garage door closing.

"Oh, 'orders' is it? Somebody may be bleeding to death out there in the park and you're talking about your orders? I don't want to hear about your orders. In fact, I've changed my mind about tonight. I don't want to stay here any longer."

"You'll have to discuss that with the Leader."

"I'll do no such thing! You can't force me to stay here against my will!" She pulled at the door handle on her right, in her mind's eye picturing how she would slip under the closing garage door just at the last second and run across the street to join Maryann.

The handle wouldn't move. She was locked in. She tried to pull up the locking button, but couldn't budge it. Then the window. It wouldn't open.

In front of her, the driver was turning around.

And she saw. Through the plexiglass, as he turned,

she caught a profile, the face behind the mirrored glasses.

The dead brown eyes.

The man with the knife.

"Try the other door," he said.

Willing her hand not to shake, Jill opened it. The door didn't swing out from the back, the way they did on most cars. The hinge was at the rear side, so that the door swung open from the center column, blocking the path to the back of the car.

Or to the back of the garage.

And here, she saw, the Gathering had refined the trap still further. The car door opened directly into an open corridor leading inside the building. So you had no choice. Either you went inside, or you stayed in the car.

A red carpet in the corridor. The man with the knife, beckoning her to walk.

50

Maryann stayed behind the parked cars on the sidewalk and walked away as quickly as she could without attracting attention, because she was afraid they were watching her from the window. Jesus, she thought, I really did it this time, I mean this is *it*, I was *right*, it's time for the story of the *year*, all I have to do is say the word to the station and they'll give me what I need to start the surveillance, maybe rent an apartment across the street, use shotgun mikes, send in repairmen to fix the electricity.

She thought, Get it wrapped up in a week or two, maybe less.

Thought, a sensation. Work our way through to the drug connection, get the cops to go in with a warrant; they return the favor and we follow them in with the cameras.

Thought. That chauffeur. And then Jill had opened her window to show herself. . . .

Jill Weston. In there. What if something happened to

her? What if tomorrow when Maryann called her she
wasn't there? Missing. Not heard from.

Go to the cops. Get a warrant, follow the cops in with
cameras . . .

It didn't play. Maryann didn't want to be the one to
say she had used Jill, put her in danger, talked her into
going there as a stalking horse. Hell. Maryann didn't want
Jill Weston in that house no matter *who* had talked her
into going there.

Should have thought of that before, she had to admit
it, should have figured something about the risk, but
how was she to know they were going to *see* her? That
she had to stand out there making herself visible, watching the limousine drive in and out of the garage, its windows blocked off, and her not knowing who was inside, if
Jill had even come in yet or not until the very end when
Jill had seen her and made her move. . . .

She turned up the collar of her trench coat and walked
across the drive at Eighty-fourth Street, heading for the
van. No more shoulda's, coulda's, woulda's, she told herself. Jill Weston was in there, and it was up to Maryann to
get her out. Or to give it the old Channel Six try, anyway.

If she played it right, she might still have herself a
story.

51

The Leader had one palatial consulting room, Jill thought,
as the door closed behind her. Antique furnishings, good
ones, too, highly polished, with leather-bound books all
the way up to the ceiling and even a ladder on a
wheeled track built into the shelves all around the four
walls, to make it easy to reach any of the books on the
upper levels. Green carpeting, heavy brass lamps on the
end tables—

The maddening thing was that it looked so *unfamiliar*.

If they had brought her to this building the last time, Jill thought, they would probably have brought her in here first. She had hoped that seeing part of the building would trigger associations with the rest, and that possibly, in the course of her last visit, she would have noticed a way out, an unguarded door or elevator or some other means of escape. But now, nothing. The room offered no memories, no clues to what she had already seen but could not recall.

But there was a pen on the desk. And she was alone. She could write down the address. Write it small, somewhere they wouldn't see it. But it would have to be somewhere *Jill* would see it, because if she didn't it would do her no good, because there was no way she was going to remember writing anything at all tomorrow morning when she woke up.

She decided on the underside of her shoe, where the sole met the heel. She was only a few feet away from the desk and reaching for the pen when the door opened behind her.

The Leader.

She knew his face at once, just the one she remembered. Noble bone structure, perfect complexion, dark eyes you could tell all your troubles to, a shining white smile that would make you forget anything had ever been wrong. For a long moment she wavered, almost not believing that this man could possibly have had anything to do with the attacks on her, the attack on Dr. Polder, the poison in her apartment. . . .

"Hello, Dr. Weston," he said. His voice was warm. "Won't you have a seat? Make yourself comfortable."

He went behind his desk as she stared at him, still undecided about what she would say.

Then she saw the file.

A neat white folder, white like the color of his tailored jumpsuit, with a label fixed to the index tab. She caught the name on the label as he sat down.

WESTON.

The file was nearly an inch thick. She had been here for only one visit. How could they possibly have accumulated that much data on her in only one visit?

The answer was obvious. They had been building that file on her before she had ever called them.

So all the rest was true.

And then, probably, what Phillip had said in his letter was also true. Which would mean that they had killed him.

"Please," the Leader said, indicating the French provincial love seat beside her. "Do try to relax. I understand you had some difficulty with Matthew."

"Matthew?"

"The man who drove you here. He said you were unhappy when you arrived. Did something go wrong?"

She wanted to come out with it then, to tell him what had gone wrong was that he'd had the foresight to put in a garage or buy a building with a garage and use it, so that Maryann, waiting across the street, wouldn't be able to identify the place for certain; she really for a moment or two considered doing just that, confessing it all to him and throwing herself on his friendly smile and merciful eyes, and then something inside her whispered that she'd already had an injection to loosen her up and he'd probably done something to her the last time she'd been here to make her feel even more trusting when she was in his presence, and if she had any brains at all she ought to know there was only one way to play it.

The way she had begun.

"I really don't want to sit down," she said. "I want to go home. I've changed my mind about taking a treatment tonight."

He nodded. Made no move.

"The man in the car was rude to me. I don't like people to give me orders as though they were prison guards and I was some sort of felon. Do you understand that?"

He nodded, at ease behind the desk, hands clasped loosely, fingers interlocked and extended, making a cradle for his chin.

"Aren't you going to say anything?"

He smiled. "Just hearing you out, Doctor. I don't want to influence your decisions in any way. I want to have you feel free to tell me everything. Everything that went wrong, everything that you did not like about your treatment, even going back to the time of your last visit. You see? It's the only way we can work together, by being completely open. I need your evaluation, your honest evaluation of the treatment, if I'm to be able to do what's best for you on this visit. And of course that treatment includes every facet of our organization, including a driver who's rather obsessed with protecting the privacy of this clinic and its patients. If he offended you, I'm genuinely sorry."

"So am I. It spoiled my evening. It changed my whole attitude tonight. I had come here thinking of this place as a kind of haven, a retreat where I could find people who cared about me, who wanted to help me, and then, all of a sudden, when I saw someone outside who appeared to need help, your driver started talking to me as if it was his personal duty to be a disciplinarian—"

Her voice was rising and she stopped, clearing her throat, hoping she sounded authentic. But at the back of her mind came the nagging fear that this man could see inside of her, that he could somehow know her thoughts, that he could easily distinguish between the shrillness in the voice born of honest indignation and the shrillness that came from being afraid she was about to be found out.

"Anyway," she said, "I don't want to get emotional about it again. I just want to go home. Perhaps another night I'll be in more of a receptive frame of mind, and we can make progress then."

He nodded politely, and she thought, He's taken the bait, he's really going to let me go, and then he spoke, casually, taking his time. "Matthew seemed concerned. He thought that perhaps you might have been passing some sort of a signal to the young woman waiting across the street from here."

Jill kept her face set in its self-righteous look. "I don't care what he thought. I'm not coming here to be concerned about his thoughts. You people are supposed to be concerned about *me!*"

"And we are. Of course we are, but you'll appreciate our position too, I hope. You know the kind of work we're doing here. Being in the medical profession, you of all people ought to appreciate the need for secrecy when a research area such as brain proteins is involved. I can tell you we've had no end of trouble keeping people away who want to learn what we're discovering—people from the drug companies, people from the military, and not just our own military either. It really is vital that we maintain the confidential nature of this location."

"I can understand that. I understood it when I was first referred here. And I understood it better, I might

add, the next morning, when I woke up without being
able to remember where I'd been. It's the injection, isn't
it? The one you have them give in the taxi. From my
experience, I'd say it was scopolamine. With an added
CNS stimulant. Am I right?"

He nodded. She hoped she wasn't overplaying it and
went on.

"As you can see, I'm being straight with you. I don't
like the secrecy, but I'm willing to go along with it, because it seems to be necessary, and because your treatment, whatever it is you're using, has made me feel
better the past three weeks. But I don't think I'm in the
mood for it tonight, I really don't. So if you don't mind,
I'd like to leave now."

"Did you see the young woman?" he asked, his voice
still pleasant.

"I wasn't watching there, I was looking farther back,
in the shadows of the park—"

She turned as she heard the door open behind her.
The big dead-eyed man. Panic on his face.

"A TV truck outside, sir. They're parking, setting up
their cameras—"

It all hit her at once, the elation that she *had* gotten
through to Maryann after all, the shock that Maryann
would take such a bold step so quickly, that she had
been *ready* to do that, without telling Jill, the memory
that Maryann had, after all, told her to try to get the
hell away as soon as she could, the frustration that she
had indeed been trying to do just that from the moment
she had arrived—

And then one thing more. She realized what her face
had been doing while she tried to cope with the news.

And the Leader was still watching her. His posture
hadn't changed, he was still leaning back, at his ease, but
the way he was looking at her said it all.

Got you, dearie.

"I guess you'd better attend to them, Matthew," he
said. "Be sure you get them well away from here."

Matthew began to smile. The Leader's voice continued
silkily, "And Dr. Weston says she wants to leave us tonight. You can take her out when you attend to the TV
people."

At home after dinner, Ted was telling Rachel about a deal he had made that afternoon with the Mariott Motor Lodge Midtown, which was replacing the TV sets in all its 155 rooms. Color TVs, Motorola nineteen-inch models, only three years old but the depreciation write-off was used up now, so they would sell to the hospital for only seventy-eight dollars and change per set. The price was a shade better than the trade allowance they could get from Sony, the kind they were replacing with, and that meant the hospital could get rid of the pay-TV people, break the lease and just move these *real* TVs into the rooms, with headphones of course, and the patients could quit having to worry about the set rental fee that would appear on their bill and not be covered by insurance.

That was a nice thing to do for the patients, Rachel said, but she thought the hospital was short of money, and didn't that come out to an expense of nearly ten thousand dollars?

Almost twelve thousand. But they'd make it back in six months, Ted told her, probably fewer than six, because when TV was free, people watched a lot more, and everybody knew that having them watch TV took their mind off their troubles, and there were studies that showed the more patients watched TV the less inclined they were to ring for the nurses, so the hospital could count on fewer calls for nurses, cut the schedule a bit, save a bundle in personnel costs—

Then Ted noticed the expression on Rachel's face. "Hey," he said. "What's with the look?"

Her eyes were rolled back a little and she didn't say anything, just pursed her lips and breathed.

Ted watched her for about fifteen seconds. "Oh boy," he said, quietly. "Oh boy."

Until she reached the front vestibule with Matthew, Jill tried to concentrate on the possibility that she might not have given herself away after all. Perhaps the Leader only mean for this Matthew to talk to the TV people, to convince them to go away, and then to put Jill into the limousine and drive her home.

Then Matthew opened the front door and wrapped his hand around Jill's wrist like steel pincers, pulling her close to him. He squeezed her fingers inside his other hand, bending them back, and the pain triggered a rush of the fear that had been growing steadily inside her. She tried to think of how she could get help, for they *were* going outside, but she realized that to a passer-by she and this man would look like a couple coming down the steps arm in arm. Only if someone looked at Jill's face would he know that something was very wrong. And no one was out walking just now. She tried to think of some other way to escape, but Matthew Garrett was bending her fingers now, making the joints scream, loosening the bones in their sockets.

He spoke softly. "A surgeon doesn't do very well without fingers," he said. "You'll want to be quiet."

The TV van said NEWS CENTER SIX. It had the side doors opened. Maryann was standing inside, along with a scared-looking boy in a worn denim suit. Maryann had on a trench coat buttoned up against the cold, and was holding a clipboard, staring. Jill guessed the boy in denim would be the driver, the one Maryann had said was so good at following people. Now he was fumbling with a shoulder-mounted camera. As Garrett and Jill came within a few feet of the van, he got it up and pointed it at them, holding it almost like a tommy gun, without focusing, his face nowhere near the eyepiece. The red glow of the light on top of the camera tinted his features. His mouth was half open and trembling, as if he were about to call for help.

Garrett looked at the camera. "Put it down."

"We're broadcasting," said Maryann. "This is a live camera. Why are you—"

"You're bluffing," Garrett cut in, still moving forward to the open doors at the side of the van. "Put the camera down, and make room for us. We're going to take a ride."

They stepped back. Maryann's eyes met Jill's. "I saw them taking you in," she said softly. "I was trying to get set up here, and make a deal—"

Her voice choked off as she saw Garrett's knife, the eight-inch blade curved slightly with a groove in the center to let the blood drain off. The tip was at Jill's throat.

"You want to be quiet," Garrett said. "You, Delvecchio. I told you before. You've used up your one mistake. Get up there behind the wheel and drive. Uptown."

Maryann got behind the wheel.

"Where do you want me?" The young driver was pale with fear. Seen from this close, he looked to be no more than sixteen.

"You sit up there next to her. And put that camera down."

The boy edged his way around the back of the passenger seat, his frightened eyes on Garrett. "The boss and I'll be quiet," he said. "We don't want any trouble." As he spoke, he set the camera down slowly, so Garrett could see it, easing it to the floor of the van in front of where Jill stood.

Garrett turned to slide the door panel shut behind him. When the boy saw Garrett's eyes were directed away from him he moved quickly. The camera was his only weapon and he gripped it, swinging it like a club, lunging forward at Garrett. The barrel of the camera and the edge of the lens cap caught Garrett on the side of the head. At the impact, Jill dropped to her knees and slipped from under Garrett's arms as he tried to get his balance. Praying that his knife would not find her, she pushed past him, her eyes on the sliding door at the side of the van. The door was still partway open. If she could reach it she would have a chance, but she was not moving fast enough. Garrett's knife hand smashed down on her with the butt end of the handle, a back-handed blow to the side of her neck that knocked her away from the door opening. She crashed painfully against the hard metal of the van's interior wall.

She looked up and saw Garrett going for the young driver, who was in the front seat trying to get his door open. Garrett's knife flashed in a powerful uppercut. The boy tried to put his hands out to protect himself, but the long blade penetrated between his fingers, moving straight up, catching him in the throat just under the point of his chin. The boy's eyes grew wide in astonishment as he felt the tip of the long blade come up into his mouth. He clawed at Garrett's arms, but Garrett had leverage and weight. He pressed the knife relentlessly upward, through the boy's tongue, through the bone at the roof of the mouth. The boy choked and fought on, even though the knife was stabbing up into his nasal passages.

Then the point of the knife broke through into the brain. Blood spurted from his mouth and nostrils in a sudden gush. His body pitched forward against the window and lay still.

Jill watched in frozen horror as Garrett pressed down on the boy's bleeding face with the palm of his free hand. He was working his knife back and forth, trying to loosen the blade from where it had penetrated the bone.

Then she heard Maryann's voice, saw the door of the van open.

"*Move!* Get out *now!* He can't chase *both* of us!"

Jill tumbled out of the van and came up running. She ran blindly, without thinking, in the middle of the street, trying to scream as a pair of headlights appeared, coming around the corner. Waving for help, she ran at the lights, and for a moment or two she thought the car would stop for her. But then its horn began to blare. She spun away before the car reached her, stumbled onto the sidewalk just outside the park.

She turned to look. The car that had nearly run her down was still traveling south. Maryann was nowhere in sight. Jill hoped she was safe, and looked hard into the shadows for the man who had tried to kill them.

The TV van was moving. Lights on, it spun around, the wheels cut hard left in a U-turn, its high beams a yellow-white glare that sought Jill out and found her frozen on the sidewalk, thinking, *Now he's coming after me.* It was a long moment before she overcame her fear and moved. When the van passed she was just scrambling up onto the blackened stone wall.

And a dark shadow broke loose from between two parked cars. Garrett. Coming in an unbelievable burst of speed. She saw his powerful arms reach for her and she pushed herself back onto the top of the wall, the stone scraping her hands as she tried to swing her legs free to jump down on the other side. But he was upon her, his grip hard on her ankle. Acting by reflex, she lashed out in a kick for his throat. The hard tip of her shoe caught him in the neck and turned him aside, so that his momentum carried him into the wall. She heard a muffled crack as his skull met the unyielding stone.

She stared at him for barely a second.

Until she saw that he was getting up.

Then she swung over the wall and ran for her life into the shadows of the park, downhill, the path of least resistance, not taking the walkway, staying behind the trees, full speed, wanting only to reach some place where she could get out of sight. She knew there were at least two of them after her now: someone driving the TV van, and the man with the knife. Was he behind her? She didn't hear footsteps, just the sound of her own breath, painful in her throat.

Ahead were concrete steps; below them a darkened archway tunneling under the end of Riverside Drive, beneath the circle at Seventy-ninth, two levels beneath the West Side Highway.

She remembered that archway and took the steps three at a time, recklessly, on her toes, hoping her leather-soled loafers weren't making enough noise to betray her, hoping she still had enough of a lead so that not making noise would make a difference, that he was not just a few steps behind her watching for his chance to leap at her again, because she knew if she could just keep the lead a minute or so longer and not fall she would have a real chance of getting away, of making it to the boat basin and getting in with Phillip's keys. Her shoulder bag was still there, she could feel the strap cutting inside her collar, feel its weight and bulk against her side, and the only thing that could go wrong was that she might lose her way going down through the monument area, not a real possibility because she remembered it pretty well from when she had come this way before,

with Phillip to see his boat, so she was in pretty good
shape. As she hit the darkness of the little tunnel she
thought of something else—that when she had fallen out
of the TV van the clasp of her shoulder bag might have
come undone and the keys might already have fallen
out and be lying somewhere in the street. But she wasn't
going to think about that because it wouldn't do any good
and she couldn't stop and check anyway, she had to just
keep running in the dark, her eyes on the lit archway
where the tunnel opened out into the wide arcade
around the big circular fountain, where the sky would be
overhead again and she would be able to see better.

She wished they hadn't given her that injection; it was
making her feel more and more disoriented because now
she was through the tunnel and into the arcade and
there wasn't much moonlight down here, it was all shadows and darker shadows, huge concrete columns and
vaulted arches like the inside of a cathedral or an ancient
temple or a maze. To find her way to the arches that
led down to the river she had to stop running. She
stopped.

Coming out to the edge of the fountain, away from the
arches, she looked up to the sky, saw the roadway on the
upper level that went around the fountain, and tried to
orient herself. The roadway up there was the traffic circle,
so the river had to be down and to her right.

Then she saw the silhouette of a van parked above
her, at the edge of the traffic circle. And below the van,
one of the shadows began to move away from the others.
The man with the knife. She knew at once what they
had done: seen from the van where she was running and
driven ahead, and the man with the knife had lowered
himself down from the roadway. Now he was waiting for
her.

In the split second that she realized how they'd gotten
ahead of her she also remembered that this was the second time; the time before, on the FDR Drive, he had let
her think she'd gotten away and then trapped her. She
wanted to scream at him but instead she thought of something better and took off across the courtyard for the shadows of the other side, away from where she wanted to go.
to the steps that led up to the south, to the roadway.
She took a glance over her shoulder as she ran and saw
he'd changed course. He was trying to head her off be-

fore she reached the steps, and that was what she wanted.

As soon as she reached the shadows where he could no longer see her, she stopped and flattened herself against one of the columns. Underfoot were some pebbles, probably broken glass too, so she was careful as she bent and scooped up a small handful, listening as his footsteps got louder. She could see the steps. Underhand, she tossed a few of the pebbles at the bottom, enough to draw attention, and then wound up and threw the rest farther up, hoping he would take the bait and sprint on up the steps after her.

He did.

The instant she saw him on the steps, she ran straight for the opposite side of the fountain and the archway that led down to the boat basin, not caring that she was out in the open, that if the driver of the van was looking out over the edge, he would spot her, because that didn't matter, he'd be yelling to the one with the knife any second now that she'd not come up that way. All that counted was speed. She had to reach the metal gate to the docks with enough distance between them to let her find the keys in her shoulder bag, get them out, open the lock, and shut the gate behind her. She was going over the movements in her mind as she burst through the archway and reached the steps.

And saw the wide, dark river, the lights of the highrises glittering on the opposite shore and reflected on the waves, pathways of light across the water to the dark outlines of the boats.

From the top of the steps she picked out the *Nirvana* right away, the biggest one there, to her right and up-river. It was facing west and looked to be clear of the other boats, so that was a break; she would not have to waste time maneuvering around, just get it started and head off. . . .

Move, she thought, and got going again, doing well until her foot slipped on the steps and she lost her balance running, halfway down out of control, full speed just trying to keep her feet under her, the bottom coming before she was ready and then it was too late, she knew she couldn't hold it any longer and crashed into the wire fence, making a racket they couldn't have missed. She shook it off and went for the keys in her shoulder bag and came up with them feeling good, so good that even when she saw the man with the knife behind her, at the top of the steps, she had the presence of mind to locate the biggest key, the only one that wouldn't be used on a boat, and get it in the lock.

She was inside and closing the gate behind her when the knife clanged against the heavy wire mesh, on the other side, making her blink because it was only a few inches from her face.

The lock clicked shut. She shook the gate once just to make certain it would hold, her eyes on the man racing down the steps for only a second, because she had no faith in the barbed wire at the top of the fence.

Running along the narrow dock, she dashed past the darkened shed where the Texaco pumps stood idle, and reached the ladder at the stern of the *Nirvana* with her heart pounding in her throat. After she scrambled up on deck she looked back at the fence and saw that someone else was also climbing, picking his way over the top, slowly but almost to where he could hang over the edge and drop down. Why wasn't there a guard? But it did no good to wish for help; she had to *move!* One key got her inside the cabin; another fit the ignition. She remembered the knob like the one on her father's Packard and pulled it out as she hit the starter, and heard the welcome roar of the diesel engines coming to life just the way it had when Phillip had been here with her. Then it was out on deck to where the boat was tied, the ropes, two big heavy ones that loosened themselves one right after the other and clattered when she heaved them away and the taped ends hit the boards below.

She saw him against the fence, getting to his feet, and she knew with an exultant rush of exhilaration that she was going to win. Unless she stalled the engine going out, she would be away before he had time to reach her, and that was where she had been smart, starting it up first, letting it idle while she cast off the lines, so it would be warmed up. She kept her eye on him as she went back into the cabin, even watching him through the window as she eased the throttle forward and felt the propeller take hold, because one thing she did not want to have to think about was whether he had managed to climb on board before she'd pulled away.

He had barely reached the middle of the jetty when she gunned the engine and saw the water appear between the stern of the *Nirvana* and the edge of the dock. Cutting the wheel hard right, the way Phillip had done, she moved the *Nirvana* out toward midstream, against the current, breathless now with relief and exhaustion, but knowing that she'd escaped the Gathering.

Now, before she did another thing, she had to finish them.

The radiotelephone was right in front of her on the control panel. She flicked the switch on, saw the yellow light over the push buttons, and pressed O. She would call the police. As she held the receiver to her ear with one hand, the other on the wheel, she decided what she would say. The address of the Gathering, of course, 88 Riverside Drive. That was the most important thing. And the death of Maryann Delvecchio's driver. They would take that information seriously tomorrow when he did not come to work at Channel Six, even if his body remained missing. And even if the others had somehow managed to catch up with Maryann.

Then Jill would give her own name and say where she was calling from, and ask the harbor patrol to send out a boat to bring her in safely.

The operator answered, a hurried, male voice that crackled through the earpiece. "Ship to shore. Your number, please."

She was looking on the dial to find the phone number of Phillip's boat when the nose of the *Nirvana* left the protected shelter of the harbor cove and caught the full force of the rain-swollen current. The wheel spun out of her grasp and the deck pitched suddenly out from under her. She fell heavily. As the *Nirvana* listed over yet farther, caught broadside in the current, Jill saw the wooden corner of the captain's chair rushing up to meet her. She tried to get her hands in front of her to protect herself, but she could not move quickly enough.

The *Nirvana* righted itself when the bow had come almost a full 180 degrees around, now heading south, downriver on the dark Hudson toward the Atlantic.

In the cabin of the *Nirvana*, Jill Weston lay unconscious.

54

The beeper.

A metallic pulse, repeated, from a great distance. The sound reached Jill faintly at first, and she was aware of the noise only dimly. Something, familiar in a way she could not quite recall, seemed to edge its way into whatever surrounded her, as though a bird were singing at dawn and she was not yet ready to wake. Then the sound grew. Continued. A tone she knew was for her. Someone wanted to reach her, though who it was and how anyone had managed to find her way down here in the dark were mysteries.

More pulses. Something was wrong. Something she had to react to, and she knew it and stirred, began to wake, and realized that her beeper was ringing her, she had to call the hospital. She found her purse on the carpeted floor beside her and opened it up, guided by touch and sound because it still was dark, even though she thought she had opened her eyes.

She got the beeper in her hand and switched off the noise.

Sat up.

Rubbed her eyes. Saw a telephone, the dial lit yellow, a window. Beyond the window, in the darkness, faraway lights.

The lights were moving up and down, with the floor—Where *was* she?

Her head throbbed and she rubbed her eyes trying to focus, wondering what had happened. She could remember the taxi, a woman inside with a veil and a hypodermic, and taking the injection and driving uptown—

And then the beeper.

Now another sound, more than one, a steady deep thrumming, an engine, and wind outside and the sound of water, waves slapping against—

She saw the wheel.

My God, she whispered, I'm on Phillip's boat. What in the world am I doing here?

She pulled herself unsteadily to her feet and looked outside. And gasped.

The Statue of Liberty. Less than two hundred yards ahead, lit up, unmistakable, majestically tall and blue-green and slowly getting closer.

She cut the wheel left, still feeling strangely detached, thinking for a moment or two that maybe this was something imaginary, that she wasn't really steering the boat, that she was somewhere else, asleep, and that if she closed her eyes and opened them again maybe the whole setting would change.

But the boat moved left, and, as she kept the wheel hard down, moved left some more, and in front of her were the lights of one of the harbor islands, and then, looming incredibly tall, the skyscrapers of Lower Manhattan, huge darkened columns with windows glowing here and there like lonely yellow outposts, and for a long minute she just stared, drinking it in, the vast quiet beauty of it all, until she realized that she had better straighten out, that she had been drifting with her hand on the wheel, and before that drifting all the way down from—where was it? Seventy-ninth street, of course; she remembered putting the keys and papers into her shoulder bag in preparation for a quick escape, because she hadn't known at all what to expect beyond the suspicion that Maryann was right and that they might be taking her to somewhere on Riverside Drive.

Had they?

She shuddered, feeling the cold of the harbor, the darkness all around her, the distance between her and the far-off lights in the tall buildings. She had been drifting down here, sleeping, half dead, and if the boat had collided with anything else in the harbor or run aground on rocks and taken on water, she wouldn't have known a thing until it was too late.

Had they put her out here and set her adrift?

She tried to sort out the possibilities. None of them were good. Whatever had happened to her, the Gathering hadn't been acting with her continued survival in mind, or she wouldn't have been out here alone. Either they had put her here and drugged her, or she had some-

how escaped them and passed out, or—No. They couldn't
be still here with her; no one would be stupid enough to
stay here on the boat while it drifted, and she knew no
one else was steering because *she* was steering, and God,
her head hurt, maybe they had clubbed her, but whatever had happened it wasn't good. She shivered as she
thought again what could have happened if her beeper
hadn't come on and wakened her—

The beeper. And she hadn't even called in yet. She
reached for the phone, found the receiver off the hook,
fished it up from the floor by its cord, keeping her left
hand firm on the wheel and her eyes on the docks off to
her left as she steered for the mouth of the East River.
Maybe she couldn't remember what had happened, but
she knew one thing. She wasn't going back to the Seventy-ninth Street dock.

She jiggled the switch hook of the phone and got the
operator. The operator wanted the number of the phone
she was calling from. Jill said she didn't know it, that it
was an emergency, they could just make it a collect call
to Madison Hospital switchboard from Dr. Weston. She
was having a little trouble steering now, because it was
upstream, the waters of the East River were pushing this
way and that, and would the operator please *hurry?*

The hospital switchboard told her Rachel Sanford was
coming in with contraction five minutes apart. Jill said
she'd be there as soon as she could. She eased the
throttle forward, and noticed that the steering became
easier as the boat picked up speed. She guessed it was a
good omen; certainly she'd had her share of good luck
with Rachel starting labor and the hospital paging her
at the right time. If she *had* escaped, probably right now
the hospital was the safest place for her to be, because
of the extra security people Ted had brought on.

When she got there, she would get Rachel stabilized
and make certain Ted was O.K. too; you had to watch
it sometimes with husbands, especially the overachiev-
ing types like Ted, who could put their wives on edge
just at the time they needed to relax most. Her mind
brought back Rachel's chart from the last office visit.
A good-sized baby, but a nice wide birth canal. The
switchboard had said Rachel had called in at 11:30.
Now it was just past midnight. There would be at least

another two hours, probably several more before she went into transition, because it was a first baby.

Nonetheless, Jill pushed the throttle farther ahead. There were docks on the Upper East Side. She had seen them when she had been jogging along the FDR Drive, but they were not the kind of docks for a boat like this.

But what the hell, it was her boat now, and even if they fined her for illegal parking or night driving or piloting without a license, she could sell the damn thing and pay for as many fines as they could throw at her. Or maybe she'd give it away, give it to a school or a kid's camp or something, and then see if the city officials were heartless enought to press for fines after that. She hummed a little, pushed the throttle up a notch higher as she passed under the Brooklyn Bridge, smiling a little at the view, and thinking she would have quite a story to tell Maryann Delvecchio when she called her in the morning.

55

Sleeping on the couch, Garrett came awake when the Leader's hand gently touched the side of his face.

"Wake up and shave, Matthew. Avery called. She's at Madison Hospital, delivering the Sanford baby."

He sat bolt upright.

"Your clothes are laid out for you in the bathroom," the Leader continued. "Come down as quickly as you can."

In just over four minutes, Garrett returned. The Leader had the door open, motioning him into the corridor that led to the garage.

"If it's Madison Hospital," said Garrett, "they're looking for me there. The security guards have my description, and there are more of them now, they've doubled the patrols—"

"Don't worry about that, Matthew," said the Leader.
"Just concentrate on driving."

As Garrett was backing out of the garage he noticed
the clipboard the Leader was carrying. As he turned
south on Riverside Drive and prepared to turn left to
go across town, he remembered his scopolamine.

"I haven't had an injection," he said. "Do you have
some with you?"

The Leader said he thought Matthew had attended to
that when he was in the bathroom shaving. Garrett felt
a pang of apprehension. "You don't have any with you?"

The Leader shook his head no. "But don't worry, Matthew. You'll do just fine without it."

"I'm feeling a little nervous," said Garrett. "They're
looking for me at Madison—"

"You're not to worry," the Leader cut in, his tone at
once authoritative and reassuring. "Not to worry at all.
The way we're going to go in there, no one will even notice who you are."

56

When Virginia Polder opened her door, she could see at
once what all the knocking had been about so early in
the day. The man waiting outside was dressed in a white
uniform, and behind him, parked on Fifth Avenue with
the motor running, was a white ambulance van. She
held the door open as far as the chain lock would allow.

"Yes?"

"Dr. Polder, please. It's an emergency." She could
see lines of strain and tension in his handsome face,
and his dark eyes shone with urgent appeal.

"I'm Dr. Polder."

"Clifton Ambulance Service, Doctor. We've a seriously injured woman in the van, and she refuses to let us
take her to the hospital until she's seen you. Says she's
a patient of yours. The name is Jill Weston."

She blinked. "By all means, then. Bring her inside."

"She conscious, Doctor, but I'm not sure we ought to move her any more than we have to. She appears to have been struck by a car while crossing the street. I'm not a physician, but it looks to me as though she's bleeding quite a bit internally. She says she can't move her legs."

"I'll get my bag," said Virginia Polder. She got her coat from the closet too, and put it on. Then she undid the chain lock and followed the ambulance driver to the rear of the van.

He opened the door for her. "Do you want me to drive while you're examining her, Doctor?"

"I think you'd better." She stepped up into the van, and saw the figure reclining under the blanket on the emergency stretcher. There were no windows and the light was only fair. "Are you still awake?" she asked.

The figure did not move.

Virginia Polder heard the door of the ambulance click shut behind her.

Then the figure moved. Sat up, the blanket falling away, and she recognized a face she had never wanted to see again; saw a glint of triumph in a pair of dead-brown eyes. Saw the muzzle of a large pistol pointed at her heart.

"You—" she said, and then the flame erupted from the barrel of the gun, and she heared a reverberating roar that hurt her ears, made her feel pain that seemed, for a moment, even more acute than the sledgehammer force that tore into her chest and shoulder.

Dorothy Weber was working her morning shift as the admissions or "triage" nurse at the Madison Hospital Emergency entrance. Mornings were generally not too busy, which was good in a way, but bad in another because the hospital administration scheduled nursing coverage accordingly. So Dorothy was alone, with the nurse's aide and the security guard for company, and the names of two residents she could page if anything serious came in.

She stood up when she saw the two ambulance men lifting the stretcher out of the back of their van. When she saw red stains on the blanket, she told the nurse's aide to get on the phone to the switchboard right away and have them page Dr. Galin and Dr. Stein, stat, which was hospital talk for "immediately."

The security guard helped her hold the door as they brought the patient in.

"Gunshot wound," said the ambulance driver. "Right out on the street, just a couple minutes ago. We saw it happen and picked her up and brought her here, because it was the nearest place."

"That's horrible," said Dorothy. "In there." She pointed to room A, the room where the blood supplies were stored, and where they had the X-ray unit.

"And she's a doctor," said the driver. "She had her bag with her. Dr. Virginia Polder. Office is just a few blocks away on Fifth Avenue. The bag's on the stretcher."

"Horrible," Dorothy repeated.

"Yeah," said the driver. He was plainly upset, standing there in the hallway while his partner, bigger and more muscular, wheeled the patient into room A.

Galin and Stein came from the elevator on the double. "Gunshot wound," said Dorothy, pointing to room A. "It's Dr. Polder."

"Son of a *bitch*," said Galin. He and Stein went into the room, almost colliding with the ambulance man. Dorothy could hear them both giving directions to the aide at once. She started to go in and help.

"The thing is," said the driver, "we were on call when we saw her get shot. We didn't get a chance to radio in, didn't have time to call the police or anything but get her the hell here. Is there a room somewhere where we can use a phone and get our reports straightened out?"

"Sure," said Dorothy. "Just down the hall and to your right. There's a phone in there. Right across from the elevator."

57

Jill cuddled Rachel's new little girl for just a moment or two before handing the baby back to her mother. They were in Rachel's room, a semiprivate, but no one was in the other bed. Rachel was just getting settled. After a long night and a labor of average difficulty, the baby had come, a normal delivery, almost exactly eight and a half hours from the time Rachel and Ted had entered the hospital.

"She's such a cutie," said Jill, and smiled. She was tired too, but not too tired to be happy for the new parents.

"Such beautiful blue eyes." Ted leaned over and kissed the little pink nose. "And so alert! Look how she's watching her daddy with those beautiful blue eyes!"

Rachel's face shone. "You can take some of the credit for how alert she is," she told Ted. "If you hadn't stayed with me, I think I'd have kept on crying for anesthesia—"

"You did just fine," said Jill. "Both of you stayed right on top of those contractions."

"I only weakened that one time, didn't I? God, I'm starting to forget already!"

"Just remember the good parts, honey," Ted told her. "And you've got the prize to show for it." He kissed his new daughter again.

"They won't give her a sedative, when they have her in the nursery, will they?" Rachel asked.

Jill reassured her that they wouldn't. "And remember it's only the first six hours that she'll be in the nursery," she went on. "After she gets her examination from your pediatrician, she'll be moving in here with you. So I suggest you both try to get a little rest when you get through with your phone calls."

"When do I feed her?"

"They'll bring her to you in about three hours and you can give her as much time at the breast as she wants—so long as it's no more than five minutes on each side. Remember there won't be milk. Just colostrum for the next day or so."

Jill moved closer to the door, because she wanted to leave them alone now with the baby for the few minutes before the nursery people came. She would not move too abruptly, however, because the new parents might still have questions. It struck her as odd that she felt just as close to Rachel and Ted as she felt with other parents she had gotten to know before a delivery, even though Ted was her hard-driving, budget-cutting hospital administrator. Professionalism, she supposed, or maybe she was too tired to feel like an employee just now.

Ted was clearing his throat. "You know, Jill, Doctor, I just want to say"—he hesitated, and cleared his throat again—"well, I guess we're both more grateful to you than either of us can quite put into words. I must admit I've thought more than once tonight how hard you've been working for us—"

"Come on, give yourself some credit too," Jill interrupted. "You were the ones who were up all night. I got to take a cat nap from time to time."

"Oh, no, it's more than that. I mean, how much you've been doing for the hospital these past weeks. And without an assistant because of our budget difficulty. What I'm saying is, you can count on having an assistant back first thing next week. And that holds true even if we *don't* get the grant money this morning."

The Marcus Foundation. Jill realized she'd forgotten about it completely. Today was the day they'd promised to notify the hospital about whether her center would be funded.

She smiled at Ted, momentarily embarrassed that he was talking of work-related matters at such a very personal time, but then realizing that Ted was quite sincere. He really *did* appreciate what she'd done, and he really was so wrapped up in his job that it was probably quite natural for him to be thinking of budgets while his daughter was being born. Besides, she thought, the roles did more or less overlap here. How many other hospital administrators would be likely to feel totally detached from their own hospital just because they were receiving its services instead of administering them? He was sitting on the bed leaning back against the headboard, Rachel and the baby snuggled up on the crook of his arm. Clearly he was in a mood to be generous. But Jill didn't want him to regret his generosity later, when he would have to get back to running the hospital.

"Why don't you keep that decision in abeyance for a day or two," she said lightly. "My father always said not to finalize any money matters when you've been up all night."

Ted didn't seem to want to take back his offer. "I guess we'll both be glad to get some sleep," he replied. "Are you going home now?"

She shook her head no. "I've got a cot in my office. And

I did get a little sleep in here while you were still in the labor room."

"May I wake you up if we get the news about the grant?"

"Only if it's good news."

As Jill was going out, Rachel held up the baby and moved its tiny arm up and down, very gently. "Wave bye-bye to Dr. Weston, sweetheart," she said. "Without her, you wouldn't have even gotten started. You tell Doctor from us that she's made us happier than"—she blinked a little, because there were tears in her eyes—"happier than we can say."

Jill got choked up too, and just blew a kiss to all three of them and walked down the hall to the elevator.

On the way down, she realized that she wanted a baby of her own. And bit her lip to make the wish go away, because there wasn't anything she could do about it just then and it didn't pay to make herself sad about things she couldn't control. Still, she remembered Jerry Chamberlain, how good he had been to her on Saturday, how much she owed him for fixing the lock and getting rid of those microphones and how comfortable, warm and comfortable, she had felt when he had kissed her.

As she was unlocking the door to her outer office she remembered Maryann Delvecchio. It was after nine o'clock now, and the Channel Six switchboard would be open. She would give Maryann a call and find out whether or not their plan had succeeded last night.

She was just inside the doorway when Matthew Garrett's powerful hand closed over her mouth. She tried to spin away, but he was too strong.

She heard the door to the hallway close behind her. Saw the inner door opening.

The Leader.

In his hand, a hypodermic syringe, with a glittering needle.

58

For a woman forty pounds overweight, Nurse Maria Eversly was moving at a rapid clip coming into Harriet Pierce's private room. She stopped abruptly in the doorway when she saw Nick O'Donnell sitting at Harriet's bedside, talking on the phone, but the look of happiness on Maria's face did not change.

"Guess you've got company," she said. "I'll come back—"

"No, come on in!" said Harriet. She was sitting up and smiling broadly, the adhesive bandages covering her head making her resemble a woman of ancient Egypt. "Don't mind Nick, here. He's my star boarder!"

Nick, still on the phone, waggled his eyebrows to say hello, and gave Harriet a squeeeze.

Maria came forward to the other side of the bed. "I was off yesterday, and they just told me the news this morning so I came right down on my break, and congratulations, honey!" She gave Harriet a kiss.

And then ooh-ed delightedly over the engagement ring on Harriet's left hand.

"You two are gonna be so happ*eee*—"

"Hey, we're pretty happy *now*, you know what I'm sayin'?" Harriet glanced up at Nick. " 'Cept he keeps runnin' the hospital from here, on the phone all the time, and nobody can call me, but I tell you it does beat sleepin' all day, that's for *sure*."

"I didn't see the guard outside," said Maria. "You two gettin' some privacy?"

A slight frown crossed Harriet's face and then was gone. "Oh, they took him off duty two days ago," she said. "They finally started to believe me when I said I couldn't remember who knocked me over the head. So I don't need protection anymore."

She looked up at Nick again, and added, "Fortunately my man here doesn't hold to that opinion. So I've got lots of company."

Nick was just starting another phone call, and both women began to listen when they heard him say, "Mr. Sanford, please," because Mr. Sanford was the boss, and the rumor was that the boss was so tickled with his new baby that he was going to recommend bonuses for the whole staff. Nick sounded happy, too. Just took a call from Marcus, he was saying, and they were definitely funding the center, not as much as they'd hoped but two hundred thousand and maybe more next year if the hospital decided to expand.

"Hey, terrific," said Harriet after Nick hung up. "Jill Weston's going to turn handsprings!"

"Yeah," said Nick. "Ted said the same thing. He wants to tell her the news himself."

59

He really did *not* like it very much, sending her out with Garrett, where any minute she might decide to risk everything and try to escape. The omicron solution was potent, he knew that, had proved it with her, even, testing the pain reflex, but blocking out pain was one thing and controlling willed behavior, giving someone a task to perform that required speech, and a certain amount of guile—that was quite another. He wished he had been able to do more work with the omicron mixture; then he could have acted this morning with a great deal more confidence. But then one didn't always have enough time. One had to adapt to circumstances. And sending her and Garrett to bring a baby from the nursery had been the best adaptation he had been able to come up with.

Not that they would ever *use* an infant as a hostage to

get out of the hospital. But the errand served well as a pretext to get Garrett out of Weston's office.

So the Leader could prepare for Garrett's death.

Lockwood drew from his ambulance driver's clipboard the handwritten confession that Garrett had made as punishment for Diana Falke. It would serve well here. "I hated her . . . even though I worked with her, I had to kill her . . ."

That would make sense to the police. The "her" would appear to be an obvious reference when they found Jill Weston's body here with the note. Ironic, he thought, that Diana's judgment of Garrett should prove more accurate than his own. There had simply been too many mistakes. Garrett had become too great a liability.

He thought how he would do it whan they returned. Best to bring them into the inner office. As soon as the door was shut, he would order Garrett to kill Weston and the baby.

While Garrett was occupied, his Leader would come behind him. A swift injection, quick paralysis . . .

And the police would have their vampire killer, dead but identifiable.

Lockwood checked his watch. They had been gone two minutes. He would prepare Garrett's injection.

Smoothly, wasting no time, he took one of the three paralytic ampules from his inside breast pocket, inserted the needle through the ampule's rubberized membrane, and drew up the plunger with thumb and forefinger, filling the hypodermic syringe with fluid. He could visualize the way Garrett would be bending over his victim, see the angle he would have to use.

No good. Garrett was too quick; too well trained to be taken by surprise. Before the full dosage could be injected, he would have reacted. And with violence. With someone else it would work, but not with a man who had Garrett's reflexes, honed to unnatural sharpness by his paranoia.

Lockwood would have to convince Garrett to accept the injection willingly. It came to him what he would say. "I've found some scopolamine *here*, Matthew, and I want to give it to you. I don't want you remembering what we do with the baby."

That would work.

And if they didn't come back with an infant?

"Now we're going to have to dispose of Weston's body, Matthew, and I don't want you remembering. I've found some scopolamine in her office; you know she was in obstetrics . . ."

That also would work. And the only other possibility was that Weston would somehow escape, that Garrett would come back alone. If he did, then what?

He knew. "Matthew, it's going to be difficult getting out of here, and we may have to eliminate people who get in our way. I don't want you remembering . . ."

He placed the full hypodermic carefully into his jacket pocket, taking care not to damage the needle.

Then he heard someone at the door.

And other possibilities occurred to him: that neither Garrett nor Jill Weston would come back; that something might have gone completely wrong; that both of them had been caught, and that Weston had been able to talk before the second injection he had given her, the rauwolfia compound, had taken effect.

A key was turning in the lock.

He thought quickly.

Putting the clipboard on the floor, where it would attract the attention of whoever was coming in, Malcolm Lockwood then moved to the right of the doorway. To the place Garrett had stood when he was waiting for Jill Weston.

The door opened. A man's voice. "Jill? Jill, are you awake?"

Ted Sanford, the administrator. Lockwood's confidence surged. Sanford, the new father, had been awake all night. His reactions would be sluggish.

As Sanford bent over the clipboard, curious, kneeling now to pick it up and read, Lockwood was on him with a clean, hard blow to the back of the neck. Before Sanford had a chance to recover, or even to turn and see who had hit him, Lockwood had shut the door to the hallway, quietly, and worked the tip of the hypodermic needle into Sanford's carotid artery, just behind his right ear.

He pressed the plunger home, infusing the paralytic solution into Sanford's brain by the quickest possible route, and had the satisfaction of seeing an immediate drop in Sanford's respiration rate.

Then he withdrew the hypodermic, took another ampule from his breast pocket, and refilled the syringe.

It had been nearly four minutes. Garrett would be
returning soon.

60

"It's been thirty seconds," said Garrett. They were outside the door to the nursery. Through the large viewing
window Jill could see the three newborns, pink and still
wrinkled in their bassinets. Two of them were asleep.
Jane Oliver, the nurse on duty this morning, was giving
the third a drink of water from a bottle; evidently it was
not yet time to take it down the hall to its mother for
feeding.

"Suppose I don't go in," said Jill. She felt strangely
calm, in control of things, even though she knew such a
feeling was totally absurd. That obedience hormone from
the Leader obviously did not inhibit *thoughts* of disobe-
dience. If anything, she felt more strongly the urge to
defeat him, so strongly that it seemed all she could do
to restrain her impulse to say aloud what she felt to be
the truth, to oppose these people openly, honestly—a
straightforward confrontation where she could once and
for all rid herself of their influence or die trying. And
yet at the same time she could see how this was exactly
what she did *not* want to do; that she would stand no
chance against Garrett unless she could think of a way to
outwit him. She supposed the second injection they had
given her, what the Leader had said was an overdose of
reserpine, a rauwolfia alkaloid that depressed CNS function, might already have started to make her feel reckless,
and that just knowing she would die unless the drug's
effects were countered within the next four and one half
minutes had stimulated her hormonal systems. They
would impel her to either fight or take flight, *now*, an
impulse that was natural, primitive, organic. And in this

case, she knew, suicidal. She would need to act with deception and, above all, with control. A plan began to form in her mind.

"You're wasting time," said Garrett. "If you don't go in, you'll die. You've got four minutes until you need the antidote."

"Suppose I *want* to die?"

"I'll give you ten seconds more. Then I'll take you into the nursery, and cut your throat, and while you're bleeding you can watch while I do the same thing to the nurse in there, and to those three babies. If you think I wouldn't you'd better think again. I killed your friend Dr. Polder this morning. Blew her heart out with a pistol at close range. It's the only killing I remember, and it was easy."

Jill bit her lip, stunned. "Dr. *Polder* . . ." Her mind spun, flooded with outrage. The ugliness of Garrett's leering face seemed unbearable.

"Five seconds," Garrett said. "Five seconds until I kill you and everyone in there."

Jill felt suddenly very cold inside. She knocked on the door of the nursery and pushed it open. Nurse Jane Oliver turned as they came in and nodded a greeting. "They're having some difficulty with one of the women in 807," Jill said. "Could you go down there and help right away? I'll cover for you here. Guess your phone must be out of order."

Nurse Oliver went off immediately.

"We'll have maybe two minutes until she comes back," said Jill. "I'm going to use one of them to sedate the baby. You stay out in the corridor and keep watch."

"And have you phone for help? I'm going to be right here watching you."

"You're being stupid," she said. Quickly she pulled shut the venetian blinds at the viewing window. "What if someone else comes in and finds us? If you're outside, you can explain that all the babies are with their mothers now, and that you're waiting for the nurse to come back. And say it loudly enough so that I'll be able to hear you."

Garrett stared at her hard for a moment. Then he went over to the three occupied bassinets and picked up one of the sleeping newborn babies. The baby was Rachel's. Holding it in the crook of his arm, he flicked open his long knife. He held the tip of the blade at the infant's throat.

"You're wasting time," said Jill.

The baby whimpered but remained asleep. Garrett turned with it to the wall telephone. Then he raised his knife, and severed the wire to the receiver.

As he was putting the infant back into its bassinet he caught her looking at him and was pleased to see the horror in her eyes.

"I'll be on the other side of that door," he said. "You've got sixty seconds."

61

Rachel Sanford heard footsteps outside her room. Someone coming down the corridor. Ted had been gone only a few moments, it seemed, but she was feeling a bit tired now after all the excitement of the baby and perhaps time had passed more quickly than she had been aware of.

The nurse came in, plump and efficient. "What's the trouble—"

Nurse Oliver's voice trailed off when she saw only one woman in the room.

"No trouble," said Rachel. "I'm having a great morning!"

The nurse looked puzzled. "Was there someone in here with you? Did they take her away?"

"No . . ."

"And this is 807, isn't it? Dr. Weston said one of the women from 807 was in trouble and they needed help. I can't think what she could have meant by that."

Rachel sat up a little straighter. "In trouble? Dr. Weston delivered my baby! She was in here less than a half hour ago. She said everything was just fine."

"Well she just told me to come down here right away. Maybe she was in one of the other rooms?"

Rachel felt uncertain, and for a moment she wished she had been watching the corridor more closely. But that wasn't her job, she told herself. Having the baby was her job, and she had done that, done it well, and everything was all right. "Maybe you should ask one of the other nurses," she said.

"Hmph," said Nurse Oliver. "I'm going back to the nursery and ask Dr. Weston herself."

"I'll come with you," said Rachel. "My little daughter's down there, and I'd kind of like to see her, just for a minute."

62

Garrett was looking at his watch.

The corridor was empty, the part that mattered, the section where he was standing, where someone could see who came out of the nursery, and whether or not they were carrying a baby. No one had come up in the elevator just to Garrett's right; no one had come up the fire stairway behind him, the route Garrett had used to bring Weston the one flight up from her office, to avoid meeting possible complications in the elevator.

Thirty seconds had passed since he had left Weston inside. Garrett thought of going in early, just to check, make certain she was not up to something. He didn't like Weston. He knew she had been assigned to him several times before, he couldn't remember how many, but he had the feeling that at some point he had made a mistake with her, that she had been one of the assignments the Leader and Falke had been discussing behind his back, one of the mistakes that Falke had tried to use against him. He didn't want another mistake with Weston and especially not with the Leader himself downstairs waiting for him to produce.

Forty seconds. He heard voices around the corner. Women, and getting closer. Soon they would be where they could see him, see the nursery, and if they stayed here maybe waiting for the elevator they would still be here when it was sixty seconds. They would see Weston coming out with the baby and maybe interfere.

The women were getting closer. His watch said fifty seconds. Probably he would have to take the women out of the picture, because he couldn't stand here waiting for Weston; in another two minutes or so she would become a walking vegetable, a falling vegetable, rather, because her legs would go first, and he didn't want that happening on the stairs. The Leader had told him to bring Weston back for the antidote.

So he would hurry things up, before the two women came around the corner and saw him.

He put his hand on his knife, ready in case she was waiting for him beside the door with some sort of weapon.

Turned the knob silently.

Opened the door fast, all the way, giving himself a clear view of the whole room.

She wasn't there. Or was hiding. Maybe behind the rows of empty bassinets, or the storage cabinets. The three babies were still there, in front of the window, the blinds still drawn, everything the way it had been when he had left her. And she couldn't be hiding behind the door, because he had it open as far as it would go, flat up against the bookcase that blocked the access door between the nursery and the adjoining nurse's office—

From the corridor, a woman's voice: "Dr. Weston! Wait a minute!"

Garrett whirled, his failure already cold and hollow in the pit of his stomach. She had tricked him and he had fallen for it, looking all around the room while she had been in the adjoining office, the bookcase pulled behind her. She had closed the connecting door, waited until she heard him come in and then made a run for it—

The two women met him in the doorway as he was coming out. One was the nurse Weston had sent away; the other was in a bathrobe, a patient.

"You," said the nurse. "You were with her. What was she doing running off that way?"

Garrett's hand was on his knife. "I didn't see her go," he said. "Did she take the stairs or the elevator?"

"Oh, the stairs," said the one in the bathrobe. "I think it was the stairs."

Garrett moved past the two women, ignoring their questions, and then he was across the corridor and had the fire door open and took the first five steps in one leap, vaulting with his hand on the rail, and another vault to the landing.

"In a hell of a hurry, all of a sudden," said the nurse as they watched the fire door swing shut. "Some people. Just too busy for their own good."

Rachel's baby was asleep. The nurse let her come in and give little Sherry a kiss and then sent her back to bed. Then, on her way out, Rachel remembered that Ted had gone downstairs to wake Jill up, because he thought she was sleeping in her office. But Jill Weston had been up *here*. Rachel had seen her. And so maybe Ted hadn't been able to locate her and give her the good news. Maybe he was at Jill's office now, wondering where Jill was.

Rachel decided she'd take the elevator and let Ted know that if he wanted Jill to hear the good news he'd better have her paged. It was only one flight down to Jill's office.

63

On the stairs, Garrett stood stock-still, holding his breath, listening for footsteps. Nothing. He leaned over the railing trying to see around the corner, but fire stairs weren't built that way. He could see only down to the next landing, where the white-stenciled number over the gray-painted door read "7."

She could have gone out there.

Or she could be hiding, just around the next landing, waiting there trapped, listening for him as he was listening for her.

He leaned far down on the rail and vaulted. A sudden, swift movement, landing hard but gently on the balls of his feet, spinning around.

To see another empty staircase. Gray-painted metal stairs, gray-painted cinder-block walls.

The weakening sense of defeat grew within him. There were seven floors she could go out on, possibly more, because he wasn't certain whether these stairs went down

to the basement level or below, and besides that, he realized, she might have gone *up* instead of down; there was
no particular reason why she should have chosen to go
down—up led to Surgery, a floor she was just as familiar
with as with the one her office was on. . . .

Sickening. He was standing here, letting her get *away,*
while on the other side of the door to Seven, the Leader
was in her office waiting, *expecting* him! Now Matthew
Garrett would have to go back and confess failure, see
the look of disappointment cross the Leader's perfect
features like a shadow, hear the quiet accusation. *Matthew, she was drugged, and it was only for five minutes!*
And he would have to answer, shamed, and worse, because he had not taken his injection, he would have to
remember—

Garrett's mind went back to the file on Weston that
the Leader had given him to look at. He had to *think*
like *Weston.* Where would she go? Where would she
feel safest?

The most recent entry in the file came back to him:
*Trust Established with Dr. Chamberlain in the Madison
Bood Bank.*

He began to run again, down the stairs, headlong and
nearly out of control in his excitement, until he realized—

The ground floor. There were those two-man teams of
security guards on the ground floor, and they had all been
given his description weeks ago. He could not come running through the corridors with that many guards on
duty.

The white-stenciled numeral on the wall told him he
was at the fourth floor. Pediatrics.

He pushed open the door and heard the cries of children. His watch said it had now been five minutes.
Wherever Jill Weston was going, she was there by now.
Conscious or unconscious. Now, before he risked an appearance downstairs, he would have to check that Weston
really *was* in the Blood Bank. Of all the places where he
could expect to get co-operation on the phone, according
to Weston's file, the Blood Bank was the one most likely.
Only four on the staff and two of them members of the
Gathering.

He ducked into the first vacant room he found, shut the
door, and found the telephone.

64

When Jill came out of the elevator she couldn't remember which way to turn to reach the Blood Bank. She had no time to look for it now, maybe no time at all, because already she could feel her respiration getting rapid and shallow, even when she tried to breathe deeply. The lack of oxygen was making her very tired, making her legs too heavy to move. She looked around for someone who might help her, but now an umbra of darkness had ringed itself around her peripheral vision, so that she seemed to be looking at an empty corridor through the wrong end of a pair of binoculars. Weakly, she started to scream for help.

And heard nothing. She stumbled once and caught herself, palms and fingertips sliding on the smooth wall. Then she saw.

Over on the right. An easel, a big cardboard poster of a grinning Easter bunny. BE A GOOD EGG AND GIVE BLOOD. Grateful for her good fortune, she moved toward the sign, and the entrance to the Blood Bank.

Jerry looked so small when she saw him, the red hair like tiny fine-drawn filaments of burnished gold, the blue eyes, widening in astonishment as he saw her, like tinted glass with a flame inside, the tiny blue-white flickerings of a welder's acetylene torch—

She opened her mouth to speak, and heard only the windy echo of her breath, emptying itself into the air, a sound that vaguely reminded her of the big pink conch shell she had brought back from the beach as a little girl. Only a hollow reverberation, her father had told her, meaningless.

The darkness that circled her vision rushed swiftly inward. What she could see of Jerry was now only a tiny pinpoint of light that glowed briefly, reaching out for her. And then, taking her with him as she fell into his arms,

Jerry was no more, vanishing into black and endless void.

On the receptionist's desk, the phone rang.

Marcie picked it up as if by reflex, staring in shock at the sight of Dr. Chamberlain as he cradled the unconscious Dr. Weston in his arms.

"Blood Bank," she said, automatically. "This is Marcie."

The voice on the other end was a familiar one.

When she had finished speaking a few moments later, she went to the entry door and locked it. Now no one could come in from the corridor until she opened it again.

She went in to the fractionalizing room, where Dr. Chamberlain had laid Jill Weston out on one of the couches and was making attempts to find a pulse.

"You can stop," she said. "That was the first of the Guardians on the phone."

"What are you talking about?"

"Dr. Weston has betrayed the Gathering. She has been given an intentional overdose of a sedative—"

"Intentional? *Who* was that on the phone?"

"I know him as Matthew," she said. "He outranks me. We're to let no one else in until he gets here, and then we're to assist him. Dr. Weston will be a member no more."

65

The five minutes were long since up.

Malcolm Lockwood walked quickly through the front lobby area, wearing a long white lab coat that had been hanging in Jill Weston's office, carrying her briefcase, his expression preoccupied, as though late for an important meeting.

The guard caught a glimpse of the plastic I.D. card dangling from the tall dark-haired physician's breast pocket and wondered briefly why he'd not noticed this

one here before. He made a mental note to remember
the face, a handsome dude, probably did all right with
some of those nurses upstairs. If he came in the front entrance again, the guard thought, he would remember that
face and not have to bother asking the man for his card.

Save time, that was the thing.

On the sidewalk, Lockwood hailed a taxi, thought
better of it, and began to walk south against the traffic.
The police would not get the opportunity to question any
cab drivers about picking up someone in front of Madison
Hospital or to learn where it was the taxi took him. Besides, it wasn't that far a walk to where he was going.

The difficult part was not knowing what had happened
to Jill Weston. Garrett had failed to bring her back; had
failed to being *himself* back, and that raised the possibility
that she had escaped him or somehow managed to have
him captured. The idea of Garrett in the hands of the
authorities did not disturb Malcolm Lockwood, because
he knew how impossible it would be for Garrett to tell
them anything that would betray his Leader. For Garrett
to turn informant would be an astonishing breach of all
Lockwood knew of the art of conditioning another human
being, and over the last seven years, Lockwood's knowledge and skill in the practice of that art had grown considerably. Theoretically it was still possible, because with
the human mind, anything is possible, but practically
speaking the chances were remote indeed. And even if
Garrett decided to tell all he knew, he still did not know
the location of Malcolm Lockwood's new and temporary
headquarters.

Jill Weston, on the other hand, was a different story. It
was conceivable that she had already been able to talk to
someone sensible before the drug took effect, and to tell
that sensible person about a handsome dark-haired man
who worked in a place unknown but was at this moment in Madison Hospital, and could be apprehended, or
better yet, allowed to go free, and followed to his lair.
He had noticed the guard looking carefully at his face
back there at the entrance. There might have been a signal given; plainclothes police in the crowd alerted, impossible for him to distinguish. They could be following
him even now, looking like businessmen, or drifters, or old
women with shopping bags—

He forced himself to walk at a moderate pace. It's all

right, he told himself. You can lose them if you try. And if you don't, even if you think you have and they've fooled you, you can find out what happened, what *really* happened, and know for certain either that you're safe or that you'd better think of something else.

He would give them time to show themselves. If they did not, he would play his card. He would call Chamberlain, the one at the hospital who Jill Weston trusted, the one who had impressed her so well Saturday morning with his chivalry, and arrange a meeting.

66

Jerry Chamberlain stared at Marcie for a long moment. When he spoke, he was standing up, and the words came slowly and distinctly.

"The hell we're going to assist him."

"Darling, I told you, he outranks *me*—"

And then she saw his eyes. "All right," she said quickly, moving away, back toward the reception area. "You can do what you want. I'll wait at my desk."

"The hell you will."

He caught her before she could get her desk drawer open. When she tried to twist away, he grabbed the lapels of her lab coat from behind and peeled them back, pinning her arms to her sides.

"You bastard," she screamed, kicking out at him. "You lying shit! You told me—"

A thick wad of Kleenex from the box on her desk. He crammed it into her mouth, cutting off her words in midsentence.

"Into experimental sports medicine, I believe you said, if we're talking about liars." Moving her across the room, into the lab, he felt the rage against the Gathering build inside him. He fought to keep it under control, because he couldn't afford emotion now if he wanted to save Jill's life. "I don't think you said a word about microphones, or wiretaps, or poisons in drinking water. Was the conditioning supposed to make me look the other way? A handful of pills to keep me happy, while you murder people by shooting them full of drugs?" He spat out the words. "You people *disgust* me."

He held her down on the lab floor, jamming his knee into her back while he found some adhesive tape on the counter just above. "If I hadn't been fairly sure you still had one more microphone in her apartment, one that was hidden too well for an amateur like me to find, you'd better believe I'd never have come back and told you what went on in there. But it was the only way I could think of to make you people think you still had me as a card-carrying, dues-paying member."

The gag taped in place, he got to work on her hands and ankles, pulling the legs up in back and binding them together with the wrists the way you'd hogtie a steer, only backward, so it would hurt more and make it harder for her to move.

"Now you'll stay here," he said, "and you won't let anybody in, and you won't get in my way. If you know what's good for you, you won't move around in here either. Too many reagents on the shelves for you to go rattling around."

A little breathless, he got to his feet. Goddamn it, he thought, he hadn't found out *what* sedative they'd used, or whether it was in her stomach or in her veins. But he remembered that little needle mark on her neck, kind of bruised, as though it had been made with her tensed up or moving away. Probably intravenous, which would make the sedative hit her all that much harder.

So it was life or death, no choice whatever, only one thing to do, just like the old days in the Emergency Room, when he had learned to sock the blood into them and do the crossmatch on the run. Only this time, he would have to be taking Jill's blood *out* at the same time, to flush out the poison. And praying that she didn't have a reaction to the new blood.

She was A-positive. He remembered that.

There was a carton of A-positive from St. Gregory's Hospital in the refrigerator, just in this morning, a repayment of a loan Jerry had sent them over the weekend. Glass bottles, but he didn't care, because he would be using the fractionalizing machines, two of them at once, for extra speed.

He set the carton down beside her couch and took out one of the bottles. The brain, that was where she would need the fresh blood right away, so he unbuttoned her blouse and found the carotid artery and went in with the widest catheter he thought she could hold, a five-millimeter, and connected the bottle to the machine and started it pumping the new blood in. Then, so that he wouldn't just be draining off the same new blood, he cut through her panty hose at the knee and found a leg vein. Another five-millimeter catheter, and he started draining away her own blood along with whatever they'd used to poison her. Before he hooked the catheter up to the machine, he filled a pilot tube with her blood, because even if it was a life or death situation, he was still going to do everything he could to see she didn't take on a unit that was incompatible with the blood she had in her.

That meant crossmatching all the units at once, and hoping that any agglutination or hemolysis, clumping or destruction of the red cells, would show up in the test tubes. Could he mix it all in saline solution, and with albumin and antiglobulin, before he'd put too much of any one unit into her?

He would have to try.

He had fifteen units of blood in the carton and one in the machine. Sixteen units to test. If she needed all sixteen, that would be a complete exchange transfusion, practically speaking, even though a small percentage of the new blood would be pumped out of her leg vein by the machine, and a fraction of her own blood would remain, diffused throughout her circulatory system. He could only hope that he would succeed in removing enough of the poisonous sedative, whatever it was, to bring her back to consciousness before there was any permanent brain damage.

Moving quickly, he went back to the lab for sterile pipettes, saline solution, albumin, and a rack of thirty-two sterile test tubes to run the crossmatch tests.

Marcie had inched her way over toward the counter. She stopped moving as soon as she heard him. Her eyes blazed hatred.

Jerry didn't say a word.

Jill had taken four units when Jerry found problems

in the test tubes. Two of the units were clumping, obviously incompatible with Jill's blood. Jerry checked the numbers on the test-tube rack, and then picked up the corresponding bottles of blood from the row he had arranged on the floor. So, he thought, a little sweat pays off. He put the incompatible units on the other side of Jill's couch so that he wouldn't confuse them with the others. He prayed that he hadn't made a mistake, that he had been quick enough.

He was putting the ninth unit into the machine when he heard her voice. Calling his name.

"Jerry," she said softly. "Jerry, what are you doing?"

She had turned herself around on the couch to try to see behind her, where he stood hunched over the machine. He looked up and saw her with the red tube taped to her neck, her beautiful blue eyes open now, and he couldn't say a word for a long moment until he got his breath, and then he was all right.

"You're doing swell," he said. "Let me switch these things off and we'll have a look at you."

He hit both stop buttons quickly, because now that she was awake he didn't want to risk putting another drop of new blood into her. He'd been lucky so far, damned lucky, and it never paid to press your luck when you weren't using fully crossmatched blood. Even as it was, with her awake now and seemingly past the crisis, he'd have to keep an eye on her for the next few hours, probably move her down to Emergency or get them to send some of the anticoagulation solutions they kept on hand for people having delayed reactions to a new unit.

He knelt at her side. His legs felt rubbery with relief. She touched his cheek; kissed him lightly.

"Thanks, Mr. Hematologist."

He kissed her, brushing her lips with his, just once. "Let me get these catheters out. Then I'm going to kiss you again, and you're going to tell me all about it."

Cotton and alcohol were in the cabinet beside the couch. He soaked a wad of cotton and applied pressure over the opening in her carotid artery while he drew the plastic tube and its sharpened hollow end out of her neck.

"Keep the pressure on, will you?" He put her hand over the cotton, giving her a squeeze. "You know what to do. Then I'll have the pleasure of holding the cotton on your leg—"

Both of them heard the noise from the reception area. Someone was knocking on the door. Hard. They could hear the voice, muffled, coming through.

"Hey! Blood Bank, open up in there. Security!"

"Where was he when I needed him," Jill said ruefully, and started to smile, until she remembered. "Let's get him in here," she said. "Maybe it's not too late to catch the two men that did this to me. They were both in ambulance driver's uniforms, and I'll bet nobody else in the hospital knows that."

In the reception area, Jerry unlocked the door, opened it a crack, saw the blue-gray guard's uniform, the black patent leather on the gray cap, the plastic I.D. badge.

"It's about time," he said, opening the door for the guard to enter. "We're glad to see you."

"Right." The guard was a big muscular guy with a dour expression. "Where is she?"

"In there." Jerry was right in the middle of pointing to the fractionalizing room when it hit him that none of the security staff knew about any "she."

A chill went through him, and he found it hard to speak as he tried to recover. "Weston's back in the lab, of course," he said. He lagged behind a moment, opening the desk drawer. "Marcie's there in the fractionalizing unit, I don't know if you want to talk to her first—"

But Garrett had already started toward the entrance. And seen Jill, sitting up with the cotton pad pressed to her neck. And watched the spreading horror come into her face.

"Jerry! No! He's the ONE!"

As Weston screamed, Garrett knew for certain, and moved. Uncoiling smoothly, he turned, saw Jerry Chamberlain, the desk drawer opened, a pointed metal letter opener in his hand. Moved again.

Jerry lunged, trying to get under his arm with the tip of the letter opener, but Garrett was too quick for him. The hard edge of the big man's hand cracked down on Jerry's wrist, setting off a stunning flash of heat that paralyzed the whole arm, all the way to the shoulder, as though the nerve had been cut. The letter opener went flying, struck the bright-yellow arch painted on the reception-area wall, and fell to the carpet, out of reach.

His right arm dangling uselessly, Jerry swept the phone from the desk, hoping to attract the switchboard, to buy time, maybe, if this murdering bastard in the guard's uniform would stop to pick it up and just maybe give Jerry an opening. This couldn't be happening, he thought, not here in broad daylight on the ground floor of the goddamn hospital, and he tried to scream too, the hell with pride, and was on the point of trying to run away, to make the son of a bitch follow *him* and give Jill some time to escape, when Garrett twisted sideways and, in a blur of movement too fast for Jerry to follow, let alone avoid, lashed out with a kick that caught Jerry in the pit of the stomach, sending the breath out of him in a sudden explosion of pain, doubling him over. Catlike, Garrett righted himself and was back at Jerry in less than a second, before Jerry could move away, catching the point of Jerry's chin with a knee smash. The impact straightened Jerry up, hurling him against the wall. He slid to the floor, a crumpled heap, unconscious.

Garrett turned away from him.

Shut the entrance door again.

Locked it.

She had curled herself up on the couch like a cornered animal. When he came into the room, she was trying frantically to get the catheter out of the vein in her leg.

"Won't do you any good," he said. "You've got no place to run."

"Get away from me."

The way her voice trembled made him feel good. "You know, I might just turn that machine on again," he said. "I think I'd like to watch you bleed to death."

She was silent, just watching, wide-eyed, as he came closer.

"But I don't think I have that much time," he went on, conversationally. "It probably won't be too long before they find a dead security guard in the Pediatrics floor, and then they'll try to make it difficult for me to leave this place. I don't want any more difficulty. I suppose I'd better kill you quickly."

His long knife was in his hand. The big eight-inch blade clicked open, flecks of red still on it from the guard upstairs.

She shrank away, one arm up, a pathetic attempt to protect herself, and he smiled.

Then he saw her eyes. They weren't looking at him. They were looking in *back* of him, an old trick, he

thought for a moment, until he saw she was trying to
look *away* from whatever was back there, trying to hide
the sudden hope that had come to her.

Reflected in the wide, dark centers of her eyes he saw
his final proof. Movement. Behind him. Something white.
The one in the lab coat, he thought, he must not have
hit him as hard as he'd thought, or maybe he'd had his
guard up, just a little, taken some of the force of the
blow on his hands, but that didn't matter. Nobody like
that doctor was going to stop Matthew Garrett, especially
when Matthew Garrett had his long knife ready.

He turned, quick and controlled, and saw. The red-
haired doctor, making another rush with only that puny
little letter opener. A piece of cake.

Then something hard caught Garrett full in the face
as Jill Weston rammed the glass container full of blood
up from where she had hidden it under her knees, punch-
ing upward with it, all her weight behind the blow as if
she were trying to take Garrett's head off with the heel
of her hand, only it wasn't just her hand, it was the
sixteen ounces of blood, and the glass that held the blood,
and the impact broke Garrett's nose as the glass shattered and the blood burst forth, shards of glass cutting
into his cheeks, his lips, his eyes as he tried to swing
the knife, but the pain was too much now and the blood
was in his eyes and the glass had cut them and he
couldn't see.

Jerry came at him, dropping the letter opener when
he saw what had happened, going for Garrett's knife with
both hands. He caught Garrett from the side, crashing
to the floor with him, hearing the screams as Garrett hit
the broken glass. And then a long, shuddering moan.

Garrett lay still.

Jerry rolled the body over with his foot. Saw the hilt
of Garrett's knife protruding from the jacket of the gray
uniform, the spreading red fluid darkening the chest.

Jill was looking at her hand.

67

Jerry had some real trouble answering when he heard the Leader's voice coming out of his telephone receiver right there at his desk, in his own office where not four hours ago one of the Leader's men had nearly succeeded in killing him.

He had an unreasoning urge to call out for the police; they had taken enough time in here with their photographs and their questions—why weren't they somewhere within range now, so he could have them pick up on his extension and start tracing this call? But at the same time, the moment he heard the Leader's voice, he knew that he was lucky the police were not listening. And the nervous sweat began to tingle on his scalp.

He had not explained to the police, or to Jill, that he had been one of the Gathering. At the time, it had seemed unnecessary, an incident of the past that did not bear remembering. Certainly not something he wanted to let Jill know about. He had made her believe he had never heard of them, and the last thing he wanted was to have her know that he had lied to her. Admittedly it was for a good cause, and it obviously had kept the Leader's people in the dark, but it was a lie all the same, and what he was hoping would happen between himself and Jill would not look nearly so promising if she knew how smoothly and convincingly he had misled her.

As soon as Jill had told him what had happened, he had thought it through, even before the police had come with their questions. He had seen immediately. For Jill to tell the full story would ruin her. The press must not connect the two deaths here in this office with Jill, other than to see her as a random hostage. Linking her with the Gathering would virtually guarantee cruel, damaging headlines that she would never live down. LADY DOCTOR KEY TO CULT SLAYINGS? The stories would follow her wherever she went, and the stares, and the whispers from the papers would live on in the minds of patients. Jill should not be hurt that way; she had suffered enough, and all she had to do was say she didn't know why the two men picked her office to hide in. . . .

He had convinced her. She and Jerry had given their stories and were now committed. For them, the Gathering had never existed.

Tragically, Marcie also would never disclose the existence of the Gathering, for she had killed herself. The police had found her in the lab, very much alive in the wreckage she had made of the lab's glassware, reagents, and equipment. But they had cut her free from the adhesive tape without checking to see the poison she had hidden in her fist. And she had been too quick for them. Mingled with his sorrow that a bright young life had been wasted, Jerry had also felt relief, for it had seemed at the time that Marcie's death ensured the secret of the Gathering.

Now, at the moment of hearing the Leader's voice, he knew he had been wrong. It was obvious that the Leader had names, telephone numbers, records. If the police found those records, they would know. They would come back to Jill with questions, and the reporters would follow the police, and the rest of the world would know. And Jill, too, would know about Jerry.

"I'm surprised to hear your voice," Jerry finally said. He reached into his desk for a cigarette. He had it lit and was drawing the smoke deep into his lungs when he realized he'd already started one a few moments earlier. Where's your will power, Chamberlain? he thought. You were quitting, remember?

"I need some information," said the Leader. "Some events happened today at Madison Hospital. I need to know about them."

"I'm not sure it's wise to talk on the phone." The knot in Jerry's stomach tightened. Was it the conditioning, he wondered, that made him sound so co-operative, or was it the knowledge of what he would have to do?

"You're right. Be at Sixty-first and Lexington at eight this evening. Be certain no one follows. Someone will find you."

The Leader broke the connection.

At eight o'clock Jerry watched the traffic outside

Bloomingdale's and kept on trying to think of another way. He was having no success at it when he heard the Leader's voice behind him.

"Take a cab to Seventy-ninth and Lexington and walk west."

When Jerry looked around, the Leader was not there.

Jerry was walking west on Seventy-ninth when a limousine pulled up alongside and stopped at the curb. The front door opened. Behind the steering wheel was the Leader.

Jerry got in beside him. "You take precautions," he said, and wondered again how he was able to *talk* to this man! Was it conditioning, or was it guile, or was it simply that Jerry was afraid of him? *You son of a bitch,* he thought, *if it weren't for Jill, I'd try to break your neck for you,* and wondered if he really would.

"Hi," said the Leader. He flashed Jerry a smile, showing his perfect teeth. "Precautions are kind of a game with me. You'll probably remember one or two of them."

He flicked a switch on the dashboard of the limousine, and a light above it glowed green. "That's the metal detector," he said. "Like the ones at the airports. Now we go with the radio scanner."

Another switch. Another green light.

"Good," said the Leader. "Now I'm sure you'll remember the injection."

Jerry looked at the hypodermic. "O.K.," he said, "but I should tell you something now. If I take that injection, I don't talk to you for the next forty-five minutes. If you want to know what happened, you'll have to wait until I'm certain you haven't put anything in there that I can't handle."

The Leader smiled. "Do you mind telling me why you thought a precaution like that would be necessary?"

"Not at all. In forty-five minutes, I'll be glad to tell you. Unless you want to toss that hypodermic out the window and forget about it."

"I like a man who isn't afraid to negotiate," the Leader said. "For the next forty-five minutes, we'll talk about other things."

Jerry rolled up his sleeve and took the injection.

By the time they reached Riverside Drive, Jerry was fairly certain the Leader had used only scopolamine in the hypodermic, along with something else, some CNS stimulant, to keep away the drowsiness that scopolamine often causes. The Leader turned the limousine north at Seventy-ninth and found a parking space a few blocks farther up, on Eighty-third.

Jerry walked south with him. The Leader slowed at a big oversize town house, a white limestone with a curved-glass front window and its own garage, and Jerry thought they were going in. But it wasn't that one, it was the one next door, 86 Riverside Drive. I'll have to remember this, he thought, knowing that he wouldn't.

Number 86 was an undistinguished brick apartment building with a narrow downstairs corridor and an elevator. They got into the elevator and the Leader pressed the button for the fifth floor. There wasn't a sixth floor.

"A small apartment," the Leader said. "I own it under another name."

They walked in. Jerry saw a nondescript living room-dining room set, the kind available through rental services. What interested him was a collection of file cards in a small box on the couch beside the telephone.

"It's nothing, really," said the Leader. "The main value is in its location. And in a special feature I designed."

He crossed the living room to the bedroom, Jerry following. On the far side of the bed was a picture of three horses on a moonlit seascape that Jerry had seen in the windows of souvenir stores on Broadway. The colors matched the blue-flowered wallpaper. The Leader went over to the window and raised it a notch. "If you'll come this way," he said, and nodded at the bedroom closet.

When the Leader opened the door, Jerry saw that the back of the closet was open too. On the other side was another bedroom; a big four-poster bed trimmed in silver. The Leader walked through and stood at the window to the right of a fireplace mantel. When he saw that Jerry was out of the passageway, he raised the window slightly and then lowered it. Turning, Jerry saw that the wall behind him had already closed.

"Nothing terribly original," the Leader said, "but it's effective. I don't expect ever to *have* to use it, you understand. It's just another part of the game I enjoy playing."

Downstairs, they went into a brightly lit, white-painted room with white-covered armless couches spaced apart, side by side. The walls curved so that you couldn't see more than one or two couches at the same time. Obviously, Jerry decided, the Leader had plenty of money, and plenty of space, and didn't want the people who were in here on the couches getting a look at one another. Probably this was the place where his "conditioning" had been given; where the Leader's face had been fixed in his memory.

The Leader smiled. "Shall we begin?"

"Another twelve minutes to go," Jerry said. "Why don't you show me around? You know I won't remember anyway."

So they went downstairs another flight on the elevator, into another white room with instrument consoles and TV screens, probably cathode-ray computer terminals, Jerry thought. "The workroom," the Leader said. "Patient records, test results, various lab studies. Gradually we're getting it off the paper and onto the computer tapes, which will save us some time. Would you like a drink?"

"Sure," said Jerry. He asked for scotch, neat, no ice, and watched while the Leader poured. "It probably won't sit too well with the injection," he said, "so I'll just ease into it. No offense, I hope."

The Leader said it was all right, he understood, and did Jerry want a cigarette? Now that you mention it, said Jerry, and got the Newport pack out of his jacket and lit one with his thirty-nine-cent butane.

"Where do you keep the blood?" he asked. "I've got a professional interest. I guess you already know that, though."

"Oh, I know."

"Maybe we could compare notes."

"It's possible," said the Leader. He got up from the swivel chair and went over to a door, and opened it. When he switched on the light, white cabinet doors shone. Glassware sparkled on white shelves. Four chromed-steel doors gleamed.

"Refrigerators?" Jerry pointed to the steel doors.

"One is. The others are ovens. Radiant heat, microwave, and ultrasound."

"Ultrasound for fractionalizing?"

"And other things. I find it accelerates certain reactions. Useful when there are compounds to be synthesized."

Jerry nodded, admiring in spite of himself. "It's a nice layout."

The Leader said yes, he spent a lot of time here, that he thought it was always more productive to work in pleasant surroundings, and that speaking of time, his watch said it had been forty-seven minutes.

Jerry checked his. "Yeah, right. O.K. What do you want to know?"

"About this morning. Do you want to talk here, or would some other place be more comfortable?"

"No, this is fine. I'm used to labs. What about this morning? A lot of things happened."

"I'm concerned about one of our people. He'd been having some emotional difficulty, and took several capsules when he should only have taken one. The effect was too much of a strain for him. When we went to Madison Hospital this morning to talk with Jill Weston, he became unmanageable. I'm afraid he caused some trouble after I had to leave."

"It was quite a scene," said Jerry. "If you're wondering why you haven't heard from him, it's because he's dead now. The police killed him, and right in my blood bank too. I had a hell of a time explaining."

The Leader's dark eyes found Jerry's gaze and held it. "Why did they kill him?"

"Marcie," said Jerry. "When he came in, the security guards were right on his tail, and she saw he was trapped. She started to say she'd never seen him before, she didn't know why in the world he'd come in there, and that seemed to drive him a little crazy. The guard wasn't strong enough to hold him. He broke Marcie's neck before they shot him."

"So. They're both dead."

Jerry nodded.

"What happened to Jill Weston?"

"That's where you're in trouble," Jerry said. "That's why I was *really* surprised to hear you call at the office this afternoon. When she got out of the Emergency Room, she told the police about you."

"I'd been concerned about that."

"So was I, when I heard what she had to say. It wasn't good. She claimed you'd asked her questions this morning and then shot her full of enough reserpine to be a lethal dose, and sent her off to get a baby as a hostage—"

Jerry watched the Leader's face as he denied it, as he told about giving her only one injection, scopolamine so that she wouldn't remember, and then turning her over to Garrett when he had to leave. Garrett was to give her an injection of a harmless sedative, wait a few minutes until it had taken effect, and then leave her sleeping in her office. "But I shouldn't have left him alone," he said. "It appears that he really panicked. I suppose after the two injections she got the facts somewhat confused. We had no reason to try to kill her."

It sounded so truthful! I hope I'm as convincing a liar as you are, Jerry thought. "I guess you can understand now why I was a bit cautious with your injection tonight."

The Leader smiled. "People have their own ways of protecting themselves. I'm never surprised to see a certain amount of reluctance to be injected. It's only natural. Where's Jill Weston now?"

"Under police protection," Jerry lied. Actually he had said good night to her at her apartment, where she was alone. She had gone to bed early on doctor's orders, with a sleeping pill, a stiff dose of Nembutal that would leave her with a headache in the morning but would give her overtaxed body a chance to rest and rebuild.

"Protection from what?" the Leader asked.

"From you. She gave them a description, and the police artist worked up one of those drawings. You should know that they're looking for you. The drawing is pretty accurate."

"I wish you'd mentioned it before. We were out walking on the street for several blocks getting here. Someone might have recognized me."

Jerry shrugged. "You also ought to know that they're hoping you make a try for her. She's the only one who can identify you, and it stands to reason that you'd want to kill her. Assuming her charges are true, of course. If they're not, I guess you could always take your chances with a jury."

"What else is she charging?"

"Oh, just what I told you. Attempted murder, attempted kidnaping, assault with intent to kill. I'm glad she's not charging me with anything."

"We can't afford a trial," the Leader said. He talked for a time about the publicity a trial would generate. About the end to the secrecy of his research. The end of anonymity for the Gathering members; their privacy invaded; their lives exposed to public scrutiny.

Jerry nodded. "I kind of anticipated that before I came. Matter of fact, that's *why* I came." Lie with the truth, he thought.

"Is there something you'd like to suggest?"

Jerry tried to look as though he were working up to it gradually, the way he would if he were the kind who really could make this offer. The trouble was, he didn't know the way that type of individual would act. He told himself that the man he was facing now would do for a model, and went on, keeping it modest and simple.

"Well, it's like I said. The police are looking for you, and they're not looking for me."

"What do you propose to do?"

"The other thing is, it looks to me as though you have a shortage of two people that worked with you pretty closely. I would imagine that those two people had some special privileges in return for what they did."

The Leader nodded, took a step back, folded his arms. "I think I understand you," he said. "You're offering to make certain Jill Weston does not identify me, and after you do that you expect to be made a Guardian. It seems reasonable. As a matter of fact, the other Guardians got their rank by doing a similar service."

"You don't quite have it," said Jerry. "The timing's wrong. You make me a Guardian first. And then I take care of Jill Weston for you."

"That's not the usual sequence."

"It'll have to do."

The Leader watched Jerry closely, dark eyes steady, curious, as though sizing him up one final time. Then he appeared to have made his decision.

"All right," he said. "As you say, the police are after me and not after you. Do you have any objections to making the conversion tonight?"

He's going for it, Jerry thought, and nervous tension began to seep from inside him, making the sweat run from his underarms in little cool rivulets. He shivered. "Tonight? I don't know. How long does it take?"

"Not long. You'll need to see some more of the equipment, hear a more complete explanation, see some documents. Say a pledge. That's all." A brief smile. "There aren't any blood oaths, if you were expecting any."

"O.K.," said Jerry. "Where do we begin?"

"I'll show you the documents first," the Leader said. "They're up in my consulting room."

The consulting room was filled with books, floor-to-ceiling, and antique furnishings that looked expensive. Jerry sat in a green-leather wing chair across from the Leader's desk. The Leader got down one of the books from the shelf, a heavy, clumsy old book about twice the size of the Manhattan telephone directory and with a cracked brown-leather binding. He handed it to Jerry.

"You can take a look at this first," said the Leader. "It starts on page eight hundred and seventy-two. Then there's one more, the one with the ceremonies."

As he thumbed through, Jerry saw that the book was an old medical textbook of pharmacology. The paper was brittle; the print difficult to read, and some of the pages were dog-eared so that the numbers were missing. He was wondering what the Leader had found in this old relic, and was flipping through the 860s, almost to 870, when he felt one hell of a stinging impact at the back of his neck and nearly jumped out of his chair.

He turned and saw the Leader holding what looked to be a large-sized staple gun in his hand. His stomach knotted up again as he recognized what it was. An air injector, used for infusions when you didn't have time to bother with a needle. Something inside him seemed to give way and he wanted to run, but he felt his legs weakening from fear. "What the hell is *in* that?" he asked.

The Leader smiled. "It's an endorphin I work with," he said. "It makes people tell the truth. Two weeks ago it worked rather well on you."

68

So it was going to be the truth. Hard to say why, Jerry thought, but the idea made him feel good even while it scared him so badly he could feel his bladder getting tight and painful. And the stuff had reached his brain incredibly fast; already he heard himself talking.

"Just fuck you," he said. "If you want the truth, I guess we might as well start there—" And he started too, started to make a dive for the Leader, spinning out of the chair and getting about halfway to his feet before the Leader's hands clamped cold down on his neck from behind, fingers digging in under Jerry's collarbones and making Jerry's legs seem to disappear from under him. He was suddenly paralyzed, as though he had no feeling at all, no control, and he realized he was sitting back down again.

The Leader stood behind him, fingers massaging Jerry's neck, kneading the flesh, working into the muscle so that Jerry wanted to scream, heard it come out: *"No! God-damn you. NO, will you stop—"*

"I think not." The voice was silky. "I think, Jerry Chamberlain, that you're going to start to enjoy this. It's relaxing you now, isn't it? My hands on you, you *like* them, don't you? Now, don't you . . ." And Jerry wanted to throw up, felt his guts churn, contract. He doubled up and gagged, the Leader's hands still on him, moving, stroking. . . .

"When we last talked," the Leader continued, "you seemed different from the way you spoke tonight. It makes me curious, and I think you probably want to satisfy my curiosity. You see, the last time you seemed to have a very deep affection for Jill Weston. It's odd that this evening you're ready to go out and kill her for me. Were you really prepared to do that?"

Jerry shuddered. "No. God no."

"Mmm. And were you really ambitious to become a Guardian?"

"Look, will you cut it *out?*"

"Don't lose your temper, Jerry. You don't want to do anything to make yourself lose your temper. You just want to tell me the truth, that's all. Now, how much of what you told me before is the truth?"

"Just take your hands off me. *Please* take your hands off me."

"And then you'll give me an honest answer?"

His flesh crawling with revulsion, Jerry told him yes. And told him what really happened.

"Mmm." The Leader sounded considerably more confident, Jerry thought, if such a thing were possible. Or maybe it was his own perception, the drug altering the way he felt about the Leader, magnifying the Leader's personal force in Jerry's mind, creating the need for Jerry to obey, and yet, Jerry realized, still allowing him the opportunity to think the way he normally would, maybe because he'd been instructed to tell the truth. . . .

". . . so tell me this," the Leader was saying. "You'd seen Garrett and Marcie dead. You'd saved Jill. Both of you were safe. Why did you come here with your little charade about wanting to become a Guardian?"

"I thought I could get in here, and then find some way to turn the tables on you. I was going to destroy your records, so when the police got you they wouldn't learn Jill Weston had ever been here."

"Oh, my!" The Leader sounded amused. "I had you down in the files as chivalrous, but that's a little too much to believe, isn't it? After all, now, you did say you were going to tell the truth. What about your own name on those records? Weren't you concerned about getting that removed too?"

"I hadn't really thought about that," said Jerry, a bit surprised he hadn't. "It wouldn't be so much of a problem for me. It's different for a woman, there's a lot of gossip about them in the medical field, I guess you know that . . ."

For some reason, he felt himself slowing down.

"You sound as though there's something else, Jerry. Tell me."

He knew it. And God he was ashamed as he said it. "I—had trouble saying no to you. You gave me an order, and I had trouble saying no. I remember at the time thinking about what kind of conditioning you must have run on me the one time I'd been here before, and it worried me. I can say that for sure, it really worried me, to think that I'd been programmed to obey *you*."

"So you knew," said the Leader. "And yet you came here anyway, trying to win some sort of victory over your own Leader. That's contradictory, isn't it? Didn't you see the contradiction? Tell me, now, Jerry, what you were going to do after you'd destroyed my records."

Jerry swallowed hard. Told him. "I was going to try to overpower you and take you in. With the records destroyed, you wouldn't have any evidence. The police wouldn't believe you if you said Jill and I had been here."

The laughter came stronger now, rolling around him in

soft, warm breaths of moisture that tickled the back of Jerry's neck and made the anger boil inside him. "Oh, Jerry!" the Leader said, his voice delighted. "Oh, Jerry, that's *won*derful! A real, macho, knockout victory! How you must have dreamed!"

Face crimson, Jerry tried to stand up again, tried to get *away*, and then the hands were on his neck again, forcing him down into the chair, and the hands were hard, their grip painful.

"I told you, Jerry, you don't want to lose conrol. I don't think you'd have much hope of overpowering me. Don't forget I had the opportunity to examine your body. I can assure you that mine is in quite different condition from yours."

"You don't have to brag," said Jerry. He felt tears of helpless rage start to come and forced them back, not allowing his voice to break. "What are you planning to do with me?"

"I think you probably know, Jerry." The hands caressed his neck again. "I'm going to take you up on the offer you made earlier. Where is Jill Weston now?"

He didn't want to say it, but the words came out. "In her apartment. Sleeping."

"Good. You'll telephone her. Use the phone on my desk. Tell her you're anxious to meet her, that you've discovered one of the police assigned to guard her is a Gathering member—"

"There aren't any police guarding her. I made that up. They're understaffed, said they couldn't spare anyone unless they knew there was a real personal intent, that she should just stay alert and not take any risks."

"Mmm. All right, that makes it easier. Call her and tell her you're coming to visit. You need to talk to her. You'll knock once, then four times, then two, so she'll know not to let anyone else in."

"Won't work. She's asleep with a Nembutal. She won't even hear the phone ringing."

"Maybe you're right," said the Leader softly. "Then again, maybe she doesn't respond that well to Nembutal. Take the phone and try. I know her number, and I'll be watching to be certain you dial it correctly. Go ahead now."

The hands released him. As if by some miracle, Jerry found he could stand up. He leaned on the desk for support, turned the phone toward him, thinking, God, what the hell am I *doing?* Jill Weston had an injection too this morning, she said she had an injection and she got away, she didn't stand there betraying somebody she loves, she got away, and he realized several things at once, as he picked up the receiver: that he wanted more than anything else to throw this phone away from him, and that the set of drapes in the big curved window were the inside of that big curved window he had seen from the outside, seen from Riverside Drive, and that there might be someone walking outside to hear the crash and ask what the hell was going on in there and maybe call a cop before Jerry died, and he scooped the phone off the desk in one motion and sent it flying into the drapes, and there was a pretty good crash before the Leader's hand came down on his neck again, really hurting like hell, twisting him around onto his back, bending him backward onto the desk top so that he nearly cried but didn't, tried to think instead, and heard a voice.

"Leader." A woman's voice was talking. "Leader, I don't think you want to do that."

They both turned. Saw. In the doorway.

Jill Weston.

Astonishingly, the Leader did not seem surprised. The only indication that he had been caught off guard was a painful tightening of his grip, his thumbs pressing down hard on Jerry's windpope.

"Come over here, Jill," said the Leader.

She stood motionless, and then, after a moment, backed away a step. Jerry saw her move, and cried out "RUN!" but the word came out in a choked whisper and the Leader's grip tightened once again.

"You can see Jerry's at a disadvantage," the Leader said, as though Jerry were still talking, as though Jill had not disobeyed him and he was only giving her the reason why she had to come near him. "You won't stay there any longer if you want to see him alive again. Have you ever watched a person being strangled? It's not pretty, Jill. The tongue, I think, is the worst part."

"Let him go," Jill said, her voice starting to tense up. "Let him go now."

"First tell me how you came here. I'll be able to tell if you're lying, so be truthful with me. If I hear a lie, Jerry's pain will increase."

Jill stared. *Talk,* she told herself, and don't look at his eyes, he did something to you this morning with those eyes and something the other time, the time that you were here, so don't look at them, tell him what you did, because you know you're tired and haven't slept, and you've got to prove to yourself that you can stand up to him! "It was easy for me to get in," she said. Her voice sounded quiet to her, so she tried to speak up. "There were two things I knew about this place. One was that it was on Riverside Drive. I was certain about that because Maryann Delvecchio said she'd be waiting on Riverside Drive at a certain place to see if I was brought here last night, and Maryann hasn't been heard from since then by anyone. So I assumed she had guessed the location correctly, even though I didn't remember whether or not I'd seen her. The other thing I knew was that this place was somewhere relatively close to the Seventy-ninth Street Boat Basin, because when I woke up after last night I was on Phillip's boat, so I knew I must have run there to escape. And if it hadn't been close, I knew I wouldn't have made it. I'd seen that killer of yours run before, and he was a lot faster than I am."

The Leader nodded. "You were thinking well, Jill. What did you do?"

"I walked up and down the sidewalk across the street. I had an idea that Jerry was going to try to do something tonight too, because he seemed really anxious to get away, but it just floored me when I saw him in his blue walking hat across the street, and walking with *you!* I tried to think why he'd be doing that when I knew that he'd saved my life, and I decided that he probably had heard me say something when I was knocked out, that maybe I'd given the location of the Gathering or your phone number in my sleep, but anyway I decided that didn't make any difference. So I followed you in to number eighty-six and watched the elevator go up to the top floor and then came up after you. I heard you talking, just for a moment, as I listened at the door, and the talking seemed to fade away. You'd left the door unlocked, so I went in. I didn't know what to think when I found nobody there, but then I decided you must have put in an entrance to the next building somewhere that I couldn't see. I went back downstairs in the elevator and noticed there was a light on in this house on the fifth floor where there hadn't been any earlier, and decided I was probably right. So I took the elevator up to the roof, walked over to *your* roof, and slid down to the little balcony outside your bedroom window. You hadn't locked your window either, so the rest was easy. I walked around, listening for voices, and finally I found you in here. I'm sorry to tell Jerry this, but I did wait in the hall while he answered the last few questions. When I saw what he did to the telephone, I knew I had to do something."

The Leader broke the silence. "I believe you told the truth, Jill. You came alone?"

"Yes, but I don't think that's going to help you, if you're planning to harm Jerry and then try to catch up with me."

"And why is that?"

"Because while I was waiting here in the hall I unlocked the front door. I made some noise doing it, but you were laughing at the time and you didn't notice. Besides that, I think I have something you want here in my jacket."

The blue ski parka. Jill unzipped the front, a little awkwardly because of the gauze bandage on her right hand. She reached in and pulled out a small file box. "I found this in the apartment next door," she said.

"It means nothing to me. And I don't hear any traffic noise. If the front door were open, I'd hear the cars outside."

"I think the box means something," Jill said. "I read a few of the cards. Maryann's name was one of them. So was mine. So was Jerry's. That's why I had to listen out in the hall. It seems to me these cards are your membership file, or some of them anyway, maybe the local ones because I didn't see any outside New York—"

The voice rose, building intensity. *"Give them to me, Jill. Come over here and give them to me."*

Just don't falter, she told herself. Just keep on, *keep talking.* "You'll have to let Jerry go. Otherwise I'm running out that front door and down those steps and there really is a policeman I can get to with these cards, he's down at the end of the block and he's probably seen the sketch of you they made—"

"DAMN you!" The Leader pushed Jerry aside and spun around, lunging for her, but when Jerry felt the hands leave his neck the miracle happened again, he

could *move,* and he got his legs out far enough to tangle
the Leader's and make him stumble, and as he slid off
the desk he got his hand on the desk lamp, a big heavy
brass lamp that seemed to cling to his palm as he took it
down to the floor with him, down to the floor with him
and the Leader, but he couldn't quite get his breath
enough to move around as fast as he should have moved,
and he saw the Leader had pinned Jill down, had her by
the legs and had somehow picked up his injection gun.

Then the muscles in Jerry's arm seemed to move of
themselves, as though he'd just knocked a glass off the
lab table and had quick-before-he-could-even-think reached
down to catch it or try anyway, only this time it wasn't
a glass he was going for, it was the back of the Leader's
skull, the hair black and shining, and it wasn't his bare
hand, the base of the lamp was in it and crashing down
hard, and then the Leader's skull and the lamp base
seemed to bounce off each other, and the Leader's body
seemed to bounce up too, twisting in a convulsive spasm
that whirled him around so that Jerry could see his
face. The blood had started to flow from the back of
the Leader's skull, spreading dark red beneath him on
the carpet, but the Leader was still alive. Jerry could not
move. He watched in horror as the Leader's hands rose
up to touch him, the teeth bared in a smile of welcome,
and the dark eyes lit, and then the powerful arms en-
folded him, pulling him down, holding him paralyzed for
a long impossible moment until Jerry nearly screamed, *did*
scream, and swung the lamp again. The blood streamed
from the Leader's smashed bone and facial tissue down
over those eyes, but they stayed bright in their horrible
red pools, alive, fixed on Jerry until he could see nothing
else.

Then he heard Jill Weston say his name.

And the Leader's eyes grew dull in their sockets and
rolled upward, now staring at eternity.

PART FOUR

NEW LIFE

69

"I'm Sarah Comfrey," the woman said. She was a pleasant-faced, modestly dressed small woman with the South in her voice. Obviously, Ted Sanford decided, she was deeply impressed by the quiet opulence of his office.

Ted got up from behind his desk and came forward to meet her, hand extended. He moved more hesitantly than he would have on a normal day, because the back of his neck still hurt. But he felt a lot stronger than he had Tuesday morning when Rachel had found him practically helpless in Jill Weston's office. Even now it embarrassed him to think about it, how she had rolled him over and seen him looking at her with tears in his eyes, and not being able to move or do anything but blink, not even able to control his bladder. Thank God it had been Rachel who'd found him and not one of the nurses, or the story would have been all over the hospital.

"I'm so glad you could come, Mrs. Comfrey," he said. "Please have a seat here on the sofa." He remembered that Mrs. Comfrey was one of the patients who had been attacked last month. She had been cooperative then, and he was going to do everything in his power to make her want to stay cooperative. The hospital had come through the horror of the past few days without too much disastrous publicity, thanks to Ted's efforts. It had really been a help that the nurse, Harriet Pierce, had been so positive in her identification of the dead man as the vampire killer, even though she'd had to request them to put a surgical mask on his face before she would say with complete certainty. And that assistant in the Blood Bank—the reporters were convinced that she had been the killer's inside contact. So were the police.

Still it would be another day or so before Ted knew how the press would really play it. The news moratorium

on the vampire killer would be in effect until the police
caught the handsome, dark-haired assailant Jill Weston
had described. Then Ted would see whether the hospital
got fair treatment. Right now the press was busy with
other local stories. A gang war in the Bronx. A big fire in
a town house on Riverside Drive that looked as though it
involved arson and probably murder. . . .

Of course, the papers would hold the vampire killer
story for only a few days at most. If the police hadn't
caught the second assailant by then, the news about him
would break too, probably, and the hospital could be in
for more trouble. Even though the one known killer was
safely dead. Not fair, but you had to face up to those
possibilities, Ted thought, when you were the man at the
helm.

Either way, Ted hoped the media wouldn't be inter-
viewing Mrs. Comfrey about the attack on her last
month, and trying to start stories of a "cover-up."

Before she sat down, Mrs. Comfrey glanced at the
painting above the sofa, a gilt-framed copy of a Fragonard
done in real oils, delicate purples and vermilions, that Ted
thought was indistinguishable from the original. "Pretty,"
she said. "I came in to talk to Dr. Weston. They told me
you were her boss, and that she wasn't here, so I came
upstairs to you. I just got back from Texas."

"Did you? I like Texas. My family has a pretty good-
size warehouse down in San Antonio." Small talk, Ted
thought. Put her at ease.

She nodded. "The reason I wanted to see Dr. Weston
was to thank her. And tell her that I'm pregnant."

"Well, congratulations—"

"—at least I think I'm pregnant. I bought one of those
test-yourself preparations they sell in the drugstores, and
I gave myself the test this morning and it said I was. So I
wanted to come in and thank her and have her give me
a real test. And then start on the obstetrical program she
told me about, with the diet and all. My husband's terribly excited."

"Oh, I'll bet he is," said Ted, his voice husky
with emotion. "My wife just had a baby girl two days
ago, and we're just still on cloud nine." He went on as
she beamed at him and said congratulations. "Dr. Weston
delivered our baby. In fact, she gave my wife the opera-

tion that made our baby *possible*. We just feel so much gratitude to her—"

"She was here two days ago?"

"Yep. Delivered the baby, and then later the same day she had a really unfortunate accident. Cut her hand on a glass bottle, a pretty bad cut. Might have hurt some of the tendons, they said, and you know what that means to a surgeon. She was a real trouper about it, of course, but I knew she was pretty upset all the same."

"Gosh," said Mrs. Comfrey. "Where is she now? I'd like to send her a get-well card."

Ted decided it wouldn't do any harm to tell part of the story. "She's off to her old home town, actually," he said. "Upstate. At least she should be by now. She called this morning to say she was going and asked for medical leave, and of course we said yes."

He left out the part about Jill still feeling afraid that the handsome man who had attacked her in the hospital might find her again. He also didn't say that Dr. Jerry Chamberlain was driving upstate with her. Chamberlain had been banged up a bit himself fighting that man in the Blood Bank, so medical leave was certainly justified there too.

But Ted wouldn't say anything about that to Mrs. Comfrey. He remembered she had a strong religious background, some odd-ball sect, and she might have serious objections to Jill Weston's traveling with a man unchaperoned.

He smiled at Mrs. Comfrey. "If you'd like to leave any cards or messages for Dr. Weston, we'll be glad to forward them. And of course I'm sure she'll be calling you as soon as she gets back."

70

The house needed some paint. There were a few trees around it to offer protection from the sun and the wind, but they were oaks. Jerry could see they were oaks, because some of the branches still had last fall's brown leaves on them. During a hard winter like the last one, a few oak trees wouldn't be much shelter for a house, especially a frame house this big. It definitely needed some paint.

Jill got out of their rented Chevy on the passenger's side, and gestured at the fields all around the house, and the barn, and the mountain behind the barn. It was a modest gesture, the more so because she was holding her purse with her good hand, and they'd bandaged the other so heavily it looked like a white gauze mitten. "This is it," she said. "Dad bought it about a year and a half ago. He said he was going to pasture some cattle on the hillside and maybe plant corn. I never had the heart to sell it after he died."

Jerry nodded, standing on the gravel driveway, taking it all in.

She reached back into the car and got out his blue L. L. Bean hat; tossed it to him left-handed while he wasn't looking, smiled when he bobbled it and held on. "What up, Mr. Woodsman, cat got your tongue?"

"Hey, c'mon, this is *it*," he said. "The real thing. Sunshine. Takes some getting used to."

Inside he found the valves to turn on the water and the gas, and she found an unopened coffee can in the pantry. She still had enough dexterity to pry the key off the bottom of the can, fit it over the metal tab, and twist. The air rushed in with a whoosh and the room smelled like fresh coffee. They sat at the big kitchen table after the coffee had perked. Jill had found ironstone mugs in the cupboard. Later on they would drive into town and get something for dinner at the market and maybe buy some more dishes. The steam would come up in the radiators by then and the house would be warm.

She sipped coffee. "Feeling better?" she asked.

"Oh, I'm O.K. Coffee's what I needed."

"You ought to quit trying to remember," she said. "It's over. He's dead, you saved my life, and it's over. We're free of him."

He shook his head. "But it doesn't *seem* over. Doesn't even seem like it happened. I can't even remember the address."

"C'mon. I told you the address."

"So you did," said Jerry. He got up and took his coffee over to the window and looked out at the mountain. There weren't any oak trees up there, he guessed, because he couldn't see any leaves at all, just the outlines of the bare trees.

Jill watched him, thinking about the other two people who had escaped the Gathering. Dr. Polder's chest wound had not been fatal: quick action in the Emergency Room had saved her life. And Maryann Delvecchio had eluded Garrett. She had phoned Jill from a friend's house where she had been hiding, her voice taut with emotion at the news of the fire that had destroyed 88 Riverside Drive. She would try to do a story, she said, but it would not be the one she had planned. And she swore that she would never include anything that could hurt the hospital or Jill. She owed Jill too much.

And Jill knew that was a promise Maryanne would find hard to break, even if ambition urged her to change her mind. All the evidence was gone. The records were destroyed. The Leader's body was burned beyond recognition.

She wondered if Maryann would keep her other promises: to do a story on Jill's clinic once it became established, and to come in for an examination as an obstetrical patient. It was hard to say when the new clinic would be started. . . .

And she wondered how Harriet and Nick would get along as a married couple, and how Rachel and Ted would grow with their little girl, and whether it might be good for Jill Weston to have a baby sometime soon. . . .

She and Jerry would stay here at least a week and maybe longer. They had vacations coming, time

enough to live here together until the spring turned the
mountain to the green that Jill remembered. They might
even stay on after that. The area needed physicians. She
just hoped that if they *did* stay, they would both make
the choice based on what they wanted to do, and not because her hand hadn't healed properly. It didn't seem
like too much more to ask, to have her hand come back
to normal.

But that was all in the future.

Then Jerry was standing beside her. "I guess I'll just
have to believe what you've told me, Doc," he said.

She kissed him lightly, and then again.

The memory of the Gathering began to fade.